JOHNNY APOCALYPSE
AND THE FIGHT FOR A NEW WORLD

MARK ROBIJN

Blue Forge Press

Port Orchard ✿ Washington

Blue Forge Press
7419 Ebbert Drive Southeast
Port Orchard, Washington 98367
360.550.2071 ph.txt

DEDICATION

To my junior high science teacher Leo (.037) Christofferson, who stopped teaching science on Fridays and read us science fiction stories instead. Thanks for instilling in me the love of writing and science.

ACKNOWLEDGEMENTS

I'd like to thank all the great writers and friends who gave me feedback and encouragement over the years, especially my good friends Carl Palmer and Rob Miller, who sadly is no longer with us. I'd like to thank Blue Forge Press for believing in me and my stories enough to take a chance on my novels. I'd also like to thank all the great authors who fueled my imagination through the years, including Jack London, Isaac Asimov, Ray Bradbury and Sir Arthur Conan Doyle. Without their great examples and inspiration, this series of books would probably not exist.

JOHNNY APOCALYPSE

AND THE FIGHT FOR A NEW WORLD

MARK ROBIJN

PROLOGUE

The days of the Great War with its Mushroom Monsters and the Great Sickness are over. Life has slowly begun to return to the desolate wasteland. Johnny Apocalypse, a boy of only fifteen seasons is chosen as the leader for his people who call themselves the Tribe because of his courage and strength. Johnny is in love with a beautiful blond, blue eyed girl named, Deb. Johnny's Tribe lived in an abandoned mall they called Sanctuary in the city that used to be called Philadelphia. Attacked by a roaming gang of cutthroats calling themselves the Doomsday Prophecy led the evil Ripper the Tribe is forced to leave and travel south to the city of Washington D.C. With the help of wise man knowledgeable in the magic of the world before the Great War they call Misterwizard, they hope to rebuild a new society on the ancient principles of democracy and freedom.

In the new city they settle into an old museum known before as the Museum of American History. They rename it New Sanctuary. But Ripper and the Doomsday Prophecy follow them, and they also find a new enemy waiting for them. He calls himself Lord Algon. Lord Algon has organized the people who wander the wasteland called Wildies into a fighting force and declared himself their king.

Meanwhile, Misterwizard tries desperately to find the secret code for the President's underground bunker where there might be medicine and supplies, because Johnny's girlfriend Deb is very sick, and his sister Carny is about to have a wriggler.

Johnny and his best friend Starbucks meet Lord Algon but don't tell him about the Tribe, but thanks to a traitor named Leader Nordsttrom, Lord Algon finds out. Now Johnny and Starbucks, captured by the Wildies, head back to Lord Algon once again, to face his wrath for not telling him the whole truth.

CHAPTER I

Lord Algon sat in his royal robes in the ruins of what used to be called the "White House" at a table in a room named the "Presidential Dining Room." Looking bored, he chewed on a cooked dog-beastie leg, ripping pieces off with his teeth.

Sitting across from him in a chair by the wall, Leader Nordstrom gazed at the dog-beastie leg with hunger. Despite his best efforts to look dignified, Leader Nordstrom licked his lips as he thought how tasty the meat looked. He closed his eyes and tried to keep from fainting. His stomach ached, and he felt miserable and wretched. Lord Algon was not giving him the respect he deserved, but he didn't dare complain, not after seeing the Lord's two bodyguards. They looked like they'd enjoy ripping him apart just for sport.

Leader Nordstrom opened his eyes and gazed about

the room. One of the few rooms with a ceiling that was intact, it was sparsely decorated. The main object in the room was a giant painting of a tall man in a black suit with a black beard and square black hat on his head. Leader Nordstrom thought how the painting took up the whole wall, the biggest painting Leader Nordstrom had ever seen. He didn't know paintings could be that large, and it frightened him. Even though it was faded and small areas in the corners were white with age, the man in the painting still looked so real it seemed like he was staring right at Leader Nordstrom. Something about the man in the painting's penetrating gaze made Leader Nordstrom uncomfortable, as if the man knew Leader Nordstrom was up to no good and disapproved. Leader Nordstrom scowled at the man and thought dark thoughts about him before turning away. He tried to sleep, and not to think about his aching stomach.

Lord Algon grinned at Leader Nordstrom with cruel humor, took another bite of the dog-beastie leg and then with a mouth full of meat said, "Be ye hungry?"

Leader Nordstrom opened his eyes with a start and began to anxiously nod, but with a supreme effort stopped himself. He knew he had to appear strong, if he was to maintain his stature as the Leader Nordstrom of his Tribe. Instead he simply gazed at the food on the table.

Lord Algon chuckled darkly, enjoying Leader Nordstrom's suffering. "Here." Lord Algon threw the Dog-beastie leg at Leader Nordstrom. It landed on the floor near his feet. Most of the meat was gone, and yet it still took a supreme effort on Leader Nordstrom's part not to leap for it. "Best grab it, matey, 'fore my dog-Beasties beat ye to it."

Realizing that he might lose it, Leader Nordstrom dove for the leg and snatched it up, to Lord Algon's amusement. Leader Nordstrom sat back down and greedily chewed on the dog-beastie leg, totally forgetting about his dignity. Lord Algon and his guards laughed as they watched, but Leader Nordstrom no longer cared. He was so hungry he would have eaten bug-beasties.

Lord Algon picked up a glass of red liquid and took a sip. "Soon, the two men ye called criminals be back. If what ye say be true of them, then ye shall eat to your heart's content." Lord Algon sat forward and stared at Leader Nordstrom, making him pause in his eating. "But if ye be lying to me, my dog-Beasties 'twill feast on ye, while ye yet be alive." Leader Nordstrom gulped and wished he could simply find a moment to slip away.

Leader Nordstrom ate what he could off the dog-beastie bone and then nodded off, weak from the lack of food but also from the tension and lack of sleep of the last few days. The smells of the roasted dog-beastie in the pot at the end of the room in the fireplace filled his nose, and it caused him to dream of a huge banquet with mounds of roasted meat and piles of potatoes. In the dream, he sat in the old food place in Sanctuary, where the Tribe gathered for special occasions. He sat all alone at one of the round white tables. Many more table surrounded him as far as he could see, all covered with mounds of delicious foods, meats, vegetables, and fruits lay, some Leader Nordstrom had only seen in pictures.

The table in front of Leader Nordstrom didn't have food on it. On it a giant mountain of small, colorfully wrapped balls rose up to above his head. There were called chocolates, a special treat he'd only seen but not eaten himself. Johnny had some once. He remembered the moment, and it burned in his memory like fire. One day in Sanctuary he passed by seeing Johnny surrounded by his friends and family, and they were all excited by something Johnny held in his hands. Without being noticed, Leader Nordstrom listened as Johnny told them about it, knowing they were something Johnny had found on one of his forbidden trips outside Sanctuary.

"They're called, "chocolates,' Johnny said, as they all gazed at the brightly wrapped balls in Johnny's hand. "Here," Johnny gave one to Deb. She smiled and looked at it, not sure what to do.

Johnny laughed. "You unwrap it, silly, like this." Johnny twisted the paper at the ends of the ball, and it fell off, revealing a small brown ball that looked somehow delicious and magical. "Now put it in your mouth."

Deb popped it in her mouth as the rest watched, eyes wide with interest. Deb bit down on it and chewed. Then she smiled, as if she'd just tasted the most wonderful thing she'd ever eaten. The rest turned back to Johnny, and he gave each one a piece! Leader Nordstrom remember being so eaten up with jealousy he felt sick. He knew he could never ask Johnny for one, because he'd always treated Johnny bad, and he couldn't lose face by pretending to be his friend then.

As if watching them all enjoy the special treat wasn't enough, Johnny even gave one to the scrabbler Sephie. A little scrabbler, enjoying something that rightfully he should have been given first! It was really the first time Leader Nordstrom really thought about how much he hated Johnny and wanted to see him dead.

Leader Nordstrom thought about those brightly colored balls, and how much he wished he knew how they tasted. Johnny's friends and family sure made them look as if they must be delicious.

Ripper and the Gangers drove slowly into the center of the city. They noticed more Wildies, big groupd of them. They filled the streets and wandered in and out of the buildings. While they were far enough away not to be spotted, Ripper raised his hand out the window and the Gangers stopped their vehicles. Ripper watched the Wildies, scratching his stubbly chin and ponded. The Wildies jabbered among themselves and jumped up and down. They seemed excited about something. As Ripper watched, the whole crowd of Wildies walked away from the Gangers in one direction, towards a large area of white buildings in the distance.

"Something's going on," Ripper said to his driver, Dog-beastie. "And I'll just bet you, Johnny Apocalypse is in the middle of it."

Facegash nodded and grinned at him. "Maybe they got him on a spit and they're roasting him."

Facegash laughed, but Ripper scowled. "I hope not. I want to do it. I want to be the one to mount him on a spit, while his family watches. Turn around. Let's park. It's time to find out what's goin' on. Facegash drove to the left to head back the way they had come. Ripper motioned out the window, and the Gangers followed in their vehicles. They turned down a side street, looking for a place to park where they wouldn't be seen.

Super ran through the dark, empty building she'd escaped into, her heart in her throat. She didn't know where to go, and the inside of the building so dark she couldn't see her hands in front of her face. She put them out in front of her, eyes opened wide and groped her way along slowly.

She touched something cold and gazed up at it to discover it was a statue of a girl in a robe, holding a book in her hands. Super's eyes began to adjust. Shelves covered every wall, all filled with books. There must have been thousands of them. She thought how much Misterwizard would love this place, and maybe Johnny, too. She shivered, for the marble floors and stone walls made the room cold. She saw a door near the wall. Slowly making her way towards it, she looked up at the sign above it. On it the words "Emergency Exit" were written, though Super had no idea what they meant. A metal bar crossed the door in the middle with the words on it, "Alarm will sound." Super pressed the bar. The door opened, but no alarm sounded. She figured it must have been disconnected ages ago. Bright sunlight covered her and made her blink and cover her eyes. The door led outside!

She hurried outside and peered around. She saw no one in sight. With a sigh of relief, she ran down the street, careful to keep watch for any Wildies or Beasties.

Now, how was she supposed to find Misterwizard and the Tribe? She saw a group of buildings in the middle of the city. They looked more important than the others, so taking a chance she took off running towards them, hoping she wasn't just getting herself even more lost.

The Tribe continued to watch the camera silently but is remained stationary. Carny held her belly and looked up at it, disappointed. "It's no use, Wizard, I don't think there is anyone there."

Deb moaned and tossed in her woozy state. Misterwizard stood before the camera and spread his hands wide. "If you do not help us, one of our members, a young lady, will die. We beseech you. If you are the descendants of the Leader Nordstroms of this land, you know it is your duty to help its citizenry. We only ask for some medicine, a place comfortable to lay our sick members and a little food."

There was no answer. Finally, Misterwizard lowered his hands in defeat. The Tribe shuffled back towards the stairs leading to the upper floors. Misterwizard returned to the door and stared at the keypad. He had to make it work.

Suddenly, as Misterwizard watched with mounting joy, the door popped open. The Tribe ran back in excitement, all talking at once, and Misterwizard put up a hand to shush them. Misterwizard stood back a step as the door swung ponderously open.

Out stepped an ancient looking man with long, gray frazzled hair and a long beard. His face was wrinkled with age and wire rimmed glasses perched at the end of his nose. He looked so old he made Misterwizard look young. The man frowned, but his gaze was not unkind, simply cautious. But when Misterwizard finally was able to tear his eyes away from the man's craggy face, he saw that he held a gun in his hand, trained right at Misterwizard's heart.

"Hello, and greetings from the Office of the President." The old man cackled at his own joke, bouncing up and down on one foot and then the other until he was seized by a fit of coughing. He bent over and wheezed, but quickly straightened up again and peered at Misterwizard threateningly.

"You must be our last remaining constituents." He laughed again wildly, and Misterwizard couldn't help but smile. The Tribe members grinned as well, all finding the man amusing. "I must say, I have to have had the longest term as President in the history of these here United States!" The old man laughed again, hooting and slapping his knee, and Misterwizard began to suspect he might be a little crazy.

"Thank you for your gracious salutation," Misterwizard said, extending a friendly hand. "I must say that I am honored and very excited to meet the current Commander and Chief, after all these years."

The old man laughed uproariously again, hopping up and down, this time at MIsterwizard's joke, and Misterwizard chuckled along with him. The old man raised the hand that didn't hold the gun and let Misterwizard shake it. Then he looked around at the Tribe, until his eyes rested on Deb lying in the corner.

"I'm sorry about the chilly reception, but you see, you are the first people I've seen in, oh let's say a coon's age, what didn't look either crazy or downright mean and ornery. I couldn't just open for anyone, you know. I've been waiting here all by myself now for forty years. I just about gave up hope of ever seeing any normal ordinary folk again."

"Well, I am ecstatic you saw fit to trust us, for our young girl Deb is in desperate need of some medicine. She has a strong case of Influenza which will take her life soon if we don't act. And we have another young lady with, well, shall we say, another very pressing matter."

"Yes!" The old man hooted with laughter. "Quite a pressing matter, as you say. She's got a bun in the oven about to pop! Even in this present dark age, a baby is still a blessing, hmm?"

"Let us in!" Thegap, Deb's father, implored. "Please, help my daughter!"

"Of course, of course," the old man said, "but not all at once." He lowered the gun and pointed at Misterwizard. "There is only me here, and I don't know you people from Adam. You could be Russkie spies for all I know, or Nazi sympathizers, or worst of all, tree-hugging liberals!" He laughed again, guffawing loudly. "Only this man who looks more intelligent than the rest of you put together, the young sick girl, her father and the expectant mother, and her father. That's a boatload already! And that's it. Any of the rest of you try cross the threshold, I'll blow yer brains out!" He waved the gun in the air for emphasis. Then he laughed again and stood back from the door.

"Please," Bathandbodyworks, Deb's mother implored, "let me go too. I'm the girl's mother."

"And I'm Carny's mother," Teavana said.

"Of course, of course," the old man said. "What kind

of a scoundrel would I be, to separate a mother from her child? Do you think I'm some kind of Communist?" He laughed again, sounding crazy. "The mothers can come, but that's it!"

Thegap ran quickly and gently picked up Deb. He and Bathandbodyworks fell in behind Misterwizard who followed the old man, and slowly they all walked into the dark tunnel beyond. Foodcourt hurried to get Carny and gently helped her walk along next to Teavana. The members of the Tribe watched from the doorway, excited and curious to know what was going to happen next.

Johnny and Starbucks reached The Capitol building again. Johnny saw the crowd of Wildies grew to double the number from the last time. Three hundred or more now milled about on the grassy lawn in front of the building. The Wildies danced and cheered, yelling and hollering. Some fought with each other over scraps of food or bottles. Wildie scrabblers ran around in circles, playing games like all scrabblers did.

"They seem to be having a party," Starbucks said. "I hope we're not the main course.

"I just hope their crazy king didn't find the Tribe. There are so many of them now. I don't think we can fight our way out," Johnny replied.

Johnny and Starbucks walked back inside the Capitol and down the same hallway towards the room at the end where they first talked with Lord Algon. Johnny kept his eyes peeled, looking for trouble. This time the Wildies didn't take them into that room but directed them to a door on the right side. As soon as they entered the dining room, Johnny saw the trouble he dreaded. In the corner of the room Leader Nordstrom glared at them with a look of pure hatred.

"Johnny!" Starbucks whispered to him.

"I see him," Johnny replied in a quiet voice, a dark frown on his face. "I wonder what that snake has been saying about us."

"Nothing good, I can promise you that," Starbucks whispered back.

Leader Nordstrom swallowed hard, though it was difficult for his throat was parched. He started to tremble, despite his best efforts to stand still. Lord Algon saw Johnny and Strabucks as soon as they entered. He smiled, drunk from the red liquid he'd been drinking. Then he put a stern look on his face. His face was flushed from the red liquid and with excitement and his eyes held a wild look.

"Lookey here, lads, here cometh our two steel beastie riders now." The Wildies peeking in through the hole in the wall laughed at Lord Algon's joke. Lord Algon pointed to Leader Nordstrom. "Yon jester tells me the tale ye spun me afore did not parlay the whole truth, but only a portion of it Ye seemed to leave out the most important details, about a certain tribe that ye belong to who've come to our harbor. This makes me wonder if ye be friend or foe and have plans to make us widows in our sleep. I hope yer tongues will wag a little more freely this time."

"Watch them, Your Majesty, they are very tricky!" Leader Nordstrom tried to back up a step, be he was already in the corner of the room. He pointed an accusing finger at Johnny. "They will tell you only what you want to hear, and then they will stab you in the back!"

Johnny approached Lord Algon, Starbucks behind him. He looked Lord Algon in the eye with confidence. Lord Algon noticed his bravery and frowned, for real bravery scared him.

"Your Majesty, it is true, we did not mention our tribe. But it was not because we intended to do you or your people any harm. We only did it to protect our tribe. We came here, seeking medicine for a sick member. Once we had the medicine, we will be on our way."

Johnny knew he was lying; their plans were to make a new Sanctuary in the city. Johnny hoped Leader Nordstrom didn't tell them all the Tribe's plans, or he'd be exposed as a liar. That most surely meant their death.

Lord Algon. "And yet lie ye did, with much skill and cunning."

Suddenly there was a commotion outside. The whole assembly turned to the door in curiosity. The door opened and a crowd of Wildies came in. At the head of the crowd an old man stood, and it appeared that the crowd was following him and watching him. The man wore a big smile of pride, as if it was the first time he had been ever been honored in such a fashion. Leader Nordstrom frowned with confusion. What was going on?

The old man walked to stand in front of Lord Algon, who wore a confused look, for the red liquid made his mind work slowly. "Gragnok, the old, useless and gray. For what reason come ye like a pesky fly-beastie to buzz in me ear, ye who have no more use than a torn sail. Have ye finally found a purpose in this world besides eating food and using precious air? Were ye not so tough of skin, ye would have been cooked and fed to your mates long ago. And ye come with a whole crew sailing alongside thee. What be the meaning?"

The old man knelt before Lord Algon and bowed his head in reverence. "My Lord, I beg ye forgive me for the arrogant act I perform, but I come with news ye will find of good interest."

Lord Algon waved his hand. "Speak on then, err I grow impatient and run me sword through your mangy heart for sport."

Gragnok smiled and told Lord Algon all about the buses. Johnny and Starbucks looked at each other, dismayed. The Tribe had been discovered.

As Misterwizard and the rest followed the old man, he picked up a smoky torch from a wall. He started down a dark, narrow passageway of stone that sloped downwards.

"Welcome to the President's Emergency Operations Center, or Peacock, as I like to call it." The old man chuckled loudly, his voice echoing off the narrow walls. "I'm afraid it's a little drafty and dark. The power source lasted for quite a few years, but, my, it's been dark in most of the facility for at least, well, how long has it been?" The old man pulled on his beard and looked up at the ceiling. "Well, it was before I got the rheumatism in my legs, and that was at least five years ago, but then it was dark long before that. At least it's warm down here!" He hooted but kept walking. "The thermal heat from below takes care of that. It does get a little stuffy, however, on the lower levels. I did manage to restore some power, but I can only spare it for my living space and the essentials, such as the food storage units.”

"May we ask your name, good friend?" Misterwizard asked pleasantly.

The old man looked back at Misterwizard with a frown of embarrassment as he continued to shuffle along. "My yes. Dear me, where are my manners? You'd think I had no training in diplomacy or tact at all. And in fact, I haven't, really!" The old man cackled again. "It's been years since I've had a decent conversation. Everyone else is so quiet lately. I guess we all just ran out of things to say." He laughed again, hooting with hilarity.

"You were going to tell me your name," Misterwizard reminded him.

"Oh yes. Rumpelstiltskin in my name. Ha, ha, ha, ha!" The old man chortled, and Misterwizard smiled and shook his head. "Just pulling your leg, Sonny. I can call you Sonny, because everyone is younger than me! My name is Reginald, or at least that's what people used to call me.

He stopped and put a finger to his chin, frowning. "Or is it Ralph? No, no, I distinctly recall it being Reginald. Or was it Rebecca? No, don't be silly, that's a girl's name!"

He started down the passageway again. "Reginald it is, unless I remember something else. I'm the son of the son of the President. Can you believe that?"

"Why, of course," Misterwizard said. "What happened to everyone else, Reginald?"

"They're all down below. You will meet them soon." Reginald cackled again. "Except for the Secretary of State. He choked on a peanut. Can you believe it? He survives a nuclear war, and one year later, chokes on a peanut!" Reginald hooted and slapped his knee.

Misterwizard chuckled. "Then there's the Vice President. He only lasted six months, just until the power went into power saving mode. One day he started saying, 'It's all over! It's all over! We're doomed!' and hung himself in the Ready Room. Reginald laughed again. "Quite a Gloomy Gus, he was." Reginald turned to Wizard. "Lots of funny stories, most of them tragic as well. And what's your name, Young Man?"

"Misterwizard laughed. "I must say, I appreciate your calling me young, though I can't be more than ten years younger than you. Everyone in my tribe simply calls me 'Misterwizard.' My real name is Adam."

"Adam the Wizard, eh?" Reginald cackled again and shook with laughter. "Well met, Misterwizard. If I need any magic potions, I know who to go to now!"

They reached the end of the passage. In front of them stood the doors to an elevator. On the right they could see a metal door. "I'm afraid we're walking, Wizard, unless you have a broom to ride, heh, heh! But then, that's a witch, isn't it, not a wizard! Fortunately, it's all downhill from here. Twenty stories downhill!" Reginald chuckled as he led them to a door. He opened it to reveal a dark metal stairway. "You're not afraid of the dark are you, Misterwizard?"

"Just hurry, please," Thegap said. "Deb needs the medicine."

"Oh, all right," Reginald said grumpily. He led the way through the door and they started to descend the staircase. Misterwizard looked down. There was nothing but a black hole as far as he could see. Reginald was moving fast, and it wasn't long before the light grew to a small flicker. Misterwizard and the rest hurried to catch up.

CHAPTER 2

Super ran down the street, hiding whenever she saw any Wildies, searching for any sign of the buses. She looked ahead and saw a strange stick-like building with the top half broken off. Ahead of the stick building she saw a big rectangular grassy field. On either side of the grassy field, tall, square white buildings stood, one after another. She decided she should probably avoid the big grassy area, for it would be easy to see her there. She walked to the left of the stick building and around the back of the first big white structure.

And then she saw the buses! All three sat right behind the first building. Her heart soared with relief. Her legs ached from the long walk and she couldn't wait to see MIsterwizard and Deb again.

She heard a noise in the distance and looked. A whole crowd of Wildies approached. At the head of the crowd stood a strange man in a long fur coat with gold things dangling from it. And Leader Nordstrom walked next to him! Then she saw Johnny and Starbucks! The walked next to the funny looking man, hands tied. They'd were still prisoners. Super had to get inside the building and warn the Tribe. As fast as she could she ran for the door before the strange man and his army spied her. When she tried the door it wouldn't open. She yelled as loud as she could.

"Misterwizard! Misterwizard! Let me in! It's Super!"

In the Museum, the Tribe had gone back to exploring. They broke open the cases and played with the items inside, and soon a party-like atmosphere developed as they tried on clothes and played with all the strange and fascinating objects. They laughed at each other as they paraded around, looking silly in weird outfits and wearing the strange artifacts.

Suddenly they heard a yelling from outside. The tribe members looked at each other fearfully.

Foodcourt turned to Johnny's mother, Teavanna. She frowned back with concern and shook her head, indicating he shouldn't open the door. The Tribe rushed to back door and stood all around it, listening. Then they heard Super's voice. Foodcourt smiled and carefully removed the bench, opened the door and peeked outside. There he saw Super, her long black hair framing her long slender face and her brown eyes staring at him.

Super peered back at him, looking frantic. "Let me in! There's a crowd of Wildies coming. Some weird guy is leading it. Leader Nordstrom looks like he's with the guy, and they have Johnny and Starbucks captive!"

Super's words put the whole Tribe in a panic once again. They all talked fearfully as Foodcourt let Super in.

Then as many as could fit peered out the door and down the street. The crowd of Wildies marched down the street, all yelling with excitement. As the Tribe members at the door watched with dismay, the Wildies swarmed the buses and piled inside them. They saw them through the windows searching the seats and grabbing all of the Tribe members' possesions.

Super closed the door and she turned back to the Tribe. "They'll be coming after us next. We have to block these doors again with everything we can find!"

The Tribe burst into fearful yammering again. "Quiet!" Super yelled. Slowly the Tribe members stopped talking. "Hurry, we don't have a lot of time!"

The members of the Tribe split up, grabbed benches and chairs and pulled them to the door for a barricade.

Foodcourt turned to Super. "What about Johnny and Starbucks? What if they want in?"

Super shrugged, frowning sadly. "I don't know, Foodcourt. I just know we can't let that mob in."

Foodcourt nodded glumly. "We have to tell Misterwizard."

"I'll go," Super said, "I'm faster than anybody else in the Tribe."

"Go, Super, find him. Let him know we need him badly! Around the corner you will find some stairs. Go to the lower floor and you will see a door leading into the darkness. Misterwizard is somewhere down there!"

Super nodded and took off running. Foodcourt turned to the Tribe. "Listen up now! Bring everything that is heavy to the door! This is our new Sanctuary, and we must defend it!"

The Tribe brought the stone benches and wooden chairs and soon a pile formed in front of the back door.

When they were done the pile reached higher than their heads.

"There!" Yelled Foodcourt. "It would take a whole mob to open that door now!"

Super ran, as fast as a deer-beastie, down the stairs into basement. She saw the strange opening leading into darkness. She stopped just outside the door and peered in. Then slowly she walked down the gloomy, unlit passageway.

After what seemed an eternity of walking, down, down, down, Reginald, Misterwizard and the others with them reached another door. This one said, "President's Emergency Operations Center. Entry by Authorized Personnel Only. Proper ID required. Deadly Force Is Authorized."

"Just ignore the sign," Reginald said. "I'm in charge now, and I say you're authorized." Reginald laughed crazily again. He pushed open the door, which turned out to be unlocked. They entered dark room stretching as far as they could see. Dark shapes filled the room. As they slowly entered they discovered long couches and tables. In one corner of the room stood a curved counter with a dark mirror behind it and shelves full of bottles.

Lush, green carpet covered the floor, but it was covered with dust and stains. A huge glass screen filled one wall on another side of the room. The visitors stood behind Reginald and peered into the dark, trying to let their eyes adjust.

"You'll have to excuse the mess," Reginald said, his

voice full of mirth. "The maid died a hundred years ago." He cackled again. "This was the Situation Room, where they talked, but mostly drank. And the situation was very dire, indeed. Ha ha!"

Misterwizard and the rest of his group stopped, mouths open in horror, for as their eyes adjusted, they saw dark shapes sitting on the couches. As they looked more closely, they realized they were the skeletons of people in ratty, moldy clothes. Misterwizard looked at the remains and counted the number in his head. Six men and four women, all sitting they died. Some lay slumped over, others sat upright, as if having died in the middle of a conversation. On man held a gun in his hand. His head lay on the back of the couch, a neat round hole in the side of it. A woman's skeleton still held a martini glass, as if she died in the middle of taking a drink.

Reginald walked to where he was standing in the middle of the corpses and smiled happily. "Ladies and gentlemen look what I've brought! New friends! Please stop sulking and greet them!"

None of the skeletons responded, they just kept staring into the darkness, seeming to smile in a macabre fashion. Reginald frowned grumpily and walked up to one corpse sitting on a couch. It wore a tattered green hat with a black brim, a green coat with colorful ribbons on the left side of its chest and green pants. Reginald scowled crossly in the skeleton's face and put a hand on its shoulder. He shook the shoulder roughly. "Roger don't be impolite. I know you think you're important, being a four-star General, but the least you can do is say hello." The skeleton didn't respond, just sat, staring off into space. "All right, General Halston. Are you happy now?"

The skeleton still didn't answer. Reginald let go of it and frowned, very unhappy. He strode over to the skeleton of a woman lying on her side on another couch wearing the remains of a shiny red dress. Wisps of her brown hair still clung to her skull, and it looked as if someone, probably Reginald, had slathered lipstick around her mouth where her lips would have been. Reginald sat her up and shook her. "Cheryl, I know you've had too much to drink, but please, you are all embarrassing me. Please don't be rude to our guests!"

Miserwizard saw Reginald was getting very upset so he said, "It's all right, Reginald, totally understandable, really. We're strangers. I'm sure they'll, uh, warm to us eventually."

"Humph," Reginald said. He turned from the skeletons as if ashamed and disgusted with them. "I apologize, Misterwizard. Over the last few years, they've become very sullen and moody. They rarely even talk to me anymore. I'm afraid it's my fault. I did something about five years ago that upset all of them greatly, and they just won't forgive me." Reginald sat down on the couch next to a skeleton in a suit full of holes and sobbed. Tears came to his eyes and he wiped them on the skeleton's sleeve. Misterwizard and the others stared at him, uncomfortable and creeped out.

Carny pulled on the sleeve of Misterwizard's short sleeve Hawaiian shirt. "Misterwizard, I can't wait!'

"Reginald, please, we must hurry!"

Reginald just sat, lost in his own sorry, staring at the skeletons. "I've begged them to tell me what I did, but they refuse to even talk to me. I still treat them like my friends, hoping they'll change their minds, but…"

Misterwizard looked at the others. Carny was about

to collapse and sweat covered her face. Deb lay unconscious in her mother Bathandbodyworks's arms, for her father Thegap was too small to carry her for long. The others looked at Misterwizard, hoping he'd do something, for Reginald was scarcing them.

Misterwizard walked up to Reginald and gently put a hand on his shoulder. "There, there, Reginald, I'm sure they will come around, eventually. Meanwhile, you have us now to talk to, don't you?"

A smile of joy spread across Reginald's face and he stopped crying. He nodded. "Yes, I do. You don't know what it means to me. I-I've been so alone. You have no idea."

Misterwizard patted Reginald on the back. Reginald gathered himself together, and soon he was his old smiling self again. "But what am I doing? You need medicine and a delivery room, and here I am prattling on like an old fool. Onward and upward!"

Reginald led them across the room. Misterwizard and the others followed as best as they could, but the darkness made it hard to avoid the couches and tables.

"Reginald, do you have no illumination in this facility?"

Reginald stopped and turned. "Mercy me! I'm so used to walking around in the dark to conserve energy I totally forgot you might need some!" He laughed crazily again, totally back to his cheerful demeanor.

"Let me fix that." Reginald walked to a switch on the wall and turned a small round dial. Slowly, lights hidden on the top corners of the walls came on, and they could see the room. It was very large, with wood paneled walls, three sets of couches, a dining room table and chairs by one wall and a small kitchen at the far end of the room.

"MIsterwizard!" Carny yelled. "He's coming!"

"Please, Reginald, some speed would be appreciated!"

"Yes, yes!" Reginald ran to a glass door at the far end of the room. Beyond it they could see a hallway lined with glass doors on either side.

"This is the way. I know where to go!" Reginald yanked the door open and ran down the hall, Misterwizard and Carny right behind him with the others following.

As they passed each door, Reginald opened each one and explained its purpose. "Game room. Pool and sauna. Auxiliary kitchen. Bathroom, what you'd call the Necessary Room, heh, heh. And here is what we're looking for, the Dispensary."

Reginald led them through the door into another hallway. The walls were white with glass doors on either side leading to exam rooms and operating rooms. The hallway extended back a long way, showing twenty or thirty rooms on either side.

"Follow me, and I'll take you to where you can put the expectant mother. By the way, who will be her attending physician?" Reginald cackled some more.

"That will be me," Misterwizard said with a smile. "I'm the Midwife for our Tribe, at the present."

Reginald looked at him and chuckled. "Well, you'll find all the things you need to deliver ten babies here, but let's hope there are no complications. We have no one to perform a C-section or give anesthesia if it's needed. Though we have all the medical supplies you could ever need."

Reginald led MisterWizard, Foodcourt and Carny to what looked like a delivery room. Misterwizard and

Foodcourt helped ease Carny onto the delivery table, where she laid back with a sigh of relief.

"How are you feeling, dear?" Misterwizard asked, his brow furrowed with concern.

"Okay, I guess. Miracle has stopped pushing for a moment. You don't think there is anything wrong, do you?"

Misterwizard patted her on the arm. "No, everything is fine. Miracle will come when he's good and ready, and not a moment sooner."

Carny smiled and put her head down. Foodcourt found a blanket to keep her warm and began wiping her wet forehead with a cloth.

Reginald watched the proceedings with a grin. "Who'd ever a' thought, another baby would be born in this place, after all that's happened. It just goes to show, Life goes on!" He laughed heartily and Misterwizard couldn't help but join in. Even Foodcourt smiled.

"She seems stable for a moment," Misterwizard said. "So please, Reginald, will you help us with our other patient, one in much more urgent need of assistance?"

"Follow me!" Reginald led them to another room with a leather bed in it. Bathandbodyworks, set Deb down on the bed and smoothed back her hair.

"By gum, you'll find what you want here I wager, for whatever ails you! All kept in refrigerated cabinets, though I daresay the expiration dates on some of them might have passed."

Misterwizard watched as Reginald searched through cabinets, pulling out medicine bottles, looking at their labels and throwing them back. "Anti-, anti-, anti-, anti-biotics!" Reginald pulled out a plastic bottle and held it up triumphantly. "Give her a couple of these, and she'll be right as rain before you know it!"

Misterwizard took them gratefully, as Thegap and Bathandbodyworks looked on anxiously. "We cannot adequately express our gratitude, dear Reginald. Do you have any water that she could take these with?"

"Of course. Water, we have in abundance. I can only drink so much by myself, and I must admit, water is not my favorite beverage, if you know what I mean. Ha, ha, ha! I'll be back presently." Reginald hurried out of the room. Misterwizard looked through the cabinets to see what other medicines he could find.

His head in the cabinet, he spoke in a muffled voice. "This is wonderful. He has a treasure trove here, everything from medicine to relieve back-ache to pills for acne!" Misterwizard had to laugh at his own joke, for it completely escaped Thegap and Bathandbodyworks. They weren't really listening anyway for they were too busy looking anxiously at Deb and waiting for Reginald to return with the water.

Presently he returned, carrying a white plastic cup filled with water. But in his hand, he held a gun, pointed at his visitors. He wore a grim, angry frown and his lower lip quivered. Thegap swallowed with fright and looked at Misterwizard, who didn't see Reginald enter for his head was still deep in the cabinet.

"MIsterwizard." Thegap said in a high-pitched voice.

"Be with you momentarily, my good man," MIsterwizard said as the sound of bottles being picked up and shaken came from inside the cabinet. "I'm looking to see if he has something for an old man's arthritis."

"Misterwizard, now!" Thegap said in a squeak.

Misterwizard's head finally popped out of the cabinet. He wore a look of curious concern at Thegap's tone as he looked at him. Then he saw Reginald, and his frown deepened.

Reginald looked at him and scowled darkly, pointing the gun at Misterwizard's heart. "Misterwizard, have I prematurely put my trust in you? I considered you friends. Are you instead interlopers here to usurp my authority and perform acts of piracy?"

Misterwizard walked forward to stand in front of Reginald. "Whatever do you mean, Reginald?" MIsterwizard's eyebrows shot up in confusion.

"I made a simple request that the rest of your entourage wait upstairs until I had time to assure myself of your true intentions. And yet, on the security cameras I see the dark figure of a young lady approaching. I this the beginning of a coup de' tat?"

Reginald took a step forward, the gun leveled at MIsterwizard's heart. Bathandbodyorks put her hand to her mouth in fright. Thegap placed himself between Reginald and Deb. "I was truly fond of you, Adam. It has been so long since I've had an intelligent personality to converse with, since the others are still angry with me. In fact, since we seemed so alike, I began to think of you as my own personal Doppelganger, a kindred spirit of sorts with whom I could share the mysteries of the universe. And yet, now it appears that you are a false friend and I will have the unpleasant task of shooting you."

Misterwizard raised his hands in supplication. "Reginald, please believe me, we spoke truthfully and with complete candor. I did instruct the Tribe. If someone approaches, I can only suspect that a calamity or great proportions forces them to disobey my instructions and seek me out."

Reginald's hand shook, and he lowered the gun

slightly. Then he smiled his old crazy smile again. "You talk just like me." He laughed, and Misterwizard and the others smiled, feeling less threatened.

"I hope you are sincere. I may look like a crotchety old man, and I admit that I might appear to suffer from a slight case of psychosis. All right, a big case. I'm crazy!" Reginald cackled darkly. "But I have enough of my faculties left to pull this trigger long before you or your fellow conspirators can stay my hand, be assured of that."

"Please, Reginald, give us a chance to prove our fidelity. You say it is a lone figure. I promise you, we will not move from this spot. My only movement will be back and forth from here to Carny's room to check on her. We will not attempt to escape. All I ask is that you give the person approaching a chance to identify themselves before you shoot them. I give you my word that if it's someone from my Tribe, they mean you no harm."

Reginald lowered the gun but narrowed his eyes, trying to look tough and frightening, but his old age, long gray hair and spindly body didn't help make him convincing. "Very well, you, and you alone, my traverse from this room to the other. If any of move in the direction of the Ready Room, I will shoot you all before you take two steps! I have six bullets and there's only, well, seven of you, but two are sick so they don't count!"

Reginald backed to the door and opened it. "I will greet this party crasher and discover her true intentions. If she is the vanguard of a larger invasion force, she will rue the day she tangled with the son of the son of the President! I am perfectly capable of defending my position. In fact, I have enough firepower to fight off the whole Polish army!" Reginald cackled again, his face lit up with laughter, and Misterwizard smiled and chuckled too. "My grandfather was not a well-liked man, for very good reason, since he started the whole shooting match. He expected an invading force to come and try to give him recompense, and so he filled this place with weaponry. We survived a nuclear war, we can survive anything!"

With these words, Reginald walked out. Misterwizard, Thegap and Bathandbodyworks waited nervously, wondering what was going to happen.

Ripper and the Gangers hid behind the broken stick building and crept up to where they could see the crowd of Wildies congregated on the grassy Mall. Ripper looked at the dirty, broken down shacks and studied the crowd of Wildies. Facegash moved up silently to stand next to him. "Look at all of them, Ripper. How we gonna take 'em all?"

Ripper smiled coldly. "They're all sheep. They won't be any trouble. All we have to do is find their Leader Nordstrom. We kidnap him and torture him a little and he'll do whatever we say. Then we'll be in charge. We'll have all these stupid, worthless Wildies serving us. Then we'll have even more people to help us take care of Johnny and his Tribe for good."

Facegash looked across the Mall to the other side at the Capitol. His eyes opened wide in excitement. He looked at Ripper and pointed at the Capitol. "Look, Ripper! That must be their king! And looks who's with him! Johnny and Starbucks!"

"And not only that, look, there's that worm-beastie Leader Nordstrom!" Lady Stabs said from where she stood a few feet away.

Ripper scowled, disappointed that it seemed like they'd arrived too late.

As the Gangers watched, Lord Algon, Leader Nordstrom, Johnny and Starbucks all walked out of the old Capitol. They strode across the grassy Mall, heading somewhere with the crowd of Wildies following, yelling and jabbering. "Johnny and the Tribe are already making an alliance with him!" Facegash said.

"I don't know," said Lady Stabs "Look, Johnny and Starbucks' hands are tied. And so are Leader Nordstrom's."

"Yeah!" Facegash said, smiling. "What do you think, Ripper?"

"That might not mean anything," Ripper said, scowling. "Knowing Johnny, he'll still find a way to make a pact with the guy. We gotta move fast. We got to create a distraction and grab the Wildies' king. Then we'll make him change his mind. He'll decide to align with us or lose some fingers or maybe some teeth."

Facegash laughed. "So, what's your plan?"

Ripper held up one of the sticks with the string. "We still have some of old Misterwizard's toys we found. It's about to get a lot more fun around here."

Ripper, Facegash and the rest of the Gangers laughed with evil glee.

Super hurried down the dark passageway. She couldn't see her hand in front of her face. She slowed to a walk and put her hands in front of her, feeling her way. The darkness was so thick it felt like a heavy blanket on top of her, smothering her. The air was stale and unmoving, and she grew scared.

"MIsterwizard!" Super yelled. The sound of her voice seemed to die two feet in front of her. It was stuffy and hot. Sweat formed all over her body and on her face. She crept along, dread filling her, no matter how much she tried to ignore it. Her heart beat fast. What if she turned the wrong way and took the wrong passage? She might wander for hours, maybe days, and be trapped, and no one would ever find her. She tried to put the thought out of her head, but it came back again and again like an annoying itch. Finally, she set her jaw in stubborn determination. She was risking a lot, maybe her life, but it didn't matter. She determined to keep going until she found Misterwizard, no matter what it took.

A cold breeze chilled her face, and the utter darkness made her feel woozy.

"Misterwizard!" She whispered loudly. "Misterwizard! Where are you?"

Suddenly a dark, sinister voice sounded from somewhere in the dark. "Who are you, to darken my halls? And what has it gots in its pocketsess?"

Super couldn't help but squeak in fear. She stopped and pulled her arms to her chest. She peered around in the dark but couldn't tell where the voice came from. She turned one way, then the other, expecting to be jumped on at any minute.

"I'm Super," Super squeaked. "I'm looking for Misterwizard. Have you seen him?"

"Super, you say? Super-duper, or Super-size? Supercilious, or Superficial? Or are you just Superior? Is that your real name, or are you just being superlative? Come, come; tell me the truth!"

"My real name is Supercalifragilisticexpialidocious." Even with her fear, Super couldn't help but smile with pride as she said her name. "It's a special name, the only one like it in the whole world. Misterwizard gave it to me."

Reginald burst into cackling laughter, so much that he sat down on the ground. Super tiptoed forward and found him sitting in the corner, out of breath with tears in his eyes. "Supercalifragilisticexpialidocious. My, my, that's a kicker! I haven't heard that word since I was a little boy! Your Misterwizard is a hoot!"

Super smiled, losing her fear as she squinted to see the strange old man sitting on the floor. "Do you know where he is? I have to find him right away! Some people are trying to break in! They have Johnny and Starbucks! The Tribe is in danger!"

Her words snapped Reginald out of his fit of laughter. "Misterwizard said it was something like that. Jingo, I'm glad he was telling the truth! Come, come, I'll take you to him! No time to waste!"

Reginald pulled a torch from under his clothes and lit it. The sudden light hurt Super's eyes and she covered them with her hand. Reginald grabbed her other hand and started running. Super had no choice but to run along with him.

"We're off to see Misterwizard!" Reginald howled with laughter.Once again down the long passageway Reginald ran, this time with Super in tow and trying to keep up.

Johnny, Starbucks and Leader Nordstrom, hands tied, followed behind Lord Algon's entourage towards the Museum. Lord Algon sat on a portable throne carried on the shoulders of four of his guards. The Wildies followed, hooting, hollering and pointing at the prisoners and having a great time, for nothing like this had ever happened in the city before. But Johnny knew that for him and Starbucks, things were very dangerous. He knew Lord Algon and the Wildies headed for Misterwizard and the Tribe, for he'd listened when the old man told Lord Algon all about the buses he found. Johnny just hoped that Super would reach Misterwizard and the Tribe and warn them about the huge mob heading their way before it arrived, or the Tribe would be totally unprepared.

Johnny turned to Starbucks. In a voice that only Starbucks could hear, he said, "Leader Nordstrom is going to do whatever he need to in order to save his own life, even if it means betraying the Tribe. We have to prove to Lord Algon what a rat Leader Nordstrom is."

Starbucks nodded. "If Leader Nordstrom convinces Lord Algon that he is still the leader of the Tribe, things could go really bad for Misterwizard."

"Whatever happens, we have to be ready to protect the Tribe," Johnny said. "Even if-"

"I know," Starbucks said, not letting Johnny finish. "Even if we die, I want to see Leader Nordstrom gets what he deserves." Johnny nodded in agreement. Then they both stopped talking and watched the road ahead.

Soon they reached the Museum and Johnny saw the buses. As soon as they saw them, the Wildies shouted with excitement, ran to the buses and climbed inside. As Lord Algon, Johnny and the rest grew closer, Johnny could see the Wildies throwing things out the windows of the buses where other Wildies quickly grabbed them and fought over them.

"Avast, we have reached the port where ye Tribe be moored," Lord Algon said from his throne in the air. "Won't be long now 'fore we discover who be tellin' the truth, and who be joining Davy Jones in his locker."

Starbucks whispered to Johnny. "I sure wish he'd stop with that weird talking jazz. It's really beginning to give me a headache." Starbucks grinned, and Johnny grinned back at him.

"Get ready. We're going to have to act soon."

CHAPTER 3

R ipper and the Gangers watched the procession wind its way behind the buildings on the side of the Mall until they reached the Museum of American History. Then they crept up to where they could see the back of the Museum and the buses.

"Look, Ripper!" Facegash yelled. "The buses! They found the Tribe!"

"Then it's time to act!" Ripper pulled out his knife and the dynamite he'd stashed. All the Gangers pulled out their guns and knives too. "It looks like they're busy looting the buses. We need to get to 'em before they get inside. When I say go, we go. It's time to start this party!"

Lord Algon lifted a hand, and his guards set him on the ground. He stood up and watched the Wildies rush to the door of the Museum. Johnny worked feverishly on the ropes tying his hands. Starbucks noticed, and started to do the same thing.

"This is it, Johnny," Starbucks whispered. "We're going to have to fight for the Tribe!"

"Hurry and get your ropes off, Starbucks. We have to find a way to slow them down!"

The Wildies banged on the doors to the Museum, but they couldn't get inside. One of the Wildies ran to Lord Algon.

"My Lord, the doors be barred from the inside!"

Lord Algon turned to Johnny and Starbucks. The boys stopped struggling with their ropes so that he wouldn't catch them at it.

"It seems your Tribe be reluctant to welcome its guests. Ye may want to help them change their minds, afore I grow angry and take it as a sign they're not the friendly sort. Then I be finding another means of entry, and those inside will suffer the worse for it."

Lord Algon turned to Leader Nordstrom, who had been attempting to slowly back up to where he could run away. He stopped now and smiled weakly at the king. "Avast, old jester, ye claim to be the true captain of these interlopers. Prove to me what ye say be true and give orders for them to unbar yon doors, and I will know of a truth it be you and the young masters here."

Leader Nordstrom smiled weakly. "Well, your Supreme Majesty, I will do what I can, but, uh, forsooth, I have been away from my Tribe for a, uh, fortnight, and forsooth, they may not hearken unto my, uh, voice."

"Lord Algon, may I speak?" Johnny asked.

Lord Algon turned to look at Johnny and raised his hand in permission.

"I will tell you the story of my Tribe, and this is the whole truth. We come from a land far away from here, a land called Fill-a-delpia. We came for medicine to help a sick member of our Tribe, medicine that can only be found in this building. Our real Leader Nordstrom is a great man named Misterwizard, and he is inside this building now, trying to find the medicine. This man," Johnny pointed his chin towards Leader Nordstrom, "was once the Leader Nordstrom of our tribe, but in a moment of danger, he fled, to protect his own life. He betrayed us and left us to die. He only cares about one person, and this is himself. If you let us, Lord Algon, my Tribe will be your allies, for we have no desire to fight with you. But you must not trust this man."

Lord Algon turned and stared intently at Leader Nordstrom. Leader Nordstrom's face twisted with fear mixed with anger. He shook with tension. He turned to look at Johnny with a scowl of hatred.

"He's a lying snake, Lord Algon! He is Johnny Apocalypse, troublemaker, and criminal! He is the reason our tribe had to flee our Sanctuary. He would never obey the rules. He always wanted to steal the Tribe from me and become Leader Nordstrom himself! He's why I had to leave. He always hated me and did everything he could to undermine my authority. With his cohort Starbucks, they roam the land, stealing and killing!"

Leader Nordstrom pointed a shaking finger at the Museum and his voice rose shrilly.

"And his friend Misterwizard, watch him, Your Majesty!" Leader Nordstrom's eyes opened wide as he talked. "He is a dangerous old man who will enchant and trick you with his spells and strange contraptions from the Time before the Great War. You have to kill all three of them, Lord Algon, before they turn the tables on you!"

There was silence for a moment, as Lord Algon looked first at Leader Nordstrom, and then at Johnny and Starbucks. Then Lord Algon burst into wild, insane laughter. The Wildies all joined him, and the sound filled the air. While they were distracted, Johnny worked feverishly on his ropes, and so did Starbucks.

Lord Algon stopped laughing and looked at Johnny with a wild, crazy look in his eyes. "The jest is on all three of thee, foolish strangers. I ne'er intended to ally with either of thee. I only played thee for sport. When gain we gain entrance to thine tribe's hideout, they too shall join thee in making excellent food for our table. For we need meat more than mates."

The Wildies cheered. Leader Nordstrom's face went white and his mouth opened wide. "Wha-what do you mean? What kind of people are you?"

"Johnny!" Starbucks yelled. "They're cannibals!"

Johnny struggled harder. "We have to get free, Starbucks, now!"

Lord Algon grinned at Leader Nordstrom. "Aye, cannibals ye may calls us. But ye, scrawny old man need fear thee not. Ye be too pasty and yellow to be very tasty. Instead, ye shall be a momentary distraction in my Arena, which ye have not yet been a witness to, but will presently. We will see how long ye last, and I wager it 'twill not be long."

"Ah!" Leader Nordstrom yelled in terror. He backed up and turned to run, but Wildies barred his way, grinning evilly at him. He sank onto the floor, shaking. Johnny and Starbucks worked feverishly at their bounds, knowing their lives hung on whether they could get free.

A scream of utter terror came from a Wildie at the very far edge of the crowd. More yells followed and suddenly the crowd of Wildie started running in all directons. Lord Algon turned and looked to see what was going on. "Avast, what be happening now?"

Johnny and Starbucks, happy for the distraction, worked harder on their bounds. Leader Nordstrom stood up and slowly inched away, trying to get behind Lord Algon's throne where he could make a run for it and not be seen.

The crowd of Wildies ran in all directions. A Wildie ran up to Lord Algon. "Your Majesty! A huge beastie be among us! It grabbeth a man and draggeth him away!"

Lord Algon laughed, amused, but made sure to move so he was behind his guards. "What a merry joke be this! A beastie taketh his portion whilst we be so busy we spy him not. Let him eat his fill, for he hast earned it, and then capture him we will. He will make be good sport in the Arena chasing yonder old fool. Then we mayhaps keep it for pet!"

"This guy is nuts, Johnny!" Starbucks said.

"How are you doing on your ropes?" Johnny replied.

"I'm free."

"So am I. When I nod my head, we run for it."

But before Johnny was could act, the Wildies at the door of the Museum ran away from it, their eyes wide with fear. What was happening now?

When Super and Reginald reached MisterwWizard, they found him in the delivery room with Carny, Foodcourt and Teavana. Miracle was on his way!

Misterwizard wore a blue gown and a funny blue hat on his bald head. He was so short his head just stood over the surface of the bed. He stood at the end of the bed as he watched Carny work at giving birth. Super grinned with joy, watching the miracle of birth. Reginald left and waited outside, wanting to give the family its privacy. Super became so entranced she almost forgot what she came for. Then she remembered.

"Misterwizard!" Super said. "Some Wildies are trying to break in through the back doors! They have some weird leader, and he has Johnny and Starbucks prisoner! And even worse, Leader Nordstorm is with them too! What do we do?"

Misterwizard looked over Carny's body and said loudly, "Push!"

"I'm trying!" Carny said.

Misterwizard looked at Super. "This is not a convenient time for an invasion!"

Super shrugged. "Sorry."

"Push!"

"I am!"

Misterwizard looked at Super again. "How many Wildies are with them? Is it merely a rabble or a more organized and formidable force?"

Super frowned and took Carny's hand. Carny squeezed Super's hand and closed her eyes, concentrating. "It looks like a lot of them, Misterwizard. A whole lot. And they seem pretty organized."

Misterwizard called to Reginald. "Reginald, good friend!"

Reginald re-entered the room.

"Now would be an excellent time for you to have decided that our intentions are honorable. We could definitely use your assistance during this new crisis."

Reginald pulled on his beard and arched his big, gray bushy eyebrows. "I really don't know you people from Adam, ha, ha, but I've always been a good judge of character. At least of the few people I knew, since I grew up in this place and only known about thirty people in my lifetime. Jumping Jehoshaphat, you have to trust somebody sometime!" He cackled with laughter again. "I suppose you want to bring your people down here, to keep them safe, tramp all over my halls, eat all my food and make a mess, get into everything, is that it?"

Misterwizard grinned in a friendly way. "That is precisely my intentions, good fellow."

Reginald cackled again. "Well I say, by gum and by golly, let's do it then! I've waited a long time to be able to complain about it being too crowded. And now I can!"

They all laughed with Reginald as continued his crazy laugher.

"Misterwizard, what about Johnny and Starbucks? That king has them!"

MIsterwizard nodded grimly. "We'll have to worry about them after the Tribe is safe." He turned and looked at Carny. "One more good push should do it, Carny!"

"I'm trying. If you would all leave and let me do it..."

"What do we do, Misterwizard?" Super asked.

"First, we need to secure the doors in the Museum well enough to gain time to help the Tribe reach the Bunker Then we'll need to secure the doors again, for an indefinite amount of time. Reginald, you're going to have visitors."

"Yee-haw!" Reginald laughed and hopped up and down.

"Super, you are going to have to take charge in my place. Do you think you can do it?"

"Me in charge?" Super said, smiling with pleasure. "You bet!"

"I'll help her, Misterwizard!" Foodcourt said. "Teavana can stay here and help you with Carny."

"Excellent."

"And I'll help them!" Reginald shouted. "I've waited years for some good old-fashioned danger and excitement!"

Misterwizard chuckled. "Now, please go about your tasks and let me finish delivering this wriggler, if you please."

"Got it!" Super shouted. Super, Foodcourt and Reginald ran out of the room.

"Now, where were we?" Misterwizard said.

"Having… a… wriggler." Carny said, her face red and sweat pouring from her face.

Misterwizard grinned. "Of course. Push!"

Super, Foodcourt and Reginald returned to the Ready Room.

"Wait!" Reginald said, grabbing Foodcourt's arm and stopping him. Foodcourt and Suepr stopped and turned to see what he wanted. Reginald smiled, lifted a finger to tell them to wait and then ran to another door. As they watched with curiosity, he walked through the door, which they could see led to another long hallway, this one with walls of concrete. After a few moments he returned, carrying small round green balls in his hands.

He walked back to them and handed a few to each of them, wearing a dark, sinister grin.

"Just in case! Just in case!" He cackled with laughter again and hurried back to the stairway to the passage. Foodcourt and Starbucks looked at each other, shrugged and ran to follow.

Back at the Museum, Super, Foodcourt and Reginald arrived to see a scene of desperation and confusion. Piled against the huge doors were the oddest assortment of items anyone alive had ever seen, from bicycles to suits of armor. And pushing against all the junk trying to keep it in place were all the members of the Tribe. Outside the doors they could hear yelling.

Cinnabon ran up to Super. "Where is Misterwizard? Wildies are outside, thousands of them, trying to get in and attack us!"

Super stood tall and tried to look important. "Misterwizard is delivering Carny's wriggler. He put me in charge!"

Cinnabon looked unconvinced. "You? But you're just a..."

"Just a what?" Super said with an angry frown.

Cinnabon looked down. "Nothing. But why didn't he put one of the Enforcers in charge?"

Foodcourt answered for Super. "He wanted someone whose knees didn't shake from fear or old age and who would do it right, that's why."

Super turned to the whole Tribe. "Hurry! We have to bar the doors and then all go down inside the Bunker!"

The Tribe members doubled their efforts to bar the

doors and some ran down the steps to the basement.

"My, my, this is quite exciting, isn't it?" Reginald said to Super, as he grabbed a chair and placed it against the front door. "Did one of your members break some taboo or refuse to marry the king's daughter or something? Is that why they're so upset?" Reginald laughed crazily again.

"I don't know," Super replied crossly, as she piled an electric toaster onto the pile. "Maybe Johnny and Starbucks did something. I sure wish they weren't prisoners. Boy, could ever use their help now."

"Johnny and Starbucks? You have a whole coffee company with you?" Reginald cackled at his joke.

Super rolled her eyes, beginning to find Reginald a little irritating. "Whatever. I sure wish half the people I knew didn't talk gibberish that I didn't understand."

From outside, the yelling grew louder, and so did the pounding on the doors.

Foodcourt turned to Reginald. "Reginald, it's getting worse!" Should we use these little balls you gave us?"

Reginald's eyes lit up and he shook his head. He took some long, silver sticks out of his pocket. "No, we'll start with these, just for fun. They're called Sparklers. My father let me light them on a special day called Fourth of July, every year when I was young. They're very special."

"Great," Super said. "Just show us how to use them!"

Reginald led Super up a set of stairs to a window above the back doors. "First, we break open this window." Reginald tore down the dusty curtain and wrapped it around his hand. Then he smashed the small window. "Next, you light them."

As Super and Foodcourt watched with fascination, Reginald took out a small, metal square object. He flipped the top section open. "This is my U.S.S Nimitz lighter. It's one of my favorite possessions."

With a roll of a wheel on the side, flame shot out the top. Super and Foodcourt watched it with amazement and delight. "Wow!" Foodcourt said. "Just like Misterwizard's magic!"

"You ain't seen nothing yet, sister." Reginald lit the first sparkle. It came to life, shooting sparks in all directions. Super's eyes lit up and she watched it, entranced. Foodcourt backed up, afraid.

"That's the most wonderful thing I've ever seen!" Super said, as the light from the sparkler reflected in her dark brown eyes.

"Yes, it is," Reginald said, watching her with pleasure. "Sadly, we have to throw it away now. But it will give our visitors something to think about!"

With that, Reginald tossed it out the window. The effect was instantaneous, as they heard a screaming and the tramp of feet running away. Reginald laughed. "That will buy us some time!"

"Neat!" Super said. "Can I try one?"

"Me too!" Said Foodcourt.

Reginald lit two more and handed them to the two friends. Foodcourt and Super held them and stared at the sizzling sparkles with wide eyes, as if they were both still little scrabblers.

"Don't touch the ends, they are very hot!"

Foodcourt tossed his out the window. Super reluctantly did the same.

From below them inside the Museum came a ragged cheer. One of the Tribe members yelled up, "whatever you did worked! They stopped pushing!"

Super, Foodcourt and Reginald walked back down to

the floor to find the members of the Tribe waiting for thm.

Reginald turned to them all. "That will only hold them for a few seconds. One the novelty wears off, they'll be back, I'm afraid."

'Well, let's be gone before they return!" Super replied. "Everybody downstairs!"

Suddenly they heard a huge explosion outside. Super, Reginald and everyone in the Tribe looked towards the back doors, wondering what it was.

"That wasn't a sparkler!" Reginald said with his usual cackle.

"It sounds like something big is happening out there!" Super said. "I hope it's not Johnny and Starbucks in trouble."

"I believe it's time to 'exit, stage right,' as the old saying goes. And possibly it's also time to blow the dust off some other toys. Let's get your people down to the Bunker. Then I shall return with some true weaponry. I haven't had this much fun in, well forever!"

Super, Foodcourt and Reginald followed the rest of the Tribe to the basement.

Lord Algon watched his Wildies run away from the door. Too many things were happening at once, and he began to feel nervous. "What be this now? Another beastie besetting us?"

"No, my Lord!" One Wildie yelled, pointing at the door. "Them what's inside possess sorcerers or witches. Evil sprites flew out the window and would have attacked us if we'd not run for our lives!"

Lord Algon snorted, unconvinced. "Sprites ye say? More like some sort of trickery."

The Wildies stopped a little way away and looked back at the Museum. "Have ye some backbone! There be nothing occurring now. Go back there and look see for yourself."

The Wildies looked, and as Lord Algon said, no more 'sprites' appeared. Slowly the Wildies walked back, fear and apprehension on their faces.

Lord Algon turned to Johnny and Starbucks. "What deviltry is this? Ye say your people be willing to make a pact, and then they attack us with sorcery."

Johnny opened his mouth to speak, but suddenly the world dissolved into chaos.

A huge explosion only a few feet away sent Wildies flying through the air. The rest screamed in terror and ran away, for this was no little sparkler attack. Even Lord Algon panicked and ran a few feet in the other direction. His guards followed him, glancing back with fear at the smoking hole where there explosion took place.

Johnny saw his chance. He dropped the pieces of the rope holding his hands. "Now, Starbucks!" Johnny took off running. Starbucks joined him. They ran towards the Museum as another explosion rocked the ground. More Wildies screamed in pain and agony and the air filled with screams of terror.

Lord Algon's slow mind was still trying to catch up to events. He looked around, taking in scenes of Wildies lying on the ground in misery and other running in all directions. No longer worried about anything but his own safety, Lord Algon ran towards the broken stick building, his guards a few steps behind him. Another explosion sent a shower of rocks and dirt into the air.

Leader Nordstrom saw his chance too and ran off, hands still tied, yelling with fear, away from the Museum and towards distant buildings in the opposite direction from the Mall. He ran into to a group of Wildies stumbling around and kicked one savagely. "Get out of my way, fool!" Leader Nordstrom looked back at the back of the Museum. He saw Lord Algon and his guards. They stood halfway between the Museum and the broken stick building. Lord Algon and Leader Nordstrom looked at each other. Lord Algon's eyes seemed to bore into Leader Nordstrom. The thought of how close he was to dying made him feel faint and almost fall to the ground, but terror drove him onward, making him run faster. He stumbled along, hardly believing his good fortune in escaping. His legs ached, his belly screamed with hunger and his head pounded, but he was alive! He concentrated on running.

Johnny and Starbucks reached the front of the Museum. A few Wildies still stood by the door looking scared and confused. Johnny yelled at them and they ran off. Starbucks turned around and looked back.

"Johnny! Look! It's Ripper and the Gangers!"

From behind the buildings surrounding the grassy area, Ripper and the Gangers ran out, carrying guns and knives. And at the back of the pack stood Ripper, an evil leer on his face.

"I should have guessed it was them. They must have followed us all the way from Phill-a-delpia. And they stole some of Misterwizard's special toys, probably when they ransacked Castle. Come on, Starbucks, we have to find a way inside before the Gangers see us!" Johnny pulled on the door handles of the Museum, but they were shut tight. He ran along the side for another way in, Starbucks right behind him.

Meanwhile, Lord Algon saw the Gangers approaching. He spied Ripper in the back and knew from experience that this was the leader. He could tell right away Ripper was a dangerous and ruthless man, for if there was anything Lord Algon knew, it was how to recognize another evil man when he saw one, being one himself. His demeanor changed from lordly arrogance to outright fear. He yelled to his four guards, "Come protect me, ye blaggards!"

The four guards looked confused and scared themselves. Then they took off in four different directions, none of them towards Lord Algon.

"Look, Ripper," Facegash yelled with a grin as he pointed at Lord Algon. "There goes their Leader Nordstrom. He's getting away!"

"Who cares?" Ripper said, for he had seen someone else. "Look who I see over there." He pointed his own finger towards the Museum.

Facegash looked in the direction Ripper pointed. When he saw what Ripper meant, he grinned with evil intent. "Johnny! Let's get him!"

Ripper turned to his gang. "New orders! Forget about the Wildies, get Johnny! And take him alive! I'm the only one who gets to kill him!"

The Gangers yelled and ran at Johnny and Starbucks with their weapons raised.

CHAPTER 4

Inside the Museum, Super and Foodcourt heard the explosions outside. They ran back to the windows and peered outside but could see nothing but Wildies running around and lots of smoke.

"Do you see Johnny or Starbucks?" Super asked, trying to see through the smoke.

Foodcourt peered out the window on the other set of stairs on the other side of the back doors. "No. But I think we should wait until Reginal returns with more weapons. Then we should try to rescue Johnny and Starbucks, if we can."

"I wish Misterwizard would finish with Carny and her wriggler. We could sure use some good advice right now."

From outside the door came a familiar voice. "Misterwizard! Are you in there? It's Johnny and Starbucks!"

"Johnny!" Super yelled, jumping up and down with happiness. "Hurry, we have to move all this junk and let him in!" Both her and Foodcourt ran down the stairs on either side to the back doors again.

"Yahoo!" Foodcourt said. "But we just spent an hour putting all this junk in place. It's going to take some time to move it again."

"Well, let's hurry! I sure hope Starbucks is with him!" Super grabbed an old suit of armor and dragged it away from the door. Foodcourt grabbed a velvet chair and threw it over his shoulder out of the way. Foodcourt looked at the pile that rose above his head. "Now I wish we didn't tell them to do such a good job!" They removed items as fast as they could to free the doors again.

Downstairs in the Bunker or "Peacock," Misterwizard had his hands full, literally, for Miracle made his appearance! Misterwizard stood at Carny's feet behind the delivery table., Teavana watched from the corner with a mixture of pure fright and joyful happiness.

"Carny, push!"

"I'm trying!" Carny's face was read as she pushed with all her might.

"One more should do it!"

The air filled with the wailing of a baby crying. Misterwizard grinned with pleasure as he held onto the newborn infant. "Eureka, you've done it! Miracle has entered the world!"

Carny's mother walked up to stand by Misterwizard ,

tears of joy on her face as Misterwizard cut the umbilical cord, wiped Miracle down and wrapped a cloth around him. Carny smiled with relief and happiness as Misterwizard brought Miracle to her and put her in Carny's arms.

Teavanna hurried over and gazed with love down at her granddauther. "Look at her. She's beautiful." She looked at Misterwizard with hope. "And she's perfect, isn't she, Misterwizard? I don't see anything wrong with her."

Misterwizard beamed with pride and wiped his gloved hands off with a towel. "She's absolutely perfect in any way. If you hadn't already named her, I'd christen her Mary Poppins."

"If you want to name her that, you still can," Carny said, smiling dreamily, for she was exhausted from the effort.

"That is totally your prerogative, Carny. Miracle is a nice name too."

"Maybe you can call her Mary Poppins Miracle," Teavana said. "That way you can both have what you want."

Suddenly in the distance they heard the dull thud of an explosion. They all looked towards the sound, curious. Teavanna turned to Wizard.

"Misterwizard, what do you think that was?"

Misterwizard took his surgical clothes off as he thought about it. He removed the blue cap from his bald head and wiped the sweat off it with the towel. "I suspect it is someone's calling card, but I sincerely doubt it is sent as a welcome.

Misterwizard looked at Carny, Miracle and Teavanna. "I am so thrilled for you, Carny. It is important that you get lots of rest now and begin to give Miracle nourishment. I would like to stay and keep an eye you two for a while longer, but unfortunately the sound of detonation we just heard leaves me no doubt my presence could be better utilized above."

"Thank you, MIsterwizard. I can never repay you for what you've done for me and Miracle." Carny gave Misterwizard's hand a squeeze.

"Seeing your happiness is payment enough. Rest now, Carny. You've had a busy day."

Misterwizard turned to leave, only to pause when he saw Deb and Bathandbodyworks standing in the doorway. Deb looked tired and weak, but she was smiling. Thegap stood behind them, smiling as well.

"Ah, my other patient. How are you doing my dear?"

Deb leaned on her mother Bathandbodyworks who held her in her arms. "I feel better."

"Look at her, MIsterwizard!" Thegap gushed with happiness. In his eyes were tears. "Her fever is almost gone, and she's getting stronger!"

"Wonderful! Well, this is turning out to be an extra-super-splendiferous day. Now, if only whatever is happening above doesn't rain disaster onto our good fortune, we can celebrate later. Little Debbie, as your treating physician I'm telling you that you need to go back to bed and rest some more. Carny, as your obstetrician, I give you the same prescription. And feed Mary Poppins Miracle, she is going to be very hungry. She worked hard as well. "

Reginald came bobbing down the hallway dressed in battle fatigues and a helmet. Across his chest a string of the same green balls hung, and he held three machine guns in his arms.

"Misterwizard! War has come once again! We are under siege! Dastardly denizens of darkness have assailed our gates. The time has come for all men to come to the aid of their, uh, Museum!" Reginald cackled with laughter.

"Then defend it we must!" With that, Misterwizard and Reginald left the room and headed back the Ready Room and the surface.

Johnny and Starbucks stood in front of the back doors of the Museum. They gazed out at the street beyond with dismay. The Gangers ran towards them, lots of them, all carrying guns and knives.

"Johnny, we can't take them all on!"

Johnny noticed Ripper at the back of the pack. Their eyes met, and Ripper grinned with evil pleasure. Johnny saw his own death in Ripper's eyes. "Well, if this is it, Starbucks, we'll go out fighting and protecting our families."

"Yep," Starbucks said. "I'll tell you what. I ain't going without taking at least a few of them with me!"

As they backed up against the doors to the Museum with their swords raised, one of the doors behind them opened! Johnny and Starbucks turned to see a very welcome and familiar face.

"You guys done playing around out there and you want to come in, or should we just shut the door and leave you alone?" It was Super!

"Super! Baby! I could kiss you! And I think I will!" Starbucks said.

"Get in here and stop talking!" Super quipped back.

As fast as they could, Johnny and Starbucks slipped in the door and Super closed it quickly.

Ripper watched with mounting fury and frustration. Why did Johnny always manage to slip away, just when he had him? Ripper yelled and stamped his feet as the Gangers stood and watched.

"Aaaah!" Ripper smashed his sword against the ground again and again taking his fury out on the grass.

"They're trapped inside, Ripper," Facegash said, just like at Castle."

Ripper smiled as he realized what Facegash just said was true. "That's right. And this time, they won't escape. We have these." Ripper held up one of the exploding sticks. "We're going to bring that building down on top of them. It will be their grave."

Inside the Museum, a very happy reunion took place. Foodcourt and Superl crowded around Johnny and Starbucks cheering and hugging them. Starbucks turned and was surprised by a kiss from Super. He grinned like an idiot, his mind whirling.

"Johnny, we are so glad you're back!" Foodcourt said. "Now we have someone to take charge!"

Super glared at Foodcourt, but he didn't notice.

"Where's MIsterwizard?" Johnny asked.

"He's downstairs in the Peacock, taking care of Carny and Deb," Super replied. "Carny's having her wriggler, and Deb is getting medicine to make her better."

"Peacock? What's Peacock?" Starbucks answered.

"It's the underground bunker," Super replied. "Reginald let us in. It's really cool, wait until you see it!"

"Who's Reginald?" Johnny asked.

"Wait till you meet him, too," Super said. "He's a

hoot, as he says."

They were interrupted by a huge explosion outside. The walls shook, and dust filtered down from above.

"Johnny, the Gangers are using Misterwizard's toys on the building!" Starbucks said. "They're going to knock it down!"

"Then this is it," Johnny said. "It's time for us to have it out with these creeps once and for all. We should have known that the only way we were going to get rid of them was to fight them to the death. Now we have no choice."

Johnny turned Foodourt. "Father, you need to get the men of the Tribe up here, with any weapons they can find. This is our new home. And if we want it, we're going to have to earn it by fighting for it. "

Foodcourt nodded. Then he ran back towards the stairs to the lower floor.

"We have to hurry, Johnny," Super said. "It' won't take many of those exploding things to knock this place down."

"I sure wish MIsterwizard would hurry up with Deb and Carny," Starbucks said. "We could sure use his brains right now."

Foodcourt returned with most of the Tribe behind him.

"They were all just waiting downstairs, too afraid to go into the tunnel, Johnny."

"Good," Johnny said. He addressed the Tribe who gathered around Johnny and his friend near the back door, all wearing expressions of fright and worry. "Listen. We can live here and be happy, but only if we can defend ourselves. Are you people willing to fight for your home? Or should we just let the Gangers win and sneak off somewhere, spend the rest of our days running?"

"We fight!" One man said, raising his fist in the air.

"We'll defend our new Sanctuary!" A woman said, a look of dark determination on her face.

Foodcourt looked at Johnny, his face full of excitement. "We'll follow you Johnny! Just tell us what to do!"

And just at that moment, Reginald ran up the steps from the basement, arms loaded with weapons. He ran over to Johnny and grinned impishly. "Is everybody ready to have some fun?"

A cheer went up from the Tribe as Reginald handed out the weapons. He doled out a few round balls to each man until they were gone and then handed Johnny a rifle he called an M-16 and Foodcourt and Starbucks ones he said were AK-47s. Then he opened the bag he carried and handed out handguns to as many men as he could. "These should put a little wrinkle in their underwear!" Reginald said, and then he hooted with laughter.

"They are so heavy!" Foodcourt said as he held the AK-47 in his hands. "How do you use them?"

Reginald took the AK-47 back from Foodcourt and demonstarted. "Just like a handgun. You point," he said, pointing the gun towards the ceiling and looking down the site, "aim, and fire!" He shot a round off into the ceiling. Everyone yelled with surprise and fear, but then with wonder as dust filtered down from above. "Whoever you point this at, you better be mean to kill, because these guns don't mess around, no siree!"

As Reginald handed the rifle back to Foodcourt, Starbucks peered down the site of his rifle, a big smile on his face. "Those Gangers are not going to know what hit 'em!"

Reginald picked up the empty bag and headed back towards the stairs. "I'll go back and get some more. We've got a whole arsenal down there. Enough for everybody to kill somebody!" They heard him hooting with laughter as he ran down the stairs, his voice echoing off the marble walls.

The Tribe members looked back to Johnny with looks of concern on their faces. A woman walked up to him. "Johnny, do we really have to kill people?"

Johnny turned to her with a frown. "I'm afraid so." He turned and addressed the Tribe. "All right, listen up people!" He held the M-16 in his arms. Even though Johnny was big for his age, the rifle still seemed huge in his arms. Johnny held it with a confidence that made him look dangerous and ready to us it. "We didn't ask for this fight, but they brought it on us, and now it's time to defend our new Sanctuary. We're going to have to shoot and kill some of them. I'm sorry about that, but they aren't leaving us any choice. Anyone that has a problem with that, we'll all understand if you don't want to. You can just fight them with whatever you have instead, clubs, knives or rocks. But you must fight. We have to show these Gangers who they're messing with!"

As if to punctuate Johnny's words, another explosion rocked the Museum. Somewhere, a chandelier fell with a crash. Johnny flung open the door and yelled, "We don't have time to wait for more guns. It's time to fight. Let's go!"

With that, Johnny ran outside. Starbuck, Super, Foodcourt and the Tribe members followed him, men and women, all wearing grim expressions and yelling war cries. The final battle for their new Sanctuary had begun.

Outside the Museum, the Gangers entertained themselves by attacking the Wildies not fast enough to escape. Others watched Ripper and a few other Gangers throw the strange, green balls at the Museum. They cheered each time one exploded and parts of the building collapsed or flew into the air.

"Take this, Johnny Apocalypse!" Ripper hauled back, pulled the pin on another grenade and let it fly. The Gangers watched it arc in the sky then descend, right on the roof at the front of the building. It rolled down the sloped roof until it landed in the gutter. Then it exploded, and a huge chunk of the gutter and a corner of the roof came flying off. The pieces landed on the street as the Gangers cheered. Ripper turned and mugged for his gang, hands in the air.

Because he was turned around, Ripper didn't see the door to the Museum open. He only knew it had happened when he saw his Gangers' smiles disappear and their eyes look past him with surrpise. He spun around to see what they looked at.

Out of the Museum the Tribe came, Johnny in the lead. Ripper's lip curled, and he raised his gun. "Go get 'em, boys!"

The Gangers stopped beating on the Wildies and ran for Johnny and the Tribe, yelling war cries. But just before they reached the, five members of the Tribe pulled the pins on their own green ballss and let them fly.

Ripper and the Gangers now knew too well what the small, green orbs were. As one they ground to a halt and turned around to run away. Some of them made it, but many didn't. Five explosions rocked the ground and Gangers flew through the air to land in screaming heaps of mangled flesh.

Johnny and the Tribe were just getting started. They raised their rifles and fired. Quickly the air filled with the rat-tat-tat of the AK-47s and the steady bang-bang of the M-16.

Some of the Gangers took off, but others simply found hiding places behind bodies or mounds of rubble. The Gangers shot back and the battle was on.

Johnny and Starbucks hid behind the tall, white columns on the porch of the Museum as bullets whizzed past them. The rest of the Tribe found other cover near the Museum somewhere on the grounds.

Gangers snuck around, trying to get behind the Tribe, and here and there those that didn't have guns engaged in hand-to-hand combat with Tribe members. Johnny and the others couldn't help the Tribe members fight, for gunfire pinned them to the spot.

Johnny called out to Starbucks. "You think we surprised them?"

Starbucks grinned back. "You bet we did. let's make 'em run!" With that, Starbucks spun out of his hiding place and pulled the trigger of his AK-47. Bullets tore up the grass and pieces of dirt flew into the air. Johnny came out and joined him, shooting his M16. The Gangers close enough to be in danger gave up. They bolted from their hiding places and ran. Foodcourt saw and came out from behind the rock he hid behind. He raised his AK-47 in the air and shook it, wearing a big grin. 'Run while you can, you Ganger scum!"

Leader Nordstrom wandered through an empty building on the far side of the Mall. Half of the building lay in rubble on the ground. The remaining half held a staircase that ended in mid-air and old desks and chairs, all covered with dust and debris. Leader Nordstrom looked through the remains for something to eat but the glass display cases held only display cases of glass held nothing but meaningless papers and pictures. His stomach rumbled. Weren't there any food places in this infernal city? All he'd seen so far were white buildings filled with moldiy old paper, desks and more desks, old paintings on the walls so faded you couldn't even see what was in them and glass cases full of worthless trinkets that no longer held any meaning.

Back in Sanctuary he was Leader Nordstrom of the Tribe, a respected man looked up to and honored; now he was just another Wildie, scrambling for scraps of food, maybe forced to eat rat-Beasties to survive. How he hated Johnny, Starbucks and that infernal Misterwizard! They took everything from him, the life he deserved, and now they would get to live like kings in their new Sanctuary, while he scraped by, cold and hungry.

In the distance in the direction of the Museum, Leader Nordstrom heard explosions and gunfire. He turned towards the sound and listened, instantly alert and interested. Something big was going on! A battle took place! He had to see what was happening!

He ran outside and gazed across the huge grassy Mall towards where the explosions had come from.

Forgetting about the danger, he ran towards the distant noise until he could see the back side of the Museum in the distance. Then remembering how exposed he was he found an old shanty building on the Mall to hide behind where he could still see. His mouth dropped open in surprise. A battle was waging, just like he suspected! He saw Johnny and Starbucks behind two columns of the Museum firing out at the Gangers who shot back at them from positions across the street behind piles of rubble.

Leader Nordstrom was overjoyed. Maybe Johnny would die after all! And the Tribe, he hoped they all were captured and tortured by the Gangers for the way they treated him. Leader Nordstrom looked around and tried to find something he could do to help the Gangers. Next to the Museum that would hold the new Sanctuary, he saw another huge white building. The roof on this building held a big gold dome, but it had fallen partially in. Trying to keep as low as possible, Leader Nordstrom ran to the building. He hurried up the steps and inside.

The interior of the building was dark and dusty and seemed to go on forever. The room he entered was empty and round, with archways that led to other rooms. The floor was cold, white marble and throughout the room marble columns stood.

On either side of each of the archways, stone statues stood of beautiful maidens or men in strange hats, all naked. Even though the faces of the statues wore smiles, dust covered the statues and in the dark they looked sinister and cruel.

Leader Nordstrom walked in, gazing at the floor carefully, for rock from the ceiling had fallen and the floor in the very middle of the room was gone, leaving a giant gaping hole to the floor below. Leader Nordstrom looked up at the ceiling. The yellow dome was hanging halfway down and a there was a giant hole next to it where he could see the sky. The building must have taken a indirect hit from some kind of bomb during the Great War, making the roof collapse, Leader Nordstrom supposed. He crept to the edge of the hole and looked down.

In the middle of the room in the floor below lay a giant dead beastie, one that Leader Nordstrom had never seen before. It had tough, leathery gray skin, huge ears, white spears sticking out below its mouth and a long gray nose. It lay on its side, as if it had been sitting on the floor above when it collapsed. Age and bug-beasties had taken their toll on the creature, for its side was caved in, showing large round bones inside.

The remains of the roof lay scattered on the floor below. Along with the display cases and other objects down there, Leader Nordstrom could see that the debris had effectively sealed up the entrances into the room, making it a place with no exit. Leader Nordstrom decided it was best not to risk falling through the hole, for there may not be a way to get back out.

Leader Nordstrom looked through the other rooms for something to use to help the Gangers against Johnny. More glass display cases filled each room, most with weird beasties or words he didn't understand. In one large space behind a glass wall, Leader Nordstrom saw some huge beastie hanging from the ceiling. It was blue on top with a white belly and had what looked like stunted wings and a giant mouth that looked so big it could swallow an old car. Leader Nordstrom decided not to get too close to it, just in case it really wasn't dead, or even if it was so he didn't risk it falling on him.

Leader Nordstrom looked at the old words on the wall telling the name of the place. It said, "Smithsonian National Museum of Natural History," though Leader Nordstrom couldn't understand them. Leader Nordstrom frowned, disappointed; there was no way he could use anything there. He looked with mild interest at the dead Beasties on display. There were some fascinating creatures, Beasties that Leader Nordstrom had never seen before. One had impossibly long legs and a long, long neck. Its skin was dotted with brown spots and it had a tiny little head with ears sticking up. Another stood in the middle of the room, but it was only bones. It had tiny little arms, but it looked like when it was alive it was a fearsome creature, for it had a huge mouth with big, sharp teeth grinning at him. Leader Nordstrom wouldn't have like to meet that beastie alive. Another was a strange looking bird with long legs, a round body with black feathers a long neck and the funniest face he had ever seen. All of the beasties were rotted, moldy and chewed on by rat-beasties and bug-beasties.

When he looked at one display, a chill ran through him. A tiger-beastie just like the one he escaped from earlier sat on a fake branch of a tree. He stood, transfixed by fear and watched it for a second, but it didn't move. He sighed with relief and finally relaxed enough to move on. He'd definitely seen enough of that particular beastie.

The place proved so interesting Leader Nordstrom almost forgot about Johnny and the battle outside, wanting to simply explore the whole building and see what new and exciting beasties he could discover. Then his stomach cramped, and he remembered how tired, weak and starving he was. His hatred and anger for

Johnny returned and he put the thoughts of the building aside.

He noticed something in the corner and walked over to investigate. One of the bombs the Gangers threw must have missed and come through the hole in the top of the building, for a small fire burned in the corner. The flames danced merrily, making shadows on the wall.

Fire; there was something Leader Nordstrom could use, but how? He looked around the room. Then he smiled. In the corner stood two Fake People wearing what looked like beastie furs. The men had big foreheads and seemed deformed somehow, but Leader Nordstrom didn't care about that. He could catch the beastie furs on fire, throw them at Johnny and Starbucks. It would create a distraction, or at the least, create a smoke screen, allowing the Gangers to get close enough to Johnny and Starbucks to finish them off. It just might work!

Leader Nordstrom hurried over to the rags and gathered them up, energized now that he had a plan. *This is it, Johnny Apocalypse,* Leader Nordstrom thought with grim hatred. *I may spend the rest of my life wandering alone, but it will be better than what the Gangers do to you and your precious family.* Leader Nordstrom couldn't wait to put his plan in action so that he could sit back and watch the Gangers have fun torturing and maiming.

He became so intent on grabbing the clothes off the mannequins that he didn't hear the low growl coming from behind him or see the tiger-beastie until it too late. By the time he realized the tiger-beastie he'd just looked at was indeed alive and turned around, it was right next to him. Its black eyes gleamed in the fading light; its white teeth seemed huge, as it looked at him and panted.

Leader Nordstrom's eyes opened in pure terror. This was the same tiger-beastie who had followed the Tribe all the way from their old city, the one Leader Nordstrom ran from earlier. Leader Nordstrom tried to scream but his fear was so great he couldn't make a sound. He turned and ran, his mind blank with fear. He was so intent on getting away he didn't realize he ran right into the hole in the floor until too late. He sailed into the open air and down, landing in a heap on top of the strange gray beastie. His arm ached, and he screamed in pain, sure he'd broken it. He turned and looked up, hoping at least his fall had helped him escape the tiger beastie; but it stood at the edge of the hole, watching him.

"Nice tiger-beastie," Leader Nordstrom said. "Go away. You don't want to come down here. Please, go away!"

But it didn't. The tiger-beastie jumped down as Leader Nordstrom tried to climb down off the strange gray bestie, his arm screaming in pain. In a second it was upon him. As he breathed his last, Leader Nordstrom finally screamed. The sound echoed through the dark, empty Museum.

Ripper hid behind an old car. A piece of shrapnel hit him in the head, and blood poured down the side of his face. He wiped his head and rubbed the blood on the grass, wondering why things always seemed to turn from victory to defeat so fast. Wasn't he just about to win? He had Johnny and the Tribe pinned, and now it looked like he and his Gangers were the ones that would be wiped out.

He shook his head, trying to make sense of what had just happened. He poked his head around the car and saw Johnny, Starbucks and Foodcourt come out shooting. The Gangers turned and ran away. Ripper knew now that there was no way his gang was going to beat the Tribe. The realization was like a heavy weight he had just swallowed that sank down into the middle of his stomach.

It didn't matter anymore. The only thing he cared about now was making Johnny pay. He looked over at the back of the Museum. The door stood open. Johnny and Starbucks moved further and further away from it as they pursued the Gangers. He looked at the weapons in his hands, just his sword in his right and one of the green balls in his left. With a dark, cold smile, Ripper ran for the door, keeping low to the ground. In a second he was at the door and inside. He slammed the door behind him and locked it.

CHAPTER 5

Inside the Museum, the men, women and children too old or too young to fight huddled together in the back at the back of the main floor. While the adults fretted and worried, the children played, unaware of the danger, The Tribe people gave the children trinkets and oddities from the display cases to play with, all things the children had never seen before. One little boy played with his first baseball mitt. Another boy banged two frying pans together, making an awful loud racket. A little girl strummed an electric guitar, unaware that she was the first person to play one in almost a century. And Sephie sat on her mother's lap with the green frog puppet Kermit on her lap, making him dance.

Misterwizard ran up the stairs from below. He looked until he found the Tribe huddled together. As he entered, all eyes turned to look at him.

"Carny has had a baby girl, and she's healthy and happy!"

All the adults cheered with joy and clapped, and the children soon joined in. "And now that my obstetrical duty is completed, I'm free to help defend our new Sanctuary."

At that moment, Reginald stumbled up, carrying another handful of weapons. Misterwizard turned to look at him. "How goes the battle, General Reginald?"

Reginald cackled with laughter. "General, am I? Well, I'm just a supply sergeant right now. The real General, it seems is your Johnny Apocalypse."

"Johnny!" Misterwizard said with joy. "Was he present?"

"Most definitely, and he and the men of your Tribe are outside fighting some fellows they labeled, "Gangers." I gave them some weapons and told them I was going to get more, but it looks like they couldn't wait!"

"Gangers. They must have followed us all the way from Philadelphia. Ripper seems intent on getting his revenge. Quite a determined fellow. I'm anxious to know how the battle is going."

"It's going great!"

Misterwizard, Reginald and the whole Tribe turned to see Super standing in the doorway, a huge smile on her face. Next to her stood Foodcourt, wearing a grin of victory.

Foodcourt said, "Johnny and Starbucks are kicking their tails, thanks to all your magic weapons, Reginald! The Gangers are on the run!"

"Wonderful!" Misterwizard said, nodding joyfully with a satisfied grin.

Another person came up from below and they all turned to see who it was. It was Deb! She looked weak but healthy. Her parents stood behind her. She smiled at them as Super ran over and helped her onto a bench.

Super smiled but looked concerned "How are you feeling, Deb?"

Deb smiled weakly. Her face was still wet, but it appeared the fever broke. "A lot better now, thanks to Misterwizard."

The people of the Tribe all smiled and spoke encouraging words.

"Don't thank me, thank Reginald," Misterwizard said, patting Reginald on the back. "It was his antibiotics that did the trick. I'm so glad to see you're feeling well, my dear."

Then Carny walked up, holding Mary Poppins Miracle in her arms wrapped in a blanket. All the ladies cheered even louder. Behind Carny and Mary Poppins Miracle stood Teavanna, both beaming with pride at her new born granddaughter. Foodcourt ran over and put an arm around Carny, gazing with joy at Mary Poppins Miracle.

"Well, well," Misterwizard said, "it appears as if developments are taking a turn for the positive around here."

A voice came from the back doorway, full of hatred and fury. "I'm sorry to spoil such a happy picture."

Everyone turned and looked. It was Ripper, and he held the stick in his hand.

"Hello, dear friends." Ripper smiled, blood dripping down the side of his face. "Now, isn't this a touching scene?"

Misterwizard moved, and Ripper turned towards him, his lip rising in a snarl. "Don't move! I've already pulled the pin on this thing, all I have to do is throw it, and you all go die."

"What do you want with us?" Teavanna asked as she shrunk back in horror against Foodcourt.

Ripper looked at her with a dark smile. "I just want to join the party. Is that all right?" He turned to Reginald. "You. Bring all those guns over here. Put them at my feet and do it fast!"

Reginald took the rifles and placed them at Ripper's feet then backed away. "I say; no need to get testy, fellow. Misterwizard, do you know this unpleasant character?"

"His name is Ripper. He's a member of a gang that call themselves the Doomsday Prochecy."

"My, quite a poetic name, I must say."

"It's not, whatever you said, and it's tough and mean that's what it is!" Ripper snarled. Then he glared at MIsterwizard. "But thanks to you and Johnny, my gang is split up. So now it's time to get my revenge!"

As Ripper, Misterwizard and Reginald spoke, Super snuck along the wall, trying to get behind Ripper and sneak out. Ripper was so intent on arguing with Misterwizard that he didn't notice her. Super watched his face and slowly, slowly moved along the wall.

"Enough talk! You and you!" Ripper pointed at Carny and Deb. "You two get over here!"

"Please," Bathandbodyworks said, "don't hurt my baby. She's sick!"

"Carny!" Teavanna called out in fear. Carny glanced at her mother with fear in her own eyes.

"Please, can I give Mary Poppins Miracle to my mother?"

"Sure," Ripper said with an evil grin. "Not that it's

going to make any difference. But hurry up. Now!" Ripper yelled. Carny handed Mary Poppins Miracle to Teavanna, who took her and held her close. Then she and Deb reluctantly walked over to stand by Ripper.

Ripper smiled. "Now we're leaving. Don't worry; I'll take care of your precious babies. You." He pointed at Foodcourt and Teavana. "You're Johnny's mother and father, aren't you? Then it's really all your fault. When your daughter is dead, and Johnny's girlfriend too, just remember it was because of your son Johnny."

Teavana glared back at him. "Johnny is a good boy, and I'm proud of him. I'm glad he's nothing like you."

"Johnny will put you in the ground, you, you malefackle!" Foodcourt said, trying to use one of Misterwizard's big words.

Super reached the doorway. She bolted out the back door of the Museum. Ripper saw her and smiled. "Go on. Tell Johnny what's happening. I want him to be here to see what I do."

Misterwizard put his hands out. "Please Ripper. It's not too late. It is not impossible for you to transform. We are perfectly willing to expunge your record and forget what happened in the past. Come join the Tribe. Together we can forge a new future. We are in a new Sanctuary, about to create a new world. You and the Doomsday Prophecy can play a part in helping us build it."

"Oh my, what a touching speech," Ripper sneered. "The only future you have, old man, is as a rotting skeleton being picked at by Beasties. You and the rest of these losers."

Ripper knelt without taking his eyes off of Misterwizard and the rest of the Tribe. He picked up an

AK-47 with his free hand and pointed it at them. He glanced at Carny and Deb with a scowl. "You two, get behind me, now!" Seeing no choice, Carny and Deb complied.

Ripper backedg up, forcing Carny and Deb to back up too.

"Well, see ya all in that place called Hell."

Ripper threw the grenade, turned and ran, pushing Carny and Deb ahead of him.

A woman from the Tribe screamed. Misterwizard ran back and tried to push everyone back in the far corner to protect them.

Reginald saw the grenade fall and skitter across the floor. With a look of sad determination, he leapt towards it. He threw himself on top of the grenade.

"Reginald!" Misterwizard yelled, but it was too late. The grenade exploded as screams of terror filled the air. The room filled with smoke.

When it cleared, Misterwizard looked around. Everyone in the Tribe seemed okay, but Reginald was gone. Misterwizard frowned with sorrow. Tears filled his eyes. "Dear friend Reginald. I am so sorry. But thank you. You were a true hero who gave his life in the defense of others. You will be remembered with honor.

"Teavana, please take the others down to Peacock while we attempt the rescue of the young ladies," Misterwizard said.

Teavana smiled sadly, nodded and gathered the people together.

Thegap ran forward. "Hurry! We have to save Carny and Deb!" The men picked up what weapons they could find and with yells of anger headed back up the stairs towards the back doors, Misterwizard, Thegap and

Foodcourt at the head of the group. They burst out the front doors and stopped just long enough to try and see which way Ripper took the girls.

Foodcourt saw Ripper and the girls in the distance heading towards the next building, the Museum of Natural History, moving away fast. He pointed. "There they are! Hurry, we can catch them!" As one the men of the Tribe yelled and ran after Ripper and the girls. Misterwizard followed as well as he could, his pockets full of grenades, hoping he wouldn't have to use them.

Johnny and Starbucks stood in the street a few blocks away from the back side of the Museum and watched the last of the Gangers run away. From the buildings up and down the street, Wildies poked their head out to see if it was now safe to come out again.

Starbucks turned to Johnny and gave him a high five. Both boys wore victorious grins.

"I can't believe it, Johnny!" Starbucks said. "Have we actually, finally seen the end to them?"

"I don't know," Johnny said, as he slung the strap of his gun over his shoulder. "I hope so. At least we'll have a chance now to get a moment to breathe and get organized."

"And man, we could sure use it. I've never been so tired in my life."

Johnny and Starbucks turned and leisurely headed back towards the Museum.

"Do you think we've seen the last of the phony king, Lord Algon?"

Johnny grinned as he looked at the burning piles of rubble strewn around the square. "He sure took off in a hurry when the fighting started."

"Good thing, too. What a bunch of freaks him and his Wildies were. Can you believe they really ate people?"

Johnny suddenly felt anxious to see Deb again, and the feelings of love for her came happily rushing back. "I can't wait to see Deb."

"Yah-hoo!" Starbucks yelled. "And I can't wait to see Super. I bet she'll give me a big kiss. We're conquering heroes!"

Johnny and Starbucks laughed and stood a little taller.

Johnny saw someone coming towards them in the distance from the direction of the Museum, running fast. He squinted to see who it was, and realized it was Super. He smiled and looked at Starbucks.

"Pucker up, buddy. I think you're just about to get a nice welcome."

Starbucks saw Super and grinned wide. "Oh yeah. Come meet your hero, Baby!"

Johnny and Starbucks laughed again. But then Johnny's smile turned to a frown of worry when Super grew close and he saw the expression on her face. It was one that said something was wrong, very wrong.

She arrived out of breath and stopped in front of them. "Johnny!" She wailed. "Ripper's in the Museum! It looks like he's going to take Carny and Deb away with him!"

Johnny and Starbucks looked at each other, grave looks on their face then they turned back to Super. "Where is MIsterwizard?" Johnny asked.

"He's there, with the rest of the Tribe," Super said in

a panting voice, still trying to catch her breath. "Johnny, I think he plans on killing them to get revenge."

"Let's go!" Starbucks yelled. All three turned and ran back towards the Museum. Inside, Johnny's guts tensed up. What had finally seemed like victory now started to feel like the darkest day of Johnny's life. If Ripper hurt Carny and Deb, he would have no real reason to go on living, let alone celebrate. Johnny put every last ounce of strength into his tired legs, willing them to propel him faster.

Ripper pushed Carny and Deb's backs with his hand, first one and then the other, forcing them to move. Still they walked slowly, for they sobbed with sorrow, crying for their families they feared had just died.

"Shut up and keep moving!" Ripper said, giving Carny a savage push. She stumbled forward, her body still weak from giving birth. She leaned against a column and Ripper raised his hand to hit her.

Deb stepped in front of him. "Stop that, you monster! She just had a wriggler, she's weak! Give her a chance!"

Ripper grinned with evil. "I'll give her a chance all right; a chance to get shot if she doesn't get moving. I don't care about how weak she is. I know what you're doing, just trying to buy time 'till Johnny gets here. But I ain't that stupid. Start moving or I start shooting!"

Deb scowled at Ripper, wishing she could slap him so hard that it hurt her hand. With an effort she kept herself from really doing it and turned back to Carny. Deb grabbed her around the shoulders and helped get moving again. "It doesn't matter what you do," Deb said, glaring at Ripper; "Johnny is coming, and he's going to pay you back for what you've done. If you were smart, you'd let us go and run while you have the chance."

Ripper laughed. "I'm counting on Johnny coming. He's just gonna be in time to watch me kill both of you. Now just how should I do it? It's got to be something really bad."

Carny stumbled along, weak and tired. When she breathed, it came in ragged gasps. Deb glanced at her, worried, but there was nothing she could do. She knew that Ripper didn't care if both dropped dead in their tracks. She just hoped Johnny reached them soon. Johnny would take care of Ripper, she knew it. She knew Johnny would come and save them. Her eyes narrowed as she thought how much she was going to enjoy it when Johnny caught up to them. Then Ripper would get what was coming to him!

In the Museum, Teavana led the Tribe to the entrance of Peacock. The people of the Tribe eyed the dark opening fearfully.

"Don't be afraid, friends," Teavana said, her mind distracted by thoughts of her daughter and Deb. "Misterwizard says it's safe down here, so we must take his word for it."

The people of the Tribe just nodded, not totally convinced. They walked gingerly down the dark tunnel.

CHAPTER 6

Johnny saw the back of the Museum of American History, New Sanctuary, in the distance. The sight spurred him to run faster, even though his legs were weak and felt like spaghetti. He wished he and Starbucks hadn't run so far in pursuit of the Gangers, for now it seemed like it took forever for them to get back to the Museum.

Starbucks grabbed him and stopped. "Johnny, look!"

Starbucks pointed off to the left. In the distance, they saw three figures walking towards the next huge white building, the Museum of Natural History. They recognized Ripper, and he held a gun on Carny and Deb! The three seemed a mile away from Johnny and Starbucks, though it was really only a city block.

"There they are!" Starbucks said.

Johnny watched Misterwizard and the men of the

Tribe pour out of the Museum of American History. They were even further away from Ripper and the girls than Johnny and Starbucks. He knew it would be up to him and Starbucks to save the girls. "Let's hurry!" he yelled to Starbucks. He turned towards the Museum of Natural History and ran faster.

Johnny and Starbucks ran towards Ripper and the girls. Ripper, Deb and Carny moved closer to the doors of the Museum of Natural History, now only a few feet away. "Run faster!" Johnny yelled to Starbucks, willing his own legs to move faster, but they ached with pain. He slowed to a walk, having no choice. Starbucks slowed too, suffering from the same exhaustion. Johnny walked for a second until his legs had a moment to rest and then forced himself to run again. He hoped that by the time they reached Ripper, he and Starbucks wouldn't be so tired they wouldn't be able to fight. He couldn't worry about it at that moment; he had to keep running as fast he could.

As Johnny and Starbucks watched, Ripper and the girls entered the building and closed the door. What did Ripper have in mind? Would Johnny and Starbucks make it in time to stop Ripper?

Johnny and Starbucks finally reached the door into the building. They stopped and bent over, panting, trying to catch their breath.

"Johnny, how many bullets do you have?"

Johnny looked at his rifle. "Only one left. How about you?"

Starbucks frowned, unhappy. "Only four. I hope they're enough."

Johnny touched his sword in its scabbard. "I still have this. If I have to I'll fight him hand to hand."

Starbucks nodded. They reached the door to the Museum of Natural History. Johnny opened the door and they walked inside slowly, looking for Ripper and the girls.

They didn't have to look far. Up ahead stood Ripper, Carny and Deb, next to the giant hole in the floor. Ripper held a gun on the girls, who stood with their hands up.

When Carny and Deb saw Johnny and Starbucks enter, they both looked overjoyed and relieved. "Johnny!" Carny yelled. "We were so afraid you wouldn't find us!"

"Yes, Johnny," Ripper sneered. "We didn't want to start the party without you. Look down there, Johnny." Ripper pointed to the floor below.

Johnny and Starbucks walked to where they could see through the hole. There they saw the tiger-beastie, padding back and forth, trapped. Next to him on the floor were the remains of Leader Nordstrom, what the tiger-beastie hadn't eaten.

Johnny and Starbucks looked back at Ripper and walked towards him until he said, "That's close enough." Then they stopped.

"Listen, Ripper," Johnny said, "if it's me you want, let them go. I'll do whatever you want. Please, Carny just had a baby, and Deb, she's sick. They're not part of this. It's between you and me."

Ripper laughed. "Oh, what a hero type speech. How sickeningly noble. You know that's why I hate you so much, Johnny Apocalypse? You put on airs, like you're some big hero, and you're just a dumb kid. You're not even a man yet, you and your good buddy Starbucks. He's not even human, look at him, he's black from the Sickness."

Johnny grit his teeth, fury filling his mind. "Don't talk like that. You know that's a lie."

"Don't worry about it, Johnny," Starbucks said. "I've heard that kind of talk before."

"That doesn't make it right," Johnny said.

Ripper sneered again. "Riding around on your fancy Harleys and pretending you're something special." Ripper pointed at himself and snarled, "Well, I really am something! I'm a man! You shouldn't play with real men, little boy. Or this is what can happen!"

Ripper pushed Carny and Deb, and they both fell through the hole to the floor below. Johnny screamed and ran at Ripper. Before Ripper could react, Jonny leapt on him. The momentum sent them both sailing over the edge into the hole. Starbucks ran to the edge and peered down. "Johnny!"

Johnny and Ripper landed on top of the gray beastie and it cushioned their fall. They rolled off it, punching and kicking. Carny and Deb fell on a pile of rubble and rolled down onto the floor. They both stood up, shaken and dirty and ran to a corner of the room, holding onto each other and looking for the tiger-beastie.

The tiger-beastie, taken back by the sudden commotion retreated to the corner of the room where it stood, eyeing all the new people who had just fallen into its temporary cage.

Johnny tried to reach for his sword, but Ripper held his arm. Ripper in turn tried to point his gun at Johnny, but Johnny held the barrel and pushed it away.

"Johnny!" Deb called out. "The tiger-beastie! Look out!

Johnny heard her, but he was too busy fighting Ripper to look. The tiger-beastie padded back and forth in the corner watching them, not sure what to do.

The doors to the Museum burst open, and Misterwizard and the rest of the men of the Tribe ran in. Soon they were positioned all around the hole, watching.

Foodcourt pointed his rifle, but Misterwizard stopped him. "Wait! Your marksmanship might be inadequate to hit Ripper and not Johnny!"

Food court lowered his gun, feeling helpless. The men of the Tribe shouted encouragement. The tiger-beastie, hearing all the commotion, crouched down and snarled, glaring up at them.

Johnny and Ripper rolled around, fighting, punching at each other, neither able to get a solid hit. Deb finally screwed up her courage. She left Carny and ran over to the boys. She gave Ripper a kick in the side. He looked up at her, turned the gun and fired. She yelled and fell back on the floor, the bullet whizzing by her head.

Johnny fought hard, but he was tired from battle and all the running. He grew weak, and Ripper began to land punches to his stomach and chin. Johnny's head grew woozy, and he desperately punched back. Each of Johnny's punches grew weaker, but Ripper's remained strong, for he was older and not nearly as tired.

Finally, Ripper landed a good solid punch to Johnny's jaw. Johnny sagged, and Ripper pushed him away. With a huge grin of victory, Ripper stood back, pointing the rifle at Johnny.

"Say goodbye, Johnny Apocalypse. I'm the winner!"

Ripper aimed and put his eye to the scope. Carny screamed and pushed Ripper as hard as she could. The rifle swung up and the fired, but the bullet shot harmlessly through the open hole in the roof far above. Ripper stumbled and fell, right in front of the tiger-beastie! And the tiger-beastie struck. It jumped on Ripper's back and bit into his neck.

Ripper screamed and fired again, but the shot was off and it only grazed Johnny's leg. Johnny rolled away as Ripper twisted and screamed, trying to shake the fierce animal off. Ripper stumbled into the darkness of a side passageway and they heard him scream in agony as the tiger-beastie roared. They heard the gun go off two more times.

Then there was only silence.

Carny and Deb ran as far away as they could in the opposite direction. The tiger-beastie walked back into view, its mouth covered with Ripper's blood. Johnny backed up as the tiger-beastie padded towards him. Johnny raised his sword, tired, bloody and sore.

"Come on, you evil tiger-beastie! I'm waiting for you!"

The tiger-beastie leapt at Johnny, as he raised his sword to meet it. Suddenly a shot rang out. The tiger-beastie fell. Johnny, Carny and Deb looked up to see Foodcourt, with his rifle pointed at the dead beastie.

Misterwizard and the rest of the men of the Tribe looked at him. He smiled with pride. "See? I'm not such a bad shot, am I?"

Everyone laughed with joy and relief. Johnny ran over and hugged Carny and Deb. Foocourt, Thegap and the other men above jumped up and down and cheered. Misterwizard simply smiled down, his face lit up with pleasure.

Deb looked Johnny in the eyes. "I knew you'd save us, Johnny Apocalypse. You're my hero. I love you." Deb kissed Johnny long and hard.

When she finally finished, Johnny looked back into her eyes. "And I love you, Little Debbie. You just don't forget whose girl you are. You're mine, forever and ever."

"I know that," Deb said with a smile, as she blinked back tears. They kissed as Carny watched with tears of her own.

Up above Super joined Starbucks, who smiled with surprise and pleasure at seeing her.

"And I owe you this," She said, and kissed him, as the rest of the tribe watched laughing.

Johnny, Deb and Carny looked at the darkness where Ripper disappeared.

"He's finally dead," Carny said. "It served him right."

"What a horrible way to die," Deb said, shuddering.

Johnny held her close to comfort her. "He brought it on himself."

"Well, well," Misterwizard said as he gazed down at them and rubbed his hands together. "This ended just like a good old-fashioned novel. And they all lived happily ever after."

Johnny, holding Deb in his arms, looked up with a wry smile. "Maybe we will, if you can get us out of this hole!"

They all laughed as Foodcourt went to find something for them to climb on.

Johnny, Misterwizard and the Tribe stood outside the Museum of American History, renamed New Sanctuary. They looked out at the buildings and huge lawn in the middle. Here and there fires still burned, and Wildies wandered about, disorganized and acting more like just ordinary Wildies with no one to lead them.

Misterwizard wrapped his arm around Johnny. "Well, Johnny, I'm hesitant to say it so as not to jinx us, but I think for the moment our troubles may be at an ebbing. We have New Sanctuary, filled with supplies, medicines, and weapons. We are at a most advantageous place to rebuild our new country, the capitol of the old. I suspect there are many challenges and adventures ahead as we forge our way, not the least of which is another encounter with Lord Algon. And I don't doubt there are many more Rippers out there to contend with. But still, I find myself encouraged and giddy with anticipation to see what new challenges befall us.'

As usual, Johnny didn't know half of what Misterwizard said, so he simple replied, "Me, too."

Johnny and the Tribe walked inside New Sanctuary.

What they didn't see was the lone figure with scars on his face and neck watching them from the Museum of Natural History, a rifle slung on his back. The lone figure walked off in the opposite direction.

CHAPTER 7

A week later, Johnny woke up to loud and ear-piercing wails. He opened his eyes, listened for a second then closed them again. It seemed all too familiar to Johnny, as if he'd never left the first Sanctuary and his room next to Carny.

He frowned at the headache he had from the noise. The wailing was so loud it seemed to be coming from inside his head, but in fact it was ten feet away, behind a curtain that divided the large room into two separate sections.

From behind the curtain, Johnny's older sister Carny spoke. "Morning, Mary Poppins Miracle. Are you hungry again?"

It was Carny's baby, all right. Johnny swore she never slept more than two hours through the night but spent most of it crying for food. Johnny had been so happy to see Mary Poppins Miracle born, but now, after a week of no sleep, he began to have second thoughts.

Johnny sat up and rubbed his eyes. His short blond hair stood up in all directions. He rubbed his hand over his head, and was pleased to see that once again, there were no bug-beasties in his hair. Since moving into the old President's Bunker below their new Sanctuary, he had discovered may wonderful things about the place. No rat-beasties or bug-beasties crawled everywhere, and dust didn't coat every surface. No Fake People watched them either. Johnny almost missed the strange statues, for they reminded him of home.

Johnny wore his favorite clothes to bed, just as he always did, his black leather pants, white cotton shirt and black leather vest. Why take them off? The only things he removed were his black leather boots. Since they'd started staying in the Bunker, Johnny's skin felt strange, weird, almost naked even when he had clothes on. Misterwizard introduced Johnny and the Tribe members to a new thing called a "shower." You actually stood in a small room and water fell on you. It cleaned all the dust and dirt you worked so hard to collect during the day off and made it disappear in a hole in the floor. Misterwizard made them use a weird bar of white called, "soap." Johnny refused to use it at first, for it made his whole body smell all sweet and flowery. But then Misterwizard found some that didn't cause him to smell that way, and Johnny reluctantly agreed to us it. These weren't the only new things MIsterwizard showed them, there were other things, amazing and almost unbelievable.

One day MIsterwizard gathered the whole Tribe into a huge room with black walls and nothing but chairs, all facing a big white wall in front. Misterwizard wore a magical grin, and everyone wondered what magic he planned on showing them. Misterwizard made everyone sit in the chairs, and then he stood at the front of the room.

As he chortled and rubbed his hands together Misterwizard said, "Ladies and gentlemen, boys and girls. I am about to introduce to you a very special treat, that I think you are going to appreciate immensely. It is called a 'motion picture.' What you are about to see will seem like magic, but I assure you, it is only technology and science at work. Our late benefactor Reginald and his ancestors stored up a veritable treasure trove of old films, over ten thousand, and I daresay we can watch movies until they become blasé. There are historical films as well as works of fiction."

The crowd grew restless and bored, and MIsterwizard seemed to go on forever, but finally he finished talking.

"And now, for your viewing pleasure," MIsterwizard said, his eyes twinkling, "I give you, Star Wars. Please sit back and enjoy. I regret to say we have no popcorn or soda, but that will be rectified in the near future."

Misterwizard left and as everyone murmured, wondering what was going to happen, the room darkened. Some grew scared and gazed around, but others smiled with anticipation, knowing it meant Misterwizard was about to do something magical.

Suddenly music filled the room and the white wall in front of them lit up. Pictures formed on it, as if they looked through a window into another world. The next few hours were some of the most magical Johnny could remember in his whole life, but also the most fun. He just kept thinking of what an amazing wizard Misterwizard was, and how fun the future was going to be if they could watch all the 'movies' they wanted. The Tribe oohed and aahed, entranced and amazed. Throughout the movie they pointed and yelled with excitement when things happened on the big wall, and when the golden man came out, someone yelled, "Look! There's that thing Misterwizard called a 'prop,' Seethreepo!" Everyone else cheered.

Johnny thought about that night now as he lay on his bed, listening to Mary Poppins Miracle cry. He wished he could go down and watch the movie again, instead of sit there with a headache.

Johnny looked around at the room he and his family, Foodcourt, Teavana, Carny and Miracle shared. It was a long, narrow room with dark black walls and not much else. One of the walls held a big flat glass plate that covered the entire thing. The door of the room said, "War Room." A huge long table had been in the room when the Tribe first arrived, but it had long ago been broken up for firewood. Now the room was bare except for two curtains they'd fashioned to give each other privacy, the beds they slept on and the items they'd collected for personal items.

Johnny rubbed his eyes and frowned, unhappy. There was no window in this new sanctuary, it was all underground so he had no way of knowing where the Red Eye was in the sky. Johnny thought coming to the new Sanctuary was going to be wonderful, but so far it was proving to be just the opposite. For one thing, it was much smaller than Sanctuary, and everyone crammed into smaller rooms. Johnny slept closer to Carny then he'd ever been in Sanctuary, and heard every noise she made, all night long. And living down, down deep in the ground made Johnny feel like they were living in a tomb.

He was missed Sanctuary, something he never thought he'd do.

Johnny figured it must be morning, so he climbed off his bed and put his feet on the ground. That was another thing. Johnny was used to sleeping on the ground. Now he was on a thing Misterwizard called a 'bed,' and it stood two feet off the ground. Johnny worried he'd roll off it onto the floor.

He reached under the 'bed' and grabbed his sword and slingshot. He put them on his belt. Then he put on his boots and yawned.

"Johnny, can you get me some water? Miracle is thirsty."

Johnny smiled. "Water spendy. Cannot waste water."

"Johnny," Carny chided from behind the curtain. Johnny knew they had plenty of water now, he just liked being ornery. Johnny stood up. "Water, water. Johnny is not Carny's slavey. But once again, Johnny go get Carny water."

Carny peeked around the curtain, smiling. They both laughed, remembering the days at Sanctuary.

Johnny walked past his parents' and Carny's sections to get to the door. Through a slit between the curtains, Johnny saw his parents still slept on their beds, Foodcourt snoring loudly.

As he passed Carny's section he spied her sitting on the edge of the bed holding a sleeping Mary Poppins Miracle in her arms, smiling at him. Johnny thought once again how beautiful Carny was, with her red hair and freckles. Johnny hoped she'd find a good mate someday, one who would care for her the way she deserved.

Johnny decided he had to go see Mary Poppins Miracle, even if his little niece did give him a headache.

He walked through the curtain, smiling. As soon as she saw Johnny, Mary Poppins Miracle, or just Miracle as most people called her, smiled and fussed, moving her little arms. Johnny's heart melted with love as he looked down at her.

He put on a frown and tried to sound cross. "Good morning, Miracle. You are noisy at night."

Carny grinned at him. "Miracle can't help it, Johnny. You made noise when you were a wriggler too, I remember."

Johnny put a finger in Miracle's tiny hand and Miracle grabbed it. Her hands were so small and dainty. Johnny couldn't wait until she was old enough to play with. They would have adventures together.

He took his hand back and walked to the door, though he could have stayed and played with Miracle for hours. He opened the door and walked out into the Ready Room to a sudden cacophony of noise and confusion, all directed at him.

Facing Johnny was what seemed to be the whole Tribe. Thegap, Deb's father, who was short and small like miniature man stood at the front next to Deb's mother Bathandbodyworks, the ugliest woman Johnny had ever seen. Next to them stood Oldnavy, a grizzled old man with missing teeth.

Bathandbodyworks complained, "Johnny, the water is running out!"

Oldnavy wailed, "Johnny, my room is too small!"

Thegap said, "Johnny, there's no more cans of food!"

Cinnabon stood holding the hand of her six-year old son Wheaties. "Johnny, this place is too dark!"

They all talked at once. Johnny backed up, hands raised, and wondered if he could duck back into his room.

Foodcourt came out of their room. "What's all the ruckus? Have the aberiginies attacked?"

An old woman named Marthastewartliving with gray hair and a big, long and who walked using an old stick for a can strode to the front and glared at Foodcourt. "We're not talking to you, Foodcourt, crazy old man, we're talking to our new Leader Nordstrom, Johnny."

Her words made Johnny angry. "Please don't talk to my father like that."

His tone quieted them all down, and they all looked scared and uncomfortable.

"Misterwizard and I will deal with all the problems as soon as we can. We are in a new place. It's going to take some getting used to."

"Well, I for one don't like this new place," Oldnavy grumbled. "It's drafty and dark. And it makes my bones hurt."

Johnny looked over the crowd at the Ready Room behind them. Johnny and Misterwizard removed the skeletons of the old occupants and cleaned up as best as they could. Now, after a week of the Tribe living there, the place was in a shamble, with food cans, clothes and just plain garbage everywhere. Blankets hung from the ceiling everywhere, dividing the room up into living sections. Johnny saw Tribe people in various sections, some still sleeping on the couches, some just talking or eating out of cans.

"You said you were smarter than Leader

Nordstrom!" A man in the back yelled, shaking his fist. "We have been here seven times of the Red Eye, and we haven't seen much!"

Johnny raised his hand and quieted the crowd. "It's true, this place is not big enough for all of us. Even the New Sanctuary above is not large enough. Today, Misterwizard and I are going to scout out a larger place, one where we can begin to build a Sanctuary out in the open and grow food for ourselves."

"But what about the Wildies?" Oldnavy asked. "They're still out there, and they are cannibals!"

"We're trapped in here!" A lady wailed.

"No, we're not," Johnny said, not sure how true what he said was. "We're going to build a new home and rebuild America the Beautiful. But it will take time."

"Meanwhile, we're going to starve!" An old woman yelled.

Johnny had had enough. He shook his head and waded through the crowd as they turned to watch him, firing questions. He had to talk to Misterwizard. He didn't know being a leader was so much of a headache.

Johnny strode quickly across the large, crowded room. Cool air blew on him from somewhere, but it was stale and musty smelling, as if it came out of a can. A crude middle passageway was fashioned between the sleeping quarters out of hanging blankets, and Johnny walked quickly so he didn't bother people sleeping.

He passed by Sephie's family's place. Sephie slept between her mother and father on a large pad on the floor. She wore a happy smile and seeing her made Johnny smile too. Then he saw a strange object on the floor next to them. It was a black metal box witha wheel on one side. Johnny tiptoed over and peered at it. It didn't seem to have much purpose that Johnny could see. Johnny shrugged and moved on.

He passed another family's area. A man and a woman sat on their mat on the floor holding what looked like miniature cars and buses in their hands. They pushed them on their blanket as if the cars were moving.

Johnny smiled. He realized the people of the Tribe members collected things from the Museum above, whatever looked interesting or entertaining. Johnny didn't care. If it made them happy and kept them from complaining, he didn't see any harm in it.

Johnny saw a short, petite woman with black hair and dark eyes making a beeline for him from across the room. Her name, Johnny knew, was Cinnabon, and she was one of the two women of families Misterwizard said were of Hispanic origin. She was a nice woman when she was in a good mood, but she had a temper, and when she grew angry she would get very excited and yell at a person really fast. Most in the Tribe learned to get along with her to avoid such a confrontation, or just go the other way when she was in a mood.

Johnny hurried his pace a little, hoping to avoid her and avoid just such a fate, but he didn't make it. She reached him just as he was getting to the hallway on the other side and blocked his way.

"Hello, Cinnabon. How are you today?"

She jabbed a finger into his chest and scowled at him with anger. "Don't Cinnabon me, Johnny! What is going on? You are supposed to be bringing us to this new place that is wonderful and full of new hope. A place where we are happy to leave Sanctuary, pick up our families, fight for our survival and leave everything we know behind! Ha!"

Johnny rolled his eyes and tried to smile. "What's the problem, Cinnabon?"

She frowned deeper and pointed down the hall. "What's the problem? My little boy, Wheaties, almost got killed yesterday when he climbed onto some big thing with wheels upstairs and it started rolling and smashed into a glass case with funny men in it. He almost fell off and it scared him. This place is dangerous!"

Johnny tried to hide his grin. He wanted to say, 'Keep control of your little brat, and he won't get hurt," but what he said was, "I'm sorry, Cinnabon. You must have been very upset."

"I am still upset. When do we get out of here? I don't like this new Sanctuary."

"Misterwizard and I are working on it."

From somewhere somebody yelled at Johnny. "The Necessary Rooms are overflowing, Johnny!"

"Well, fix them then!" Johnny said grumpily. "I don't have to do everything!"

Johnny frowned grumpily walked away, leaving Cinnabon with a surprised look on her face. "Leader Nordstrom would know what to do," she said in a parting shot. *Well,* thought Johnny, *Leader Nordstrom was a snake who betrayed you to the Gangers. And if it wasn't for me, you'd all be dead, killed back at Sanctuary.*

Johnny hurried to find Misterwizard. Things seemed to be getting out of control, and Johnny began to wonder if he was cut out to be leader after all, or if he even wanted to be.

CHAPTER 8

On a lonely, deserted street on the other side of the city, a girl in a black leather jacket wandered down the road. On one side of her head long blond hair cascaded down. The other half of her head was shaved and a tattoo of a red skull placed where her hair had been. She wore black leather pants, a black leather jacket and a glove with spikes on the back on her right hand. Her name was Lady Stabs, and until recently, she'd been a member of the Doomsday Prophecy.

Now she wandered the street, holding a knife in her hand, trying to keep an eye out for Wildies or Beasties, and hunting for food. Her sad frown told of her unhappiness and disappointment at what had happened to her gang lately. If they simply not listened to stupid Ripper and stayed at Misterwizard's Castle, they'd be living it up right then. But because of Ripper's constant grudge against Johnny they followed the Tribe all the way to this new city to get revenge, and now they were all scattered and lost, each one out for themselves, left to search for food just like the Wildies.

She walked down the street, peering at the dark interiors. Lady Stabs tried to look tough and she'd built a reputation of not being afraid of anything. The truth was she just acted like that because she was always afraid. She never really fought anyone if she could avoid it, just talked a good talk, then managed to find a place to hide when the real fighting began. She didn't really like fighting. The minute someone came at her with a knife, her insides turned to jelly and she stopped thinking. She hated violence and it tore her up inside when Ripper or the Gangers tortured somebody. What she really wished for was to leave the gang and join Johnny's tribe. The problem was she grew up in the gang. Her father and mother belonged to the Doomsday Prophecy and from a little scrabbler, it was the only life she'd ever known.

She walked up to a two-story brick building with no door. On the wall next to where the door should have been there was writing and a picture of a man in an apron holding a round disc that looked like some kind of food. It made her hungry. She hadn't eaten anything since the day before, and that had only been some apples she found growing in a small patch of dirt next to a building. Her insides groaned with hunger, twisting and aching.

Then she stopped and thought. How hard would it be for her to go back to Misterwizard's Castle alone?

Hard. She remembered it took a long time, and that was in the strange metal beasts. On foot, it would take forever. *Where were the metal beasts?* she thought. Back near Johnny's Tribe, and most had been on fire when she ran away. Besides, she'd never learned to drive one.

She walked into the dark building, her heart pounding, afraid a Barker or a Beastie would jump on her at any moment, or even worse, a Wildie with fierce eyes stronger than her who would knock her to the ground, kill her and eat her.

The interior was dark and scary. Large metal racks stood all over, covered with dust and dirt. The light from the doorway only penetrated a few feet, then there was nothing but black. Slowly she shuffled through the room, looking for something, anything to eat.

She reached the back of the store and stood in total darkness. She saw stairs leading up to the second floor. She started up them, hoping there was something on the floor above that might help her.

Suddenly she heard a noise. She turned and looked. A shadow filled the door to the street, the shadow of a man. Someone was there. Had the person seen her, and was he coming to kill her? She felt alone and small, afraid. Fear twisted her insides, and she looked for something to use as a weapon. She shrunk down, trying to make herself as small as possible, wishing once again she was a member of the Tribe, and Johnny was there to protect her, the way he did his girl Deb.

A deep, cold voice spoke to her. "Hey, Lady Stabs."

She smiled with relief, recognizing the voice and stood up. "Hey, Facegash."

She could see him now. Even though she knew he was on her side, because of the scar running down his face and his dark smile, he still looked scary, and her heart thumped hard and fast inside her.

He walked towards her, and for a moment she didn't

know if he was going to be friendly or not. But then he grabbed her arm and pulled her towards him.

"You made it, I see."

"Yeah," she said, eyes wide open in fear. "I ran, like everybody else.

"We all didn't run," he said quietly, almost hissing. "Some of us stayed and fought."

She snorted disdainfully and glared at him. "Is that why you're alive? And I don't see any new scars on you, only the old one on your face."

He spun her towards himself and scowled at her. "What are you saying?"

"Nothing," she said fearfully, remembering that Facegash could get angry fast, and when he did he was dangerous. "I did just like you. Ran when there weren't no other choice."

He let her go. She sighed silently with relief and rubbed her arm. He turned and surveyed the store with a look of disgust. "Ripper's dead. So are a lot of the gang."

"Look, Facegash," she said, looking into his eyes. "Let's leave. We can go back to Misterwizard's castle. It's empty. We can live there and do whatever we want."

Facegash looked at her intently, and she felt the fear coming back. "You'd like that, wouldn't you? Run with our tails between our legs. Let Johnny win. Let him kill Ripper and get away with it."

"Who cares about Johnny?" Lady Stabs scowled now too. "I'm hungry and tired. If it wasn't for Ripper's stupid obsession with Johnny and his Tribe, we could all be living it up right now. We're all that's left, Facegash. The Doomsday Prophecy is gone. We need to think about us now."

Facegash walked over to one of the metal tables. He

picked up a metal circle and flung it against the wall. It crashed with a loud bang that made Lady Stabs jump. Then he looked at Lady Stabs again.

"We're a long way from Castle. We ain't got no food or way to get there. And the Doomsday Prophecy ain't done. We're just scattered. I tell you what we're gonna do."

He walked over until he stood in front of her. His eyes shone with a dark light, and his face shined with sweat.

"We're gonna find all the Gangers and rebuild the Doomsday Prophecy. We're gonna be bigger and meaner than before, and we're gonna pay Johnny back for Ripper."

Lady Stabs backed away from Facegash and headed for the door. "We couldn't take Johnny when there was a whole bunch of us. I ain't stickin' around to watch you rebuild the gang just to watch us get beat all over again."

Facegash ran and blocked her way. He put an hand on her shoulder. "Listen. We don't have to fight the Tribe and Johnny again. All we have to do is show them freak cannibal Wildies and their crazy Lord the way in to 'em."

She pushed his hand off of her shoulder roughly. "Is that all?"

"That's all." Facegash took out his knife and moved it in a circle in front of her. "You in, or out?"

Lady Stabs wanted to be out, but once again she felt trapped in the only life she'd ever known. She tried to resist, but knew she really had no other place to go. "I'm in."

Facegash smiled. "Good. Now let's go find something to eat and round up the rest of the Gangers. We got a lot of work to do."

The Bunker, or Peacock as Reginald had called it, had five doors to hallways from the Ready Room by the secret entrance. One hallway had words on the wall that said, "Dining Room and Kitchen." Another said, "Dispensary," which was where Deb and Carny had been taken when they first arrived.

A third, the one Johnny walked down, said "Bedrooms." He headed down it to Misterwizard's room, glad to leave the Tribe, who he could still hear chattering and complaining to each other behind him. What Johnny wanted more than anything in the world was to get his Harley and ride out on an adventure, leaving them all behind to fend for themselves. If only the Tribe didn't need him, and if only Lord Algon didn't have his Harley. The thoughts depressed him even more.

The door to Misterwizard's room was large and elegant, made of dark wood with gold letters on it. On the door were the words, "Executive Quarters."

Slowly Johnny opened the door and peeked inside. What he saw was a sumptuous room full of beautiful furniture and rich and fascinating paintings. His eyes opened wide with marvel, and he stepped inside.

This, so Misterwizard had told him, was the Presidential Suite. The main room was so large Johnny couldn't see the other side in the darkness. Doors on walls led to a private kitchen, its own Necessary Room and the large bedroom.

Big leather couches sat in a semicircle in the middle of the room on a soft, dark blue rug. Glass tables stood in front of the couches, some with golden statues of beautiful women or dark wood ones of eagle-beasties and cat-beasties.

Next to the couches small tables held metal objects with white round things on top, carved and elegant. In the corner of the room stood another curved counter with bottles on shelves behind it like the one in the Ready Room.

Johnny toured the room, looking at the furniture and the paintings. One was of a man in strange clothes, white pants and a blue jacket with yellow buttons. His hair was white and he had a pleasant half smile. Johnny gazed at it, feeling like the man was almost alive and would talk to him at any moment.

He moved over to another painting. This one puzzled Johnny. It seemed to have the same man from the other painting, but he was with a group of other men and they sat in some kind of wooden contraption. They were on what looked like water, a lot of it, and they held sticks in their hands which they held in the water. Johnny would have to ask Misterwizard what it meant, for it was very strange.

Johnny walked towards the bedroom. From inside he heard loud snoring. He laughed. Misterwizard slept soundly. Johnny pushed open the door and looked inside.

The bedroom seemed as big as the main room. Large wooden boxes stood next to the walls, with knobs on them. A large bank of metal and glass boxes filled one whole wall. Johnny knew they were some kind of electronic junk, long dead.

In the middle of the room stood a huge four poster bed with black curtains hanging down at the four corners. The covers on the bed looked rich, thick and warm. And under them, Misterwizard lay, mouth open, dead to the world.

Johnny grinned, but with a bit of unhappiness. A small amount of jealousy filled his mind as he saw how nice a place Misterwizard had all to himself while Johnny was crammed in with his family in a bare room. He quickly forced the feeling away, reminding himself Misterwizard deserved the best. He was their real leader, and if it wasn't for him, they would all be dead. There was no way they could ever pay Misterwizard back for all he'd done for the Tribe.

Johnny walked over to Misterwizard, reluctant to wake him. He watched him for a few minutes, then decided he had no choice. Things were getting out of hand outside.

Gently, Johnny put his hand on Misterwizard's arm and shook him. At first, Misterwizard didn't respond, and Johnny wondered if he was going to be able to rouse him from his sleep. But finally, after shaking harder, one of Misterwizard's eyes popped open and he stopped snoring.

He sat up with a pop, and Johnny saw he was dressed in a blue fluffy robe and pink bunny slippers.

"What rascal dares to intrude upon my slumber? A curse on them!"

Johnny frowned, worried that he'd done something to get himself in trouble, but then Misterwizard saw him and smiled.

"Johnny! Good morning! Forgive me. I often awake with an unpleasant demeanor, for I am not a morning person. But I've had the most wonderful night's sleep. Like a wriggler!"

Johnny frowned grumpily. "I'm glad for you." Johnny thought about how he hadn't had a good night's sleep since he started rooming next to Carny and Miracle.

"Isn't this place splendiferous?" Misterwizard said. "A magnificent abode, full of luxurious accommodations and fine dining."

Johnny shook his head. "It may seem that way to you, MIsterwizard, but the Tribe is doing nothing but complaining. We're running out of food and water, the Necessary Room is backed up, and we're crammed together like rat-beasties under Sanctuary."

Misterwizard chuckled gleefully and patted Johnny on the arm. "Minor inconveniences, my boy, which we will endeavor to resolve today. I admit I didn't realize how fast the food and water would dissipate, or I would have suggested you initiate rationing. No worries, however. This is a large city. We must simply expand our territory, go on a mission of seizure and reclamation."

"We need to find a bigger place," Johnny replied, not sure of half of what Misterwizard said.

"Yes indeedy." Misterwizard hopped out of the bed on the other side and skipped over to a group of colorful painted boards with fabric on them in three panels. He zipped behind it and Johnny saw his robe go flying.

"Just let me get dressed, and we'll start our adventures. I have a lot to show you today, and we have a lot to discuss. There is a lot to know as leader. You may discover performing Leader Nordstrom's functions as leader are not as simple as you surmised. It might even and elevate your opinion of him slightly."

"I already find it not as easy," Johnny said, and once again felt a strange unhappiness inside, almost a feeling of gloom at the thought of being leader.

Misterwizard emerged, and now he was wearing even odder clothes. He wore green shorts, an orange shirt with funny trees with long stalks and three leaves at the top and shoes that were open in front and had two straps holding them on his feet.

MIsterwizard spun around, his short, round body hopping on his two short legs. "How do you like my outfit? The President was quite a snappy dresser. This Hawaiian shirt has real clamshell buttons, and these shorts are quite comfortable."

Johnny stifled a laugh. Misterwizard saw and laughed himself. "And look at this."

Misterwizard led Johnny over to a strange long bag standing upright with metal sticks in it. He took one of the sticks out and swung it. Johnny stepped back just in time, or he would have been hit. "This is called a 'nine-iron.' It is used in a game called, I believe, "Golf." It was a favorite pastime of the wealthy and socially upwardly mobile. I may try to learn it myself."

"Johnny!" Somebody down the hall yelled. Johnny rolled his eyes and groaned.

"Can you help me find a way to escape, just for a few minutes at least?"

"I most certainly can," Misterwizard said, as he put the metal pole back into the bag. "And it is exactly where I intended to take you. Let me introduce you to the other entrance into the bunker, the one leading to a building called The White House."

CHAPTER 9

Deb woke up in a big, fluffy bed lying under soft, silk sheets. She sat up and stretched, raising her arms up in the air. She looked around a smiled. She felt wonderful. The sickness seemed to be almost totally gone and she felt full of energy, and hope.

The place in Peacock Johnny chose for her and her family was one of the best in the Bunker. It was very similar to Misterwizard's Presidential Suite, for it was made for the Vic President. Johnny insisted Deb and her parents should have the room, so Deb could fully recover from her sickness. Deb and her parents each had their own room with a big, soft bed, and like Misterwizard's room, the suite had a small kitchen of its own and a living room full of couches and chairs.

Many people in the Tribe grumbled when Johnny said the room would be for Deb and her family, but Johnny was leader now, so he got to decide.

Deb couldn't wait to show Johnny how much better she was. She climbed out of bed and dressed in a nice, new pair of green coveralls she'd found in the gift shop of the Museum and a shirt that said, "Lincoln slept here," though she had no idea what it meant.

She put on a new pair of white shoes and looked down at them with pleasure. They were soft and pretty, but they felt good and strong when you walked in them. They were called "tennis shoes," and she'd never had any like them before. They were tight and snug, and they made her toes feel good.

She ran out of her bedroom into the kitchen. She grabbed two cans from the shelves above the counter for breakfast, a can of green beans and another one of something called 'chili.' She remember how low they were on food, but she knew Johnny would take care of it. He was smart and courageous, and there was nothing he couldn't do.

Deb's long blond hair was all mussed up, sticking up in curls,so she combed it with her hand. Then she dumped the contents of both cans into one bowl and called out, "Breakfast is ready!"

Thegap, Deb's father, and Bathandbodyworks, her mother, shuffled out of the other bedroom in fancy bathrobes with gold letters on the them, each smiling sleepily. Thegap looked at Deb and said dreamily, "Good morning, darling! You look so much better today!"

Deb smiled as she portioned the food out onto three plates

"Are you going to have more adventures with Johnny today?" Bathandbodyworks asked.

"Of course. He's going to need help figuring out

where we should live next. We can't stay here much longer, we're running out of food."

Thegap nodded and frowned. "Yes, that's true. We need to find a place to plant crops, and hunt for beasties. But with those Wildies and Gangers still around, it's going to be difficult."

Deb grabbed her plate and a spoon, walked over to one of the big, comfy couches and sat down. "Johnny will figure it out." Then she started to eat.

"Johnny's a good man. I'm glad he chose you," her mother said, picking up her plate and a spoon.

"Johnny did it," Thegap said, a smile on his small, intelligent face as he thought of recent events. "He really did save us from the Gangers and find us a new place to live. He's truly a courageous young man."

There was a knock on the door. All three looked up, curious. Deb put her food down and went to answer. She opened it to find Super standing there.

"Super!" Deb yelled. She quickly hugged her friend, who hugged her back.

"Starbucks and me can't find Johnny, so we're going to go exploring down the street behind the buildings on the other side. You want to come with us?"

Deb thought about it. Something told her it wasn't a smart idea, but she didn't want to look like a cowardie to Super. Besides, she'd been cooped up in a smelly old bus and then the dark, dreary bunker for a long time. She longed to see the sun and feel fresh air on her face. And really, Johnny didn't invite her to go look for a place with him, she'd just hoped he would. *Better to go with Super and Starbucks on a sure thing than risk being cooped up for another day in the dark, dreary bunker*, she thought.

"You bet!" Deb said. She walked out the door and

called back to her mom and dad, "See you later!"

"Be careful," Thegap called back. "It's still dangerous out there."

Misterwizard led Johnny to a closet in the bedroom. He opened the closet door and pushed the suits and other clothes on the rack to the sides, so a gap opened they could see past. There at the back of the closet stood a door. On the wall next to the door, a square black panel held colorful square buttons in orange and white. Some of them blinked, others were dark.

Misterwizard turned to Johnny then looked back at the strange door. "This is how the President most likely came into the bunker on that fateful day so long ago."

Johnny peered at it with interest. "So, what happened, Misterwizard? Why did they have the Great War?"

Misterwizard stroked his beard and looked thoughtful. "I've spent many hours trying to decipher that riddle myself, Johnny. From what I can gather from the newspapers I've seen, it seems times had begun to be very difficult. The sheer volume of people in the world and the lack of resources due to deforestation and global warming left most of the world starving and on the verge of chaos. The President decided to declare a state of emergency. He instituted something called "martial law,' invalidated the constitution and declared himself king. Then he proceeded to annex the countries around him.

"He took over Mexico with little argument, then proceeded to take over all of South America. But when he tried to do the same to Canada to the north, it became the 'last straw that broke the camel's back,' as the saying goes.

"England declared war on the United States and the President launched nuclear weapons against it. Russia saw the 'writing on the wall,' as they say, and realized the President would attack them next. They launched missiles against the United States. Soon all countries with nuclear weapons became involved, until there was little left."

"That's terrible, Misterwizard. And seems so pointless."

"It was pointless, Johnny, and insane. But as you know dealing with Ripper, some men let their evil natures inhibit their ability to think rationally."

Misterwizard walked back to the closet door and took out a piece of paper from his shirt.

"I was able to find this combination in the desk in the living room. I believe it is the code to open this door. We shall see if I'm right."

Misterwizard pressed some of the buttons and stood back. They both watched the door. At first nothing happened. Then with a soft click, it sprung open. The door swung wide, revealing a long, dark tunnel with recessed light at the top corners of the walls. It seemed to go on forever, straight and narrow.

Misterwizard chuckled with glee and bounced back and forth. "Are you ready for another adventure, Johnny?"

Johnny grinned with joy. "Bring it on!"

They slowly entered the tunnel and disappeared into the darkness.

On the other side of the river that split the city in two but still not far away from the Museums and Mall where Johnny and the Tribe lived, a strange and macabre scene unfolded.

A large grassy area filled with small stone slabs stuck in the ground was surrounded by a tall, brick wall. At the front of the brick wall an iron archway curved over an iron set of gates. The archway had the words, "Arlington Cemetery" written on it in metal letters. This was Lord Algon's real fortress, where he started his reign of power and where the building stood he declared his castle. Large and square and made up of white stone, the building stood two stories high surrounded by wild flowers and overgrown hedges. Large windows filled the sides of the building, some broken but many still intact. A white staircase led up the front of the structure to two large oak doors.

Lord Algon sat on his real throne now in the large main room of the building, his Throne Room. The walls of the room were decorated with the finest paintings he could find, most depicting battle scenes or ones of death and cruelty. A few showed old wooden vessels with large white sails on roiling seas, for Lord Algon had a good reason to love the sea and ships. Statues lined the walls, ones of beasties or strange monsters. A red carpet ran down the middle of the room to his throne. Lord Algon wore an elegant black robe embroidered with bird-beasties and tiger-beasties.

Four new guards stood behind him, men as fierce as his first guards. Two of them were black men with rippling muscles. The other two were shorter men, one oriental, the other white, but both with thick bodies and strong arms. Also next to Lord Algon stood his First Mate, a tall, strong man in leather clothes ripped and painted to look scary. His name was Hardhitter, and Lord Algon chose him because even though he was strong and knew battle tactics, he wasn't very bright.

Lord Algon's first four guards knelt in front of him. Their hands bound, they stared at the ground in terror. Even though they were large, muscular men, they trembled and shook with fright.

Lord Algon's subjects, the Wildies , filled the Throne Room, standing all around the room and watching the spectacle unfold. Lord Algon stood up and all eyes turned to him.

"What think ye, mates? What shall be done with these cowardly vermin, who ran and hid instead of defending their lord and captain?"

"Kill them!" An old Wildie man said, waving his fist in the air.

"Torture them!" An old lady said as she spat at the guards.

"Eat them!" A little boy said, a big grin on his face as he got into the spirit of things.

Lord Algon smiled as he looked at the abject terror on the guards' faces. He walked up to the men and then strode around them in a circle.

"Of a truth, we have not had a good roasting in a while. And a good meal would suit us well!"

The crowd cheered. One of the guards looked up at him imploringly.

"Please, milord, we meant not to betray thee. We grew frightful, like all, when we saw the strange magic of the Newcomers."

"The Newcomers?" Lord Algon said. "Aye, the Newcomers. Well, we have some what to show these Newcomers, don't we my people?"

The crowd cheered. Lord Algon walked down the red carpet, his new guards falling in behind him. The guard prisoners were forced to their feet and made to march along behind their king, with the Wildies following.

Lord Algon left his castle and walked across the grass, past many of the stone tablets in the ground. The crowd followed. He reached four large metal cages. In the cages, beasties padded back and forth, snarling. In one a bear-beastie stared at the crowd and roared. In another, a huge, long snake, its body as thick as a man's arm, lay with its coils piled up on a heap and its head dancing back and forth. Its tongue darted in and out as it stared outside the cage. In a third, a lion-beastie, with tawny brown skin and a full mane, twisted its head, snarled and flicked its long brown tail. And in the fourth, a giant ape-beastie stared out, its long, big hands gripping the bars and shaking them.

"Afore long, our good pets with make good sport with the Newcomers. 'T'won't be long afore the Newcomers will wish they'd never set foot on our shores!"

The crowd cheered again, and Lord Algon smiled, enjoying the sensation he caused. He looked back at the guards.

"And now to these cowardly dogs."

The guards looked up at him, their eyes begging for mercy.

"We shall not eat ye all."

Hope flashed in their eyes.

"Nay, we shall only eat two of ye. And the others shall make good entertainment playing with our pets, though I doubt for very long!"

The crowd yelled and rushed forth. As the men screamed, the Wildies grabbed them and dragged them off, two to the cooking pot, and two to the Arena of Death, the place of sport set up by Lord Algon.

CHAPTER 10

The tunnel from the President's bedroom, though lit dimly by light high on the walls, still seemed tiny and stuffy to Johnny. He felt as if the walls and ceiling were about to crush him at any moment. They had left the bunker far behind, and whether he looked forward or behind, all he saw was black tunnel.

"Is this tunnel safe?" He asked.

"Relatively, my boy. It is undoubtedly reinforced to prevent collapse in the event of a nuclear attack, and even after one hundred years I suspect it is still trustworthy."

Johnny wasn't so sure. It felt like there was no air, and he breathed harder, as if he couldn't get enough to fill his lungs.

Misterwizard talked on in front of Johnny, his voice echoing off the close, dark walls. "Once we have truly created a safe and stable domicile for the Tribe, it will be time to start teaching again. I will begin classes in English, mathematics, politics basic engineering and animal husbrandry. And history, of course."

"If you say so," Johnny said, feeling grumpy and depressed because of the tunnel.

"I will teach you, Deb, Starbucks and Super first, since you are the leaders of tomorrow. And I think I will teach your parents next. Foodcourt, no matter what people think of him, is a very intelligent and trustworthy fellow. So, I suspect is Thegap, Debs' father. You in turn can teach others, creating a domino effect of learning and knowledge sharing, for future generations."

Johnny wished Misterwizard would stop talking, and that the tunnel would finally end. It seemed to go on forever, and the further they traveled, the more Johnny felt trapped. "Are we almost at the end?"

"Yes!" They walked around a curve in the tunnel and finally came to a metal door similar to the one they went through at the bunker. This door was open and hung ajar.

"They must have been in such a hurry during the War they didn't bother to close it. Or someone else has been tinkering with it. Either way, this makes it easier for us, but we need to be careful in case we find interlopers above."

Johnny nodded, not knowing what interlopers were, but knowing exactly what Misterwizard meant. He took out his sword and held it ready as they walked through the door.

Deb walked upstairs to the Museum of American History to find chaos, Tribe members broke into display cases and fiddled with all the things they found, breaking things or turning them upside down and spilling their contents. One carried an odd thing that looked like a peanut, but it had eyes, arms, llegs and a big, tall black hat. Another held a stick that ended in a big loop with strings in both directions in the middle making a cross-hatch pattern. The man was using it for a walking stick.

Another sat on a strange metal contraption that looked like Johnny's Harley with two large wheels, on in front and one in back, but there was no machine in the middle. Instead it had petals on either side. The man had his feet on the on the petals and he pushed them, and the contraption moved around the room! The man smiled with pure enjoyment as he held onto a metal bar on the front. Deb watched him roll by with fascination.

Deb saw other Tribe members standing on couches or chairs and peering out the windows, though no one seemed to be going outside, as Johnny had ordered.

Sephie walked up. "Deb! Look at this!" Sephie held something up in her hand for Deb to inspect. It was the green little frog Johnny had showed her when they first arrived.

"Johnny said I could have him. Isn't he cute?"

Deb smiled and knelt down. She took the doll and inspected him. "He's wonderful. I'm glad you get to have him."

Super grabbed Deb's arm. "Come on. Starbucks is waiting outside for us."

Deb reluctantly followed but said, "But didn't Johnny say no one in the Tribe was to go outside until we made a plan to protect us against the Wildies?"

"That's for the Tribe members, not us. We're the leaders."

"I don't know if Johnny would agree to that," Deb said.

Super dragged Deb back to the main room and the large doors. After they had won the battle against the Wildies and the Gangers, Johnny and Misterwizard told the Tribe to rebar the doors until the Misterwizard and Johnny decided what to do next. Chairs and couches still lay propped against the doors.

Super moved a couch and some chairs, allowing one door to be swing open. She pushed the door and bright sunlight streamed into the room, along with a pleasant warmth from the morning Red Eye. "Starbucks thinks he knows where Lord Argon left the Harleys. He wants to go exploring and see if we can find them."

"I don't know," Deb said, unsure if they should venture out on their own. "I wanted to check with Johnny. He said to stay put."

Super put her arm through Deb's. "We'll be back soon. We won't go far. If we can't find them, we'll come back right away."

Deb looked back at the Museum of American History and at all the Tribe members exploring. An alarm bell rang in her head, but she's look like a little scared scrabbler if she turned back now. She smiled at Super and allowed herself to be dragged out the door. "Only if it's close and for not very long."

CHAPTER II

Facegash and Lady Stabs walked down the empty street. Gutted buildings on either side of the road, their windows long ago smashed out and only empty holes facing the street, looked like skulls with eyeless sockets staring at them. The rusted hulks of cars lined the sides of the street, some still with a little color mixing with the red of the rust, and some still with seats and steering wheels. Some still had the remains of skeletons inside, with bits of clothing or hair stuck to them.

Facegash grabbed Lady Stabs' arm. "Look!"

He pointed to the entryway of a deserted building. Two Wildies sat on the ground, eating something.

"Let's see what they got."

They took out their knives and advanced on the Wildies. The Wildies were so intent on their meal they didn't see Facegash and Lady Stabs approach. Facegash smiled. It was only a woman and her two children, each younger than five. He peered over their shoulders and saw they were eating a young deer. The deer was raw, and they tore it open with their bare hands. They pulled out its guts and ate them.

Disgusted, but so hungry he didn't care, Facegash yelled.

"Yah!"

The woman and her children looked up with fear. They saw him and instantly jumped up. They backed away, their faces and hands covered in blood.

"Oh, gross, look at them, Facegash. They're like wild animals."

"Yeah, but they got food. Facegash advanced on them and waved his arms. "Get out of here, you Freaks!"

The three just stared, their eyes motionless, unblinking.

"They're creepy, Facegash. Let's just get out of here."

"Ain't you hungry?"

Lady Stabs looked down at the half-eaten raw deer. Despite how disgusting it looked, her stomach rumbled, and she found herself feeling like a savage, ready to grab pieces of meat an stuff them in her mouth.

"Yeah," she whispered.

"Well, then, this deer is now ours." Facegash advanced on the three Wildies. He raised his knife. "Get out of here, now!"

They didn't move. Facegash smiled grimly. "Okay, if that's the way you want it."

But as Facegash reached them, he saw another figure behind them. A man, the biggest man he'd ever seen. He had broad shoulders and a huge square head. And big fists. He stood at least six feet tall, and he looked deadly.

Facegash backed up, fast. Lady Stabs saw him coming back, having a hard time keeping her eyes off the tantalizing deer carcass. "What's wrong, Facegash?" Facegash didn't answer. He just turned and ran. Lady Stabs looked at the three Wildies, wondering what about the woman and children had spooked him. Then the man came out of the shadows, advancing towards Lady Stabs. She took one more longing look at the deer and then took off after Facegash, holding her aching stomach.

Misterwizard and Johnny crept through the door, Johnny in front and Misterwizard in his shorts and orange shirt following close behind.

"Be careful, Johnny. Who knows what evil lurks ahead?"

"I will," Johnny said, annoyed because he was nervous and Misterwizard's words made it worse.

They entered another small tunnel with stairs that led up to a wooden door. This one didn't seem to have a lock, just an ordinary metal latch. It was closed.

As they reached the door, they paused and listened. Something moved around inside the next room, banging into things and knocking things over.

"Wait here, Misterwizard." Misterwizard nodded.

Slowly, Johnny opened the door and peered inside. The room had curved walls with a desk on one side and couches in the middle. The roof was gone, and bright daylight shone down. The carpet, which had once been blue, was faded to black. It had once had a symbol on it, but the carpet was so faded it was hard for Johnny to make out what it was.

The door he entered through was part of the wall and didn't look like a door at all. As he walked into the room, he saw where the noise had come from. A deer-beastie, a large beautiful one with big antlers, had somehow stumbled into the room. It tramped around, knocking over tables and chairs in an attempt to get out.

"It's just a deer-beastie, Mistewizard," Johnny whispered back.

"Oh!" Misterwizard said, and he walked up and looked past Johnny.

"It's beautiful!" Johnny said, looking at its soft brown hide and long, slender legs leading to its black hooves.

"Most assuredly, Johnny," Misterwizard agree. "However, I'm afraid we are going to have to kill it. The Tribe will need the meat. From now on, hunting is going to be one of our main sources of food."

Johnny hated the thought of killing the magnificent, noble creature, but he knew Misterwizard was right. With a heavy heart, he ran over to the deer-beastie, sword drawn.

Misterwizard followed close behind Johnny, watching. "Be careful of its hooves, Johnny, and its antlers. It can do considerable damage if you let it."

As soon as the deer-beastie saw them, it redoubled its efforts to escape, running around the room. Johnny had to back up to keep from being knocked over. He chased the deer-beastie around the room, but it was fast and he couldn't keep up with it.

Misterwizard grabbed a chair and tried to block the deer-beastie's path. It stopped the deer-beastie for a moment. It stood still, panting, eyeing Misterwizard nervously.

Johnny approached, sword held in front of him, ready to stab the beastie in the side. But suddenly, as if by magic, the deer-beastie leapt straight up, out the hole in the ceiling. It landed outside on the sloping wall and slid down. Then as Johnny and Misterwizard watched in amazement, it bounded off. Johnny and Misterwizard looked at each other and Misterwizard chuckled. "It seems the deer-beastie was truly motivated. We shall have to get better weapons than your sword to hunt, or we shall find ourselves being very hungry."

They both laughed. Then Misterwizard walked over to the desk and sat on the edge of it. "Come here and sit in the chair, Johnny. The chair of the President."

Johnny walked over, looked at the chair for a moment then sat in it. It was old and moldy, but it seemed to hold his weight.

"So, this is where the Leader Nordstrom of the United Sate sat?"

"The United States, Johnny, and yes, but he wasn't like the Leader Nordstrom you knew. He was chosen by the people. They all voted and decided together if they wanted him to be their leader."

"That seems like a good idea," Johnny said, rubbing his chin and gazing around at the room, wondering what it must have been like, before. "Were presidents good leaders?"

"Some in the affirmative, others doubtful. And each only stayed Leader Nordstrom for four years, what you would call seasons. Then a different man would be voted in, though the first one could be voted in again, for a total of eight season. And he didn't have ultimate power. He would suggest laws, but they had to be agreed to by Congress."

"Congress," Johnny said, his brow furrowing in confusion.

Misterwizard searched the desk drawers as he talked, his big, squat body hunched over, so all Johnny could see was his bald head. "You see, Johnny, there were three branches to the government. The Executive branch, which contained the President, the Legislative branch, which included the Senate and the House of Representatives, and Judicial branch, the judges."

"Judges," Johnny said, getting a headache again and wishing he'd never asked about it.

Misterwizard found something he liked in a drawer and pulled it out. It was a small wooden box. He opened it and peered inside. "Judges settled disputes between people and decided the punishment for wrongdoers. They also had a say in the laws that were passed, to make sure they were fair."

Johnny looked around the remains of the room, at the pictures not destroyed on the walls and the books lying in the rubble. "Was it always that confusing? Misterwizard, I'm beginning to think I'm not the right man to be a leader."

Misterwizard pulled a short brown stick out of the box, held it sideways under his nose and sniffed it. He closed his eyes and sighed. Then he said, "Governing people is always a hazardous and complicated business, Johnny. It is not for the weak or simple minded, and the rules for governing must be written to prevent skullduggery. But I promise you, you will rise to the challenge. I have ultimate faith in you. Ah, now if only I had a light!"

Misterwizard gazed at the small stick in his hands with pleasure. "Amazing that they survived this long.

Fortunately they were sealed and kept in a moisture free environment. A truly spectacular find. A match! My kingdom for a match!"

Misterwizard searched around again. Johnny heard a noise. He walked over to the broken wall and looked out.

"Misterwizard, Wildies have begun moving back into the shacks on the grass. And Lord Argon is still out there, somwehere."

Misterwizard walked over and looked out as well. "Yes. We need to reach an understanding with the Wildies. They will be required to Lord Argon, abandon their cannibalistic ways and join us, or we will have no alternative but to run them off. Let's go back to Peacock, shall we? It's time for us to talk to the Tribe and come up with a plan of action."

Misterwizard put the stick back in the box, stuck the whole box under his arm and strode off back towards the tunnel with Johnny following close behind.

CHAPTER 12

Starbucks waited for Super and Deb on the steps of the Museum and met them when they came out. The Red Eye sat a quarter of the way into the Eastern sky, and half the large grassy Mall lay in shadow.

Deb looked to her right at the big, white stick like building with the broken top. Then she looked to her left at the building with the round dome way at the other end of the Mall on their left.

The Museum of American History, presently called New Sanctuary, sat on one side of the long, rectangular lawn called the Mall. Next to it on Deb's left sat the Museum of Natural History, where Johnny and Ripper fought, and Ripper had died.

Across on the other side were more white buildings. And on the grass, itself sat hundreds of shacks, the Wildie encampment.

"What if the Wildies catch us out here, alone?" Deb asked.

"I have this," Starbucks said, holding up a rifle from the bunker. "It's only got two shots left, but it'll scare 'em long enough for us to run away. And if we still need something," he pulled out his sword and swung it around to impress them, "I have my trusty sword."

"Your sword is so cool, Starbucks." Super said, looking at it with pleasure. His sword was long and curved, with some strange beastie with wings, a long tail and sharp teeth on the handle.

"Isn't it, though?" It's not as cool as Johnny's. Johnny and me found our swords a long time ago, back in Pilladepia. We had our pick, and I picked the coolest."

He put his sword back in his belt and slung the rifle over his shoulder.

"And I brought these for you two, just in case." He handed each girl a short knife.

"They'll do good in a pinch. Nobody will dare mess you with while you have those."

Deb looked at the knife he handed her. It was heavy, almost a foot long, silver with a black handle that had some strange silver twists in it.

"That one you have, Deb, was in a case inside with some letters on it, and I can even tell you what they said, because I've been learning from Misterwizard how to read, just like Johnny. It said "Sting." I think it has magical powers."

Deb held it up and gazed at it. Somehow holding it made her feel more confident, braver. She smiled.

"It's heavy," she said.

"You'll get used to it," Starbucks said nonchalantly. "And yours, Super, is really cool."

Super looked at her knife. It was shorter, but the blade and handle were curved and sharp.

"Yours was in a case with a picture of some weird, freaky guy in a silver suit with a head that had ripples on the top. It had the letters Cling-on or something on it."

"Cool!" Super said, and she swung her knife in the air, a big smile on her face and her eyes bright.

"We shouldn't be here," Deb said. "We're going to bring danger to the whole Tribe."

"Well then, let's go!" Starbucks started walking down the steps towards the white stick building, away from the Wildie encampment.

Deb watched him for a moment. "That isn't what I meant, Starbucks."

Starbucks just smiled and kept walking. Deb and Super looked at each other, stuck their knives in their belts as best they could and followed him.

Super caught up to Starbucks and put her arm through his. "So, you think you know where the Harleys are?"

"Sure do," Starbucks said. "The Wildies really don't care about 'em. It was only Lord Algon who seemed interested, and he's gone."

Deb hurried to catch up, annoyed at them for forgetting that she'd recently been sick and wasn't as fast and healthy as they were. "This is so dangerous," she said, glancing back at the shacks behind them.

"Starbucks knows what he's doing," Super said, and grinned at him. Her confidence and compliment made Starbucks stand up a little taller and he grinned at her. She grinned back and then gave him a kiss.

Deb rolled her eyes. It was all good and fine for Super to believe Starbucks, she was gaga over him. But she knew better. They were only headed for trouble.

They reached the white stick building. It rose up forty feet in the air and then came to a jagged end. On the ground around it, white stone rubble gave mute testimony to what had happened to the rest.

"We have to circle around behind those buildings on the other side of the big grass," Starbucks said. "During the battle, I saw some Wildies rolling the Harleys behind those buildings. I bet they're still there."

A Wildie appeared around the corner of the building, making Deb's heart jump. He had wild eyes, long wild gray hair and a large gray beard. He wore a long dirty overcoat and his face was covered with dirt and grime.

"A Wildie!" Deb said, pointing.

Starbucks steered them around towards the other side of the building. "Just one," he said, but he didn't sound as confident as before.

They passed around the side of the stick building where they couldn't see the Wildie anymore, and Starbucks walked faster. Super and Deb hurried to keep up.

Deb begin to feel a little woozy. She still wasn't totally healed, and the trek out looking for the Harleys was already a lot more tiring than she'd expected. She wished Johnny was there with them. She felt so alone without him, even with Starbucks and Super nearby.

Facegash and Lady Stabs kept walking, almost stumbling form exhaustion and hunger. Lady Stabs kept glancing at Facegash, wondering if she could walk slow enough to get some distance from him and then run away. She could go to Johnny and the Tribe and beg for mercy. She had no doubts Johnny would forgive her and let her join them, for Johnny was a good man.

She walked slower, and soon the distance between them grew. Lady Stabs pretended to look at the ground and shuffle along like Facegash was doing, but really, she watched him, looking for her chance.

Suddenly they heard a whole crowd of voices. They both stopped, instantly afraid. Facegash backed up and walked over to the nearest building, a big square one with its roof caved in. Lady Stabs joined him.

He looked at her with meaning. She nodded. Slowly they crept forward. They came to a building that was just a shell, with large white columns outside and arched doorways but only two walls standing, the front one and the one facing them.

They crept up to the windowless opening and peered inside. They saw a group of men and women standing next to a fire on the ground, eating something. Something that smelled delicious.

Then Facegash recognized them and he smiled with relief and pleasure. They were Gangers!

He grinned at Lady Stabs. "It's our guys."

She wilted with relief and joy. "Yeah," she said, hoping she didn't sound as weak and frail as she felt. She wanted to cry with happiness, at least they were familiar faces.

Facegash strode into the building as if he owned it with Lady Stabs right behind him. The Gangers all looked up at him.

"You better have left some of that for us," he snarled, already back to his old, cocky self.

"Facegash!"

"Lady Stabs!"

"Hey guys!" Lady Stabs waved as if she was cool and relaxed.

The Gangers all smiled at them as they walked in. Facegash slapped arms with some of the guys and Lady Stabs hugged one of the girls she knew.

"Hope you like squirrel-beastie," said a short, thick Ganger with a square head and a big flat nose named Trashcan. "'Cause that's all we got."

Facegash grabbed some squirrel out of Trashcan's hand and chewed on it. "It'll do for now. Until we give Johnny and his Tribe what's comin' to 'em and then we'll be feasting on their guts."

Trashcan nodded, not really believing him, just taking it for what it was, the usual tough banter they always talked.

A girl with spiky green hair in black leather shorts, a red shirt and a black leather jacket with metal studs all over it named Curlygirl spat out a piece of squirrel tail and said, "Facegash, we ain't got no way to 'pay Johnny back.' Ripper's dead, and we're eatin' squirrel-beastie. We got to go back where we belong before Johnny comes lookin' for us."

Facegash scowled, putting on his fiercest look. He strode over to Curlygirl and glared at her, making her shrink back slightly. Then he looked at the rest of the Gangers.

"If anybody here thinks I ain't the man to take over for Ripper, he better say so now. Then I'll show him who's in charge. And since I'm now in charge, we ain't goin' back with our tails between our legs. We're gonna stay here and rebuild. Then we're gonna find a way to take care of Johnny Apocalypse, if for no other reason than to avenge Ripper. Anybody got any questions?"

They all looked scared and nodded.

Facegash grinned darkly and with pleasure. "It may take us a thousand years, but we're gonna make 'em pay. There's a crazy guy named Lord Algon out there, and he eats people. All we got to do is let him at the Tribe, and he'll eat Johnny. And that's gonna be a sight to see."

They all cheered and high-fived each other and went back to eating their squirrel-beastie.

A door into the Museum of American History opened. Foodcourt, stuck his head out the door and looked around. He didn't see any movement in the shacks on the lawn, in fact they looked deserted. He gazed up at the rising Red Eye and the fading shadows and smiled.

"It's all clear."

Johnny's mother Tevanna, thin and tall with long black hair, stuck her head out as well. "Do you really think it's safe for us to go outside? I am getting so tired of this dark, dreary old place."

"As long as we're careful. We can at least sit out here on the porch and get a breath of fresh air."

With that, Foodcourt strode outside with confidence and a steady gait, his head held high. Teavana stayed in the doorway and watched him, nervous.

Foodcourt gazed around at the grassy Mall and the white buildings on either side, some intact but most crumbled or broken in some fashion.

"This place is all broke up. But it'll do until we finally

head to Australia."

Foodcourt walked over to one of the large white columns at the top of the stairs and leaned on it. "Coming, Mother?"

Teavana finally ventured out, and when she did three other faces took her place at the doorway, all watching with wide eyes.

Teavana tiptoed over to Foodcourt and grabbed his arm. "We should really have asked Johnny before we did this."

"Nonsense. This is our home now. We own this place." He raised his hand and waved it around at the city around them. "Soon we'll build a new country, just like Johnny said. And then maybe we can put off going to Australia, it will be too nice here."

Two others ventured outside, Bathandbodyworks, Deb's mother, and the old man Oldnavy. They gazed around at the landscape, smiles spreading on their faces.

"To think, we can live outside, without fear of the Sickness," Bathandbodyworks said happily. "Enjoy the light of the Red Eye and fresh air, and not be afraid. It's like a dream come true."

"And it's all because of my Johnny," Foodcourt said with an air of pride.

Forgetting about the shacks and any danger, they walked down the steps and gazed around.

"We should explore our new home," Foodcourt said. "Let's go look inside that next building to start with. I want to see where Johnny killed that evil Ripper again."

Foodcourt strode off purposefully towards the Museum of Natural History. Teavana, after a nervous glance back at New Sanctuary, followed.

More Tribespeople came out, cautiously and slowly,

but soon with less fear and more excitement. The large stone porch filled with people, all gazing at the view with amazement and delight.

They were so engrossed in what they were doing, they didn't see the rotted, wooden doors of not one, not two but five of the shacks below open and eyes peer at them from inside.

CHAPTER 13

Starbucks was so interested in finding the Harleys that he walked faster than the girls, soon putting quite a distance between them. He gazed ahead at the street looking for any sight of the bikes.

They passed piles of rubble and the old buildings, most one-story business offices with dark interiors, but an occasional two story or higher structure. Most of the buildings had fallen in on themselves from the decay of years, though a few were still intact.

Starbucks came to a place where the street was broken up and cracked. The nearest building looked destroyed too. The whole front of it was gone, and it its place big pile of rubble lay on the ground, almost reaching to the second floor. Only a jagged piece of the outside wall on one side remained sticking out towards the street, and on the other side the wall had a big round hole in the middle, as if someone had purposefully broken it out. The building had three floors, and Starbucks could see all three from the street, but only half on each level remained, the edges of the floors ragged with pieces of round metal sticking out of them. On the second floor of the building, old pieces of furniture stood in the corner, a desk and some chairs, as if nothing had happened and they were just waiting to be used. A painting hung on the wall next to the desk. It showed a house with two sticks on the front in a "X" pattern near the top. A little girl in a funny looking white hat with what looked like wings stood in front of the building with flowers in her hand.

He looked back at the street. Cracks in the pavement made a spider web pattern everywhere he looked. In some places chunks of street were missing altogether. The cars on the street looked like nothing more than mangled metal, and some were in two or three pieces. Starbucks surveyed the scene with interest. "This area must have been hit by some of Misterwizard's special weapons during the fight," he muttered to himself.

He walked more carefully. He stopped and looked back at the girls. They were just dots in the distance. He frowned, annoyed, impatient to go but knowing he should wait for them.

He looked into the distance. No sign of the Harleys yet. He heard a noise and looked to his left, instantly on alert.

A little Wildie scrabbler, not more than five seasons, stared at him from a doorway. The boy looked intently at Starbucks with a frown. The boy seemed to be all alone, but his presence made Starbuck nervous. Where there was one, there would probably be more.

"Avast, ye scurvy knave. Strike thy colors or I will run thee through with my trusty sword."

The boy held up a stick, sharpened to a point on one end. Starbucks smiled. "You win, fella. You're too tough for me."

The boy smiled with victory. "Ye be one of the varlets that come to occupy the house back yonder, be that the truth?"

"Maybe," Starbucks said, not sure if it was wise to tell the boy too much.

The boy grinned. "It be quite amazing the show ye put on before, with loud noises and lots of fighting. It be a grand time, and there not be the likes of it in a long while."

"I'm glad you liked it," Starbucks said. "We don't mean your people any harm. But we won't be dinner for ye, ah you either."

"Not all of us be the way of the maneaters. That be Lord Algon's doing. 'Twas when he arrived the eating of people started."

"Well, let me tell you something about your Lord Algon, friend…"

But the boy was gone. The doorway lay empty again. Starbucks shrugged and looked back at the girls again. They were still so far back. How he wanted to keep moving! He decided he would run really fast ahead, see if the Harleys were anywhere in sight and come back. At the pace they were going, he'd still be back to greet them before they even made it to the spot where he stood. He didn't think the boy would be any threat to them, or even his family if they showed up. In any case, Starbucks would be really, really fast.

He took one more look back them. They stopped!

What were they doing? He wasn't going to wait any longer. He turned and ran ahead as fast as he could, looking everywhere for the Harleys, confident that the girls wouldn't even know he'd left them for a brief time.

Deb and Super walked down the street, looking around with interest and enjoyment at the broken buildings, junk cars and bushes growing out of flat surface. It seemed like the forest took over the city again, and everywhere grass sprung up and little trees grew. Even in the cracks of the street grass sprouted, and through the broken windows of houses they could see trees inside. Many of the buildings were square and made of white stone with large white pillars in front. The interiors of the buildings were all dark and gloomy and looked empty and scary. The girls peered into them as they passed, looking for any signs of Wildies watching them, but didn't see any.

Deb tried to keep up with Super, but Super seemed to have twice as much energy. Super walked ahead then came back, walked ahead again and came back, talking to Deb at a hundred miles an hour. Deb began to wish she'd never joined them on the little excursion, though she did enjoy being with Super.

"Starbucks says there's a whole country to explore, Deb. He says it goes so far, it would take a whole cycle of the seasons to get from one end to the other. He says there's an adventure around every corner. He even says there are monsters out there somewhere that eat people and are ten feet tall, and tribes that are freaks because of the Sickness."

"I think Starbucks is a good story teller," Deb said with a grin. Where was Starbucks? She looked ahead and saw him far in the distance. "Why isn't he waiting for us?"

Super looked ahead at Starbucks too. "He wants to find the Harleys to surprise Johnny."

"Well, he should stick with us. What if something happens?"

"Nothing is going to happen. And we're going to get to ride back. I've learned to ride, so I can ride Johnny's. Unless you want me to give you a lesson so you can, Deb."

Deb liked that. "It would be nice to surprise Johnny someday and show him."

"Yeah!" Super said.

Suddenly they heard a noise from the house on the right. They both stopped and looked. Something was moving inside.

"Oh, oh," Deb said.

"It might be nothing," Super said, but both of them backed up the other direction.

A dark shadow moved inside the building. Then two shining eyes gleamed through an empty window frame. The girls took out their knives and held them in front of themselves.

The eyes moved towards them and they saw what it was. A big, furry wolf-beastie, thin and gaunt but with big sharp teeth and a look of ferocity.

"We have to get to the building behind us," Deb said, slowly inching back.

"Starbucks, come back," Super whispered to herself. "We need you."

Suddenly there was a large crash. The girls fell

through the air, screaming. It seemed like they fell forever. Deb's mind was blank with shock and surprise, wondering what was happening.

And then they hit hard rock, and something wet. They both fell unconscious.

Johnny and Misterwizard walked back down the long, dark tunnel. Johnny was more used to it this time, but it still seemed to go on forever, and he still didn't like it.

"So Misterwizard, Johnny said, peering ahead at the dark shape of his friend ahead of him. "So, tell me more about the Great War. You said the President took control. Did he become like Leader Nordstrom?"

Johnny saw Misterwizard's head nod. "Yes. From what I've read in the newspapers and official documents, after the President seized power, some countries across the ocean formed an alliance, countries called Russia, China and North Korea to name a few. Others formed an alliance of their own, countries like England, France and Germany. Soon what the President did didn't matter anymore, it became every country for themselves. Each Alliance hurled nuclear bombs, the mushroom monsters as you call them, at the others to destroy them. Most of Europe, another place across the ocean, was decimated as well as most of the large cities in the United States. In retaliation for the attack on the United States, the President launched missiles at just about everyone else, causing total annihilation.

"Once the bombing was over, most of the governments were destroyed and the countries lay in chaos. Radiation and contamination wreaked havoc on the survivors."

Johnny scratched his head and thought about what Misterwizard had said. Just like Ripper and the Gangers, causing death and suffering, and for what?

They came to the other door and stopped. Misterwizard looked back at Johnny.

"At the end, the President and his cabinet hid in the Bunker and sealed it off, and there they remained, until they died. Our poor friend Reginald, who gave his life to help us, was the President's grandson. He filled in a lot of the history to me before he died."

"He must not have been like his father then," Johnny said.

"No," Misterwizard replied. "I think he was more like the President could have been, if he hadn't let greed and power corrupt him."

Misterwizard turned to Johnny just before they entered back into the Bunker. "Johnny, I've found some papers in the Bunker, and they refer to a new kind of strange weaponry the President was building to retake the planet. There were no details as to what kind of weaponry it was, they simply referred to the "Goliath Initiative." The papers hinted the weaponry lay hidden somewhere in Washington D.C. I don't believe anyone has discovered this new weaponry yet, or even if they did they'd know how to use it. But we need to keep an eye out for it. If we can find this new weaponry and find out how to utilize it, we may find it very useful. In any case, we need to find it before one of our enemies does"

Johnny nodded, not sure what Misterwizard was even talking about. He rarely knew what MIsterwizard was talking about, but somehow it always became clear in the end.

They walked back through the door into the President's bedroom to find Carny waiting for them, holding Mary Poppins Miracle in her arms.

"Johnny, you better get up to the Museum. Most of the Tribe has gone back up there, and I think they're going outside."

Misterwizard stroked his beard and looked thoughtful. "It may be of no consequence, the Wildies have been quiet and scarce of late. Still, a reconnaissance of the situation is definitely in order."

"Yes, and we should also find out what they're up to," Johnny said.

CHAPTER 14

Starbucks walked around the corner of a white building with statues of naked women with long cloths wrapped around them. He gazed at the statues for a moment, thinking how life-like they seemed, almost alive. The women smiled, looking happy and content, and Starbucks wondered when the statues were created and who made them. One looked like Super, and Starbucks couldn't wait until her and Deb arrived and saw them.

Across the street stood a building made of red bricks with the whole front wall gone. Starbucks could see into the room, where old moldy couches sat and faded paintings hung. One of the paintings was of a man in some kind of uniform. Most of the picture was so faded he couldn't make it out, but the man's eyes stared at Starbucks, as if in surprise or dislike. Starbucks decided he didn't like the painting at all.

Then he saw something else much more important sitting in front of the house and smiled with excitement. It was the Harleys! They lay on the ground on their sides just like the Wildies must have abandoned them.

Forgetting the girls for the moment, Starbucks ran up to the Harleys and looked them over. They didn't seem damaged. He frowned though as he stood them up and lowered the kick stands, mad at the Wildies for just dropping them and risking scratching them up.

He examined them inch by inch, but they seemed to be perfectly intact. He smiled, happy.

He looked back down the street, wondering what was taking the girls so long. He couldn't wait to show them the Harleys and go for a ride.

Then it dawned on him. He couldn't see them at all anymore. Mild alarm bells went off inside him, wondering if something had happened to them, and feeling bad because he left them so far behind.

He hurried to his Harley and started it up. It roared to life, and despite the possible emergency, Starbucks felt a thrill of joy. He hopped on his Harley with a smile and motored it around so that he was facing back the way they'd come.

And then he saw the wolf-beastie, watching him. It was lean and savage, and saliva dripped from its fangs. Starbucks' heart pounded, and he looked close at the creature to see if he saw any blood on its mouth. Had it attacked the girls while he was playing around and having fun? The thought of him leaving them to be killed made him feel terrible. If he'd lost Super because of his own selfishness, he didn't know if he could live with himself.

But just then he had other things to think about. The wolf-beastie bounded towards him. With no other option, Starbucks turned the Harley around and sped off, with the wolf-beastie in pursuit. He had to lead it away from the girls, kill it and hope he could circle back and find them, if they were still alive.

Facegash and the remnants of the Doomsday Prophecy walked along a deserted street. The squirrel-beastie had barely taken the edge off their hunger, but Facegash knew if he couldn't find food for them they wouldn't stay his gang very long.

Up ahead a group of Wildies stood over fire pit, warming their hands. As they grew close, Facegash saw something that made him smile. There was a pot on the fire. That meant food.

He looked at the others and counted them. Ten left, ten of a whole gang. But they would grow, grow until they were in the hundreds, maybe thousands. They would be kings, after they killed Johnny and the Tribe.

The Gangers looked up at him. "They got food ahead. What are you waiting for?"

The Gangers hollered and whooped and took off towards the Wildies. Facegash grinned. It was almost like old times, terrorizing someone weaker than them. He ran to join them.

When he arrived, he saw the Wildies running away and his gang investigating the pot. An old Wildie ran away but slowly because he had a bad leg. Facegash ran over to him and knocked him to the ground. The man yelled and put his hands over his face. Facegash stood over him and grinned down.

"I ain't gonna hurt you, old man."

"Please, kind master, take what ye wouldst but have mercy, I am but a poor old wretch what done no one any harm."

Facegash chuckled. "You know, I'm getting real tired of that gibberish you people talk. What I want to know is, where is that phony king of yours?"

The man kept his hands in front of his face and shook. "Of a truth, he and his guards weighted anchor and sailed off, I know not where."

Facegash kicked the old man in the shoulder and the old man yelled. "That nonsense is giving me a headache. Tell me where he's at or I'll, I'll shiver your timbers or something."

The old man frowned with fright. "I know not but can suspect. He be on the other side of the running water, where his true castle be, where the stones stick up out of the ground and the stone people stand. That be where he holds court and makes sport in the Arena he fashioned."

Facegash was getting really annoyed at the way the old man talked, mainly because it made him feel stupid. He grabbed the old man and pulled him to his feet.

"I don't know what you're talking about, you crazy old spook. But guess what? You just volunteered to take me there, Matey."

Facegash dragged the old man back to the Gangers. When he got back, he found them all staring at him.

"What?" He said.

Lady Stabs nodded towards the pot. Facegash looked inside it. Floating in the water was part of a human torso, a leg and an arm. Facegash's face changed to a look of disgust. He looked at the old man and shook him. "You people are freaks, you know that? Where'd you get the body, old man?"

"They be what's left of the tragic victims of the battle, me lord. Waste not, want not, we always say, and Fate provides for us in times of need."

Facegash looked in the pot again. And this time he saw a tattoo on the arm. The arm was from a Ganger, and he knew who it was, a friend of his.

He grabbed the old man and shook him, raising his fist. The old man cowered, putting his hands over his head. Facegash was about to hit him, and then he thought about it. The Ganger was dead, and he knew how hard it was to come up with food in the empty barren city. And he was hungry himself.

He gazed at the rest of the gang then back at the old man. "Where's the rest of the body? The head, and, well the rest?""All eaten, my lord, in the bellies of lads and lasses, I wager," the old man said.

Lady Stabs' lip curled. "I ain't eatin' no people, Facegash. That's just sick."

Facegash scowled, "Then you can starve. I know we don't like it, but we got to get strong so we can fight Johnny. If the Wildies can do it, so can we. No Wildies are tougher then the Doomsday Prophecy."

Facegash released the old man. The old man crawled over to a corner and cowered. Facegash smiled and looked at the pot again, smelling the sick but tantalizing aroma. "Who knows?" he said with a grim smile. "Maybe we'll start to like it, and then when we make Johnny's Tribe our slaves, we can eat them like cattle. Step up. Soup's on mates."

Foodcourt and Teavana peeked their heads inside the lobby of the Museum of Natural History. The vast cavernous room seemed to stretch on for miles and rise above their heads into the sky. It was dark inside, even with the crack in the ceiling, and the marble floor and walls made it cold. Teavana shivered, wrapping her thin arms around her tall thin frame. The shivers weren't just from the cold but also from the creeping fright that threatened to make her turn and run back outside.

In the semi-shadow, they saw the hole in the floor in the middle of the room. A breeze blew through the room, causing Teavana to shiver.

She frowned darkly. "I don't like it here, Foodcourt. What if there are some more beasties like that tiger-beastie inside?"

"Then we run," Foodcourt said with an impish grin, "but not before we look down in the hole again look at the dead tiger-beastie."

"You are so proud of your son Johnny, aren't you?" Teavana said, looking at him with a smile.

"He's a hero," Foodcourt said, puffing out his chest. "Come one, let's go look."

They crept over to the big hole in the floor and peered over the edge. Sure enough, the tiger-beastie still lie there, but something was different.

"Look, Teavana said. "The body has been torn apart, and all the insides are gone."

"Yes, somebody was eating it," Foodcourt said. "Which is what we should have done, if we were smart."

"And where's Ripper's body?" Teavana said. "Shouldn't he be there too?"

"Maybe whatever ate the tiger-beastie ate him too," Foodcourt said. "That would serve him right. I hope it was some rat-beasties."

"I don't see Leader Nordstrom's body either," Teavana said. She shook her head disapprovingly. "Let's go." She glanced about the Museum nervously.

Foodcourt frowned at her, irritated. "What are you so afraid of? I want to explore this place."

"You're going to get us killed," Teavana complained.

Foodcourt put his arm through hers and led her away, towards the hallway leading into the Museum. "Just one quick tour around. I bet we find some beasties in here from Australia."

As they left the main room, they didn't hear the strange scraping sounds coming from down below in the hole, somewhere in the rubble next to the tiger-beastie's body.

Lord Algon lounged in his new throne on top of the wall of the Arena of Death and listened to the cheers of his people. An electricity and excitement filled the air. Rarely did they have as big a spectacle to enjoy as they were about to in a few moments.

The throne he sat in was not as nice as his portable one the guards carried him on when he traveled. He left that one at the Museum after the fight with the Newcomers. This one wasn't made of dark wood and carved with beasties like the other. Instead it was made of white wood with a red seat and back in some kind of soft cloth. It was adorned with little men wearing funny hats, strange men with round bodies and heads and goofy smiles, crooked white sticks with red stripes up and down them and bells with ribbons. It was much less dignified and scary, and almost looked like a little scrabbler's chair, but it was large with a tall back, and so it was better than nothing.

He had made the best of it, though, and adorned it with skulls and bones. Now he smiled with pleasure and waited with eager anticipation for the start of the fun about to begin.

After the battle he retreated back across the bridge over the river to his main fortress. Situated on a large grassy field full of strange stones with rounded tops that stuck up from the ground and the stone people with wings and sad faces, it was an ideal location because it had stone walls surrounding it with gates at the entrances. A huge stone building with big, tall columns stood right in the center. Lord Algon had turned this building into his castle, filling it with beautiful and terrifying things, and his real throne sat there in his main hall.

Here he ruled with fear and might or had until the Newcomers arrived. The very thought that they had bested him and made him run like a cowardie away burned his insides as if he was being tortured by a hot iron. He had to destroy them, show his people he was still the supreme ruler of Algonia. He knew it wouldn't take long for doubt to creep into the hearts of his followers, and then someone might try and kill him to steal his throne. The thought of his people killing and eating him filled him with a fear he could barely stand thinking about. He had to act, fast.

The Arena was fashioned by taking the stone slabs from the ground and piling them on top of each other in a circle with a large grass area in the middle. Held together with mud and grass, the slabs rose up to a height of ten feet and then a walkway was fashioned on top. So many of the stones had been piled up they were three wide which made a surface at the enough for the Wildies to stand on or sit on chairs. Other stones made steps to walk up to reach the top.

A small gap on one side of the Arena held a gate that could be closed and locked for the entrance of the poor, helpless contestants. Another larger entrance on the other side allowed the beasties to be let in. On the side of the beastie entrance, four cages sat. In one, a lion-beastie paced back and forth. In another, a huge python snake-beastie lay on the ground, curled up in a circle. In a third, a huge black bear-beastie stood on its hind legs and roared. And in the last, a monstrous gorilla-beastie stood, holding onto the bars and exposing its sharp teeth in a grimace. All four of the beasties snarled and looked ready to kill, agitated by the yelling and activity.

Lord Algon's new portable throne sat on the wall in the middle. On either side of him, beautiful Wildie girls sat on cushions and held his hands.

The center of the Arena was large enough for a hundred men to stand, though usually only one or two stood in it at a time fighting or dying. Old junk cars and gravestones lay scattered inside the Arena for places to hide and fight from. Both the cars and the gravestones were stained with old blood, as well as scrapes and dents where swords or clubs had hit them.

At the head of the Arena inside stood a giant statue.

It was made of bits and pieces of broken buildings glued together with mud. Shaped into the image of a terrifying monster with a deformed head and claws, it was the Wildies' god, the great lord Nucleer, who swallowed and ate all but the strong and courageous. It was Nucleer, according to the legend started by Lord Algon, who chose him to be the king of the Wildies, for his courage and strength.

The two guards, huge men but now docile and timid, wore nothing but cloth loincloths. They shuffled towards the gate into the Arena of Death slowly, reluctantly, with their hands ties and spears pointed at their backs by four Wildies.

The guards were pushed inside the Arena. They both ran over to kneel in the grass below Lord Algon's throne, their hands clasped in supplication. Though they were big and strong, they both shook with fear, their eyes wide.

"Please, me Lord, may thee and our great god Nucleer have mercy," one said. "I beseech thee, show us the kindness and compassion we know ye have in thine heart. We have ever been thy faithful servants protecting thee from any that might wish to harm thee."

Lord Algon laughed and the crowd joined him. The girls next to him smiled at him with amusement. He stood up and turned to the left and right, milking the moment for all it was worth. The people cheered. Then he looked at the guards, but really spoke loudly to the Wildies.

"Ye would rob my people of their sport today?"

The Wildies roared with laughter and cheered. Lord Algon looked at them, arms outstretched.

"Be it not true, my people, that our great god Nucleer destroys all who have not courage and strength?"

The people nodded and cheered some more.

"Nucleer has no stomach for cowards. He eats them whole!"

The crowd cheered, loving the spectacle.

"Please, my lord," the other guard wailed, crawling forward in the grass as close to the wall as he could get, "ye but only have to command us, and we will be thy slaves forever."

Lord Algon scowled at them. "And what manner of slaves would ye be? At the moment when I truly needed thee most, ye fled like scurvy dogs. Ye left me to fend for meself agin the strange visitors and their magic. Ye thought only of thine own hide, and not that of thy master."

"We all fled, master, every one of us, as ye recall," one guard said. "Even my lord ran from the Newcomers and their magic."

Lord Algon's eyes narrowed in fury, and the guard realized he'd made a mistake.

"Be ye accusing me, your lord, of being a coward, here before our god Nucleer? For that ye shall die horribly!"

"No, my lord, I meant it not!" The man quivered and fell over on his side.

Lord Algon ignored him and turned to the crowd. "What say ye, my subjects? What shall be the fate of these traitorous whelps? Shall we spare them, pat them on the head and tell them, 'well done'?"

"No!"

"Kill them!"

"Feed them to the beasties!"

"Teach them a lesson!"

Lord Algon smiled, glad the Wildies had forgotten

that he too had run in terror, as had all of them. The Newcomers had powerful magic, and Lord Algon was terrified of it. But he knew that if they could somehow steal the magic, it would make him the most powerful king in the land, maybe the world.

The guards looked up at the crowd, their eyes begging for mercy, but only cold, hard eyes looked back at them. Lord Algon raised his hand and the crowd quieted.

"Let this be a lesson to thee of the price that comes from disloyalty and cowardice. Across the running water and over the bridge awaits our new enemy sitting pretty in our abode. They have taken what be ours, and think we have no stomach to take it back because of their magic. But this be our land, the land of Algonia!" The crowd cheered. "We will kill the Newcomers and take their magic for our own. Then I, I mean we, will be the rulers forever!" The crowd cheered louder, jumping up and down. "But now is the time for sport and entertainment!" The crowd cheered yet again. "Give them weapons, err they die too quickly!"

Two small swords were thrown down into the Arena. The men ran and seized them. They stood back to back, shaking with fear and tension.

Lord Algon smiled. "Listen ye varlets. If one of ye strikes the other and the beasties eat him, perhaps I will find mercy in my heart to spare the other."

The men looked at each other and backed away from each other, now suddenly mortal combatants.

"Let the first beastie in!"

The gate was opened. The cage with the lion-beastie was opened. As the crowd roared, it bounded into the Arena, looking for prey.

CHAPTER 15

Johnny and Misterwizard hurried through the bunker towards the long, dark steps up to the Museum. Johnny ran faster than Misterwizard, who was much older, and reached the stairs before him.

"I'm coming, young man. I'm not as spry as I used to be." When Misterwizard reached the stairs, he stopped to catch his breath. He waved to Johnny.

"You proceed and see what mischief the Tribe has managed to create. I will join you at my more leisurely pace."

Johnny nodded, not knowing what Misterwizard said but figuring it meant, 'go on ahead.' He opened the door to the stairs and bounded up them two at a time. Misterwizard watched him until he disappeared in the darkness above, then he started up at a much slower pace. "Oh, to be young again," Misterwizard said, as he took the steps one at a time.

Johnny ran as fast as he could, but even he grew tired after a few minutes and had to slow to a walk. It was pitch black. *Why,* he thought, *did so many places in their new city seem to have long, dark, stuffy tunnels?* He began to wonder if it was just something he was going to have to get used to.

Up, up, up he went. Each time the stairway curved, only to reveal more stairs. Finally, Johnny reached the Museum again. He entered the basement room and stood by the statue of George Washington that at one time hid the door to the Bunker. No one from the Tribe was around. Worse, he didn't even hear any sound. Where were they all?

Johnny ran up the curved stone stairs up to the main floor. With relief he saw some of the Tribe milling about, but only a few. He hurried through the Museum, looking for someone in charge, like Foodcourt or Thegap.

"Johnny, look!" Johnny turned to see Sephie holding the green frog up to show him. "It's mine now!"

Johnny smiled and knelt down in front of her. "That's wonderful, Sephie. Where are you mother and father?"

Sephie smiled and pointed towards the main doors. "They went outside with everybody else. They told me I had to stay inside because I was too young." Sephie frowned.

"Everybody else?" Johnny said, closing his eyes and looked pained. He opened them again. "Stephie, do you want to do something for me?"

"Sure, Johnny," Sephie said, her face lighting up with a smile.

"Good. Go downstairs and wait for Misterwizard to come out of the opening to the Bunker. Tell him I went outside to get the people back in before they get themselves into trouble. Can you do that for me?"

Sephie nodded. "I like Misterwizard."

"Thanks, Sephie. I like him too." Johnny let her go and watched as she ran down the steps to the basement happily. Then Johnny hurried to the door to the Museum, hoping he wasn't going to have a big headache ahead of him.

Deb woke up to a splitting headache of her own. Her arm hurt bad and her leg was cold. She opened her eyes and looked around, but wasn't sure if she really had, for it was just as dark as if she kept her eyes closed.

"Are you all right?" A voice in the darkness spoke. It belongs to Super.

"What happened?" Deb asked. "My arm hurts. And so does my head."

Slowly her eyes adjusted to the darkness, at least enough until she could make out the dark form of Super peering down at her. Beyond Super was only black, pitch black, so dark that it looked alive.

The head of the shadow that was Super looked straight up. Deb looked up too and saw a small circle of light surrounded by a jagged edge. It was high, impossibly high, and seemed like there was no way they were ever going to reach it.

"The street just fell apart and we dropped in here. Luckily, we landed in some water, or we'd be dead. How do you feel? Is anything broken?"

Deb did a mental check of her body, and though she

ached all over, she didn't think anything was broken. The only way to really know was to stand up. She put her hand on a broken chunk of rock next to herself and tried to push up. Her head immediately felt woozy, and she thought of how the fall wasn't going to help her recovery from her illness happen any sooner. After trying twice, she finally stood on wobbly legs. Her arm felt wet. She rubbed it with her other hand and something slick and dark came off. The feel of it told her it was blood, her own. She had no way to tell how bad she was cut. She just had to hope it was minor.

She hobbled over to Super. "I think I have a cut. How about you? Are you okay?"

She saw Super's head nod again. "I landed right in the water. It was nasty and smelly, and I'm wet and cold, but otherwise okay."

A growling sounded above them. They looked up to see the dark outline of the wolf-beastie's head against the dim light of the hole. It sniffed and snuffled and peered down at them.

"Well, at least it can't get to us," Deb said.

"Let's hope it's not hungry enough to jump down here."

They pulled out their swords and waited, watching the wolf-beastie as it moved around the hole, peering down, sniffing, then moving again to another spot.

"Go away, you rotten monster," Deb said, feeling lost and alone.

"Where is Starbucks?" Super asked. "I hope the wolf-beastie doesn't get him."

They heard a distant roar and smiled at each other in the dark.

"Starbucks found the Harleys!" Super said.

Deb grinned with relief, but then she remembered the wolf-beastie, and where they were. "But how is he going to know where we are?"

In response, Super started yelling. "STARBUCKS!"

Deb joined her. "STARBUCKS! WE'RE DOWN HERE!"

The wolf-beastie's head jerked up. It ran off.

"Oh, no," Super said. "I hope we didn't just get Starbucks killed."

They both listened intently, hoping to hear anything. But there were no more sounds, only the pervading silence and blackness around them.

"STARBUCKS!" Super yelled again. No answer.

Deb looked around at the darkness. It seemed to be getting closer, almost as if it was filling their souls. "Well, we better start looking for a way out."

"How can we?" Super replied, and Deb saw her peering around. "We can't see our hands in front of our face."

Deb put her hand in front of her face, and even in the dim light from above, she could barely see it. "We have to do something. I don't think Starbucks is going to find us."

"Who are you?"

The girls froze and stared into the darkness. The voice didn't come from one of them. There was someone in the dark with them.

Facegash and the Gangers stood by the stone wall outside Lord Algon's complex listening to the cheers. A tall, thin Ganger named Badluck with long, black, greasy hair that was plastered to his head and a black eye patch walked up to Facegash. He was named Badluck because nothing seemed to ever go right for him. He lost his eye one day while simply running down the street, tripping on a metal spike in the road and falling right onto another spike that poked his eye out. He lost three fingers on his left hand by putting his hand in a hole in a building one day where there just happened to be a hungry dog-beastie on the other side. He always seemed to be the one to stumble into the worst of any fight or predicament. So, they named him Badluck, and nobody wanted to be around him too much for fear the bad luck would rub off.

Badluck wore a pair of jeans with holes in them, black army boots he'd found somewhere, a filthy tee-shirt that had once been white, and a faded black leather vest. As he walked up, Facegash scowled at him, not liking him to be so close.

"Listen, Facegash," Badluck said. "Something is sure going on."

"And guess what?" Facegash said, smiling. "You just got elected to find out what."

Lady Stabs walked up and jabbed a finger in Badluck's direction. "You sure he should go? You know what happens to him."

"That's why he's going. If there's gonna be bad luck, Badluck will take it first. Then the rest of us will be free and clear."

Badluck put on a dangerous look. "What if I say I ain't goin'?"

Facegash walked up to Badluck, making Badluck flinch and move his head away as ifhe was afraid Facegash was going to hit him.

"Then we throw you over the wall and let 'em eat ya. Got it?"

Badluck nodded, looking scared. Lady Stabs punched him in the arm playfully. "Don't worry, Badluck. Your luck's gotta change some time."

Another Ganger, a big burly man with red hair named Mushface because his face looked like it had been mushed in by a wall, walked up to Facegash.

"I say we get out of here, before we're spotted."

Facegash scowled at Mushface. Mushface was big, but he was slow, and not only that, he was slow-witted. If it wasn't for these facts, he'd probably be the leader, but as it was, Mushface was happy to go along. So Facegash knew Mushface wouldn't argue too much, he was just trying to act tough.

"Be quiet, Mushface, before I mush your face into this here wall." That made the other Gangers laugh. Mushface's face turned from tough to looking scared.

"But I'm scared, Facegash. If they catch us, they'll eat us."

"We got to find out what these weirdos are up to," Facegash said. "There ain't no other way we're gonna take 'em over, and if we can't take 'em over, then we's gonna have to leave."

Facegash tried to look fierce. "And Ripper would spit on us if he knew we let some freaks run us out of town." He turned to Badluck. "Get up there, Badluck, before they do spot us."

They all gathered around Badluck and Lady Stabs made a stirrup with her hands. Badluck stepped into it and Lady Stabs lifted him up until he could reach the top of the wall. He hosted himself up and lay flat on the top. The Gangers all looked at him, waiting.

"What do you see?" Facegash asked.

Badluck's mouth opened wide as he stared into the distance on the other side of the wall. "You wouldn't believe it!"

"What?" Facegash said, growing irritated.

"I've never seen anything like it," Badluck said.

"Well, describe it to us, Stupid," Facegash said.

"Well," Badluck said slowly, "there's this big, I don't know what it is, in the middle, and the Wildies are all, like standing around it."

Facegash scowled and looked disgusted. "Be more specific, Dummy."

Badluck stared in amazement. The Gangers watched him, growing more anxious to see for themselves. "It's like amazing. Those poor guys in there are gonna die."

"That's it," Facegash said. "That's what you get for sending a moron to do your looking for you. Help me up."

Lady Stabs made a stirrup again, and Facegash climbed up. The other Gangers couldn't wait, and they all helped each other climb up too. Lady Stabs was the last one, and one of the other Gangers grabbed her hand and pulled her up.

The Gangers all lay flat on the top of the wall, scanning the area for people who might see them. They didn't have to worry, however, for all the Wildies were too busy watching the spectacle.

As the Gangers saw what Badluck had seen, they all grew amazed as well. Smiles appeared on their faces and looks of interest.

"Look," Facegash said. "There's their phony king."

"And look at that place they built," a Ganger said as he stared at the Arena. "It's cool."

"See those guys fighting the beasties?" Badluck said. "I sure wouldn't want to be them."

"They ain't gonna live long, that's for sure," Facegash said.

"These guys are organized, Facegash," Lady Stabs said, fear creeping into her voice. "And scary. I think we should get out of here before they see us."

Facegash smiled. They Wildies were much more ferocious and dangerous than the Gangers realized when they first arrived. And there were more of them than they ever could have guessed. Which meant one thing: they could easily destroy Johnny and his Tribe, if they just had a little help.

"Which means Johnny and his stupid Tribe got trouble comin' their way. Okay, let's get out of here. We got to plan."

The Gangers crawled backwards and dropped off the wall outside where they came from. Facegash was the last one. His feet hit the ground, but before he could even turn around, he felt Lady Stabs' hand on his arm. "Facegash, we got big trouble."

Facegash turned around and saw what she was talking about. In front of them stood a whole group of Wildies, holding spears on them.

Facegash scowled. "See what comes of hanging around Badluck?"

CHAPTER 16

Out the door they walked, first one, then two, then most of the Tribe. As they fearful ones inside saw the boldness of the ones who had walked out, they grew less afraid themselves and followed them. Soon the large, stone porch of the Museum was filled with people of the Tribe, all gawking at the scenery and the beautiful sunrise.

Thegap and Bathandbodyworks, Deb's parents, came outside. Microsoft and Abercrombie, Sephie's mother and father, did too. Cinnabon and her son Wheaties, who was only six seasons old, stood near one of the large pillars.

"Where did Foodcourt and Teavana go?" Abercrombie asked as she scanned the horizon.

"Into that building," Microsoft said, pointing at the Museum of Natural History.

Thegap asked, "Where did Starbucks, Super and Deb go?"

"I don't know," Bathandbodyworks said, looking around. There was no sign of Starbucks and the girls anywhere.

Marthastewartliving hobbled outside on shaky legs with her cane and peered to the left, her eyes narrowed. "That's where Ripper died," she said in a serious voice, pointing at the Museum of Natural History.

"I want to know where Johnny is," Cinnabon said, frowning. "And if he's bringing us some food."

"I agree," said Microsoft, touching his big belly. "I've never been so hungry in my life."

"You could use to lose some weight, dear," Abercrombie said. "We both could."

"Well, I'm doing it, whether I want to or not," Microsoft grumbled.

Bathandbodyworks walked towards the Museum of Natural History. "Come on, Thegap, let's go see where it happened."

Thegap smiled and ran to catch up with her on his short little legs. "And see if we can find Foodcourt and Teavana, or Starbucks and the girls."

The rest of the Tribe watched them, afraid to follow. Cinnabon started off in the opposite direction, towards the big, tall white broken stick building.

"Where are you going?" Marthastewartliving asked.

"I'm going to look in that big tall white thing," Cinnabon replied, pointing at the stick building. "Maybe it has some food."

Marthastewartliving looked around, feeling deserted. "Don't leave me here alone!" She looked both ways and then finally followed after Thegap and

Bathandbodyworks, hobbling along with her cane.

In the Museum of Natural History, Foodcourt and Teavana walked through the rooms gazing at the displays of strange animals. Each one they passed seemed more amazing and weird than the last.

Teavana pointed at a weird creature in a glass case. It seemed suspended in midair, surrounded by a wall painted like blue water and rocks. It had a big, fat, gray body and strange flippers for arms. It didn't have any legs, but instead had a weird big paddle at its bottom. And it had two long, white teeth that stuck out from its mouth and hung down almost to its middle. The teeth were sharp and round like spears.

"Look at that, Foodcourt! Do you think it was a real beastie?"

Foodcourt stared at the creature, mouth open but a big smile on his face. "I suppose so, though I don't think I'd like to meet one. It doesn't look very friendly."

"How could it walk?" Teavana said, her face wrinkled in puzzlement. "And how did it eat, with no hands?"

"I don't know," Foodcourt said. He looked at the bottom of the case. "It has some scribbling here at the bottom. Johnny says Misterwizard is going to teach us all the ancient words. I can't wait. It drives me crazy seeing it all over and not knowing what is says."

They stared at the creature for a few minutes then moved on, entering into a large dark room full of more glass cases. They looked up towards the ceiling and gasped.

Hung above them was the biggest creature they had ever seen. It looked like the gray beastie but was as big as a bus. It was black and white with a huge flipper at its end. Its mouth didn't have spears like the other one, but it was open showing two rows of sharp white teeth and a pink tongue.

"Look at that!" Teavana said, smiling with excitement. "It's so big!"

Foodcourt looked up at it nervously, wondering if they passed under it whether it was going to fall on them. "We're going to have to get Misterwizard to come here with us."

"Wouldn't that be wonderful?" Teavana said, looking at him and nodding. "He could tell us all about all these strange beasties."

Something in the darkness in front of them made a noise. It sounded like someone laughing. Foodcourt and Teavana both frowned, instantly afraid. They glanced at each other and then at the darkness. Teavana moved over to Foodcourt and he put his arms around her.

"Is someone there?" Foodcourt yelled. "Johnny, is that you?"

There was no answer. "Maybe we should go back," Teavana said, looking back the way they came uneasily. "We didn't even think to bring a weapon."

"It's probably just one of the scrabblers from the Tribe, playing games," Foodcourt said, but his voice didn't sound like he believed it.

"Johnny…Johnny…" A mocking voice came from the darkness.

Foodcourt's face clouded in anger. "Whoever that is, we're not afraid of you." Then he steered Teavana back the way they'd came, glancing over his shoulder towards the strange voice.

Suddenly something came skittering across the floor into the dim light. Foodcourt and Teavana looked down at it. When Teavana saw what it was, she screamed and grabbed Foodcourt.

Lying on the ground before them was the tiger-beastie's head.

"Foodcourt! Look!"

"Keep moving," Foodcourt said.

They hurried back to the main room, past the huge hole in the ground. They both looked down at the tiger-beastie. Sure enough, its head had been cut off.

They stopped at the hole and peered back down the dark hallway beyond it.

"Who would do such a thing?" Teavana asked. "And how did they get down in that hole and back out?"

"I don't know," Foodcourt said. "But it's not a very funny joke."

The door to the Museum opened and Thegap and Bathandbodyworks entered. They saw Foodcourt and Teavana and smiled and waved.

"We came to join you."

"Good," Foodcourt said. "Do you have a weapon?"

Thegap frowned, instantly afraid. His short, thin body shook. "Why would I need a weapon?"

Foodcourt strode over to him and motioned towards the dark hallway. "It doesn't matter. They wouldn't dare do anything with two of us. Come on, we need to see who's in here."

"In here?" Thegap said, frightened and reluctant. "Why? Who's in here?"

"We don't know," Teavana said. "Somebody threw the tiger-beastie's head at us."

"Then we should leave, right away!" Bathandbodyworks said, grabbing Thegap's arm.

"Nonsense," Fodcourt said. "There are two of us, and this is our home now. We can fight. Or," he said, leaning towards his wife and talking low so only she could hear, "we could just let Bathandbodyworks go back. Her looks would scare anyone." Teavana gave him a reproachful look and elbowed him.

Foodcourt looked around and found two long sticks, pieces of old display cases. He picked them up. Then he walked over to Thegap and thrust one in his direction. Thegap grabbed it without thinking and held it up, staring at it. Foodcourt grabbed Thegap's arm and dragged him towards the hallway.

"I don't know, maybe we should wait for Johnny." Thegap planted his feet and best he could, holding the stick awkwardly. He wore an expression of fright. He wasn't strong enough or big enough to stop Foodcourt from pulling him along, so without moving his feet she slid on the marble floor.

"We can't make Johnny do everything. Are you a man or a mouse-beastie?"

Thegap looked at the women and tried to straighten up and look tough. "It's not that I'm scared or anything, I'm just not, as you would say, tall of stature. Being a small man, I…"

"Well then, let's go!"

Thegap finally relented and joined Foodcourt walking towards the dark passage. Just before they disappeared into the darkness, Foodcourt said, "You ladies stay here until we make sure it's clear. If we don't come back in a reasonable amount of time, go back to New Sanctuary and get Johnny."

"Why wouldn't we come back?" Thegap said in a frightened voice as Foodcourt dragged him towards the dark passageway.

"I don't like this," Bathandbodyworks wailed. "Thegap, you be careful. You're no Johnny Apocalypse. You see something, you just run!"

"You bet I will," Thegap said, just before he and Foodcourt disappeared into the darkness.

CHAPTER 17

Who are you?" The voice seemed to come out of nowhere, a floating apparition. Already Deb could feel her senses playing tricks on her as the darkness messed with her mind.

Deb and Super took out their swords and stood back to back. The swords gleamed in the dim light from above.

"Who are you?" Deb asked in response.

"I asked first," the voice said. Deb began to realize it was a soft, falsetto voice, the voice of a young boy.

"We're Deb and Super," Super said. "You try to hurt us, and we'll stab you. Got it?"

"Where did you come from?" The voice asked, seemingly in real confusion.

"From that hole up there," Deb said, pointing above them. "And we need to get back up there, right away. Can you help us?"

A face materialized out of the darkness. Just as Deb thought, it was a young boy of about ten seasons, but he was not like any boy she'd ever seen before. His skin was pure white, and his eyes were big and round and black. He had long, tapered fingers, and he wore nothing but a loincloth around his waist. He had no hair and he reminded Deb of a slug-beastie she'd seen on one of the plants back in Sanctuary.

"Out of the sky?" The boy said, looking up at the hole with amazement. "You fell out of the sky?"

"It's not the sky," Super said. "It's just the land above this place."

"And we need to get back there, but it's a long way up. Is there another way out?"

The boy sat down in front of them on a rock and turned his head this way and that, looking them over, as if having never seen anyone like them before. He smiled, as if liking them. Deb and Super smiled back. It didn't seem as if the boy meant any harm, he just seemed curious, as if he'd never seen anyone like them before.

"That is the sky. You cannot climb to the sky."

"Listen, it's not the sky, okay?" Super said, growing irritated. "It's just the street. Haven't you ever been on the street before?"

"I don't think he has, Super," Deb said, studying the boy. "I think he lives down here."

"Gross!" Super said. "How creepy is that?"

The boy smiled at them. "You are beautiful. Are you angels?"

The girls looked at each other. Realizing they were still pointing their swords at the boy, they both lowered them and put them away, but they remained cautious.

"What's your name, little boy?" Deb asked.

He pointed at himself. "Loki. Do angels have names?"

"We're not angels, Loki,' Deb replied, smiling gently at him. "We're just girls. My name is Little Debbie, or Deb for short, and this is Supercalifragilisticexpialadocious, or just Super."

"Super-cali-fragi-listic-"

"Why'd you tell him that?" Super said. "Now he's going to spend an hour trying to say my name. We need him to show us the way out of here."

Deb grinned and looked at Loki. "Just Super, Loki. Loki, we need to get back up through that hole. Do you have any ladders, or boxes, or rocks we can pile together to get up there?"

Loki laughed gaily and rolled around. "Ladders, and boxes and rocks. Ladders and boxes and rocks."

The girls rolled their eyes. Super looked at Deb. "I don't think he's going to be much help."

"But Super," Deb said, looking worried, "if he lives here, that means he's got a tribe here too. They may not be as friendly as Loki is."

"Yeah." Super turned to Loki. "Loki, are your people nice?"

"Nice. Nice. Nice. Nice."

The girls looked at each other.

"This kid is beginning to annoy me," Super said.

Suddenly, somewhere in the darkness from the opposite direction that Loki had come from came a scrabbling sound. Loki instantly jumped up with a look of fright.

"Come!" He grabbed Deb's hand and tried to pull her along. Deb resisted, staring at the darkness where the sound had come from. "Loki what's the matter?"

"Rat People!" Loki said. "Hurry, or they'll eat us!"

Loki tried to pull Deb along again, and she began to reluctantly let him, staring into the darkness ahead of them. "But we can't see, Loki. It's too dark!"

The sound of a thousand little feet scrabbling on rock and squeaks from a hundred rat-beasties came from the darkness behind them.

"Hurry! Must go! Now!"

Super pulled Deb's hand, and slowly sheet Loki drag her into the deep, inky blackness, with Super tagging behind.

Cinnabon and Wheaties stood in front of the strange, tall white stick building. Around its base, white rock in a pile lay, the remains of the building's top half. Cinnabon craned her neck and looked up, and Wheaties did too.

"What a funny building, like a big spear in the sky." She lowered her head and looked at the door leading inside. The interior was dark and foreboding.

"I'm scared, mother," Wheaties said. "Let's go back."

"Don't be afraid, Wheaties," she said. "Never be afraid."

She grabbed his hand and started pulling him towards the door. "Let's go see what's inside." She walked until they were ten feet from the entrance.

A Wildie walked out from behind the building with a gray, grizzled beard, a ring of hair around a bald spot on the top of his head, and brown skin from being in the sun. He wore a dirty, torn gray suit but bare feet.

Cinnabon stopped and stared at him. Wheaties looked at him with wide eyes of fear. Suddenly another

Wildie appeared, a woman with wild gray hair and then another, a girl in her teens with frizzy black hair wearing a dirty pink dress.

Cinnabon spun around and dragged Wheaties back towards the Museum, fast.

"Mommy, who are they?" Wheaties said, looking back over his shoulder as they walked.

"I don't know, son, but we are not waiting to find out."

Suddenly from a building on their left more Wildies appeared. Cinnabon glanced at them and her eyes opened wider. She walked faster, and Wheaties tried to keep up.

From the tents on the grassy Mall, Wildies walked out. Cinnabon grew afraid. She picked Wheaties up and started walking very fast.

"Mommy, are they going to attack us?"

"No son, we'll be fine." Then to herself she said, "This is all Johnny's fault. He should be here to protect us!"

She ran as fast as she could with Wheaties in her arms. Behind her, the Wildies gathered, until there was a whole crowd. Then they followed after her.

Johnny reached the entrance to the Museum. A few people stood by the door, peering out. When they saw Johnny, they smiled with glee, knowing the others were going to be in trouble.

"We stayed in here like we were supposed to," old man Dellcomputers said with a smile that showed his missing teeth. "They went outside, probably got killed."

The other nearby all looked horrified and whispered to each other. Johnny just smiled.

"No one is going to get killed. But we have to get organized and have a plan before we start going out, or we're going to end up scattered."

Johnny walked outside. A few more tribesmembers stood on the porch, peering out at the Mall and the buildings beyond it. They turned and saw Johnny and ran to him.

"Johnny!" A tall thin woman with stringy blond hair named Searshomeandgarden said with excitement. "Everybody is going everywhere. Some went that way," she pointed towards the Museum of Natural History, "and some went that way." She pointed to the tall, white stick building.

Johnny addressed all the people still within earshot. "Please, everybody, go back inside. When we get everyone together, Misterwizard and I are going to talk to you and set down some rules so nobody gets lost or attacked."

The people nodded and headed back inside, talking to each other. Johnny looked around, wondering how he was going to find the people who wandered off. He remembered trying to get the Tribe from Sanctuary to Castle, and how he thought it was like herding cats. This would be even worse. He turned to a young boy of seven with black hair named Searshomeandgarden. "Do you know how many people left and where they went? "

Searshomeandgarden smiled, happy to be asked something important. "Well, your friend Starbucks and two girls went that way." He pointed off to the right, past the white stick building. "And later, Cinnabon and Wheaties went that way too. But…"

He turned and pointed the other way. "Your crazy father Foodcourt and your very tall mother Teavanna, and old lady Marthastewartliving went that way, into that old building."

Johnny frowned, trying hard not to be angry at her calling his father crazy. He was really getting tired of people calling his father that, when all his father really wanted was to go to a land he'd heard of, one where they'd be safe and happy, the mythical land of Australia.

Johnny didn't know which way to go. The thought that alarmed him most was Starbucks and 'two girls,' who were surely Super and Deb, going off who knew where by themselves. But he was also worried about his father and mother.

He decided the best thing would be to follow after Starbucks and the girls. His mother and father weren't really far away, and they were inside a building. He had no idea where Starbucks and the girls wandered off to.

"Listen, Searshomeandgarden, can you do something really important for me?"

Searshomeandgarden smiled and stood up straighter, proud to be being put in a position of authority. "Of course, Johnny. You can tell me to do anything, and it will be done right!"

"Good. When Misterwizard comes to the door, tell him about my father and mother. And help him round up the rest of the Tribe, all right? And most important, tell him I'll be right back. I'm just going to look for Starbucks and the girls. Can you remember all that?"

"Sure, I can!" He said, raising his fist in the air. "I have a perfectly perfect rememory."

Johnny smiled at him and walked away. "Thanks, Searshomeandgarden. I knew I could rely on you."

Johnny headed off in pursuit of Starbucks and the girls. Searshomeangarden tramped off, as if full of purpose, back to the door of the Museum to wait for Misterwizard.

Facegash and the Gangers held their hands up in the air and stared with fear at the Wildies, all except Mushface, who lay on the ground next to the stones of the Arena wall, covering his head with his hands. He looked strange, a big, strong man so afraid.

"I told you, Facegash! I told you! Help! Help! Mommy!"

Despite their fear, the Gangers couldn't help but laugh at how chicken Mushface was. The Wildies pointed at Mushface with looks of hilarity on their faces, laughing out loud.

Laddy Stabs stopped smiling and frowned with fear. She looked at Facegash. "Are they going to eat us, Facegash, like Mushface says?"

"How do I know?" He said, scowling, but with fear written all over his face.

An old Wildie woman with wild white hair, a long, hooked nose and wrinkles wearing a black dress said, "Speak quickly, or lose yer tongues. What be ye doing spying on us from our very own wall?"

"We mean ye no harm," Badluck said. "Please don't eat us."

"Shut up," Facegash said, trying to sound ferocious. "I speak for the Gangers." Facegash looked back at the old lady. Though she was old and weak, Facegash had never been so afraid before. His legs trembled, and he felt like he was about to fall down, but he tried to act tough and unafraid. "We come to parlay with your leader man, Lord Argon, oh lady who speak like crazy woman. We have news of what he might find mighty interesting, by golly."

The old lady smiled and looked at the others, who smiled and laughed back at her. She turned back to Facegash and scowled darkly. "Ye make sport of the way we speak do ye, ye scurrilous, scurvy knave?"

She strode forward and kicked Facegash in the leg. He lifted his leg and grabbed it, hopping on the other one and howling.

"Methinks perhaps I be inclined to gut you like a fish, spill your liver on yon grass just for fun and let my mateys cook the rest for supper What make ye of that?"

The Wildies all cheered and laughed, and Facegash felt faint. Mushface let out a yelp of fear and cowered down even further. The rest of the Gangers looked terrified, thinking they were about to face death.

"Please, milady," Lady Stabs said. "We meant no harm. We just don't talk like you is all. We're not sure how to talk like you, even if we wanted to."

The old lady peered at Lady Stabs. She looked at her hair. "Forsooth, ye be a strange lassie, but I like yee. Me own daughter ye be like, though with more teeth and more hair."

She looked at Mushface and laughed again. "If ye all be like this gentle lamb, you'd all be in the pot by supper. But seein' some of ye have spirit may perhaps has spared thee, for anon."

She lowered her spear and motioned to them with her hand. "Strike yer colors, and don't be trying no tricks.

I wager it might be more entertaining to see what Lord Algon does with thee, any ways." She laughed with a cackle and walked away. The Wildies used their spears to poke and prod the Gangers into motion. The old lady poked Mushface until he got up and joined the others, sobbing and looking frightened. The Wildies surrounded them and led them to Lord Algon.

CHAPTER 18

Starbucks circled his bike around the big, white building, looking for the wolf-beastie in his small, round side mirror on the side of the Harley. He couldn't see a lot in the mirror, it was so small, and as he bounced and rode, the sight in it kept changing. His heart was racing, and his mind screamed at him, terrified that the wolf-beastie had hurt the girls.

He stopped the bike and turned his head and upper body around to look for the wolf-beastie, all the while yelling at himself mentally for leaving the girls so far behind. Suddenly he saw it near a building to his left, and it was running right for him!

He gunned the engine and took off, just in time as it leapt for him, landing right where he had just been and skidding to a halt. It took off after him, going slower but steady.

He knew the only way to get back to the girls was to kill it. He spun the bike around and stopped, looking for the wolf-beastie. It ran down the middle of the road, its teeth bared and a look of ferocity on its face. Starbucks put on a look of ferocity of his own and gunned the engine. He took off in a shower of rocks, headed right for the wolf-beastie. He sped towards it, eyes narrowed, concentrating. He knew that if he missed it and the bike spilled, he'd be easy prey.

The wolf-beastie realized what was happening at the last minute and stopped. It tried to turn and run, but before it could, Starbucks was on top of it. He yelled as he slammed the bike into the wolf-beastie. It yelped and fell to the side as Starbucks sped past. He had to make a big circle to turn around because of the debris and old cars in the road. When he finally was able to return to the spot, the wolf-beastie was gone. Where he hit it, he saw a pool of blood. A trail of blood headed off towards the nearest building, stopping at the dark open door.

Starbucks nodded. He didn't have time to make sure it was finished. He had to get back to the girls. He hit the Harley's throttle and took off as fast as he could, back to where he'd last seen Super and Deb.

Foodcourt, now confident with strength in numbers, strode ahead with purpose, while Thegap reluctantly followed. Thegap's stick shook in the air, mainly because Thegap shook all over with fright.

"Who's in here?" He asked, in a squeaky voice, his small face scrunched up in fear.

"We don't know," Foodcourt said in a dark, dramatic voice, "but it might be a Ganger or a Wildie."

"A Ganger or a Wildie?" Thegap squeaked as he looked back longingly towards the main hall and the women. "What if there's a whole pack of them? We'll be outnumbered!"

Foodcourt tiptoed down the dark passage with Thegap following, past broken display cases with molding beasties in them, some eaten by bug-beasties or fallen onto the bottom of the cases, staring up with lifeless eyes.

"Don't be such a cowardie," Foodcourt said. "If we're not going to Australia, this is our place now. And no Gangers or Wildies are pushing us out."

Thegap looked nervously at Foodcourt. "That's right, you're the crazy one, aren't you? Always talking about that place. I'm about to get killed with a crazy man."

Foodcourt turned and grinned at him, his eyes wild. Thegap's eyes widened in fear as he stared back. "That's right," Foodcourt said, looking crazy. "And if you don't help me defend this place, I'll feed you to the dingo-beasties."

Foodcourt chuckled and moved on. Thegap gulped nervously and followed, not sure if Foodcourt was kidding or not.

Despite his fear, Thegap couldn't help but goggle with amazement at some of the beasties they passed. He stopped and stared at one. It was huge, bigger than the old cars outside. It was covered on the top with shaggy fur and the bottom side of it was bare. It had a huge head and little beady eyes. On its head, two small horns stuck up.

"What is that?" Thegap asked, pointing. Foodcourt

scowled, grabbed Thegap's arm and pulled him along. "I don't know," he barked back, "Misterwizard hasn't told us yet. Keep up!

Thegap let himself be dragged along, until he saw the next beastie. It was even stranger and more fascinating than the last. It was huge and gray, with tiny little eyes and a huge, sharp looking horn coming right out of its nose.

"What's that?" Thegap said, stopping and pointing.

Foodcourt rolled his eyes, growing irritated. "I don't know! You're worse than Carny. Let's go!"

Once again Foodcourt dragged Thegap along, this time a little more forcefully. Thegap had almost forgotten his fear in the excitement of discovery. He turned this way and that, trying to see all the weird beasties at once.

He was so interested in the displays he didn't even realize that they had stopped until a few seconds had passed. Then he turned to see Foodcourt staring at something, his face grim. When he saw what it was, he let out an involuntary yelp.

In a display case in front of them hung the remains of Leader Nordstrom, strung up and hanging like a ragdoll. His face and body had been chewed. Half his face as well as his left leg was gone. Rat-beasties stood below him, reaching up and chewing on his remaining foot.

"Aah!" Thegap yelled. He bent over and threw up. Then he turned and ran, right into a display case. He fell over the weird beastie inside and a puff of dust rose in the air. He screamed as he touched it, horrified again. He went into a fit of coughing, so many times he forgot to breathe. He stumbled back and fell on the floor, passed out.

All the while, Foodcourt just stood and stared at the remains of Leader Nordstrom. "This is meant for us," he said to himself. "Somebody is telling us they're out to get the Tribe. We have to show this to Johnny."

Suddenly, from somewhere far away near the main hall, he heard a scream. Leaving Thegap lying on the floor, he hurried back towards the entrance. The one lifeless eye Leader Nordstroms had left stared after him.

Deb and Super walked slowly in the dark, feeling out of touch with reality. The dark was so thick they felt it on their skin like a living thing. Loki led them along, talking in an excited way, not the least affected by the dark. Deb's heart pounded. She didn't know how much longer she could take the blackness.

"Loki, please take us back. I have to have some light."

"Can't go back," Loki's voice sounded like a floating ghost in the darkness. "Rat people will eat you."

"Don't your people ever use torches, light to see?" Super asked. From the sound of her voice, Deb could tell the dark was freaking her out too.

"Light is for special times only, not regular use."

"Loki, we are not like you," Deb said, with a touch of panic. "We need light. Please. Don't you think finding us would be a special time?"

There was silence for a moment, as Loki thought about it. The silence was the worst for Deb, it made her feel like she was floating out of her body, losing any touch with where she was. She had to say something or go crazy. "Loki, did you hear me?"

"I get in trouble."

"Please, Loki," Super said. "We will tell them we made you do it. It was our fault." Super knew that they may be getting themselves into real trouble by asking for a light, but just like Deb she couldn't stand the dark much longer.

"One light. That is all."

"Thank you!" Deb said, willing him to hurry.

Suddenly a bright light blazed forth. The girls shielded their eyes from the sudden brightness, but it was only bright because of the darkness they'd endured before. It was actually a very small torch, flickering in the cool air. In its light, they could see the pale white form of Loki, holding the torch aloft, his dark eyes shining.

They both sighed with relief. "Thank you, Loki. I know you're taking a big chance for us."

Loki grinned in the dim light, looking slightly devilish. "It's okay. I like you. You're angels. Come, let's go."

Lokie took off again, dragging Deb with him and the girls hurried to keep up. They splashed through water, not very deep but enough to get their shoes wet. Loki had no shoes, his big, flat feet treaded the water as if he'd done it all his life, which he probably had.

In the dim light, they could see now that they were in a huge tunnel with a curved top. At their feet a two strange metal lines ran, a few feet apart, all the way down the tunnel and back behind them. Under the metal lines pieces of wood lay crossways, each just long enough to sit under the rails and each about a foot wide.

As Deb looked around, she could see they were in a lower place, and on either side small walls rose three feet up to platforms on either side. The platforms were ten feet wide before they reached the sides of the curved tunnel. Wood boards on stands stood everywhere on the platforms, most with ragged papers attached to them. On the walls pictures, torn and faded, showed the faces of people from the Ancient Times doing odd things. The girls could only guess what those things were.

"Loki where are we going?" Super asked. "And what is this place?"

"Home," Loki said, as if it was obvious. "We'll go to Slon now. Slon will be proud of Loki. Maybe even Harp will see. Loki brings angels to the Undergrounders and they will think Loki is a hero."

Deb and Super looked at each other and then back at Loki. "Loki," Deb asked, "Is that what you people call yourself, the "Undergrounders?"

Loki nodded with a smile. "Undergrounders. We are the smart ones, safe from danger."

"Is Slon your leader?" Super asked.

"Slon is leader since Moth is gone." Loki looked serious and sad. "Moth was eaten bythe Rat People. Rat People will attack if you go out alone. Moth left our village and never came back. But Loki is not afraid. Loki is too fast for the Rat People. He knows where to hide."

Deb glanced at Super, who was busy looking around at the dark, depressing tunnel as Loki continued to drag them further away from the hole to the street, the only way they knew to escape.

"Loki," Deb said, "Is Slon nice?"

Loki stopped for a second, thinking. Then he shook his head and walked on.

"Slon is not as nice as Moth. Slon yells all the time. But Slon is in charge. Somebody must be in charge. You will make Slon happy. Slon will know what to do."

Deb and Super looked at each other, both thinking

the same thing.

"What should we do?" Super said.

"What choice do we have? If we want out of here, and don't want to get eaten by the Rat People, it looks like we are going to have to meet Slon."

They looked at each other and Deb glanced meaningfully at their swords. Super nodded, knowing what she was thinking. They could defend themselves if they had to.

Teavana and Bathandbodyworks watched Foodcourt and Thegap disappear down the dark passageway. They both looked around, not sure what to do.

"I feel so helpless, just standing here," Bathandbodyworks said.

"Me too," said Teavana.

Teavana walked over and peered down into the hole again. Bathandbodyworks joined her. They both stared down at the remains of the now headless tiger-beastie.

Bathandbodyworks looked at Teavana. "Maybe we shouldn't wait. Maybe we should go get Johnny now?"

"And leave them alone? What if they need us?" Teavana replied. "I'm waiting here until Foodcourt returns."

"Well," said Bathandbodyworks, looking around. "At least maybe we can look around a little." She'd been anxious to explore the Museum, but with everything that had happened she'd almost forgotten.

"I suppose it wouldn't hurt, as long as we stay close, and don't wander too far. We don't want to get into trouble ourselves."

Bathandbodyworks smiled, her big, long face glowing. She pointed with a bony finger towards one of the archways. "Let's go down that one!"

Teavana smiled, Bathandbodyworks' excitement infecting her. "All right. I haven't been down that one yet."

Together the ladies hurried over to the archway. When they reached it they both slowed down as if by signal. Then, holding each other's hands, they tiptoed into the dark recesses beyond.

Marthastewartliving poked her head carefully past the door into main hall of the Museum of Natural History, "Hello? Anyone home?"

There was no answer. She peered around the dark, dusty interior. A small raised platform flanked by tall white columns led to a large main room filled with glass cases. In the middle of the room she saw the huge hole in the floor surrounded by rubble and remnants of the roof. Beyond it, she looked with mild alarm at the giant bones of some monstrous creature standing in the middle of the room. It seemed to be looking at her with its eyeless sockets, its giant mouth full of large sharp teeth just waiting to snatch her up and swallow her. But then, she thought, she'd just fall to the floor, for it had no stomach or body at all for that matter. Still, she thought, the teeth could chop her up into little pieces. It wouldn't be a pleasant experience, not at all.

She tiptoed in, careful to keep an eye on the bony

creature. She smiled, excited at the thought of herself getting to see where the great battle between Johnny and the Ganger Ripper took place. She'd been hiding in the Museum during the fight, in a corner, afraid to move, terrified until it was all over. Now that things were calm and free from danger, she felt free, unafraid, and ready to get to know their new home.

She walked gingerly over to the hole and peered down. It was dark down there, and she couldn't see much. She felt disappointed, expecting to see the Ganger's dead body and maybe even the tiger-beastie. There were some remains in the corner, but it was hard to tell what they were. They were piled up in a heap, just looking like any other beastie carcass, even a dog-beastie or rat-beastie.

There was no sign of the Ganger leader at all. Bored now, Marthastewartliving looked around for something else of interest. She peered at some of the glass cases. They had the ancient words scrawled in them, and dark objects on shelves. They looked like strange beasties, ones she'd never seen before.

Excited again, she walked towards the nearest case.

"*Hey.*" A deep, hushed voice came from the shadows on her right.

She froze in mid step instantly, terror seizing her. Her whole body started to shake and she was afraid she was going to fall down.

"*Are you all alone?*"

Marthastewartliving's lip quivered, and she mentally berated herself for begin stupid enough to venture out alone.

"No, I most certainly am not!" She barked back in her harshest tone, trying to sound angry and not afraid, like she really was. "I am here with...Johnny. He's just outside. I think I'll go fetch him right now."

"Johnny...Johnny...Johnny...Johnny..."

Marthastewartliving spun on her heels and as fast as she could, she tramped back towards the front doors.

She almost made it.

No one heard her screams as they echoed off the bare marble walls, and the only one watching was the giant, ancient beastie with its sharp claws and huge, empty holes for eyes.

CHAPTER 19

Misterwizard tramped up the dark passageway out of the Bunker towards the Museum. His bones ached and he felt tired. He smiled to himself. It was not fun getting old. He would be glad, he thought, when they were all finally settled and things quieted down. He looked forward to spending his last days watching the Tribe grow and prosper and Life return to the empty wasteland.

He knew there was a long road ahead before that could happen, however. He had to teach the men and women of the Tribe how to read and write. He also needed to teach them basic farming skills. Life would return, but it would start basically, simply, like in the days of Castles and Kings, before modern technology. It was almost as if the world had traveled back in time to the Feudal days, the days of knights and Lords. He hoped it wouldn't return to the ancient days of each king fighting with the kings of the neighboring kingdoms, but he suspected until a centralized government could be set up, that might be just what transpired.

If the world was to return to those days, then the Tribe needed to build a stronghold where they could defend themselves. Misterwizard had already been thinking about it, making plans. He sighed as he trudged up the stairs. "And miles to go, before I sleep," he said out loud, quoting one of his favorite poets Robert Frost. His words echoed off the dark, close walls. Then he smiled and wished he could go back to bed.

He finally reached the door to the Museum. He sighed in happy relief. And then he smiled even wider when he saw who waited for him in the doorway. It was Sephie, clutching the green frog she'd been wanting since they arrived.

"Well, hello Sephie!" Misterwizard said with affection. "Are you waiting for me?"

Sephie smiled and nodded, her face lighting up with joy at seeing Misterwizard.

"Look!" She said, holding up the green frog.

"Yes!" Misterwizard said, chuckling and taking the green frog from her. He examined in as if he was inspecting it critically. Then he spoke to it.

"Well, Kermit, it seems you've got a new job to do. You take good care of Sephie, do you hear me?"

Misterwizard returned Kermit to Sephie, who grabbed him and clutched him tight. "I love him. He's my best friend, next to Johnny."

Misterwizard put on a pretend look of hurt. "And what about me, young lady?"

"You're my best friend too, Misterwizard. I didn't

mean to say you weren't." Sephie looked alarmed at her mistake.

"I know that," Misterwizard said, taking Sephie's hand.

Misterwizard looked around and saw there was no one in the basement. He didn't hear any sound coming from above, either. "Sephie, what's going on? Where is everyone?"

Sephie's face changed to a look of seriousness. "Johnny sent me for you. Everybody's run away!"

"No," Misterwizard said, suspecting she was exaggerating, "everybody?"

Sephie nodded and led Misterwizard towards the stairs. "Johnny told me to find you and bring you upstairs. He said you needed to meet with the Tribe and tell them what to do."

"Well, let's go accomplish that task, shall we?" Misterwizard said. He grabbed Sephie and hoisted her onto his shoulders.

"Whee!" Sephie said as Misterwizard started off, an elated Sephie riding on him like a queen on her mighty steed. She pointed up the stairs. "Onward!"

Johnny walked quickly towards the white stick building in the direction he was told Starbucks and the girls had gone. He wondered why they would have gone off on their own. He grew angry thinking about how everyone was scattered and going off in all directions, nobody waiting until they could all get together and get organized. It was going to make it doubly hard to get anywhere if everyone kept going off on their own little adventures.

How far had Starbucks gone, and why did he just take off without talking to Johnny first? And why had Deb and Super gone off with him? It made Johnny nervous, wondering what prompted his friends to leave so mysteriously.

He scanned the horizon and didn't see anyone. The long, rectangular grassy area called the Mall was full of the Wildie's shacks, but there seemed to be no movement or people there. They almost seemed deserted, probably during the large fight the week before with the Gangers and the Wildie king, Lord Algon.

He looked towards the white stick building and the rubble around its base. There were no buildings near it. It seemed to be all by itself surrounded by a large sea of grass. The only objects around it were some metal sticks in a circle with little bits of cloth at their tops. Some of the sticks lay on the ground, others were bent and broken, probably hit by the falling pieces of the building. The pieces of cloth at their tops waved in the breeze, each a different color with strange symbols on them. Johnny would have liked to ask Misterwizard what the symbols meant, but now was not the time to sit back and ask questions. Johnny hoped things would someday settle down to where they could start to learn and explore without fear of some big fight or crisis, but that day seemed to be a long time off.

Suddenly Johnny saw a person far in the distance running towards him. Then he saw it was two persons, a woman and a little boy. As the figures grew closer, Johnny realized who it was, Cinnabon and her young son Wheaties. Johnny groaned inside. They were the last thing he needed just then. *Another pair going off on their own,* Johnny thought with annoyance. He began to think the Tribe didn't deserve his constant help. If they were going to do their own thing and not accept him as leader, then maybe he should let them, and they could face the consequences.

As Cinnabon and her son grew close, Johnny steeled himself. He wasn't going to be nice this time, he'd be just as grumpy and unpleasant as she was. That would surprise her, and maybe give her something to think about.

But as she reached him, Johnny could see she was scared. Her eyes were wide open and she dragged Wheaties along, him half walking, half being dragged by her.

"It's about time you show up, Johnny! We are in danger, and you are out having fun!"

"What are you doing so far from Sanctuary, Cinnabon?" Johnny shot back. "Don't you realize how dangerous that could be?"

"I was out looking for food, something you as leader should be doing."

In the distance behind Cinnabon, Johnny saw other figures come from inside the stick building. Cinnabon saw where he was looking. She turned and pointed.

"Look! Wildies are coming our way! It's an attack!"

"Get back to New Sanctuary," Johnny said. "And stay there. I'll check it out."

Cinnabon scowled at him and walked stiffly past him towards the Museum, dragging Wheaties along. "I'm going, all right. Some people are so pushy."

Johnny grinned, thinking about what he'd like to say back to her. Then he forgot about her and concentrated on the figures approaching from the stick building. Three people approached, grouped together like a family. As they grew close, Johnny saw they included a balding old man with a beard, an older woman with wild, gray hair and a girl about Deb's age with frizzy black hair.

They didn't look very dangerous, but Johnny put his hand on his sword just in case. He looked beyond them, and far in the distance next to the door into the white stick building, a small crowd of Wildies stood. They didn't seem to be coming towards Johnny, just watching the other three approach, almost as if the three were some kind of spokespeople for the group.

Johnny turned his attention back on the three coming towards him with interest. Their faces showed fear and tension, but no real anger or ferocity. Johnny began to think they weren't coming to fight, but simply to talk.

Though Johnny didn't see her, Cinnabon and her son Wheaties stopped to turn and watch, far enough away they could run if they had to, but close enough to see what happened. The three Wildies reached Johnny. They stopped ten feet away. Then they just looked at him, not moving.

"Hello," Johnny said in a friendly tone. "My name is Johnny Apocalypse. Who are you?"

The old man with the balding head smiled in a clumsy way, as if he wasn't used to smiling very much. "I be Yellowtooth. This be my wife Marbleskin and our daughter Funnygiggle."

Johnny tried not to smile at their names. They were worse than the names Misterwizard picked for members of the Tribe.

"We hear tell ye and your tribe be good people. Do this be of a truth, be ye good people?"

Johnny felt his fears ease and a warmth spread in his heart. These people weren't bad people at all. "We try to be good. We are not here to hurt anyone. We just want to rebuild the great county America, so we can have a good place to live again."

The man smiled and turned to his wife, who smiled in return, as if this is what they hoped Johnny would say. Then they both looked at him again.

"'Tis as we hoped. Not all of us be like Lord Algon. Many despair of the killing and such and be like ye, only wanting a good port to call home. We be no eaters of manflesh nor brigands, but merely be forced to do Lord Algon's bidding. But we'll be mighty happy to strike our colors and lay anchor with thee, if ye be willing."

Johnny didn't understand everything the man said, but enough to make him smile with happiness. "We'd be glad to have all the Wildies who want to come join us. As long as they are willing to do so in friendship and peace."

All three of them jumped for joy, making Johnny chuckle. The man smiled, his face full of happiness. "'Twas what we hoped for. For too long have we lived in fear of Lord Algon. He is truly a cruel captian, who tortures not only his enemies, but his own with no more conviction."

"You must understand," Johnny said, "that if you join us, you will have to obey me and the leaders of the Tribe."

"That we will, be no mistaking of that," the man said, nodding his head up and down. "We be like lambs to be led, and not a peep will ye hear from us in complaint."

"In that case, we're happy to have you join us. In fact, the more numbers we have, the easier it is going to be to rebuild."

"Of a truth, ye be wise in sayin' that,' the wife said. "You be a smart and good man, Johnny Apocalypse."

The man looked at Johnny and pointed at the people waiting at the white stick building. "May I tell the others to approach?"

Johnny looked back at the crowd by the white stick building. It was growing to be quite a group.

"Maybe you and your small family should talk to our Tribe first, so as not to scare them. Then when they understand that you mean them no harm, we can bring your group over."

The man nodded eagerly. "As ye wish, milord. Ye be our leader now." The three Wildies joined Johnny and together they walked back towards the Museum. In the distance, Cinnabon and Wheaties saw them coming. They turned and ran themselves back towards the Museum to get there first and spread the news that something new and exciting was about to happen.

Suddenly Johnny heard a loud rumbling sound, familiar and music to his ears. It came from his right, way on the other side of the grassy Mall. He stopped and turned immediately to see where it came from, for it was the roar of a Harley, just like Johnny's.

What he saw filled him with joy and happiness. On the street behind the white buildings on the other side of the Mall, Johnny caught a glimpse of someone riding a Harley, and that someone was Starbucks!

Johnny turned to his newfound friends. "Listen. I have to go somewhere, it's very important. You just go to that white building there," Johnny pointed to the Museum of American History, "and tell them Johnny said to have you talk to Misterwizard. You tell Misterwizard just what you told me."

"Be ye certain he will be of the same mind as ye?" The man asked with a look of worry.

"Don't worry," Johnny said. "Misterwizard is even nicer than I am. You're going to like him a lot."

The Wildies smiled and looked at each other, wondering.

Johnny didn't wait to talk to them anymore. He took off running across the grassy Mall as fast as he could, darting past the shacks on his way to the buildings on the other side and the street beyond. He just hoped he could get there before Starbucks was gone. He couldn't wait to see what Starbucks and the girls had been up to.

CHAPTER 20

Facegash and the other Gangers shuffled along, surrounded by the Wildies. On the top wall of the Arena, Wildies stood, their backs turned away from the Gangers looking into the center of the Arena. The air was filled with cheering and shouting. Wildies jumped up and down, waiving their fists in the air, laughing and joking with each other as they watched the men inside fight for their lives. The Gangers looked with terror at each other, no longer pretending that they weren't scared to death.

Facegash knew he had to come up with something to convince the Wildie's crazy king not to kill them. Lady Stabs looked at him, fear written all over her face.

"Should we try to run, Facegash?"

Facegash tried to look tough, and he spat on the ground. "Ain't much chance to get away."

"What are we gonna do then?" Badluck said.

"We're all gonna die. We're all gonna die!" Mushface moaned.

"Shut up, Mushface!" Facegash said. He turned to Lady Stabs. "We got to convince this crazy king that we can help him fight Johnny. If he thinks we're valuable, he won't kill us. Then we find a chance to "he glanced up at the old lady Wildie and lowered his voice to a whisper, "to kill him and take over. Got it?"

Lady Stabs nodded, looking scared, wishing for the hundredth time that she'd ran and joined Johnny and the Tribe instead of getting involved with the Gangers again.

Facegash looked over the other Gangers. There was twenty of them, men and women, all that he'd been able to find of the Doomsday Prophecy. He knew there were more out there somewhere scattered around Washington Deecee, Gangers who had ran away during the battle. But at that moment, this twenty was all they had. It would have to be enough.

The Wildies led them up the ramp of stones to the top of the Arena wall. When they reached the top, they could see inside the Arena. They stopped and stared at the grisly spectacle taking place.

Only one guard was still alive. The other lay on the ground, being eaten by the lion-beastie. The remaining guard had a cut in his side from which blood poured. He was hot and sweaty and looked exhausted.

Facegash looked at Lord Algon. The Wildie king lounged on his throne, having a wonderful time, drinking wine from a silver cup and watching the fight with a satisfied smile on his face. Behind him, his four new guards stood, arms crossed, smiling. Facegash realized the Gangers were in real danger. The chances were good they would end up in the Arena next, unless he was a real good liar.

The crowd roared with excitement as the remaining guard approached the lion-beastie from behind to tried to stab it. The lion-beastie didn't see him, for it was too busy eating the other guard. The guard snuck up slowly, sword raised. The crowd leaned forward, eager to see what was going to happen.

At the last moment, the lion-beastie turned, but the guard lunged. He stabbed the lion-beastie in the shoulder. It spun, snarled, raised his claws in the air and rushed the guard. The crowd jumped up and down as the lion-beastie jumped on the guard. They both went down in a heap, the guard underneath the lion-beastie. Even the Gangers, scared as they were, couldn't help but smile and get into the spirit of the titanic struggle. They moved to the edge of the Arena wall, wondering like all the others watching whether the guard was dead.

The lion-beastie roared and clawed at the poor guard, who struggled and stabbed at it from underneath and struggled to get free. As the crowd watched in hushed anticipation the deadly struggle continued. Even Lord Algon rose to his feet and watched silently, waiting to see if the guard would live or die.

Finally, the guard threw the lion-beastie off. It was dead. The crowd jumped up and down and roared its approval, waving their hands in the air and smiling at each other. Even Lord Algon smiled, nodding his head.

The Guard's face was covered with gashes. His left arm was torn open and bleeding. He staggered forward and dropped his sword on the ground. Then he fell to the ground, exhausted and near death. He lay there, not moving, eyes closed.

Lord Algon turned to the crowd.

"What say ye, mates? Hath this man fought bravely enough to win mercy from his Lord? Speak now with a show of the finger."

The crowd yelled and laughed and looked at each other. They looked at the guard in the Arena and talked among themselves. Then they raised their hands. The majority showed a 'thumbs-up,' a sign that seemed to indicate they wanted to give the Guard mercy.

Lord Algon knew this was most likely going to be the crowd's decision. He knew if the guard was allowed to live, he would be a dangerous threat to Lord Algon, constantly wanting revenge. But Lord Algon had already planned for the crowd's reaction.

"It seems ye have a softness and a tenderness this day, and this be not always a good thing. Still, cotton to thee I will, and spare this miserable cur's life, if he manages to survive his wounds, which be mighty doubtful."

The crowd cheered as men put the unconscious guard on a stretcher and carried him out of the Arena. The Gangers were prodded back into motion and they walked towards Lord Algon, waiting to find out if they were to be the next to di in the Arena.

Deb and Super stumbled along in the long, dark tunnel. They followed the strange metal rails on the ground, but it was hard going because the wood slats were just spaced apart far enough that the girls had to stretch to reach each one with their foot, which was hard to do in the gloomy darkness. It was either that or walk on the sharp stones underneath the wood slats that hurt their feet.

The torch Loki carried made dancing shadows on the walls and the curved ceiling far above their head, as if strange, ghostly beings followed them. The light from the torch only shone a few feet in any direction before being swallowed up by the darkness. The girls seemed to be in an endless abyss of darkness that waited to swallow them whole if the torch were to accidentally go out.

Deb's heart thumped in her chest and she found it hard to breathe. It seemed like they'd been walking for hours, though it had probably only been a few minutes. Each step was a trial, for they had to stretch their legs and step into the darkness, hoping the next wood slat was there. More than once Deb twisted her ankle a little, and each time she did her breath caught fearing she was going to break her ankle or twist it so bad she wouldn't be able to walk anymore. Deb's spirit seemed to shrink inside her, and she felt small, weak, and totally alone in a strange , dark world. When she looked straight up, she saw places where the parts of the ceiling had fallen, exposing dirt and roots. She wondered how long until the tunnel collapsed altogether, becoming a dark, horrible tomb. She looked at Loki and couldn't imagine how he and his tribe had survived in the dark, airless space. How long had they been living down in the dark, for as long as her Tribe had been in Sanctuary? Suddenly Sanctuary didn't seem so bad.

Deb and Super held their swords in front of them, though it was so dark, Deb didn't think they'd be able to see anything to fight it. The tunnel stretched off into the distance, a black nothingness.

"Deb, how's your leg?" Super's voice suddenly coming out of the darkness startled Deb, but after her surprise she found it comforting. "It hurts a little," she replied, "but it's getting better."

Deb noticed something on the raised platforms on either side. Strange metal fences, only about waist high and made of round poles stuck together, stood all over in what looked like random patterns. And beyond them she saw dark tunnels leading away to who knew where. She wondered if they led to doors out of the dark maze.

She whispered to Super, looking towards her friend's shadow. "Super!"

The dark outline of Super's head turned, showing Super was listening to her. "Yeah?" Super said.

"Did you see those doorways?" Deb pointed to one.

"Yeah," Super said. "You think they lead out?"

Deb nodded and Super nodded back.

"Loki," Super asked. "Where do those tunnels lead?" Loki glanced over to one of the tunnels. "No tunnels" he replied. "They are all filled with rock, like every place."

Deb and Super frowned at each other with disappointment. The tunnels led tot dead ends. Deb glanced behind them every few minutes, her ears straining to hear the Rat People, but there was only silence. The thought of them behind the girls made her hurry a little more. If the Rat People attacked, they would be totally helpless, surrounded by nothing but open air.

"Loki," she finally asked, "will the Rat People follow us here?"

"Maybe," Loki said, not stopping or turning around. "Maybe not. Sooner or later they will come, but if we stay in the village, we are safe."

Deb thought about what Loki said, but her thoughts ended abruptly for suddenly a huge dark hulk became visible in the dim light of the torch. Like some kind of giant dead beast lying on its side, it lay right in the middle of the path on the metal rails. Rounded at the top, it was twice as tall as the girls and stretched on as far as they could see in the distance.

"We're close to home now!" Loki said, turning and smiling at them, his eyes glinting. Deb and Super glanced at each other, wondering what was going to happen to them next. They gripped their swords tighter, ready for a fight.

As they grew close to the object, Deb realized it was not a beastie at all, but some kind of metal vehicle like the buses they had traveled in. But it was much bigger and longer then the buses, and Deb thought it must have been able to carry a whole tribe inside, maybe two or three tribes. It leaned to the left, as if it had fallen over, and it was covered with dirt and rust.

At the back of the huge metal thing Deb saw a doorway. On the ground in front of it lay a piece of metal that looked like it had once been the door for the hole. Deb peered inside. The interior canted to the left and looked except for benches running along the walls and what looked like metal poles running from the floor up to the ceiling. The floor inside looked filthy and papers and trash covered it. Here and there, small boxes lay on the seats or floor, some open but others closed. One open box seemed to be filled with dirty, rotted clothes.

Loki stopped and turned towards them.

"I must put out the torch now. But don't worry, there are lights inside. You'll see!"

Without waiting for a reply, Loki dropped the top of

the torch into a puddle. It sputtered and quickly went out, and once again they were pitched into total darkness.

"Loki, no, we can't see!" Deb yelled.

"What lights?" Super said. I don't see any lights."

Deb felt Loki reaching for her hand and she grabbed it. Then she felt around and found Super's hand.

"Strange angels, not able to see without torches." Loki sounded confused.

Deb said, "Loki, we're not-"

Suddenly Super squeezed her hand, and she stopped. Deb looked over and Super shook her head in warning.

Super finished Deb's sentence. "We're light angels, Loki. We need the light to give us power."

"Oh!" Loki said. His small white body turned and his pale face moved close to Deb's face, making her feel uncomfortable. "I never met an angel, so I don't know much about you. You have power? Loki can't wait to see."

Loki pulled them up three steps and they could feel they were entering inside the long, metal tube. Inside it was even darker, and the air was stale and unpleasant. Deb and Super looked around but couldn't see anything. The sound of their feet on the rusty old metal of the tube sounded loud in the darkness.

Loki stopped in the middle of the long, metal compartment. He reached over to the wall for something. Suddenly all along the walls near the ceiling, long bars began to flicker and glow with the faint white light.

"We are not supposed to use the lights except for very special times, for they have only a little power left.

But this is special time for sure. Only time we have ever had angels visit!"

Deb and Super sighed with a small amount of relief, for finally they could see in the long, dark metal tunnel. On either side of the tunnel the benches ran, with old boxes and other pieces of junk on them. Deb saw a wide-brimmed hat sitting all by itself. She saw a stick with cloth in strips along the bottom and a curved handle at the top. And she saw skeletons.

Some of the skeletons still had ragged bits of clothing on them. One that must have been a woman had a red hat on with feathers, but the hat was so old it had a hole eaten out of it. On skeleton in a blue suit with yellow bars on his sleeves lay on the floor right in their path.

Super said was Deb thought. "Ooh, this is creepy. Are those members of your tribe, Loki?"

Loki laughed. "No, those are the old people that lived before. We do not touch them out of respect, for they were here before us."

Loki walked down the passageway past the benches. He stepped over the skeleton on the floor as if he'd done it a thousand times, which he probably had.

Loki pulled them along again, and Deb glared at Super. "Way to go with that power thing," she whispered, "what if his tribe wants us to show them we're angels?"

Super shrugged, though Deb didn't see it. Then Super whispered, "I guess we find a way to show them." Super lifted something out of her pocket. She touched Deb's side and Deb turned to see what she was holding. In the dim light, Deb could just barely make out what it was: one of the green balls from the Bunker.

Super whispered, "I brought it along with us, just in

case we had to fight a beastie or some Gangers."

Deb peered at Super's face, which was ghostly in the pale light. Super put the small, round bomb back in her pocket.

"Let's hope we don't have to use it," Deb whispered back.

Starbucks finally made it back to the last place he'd seen the girls. There was no sign of them anywhere. He stopped his Harley and climbed off. The street was quiet, not a sound, not even the squeak of a rat-beastie. He grew very worried, wondering what could have happened to them. He walked down the street, looking every direction for any sign of them.

He saw a building to his right. It was a two-story gray structure and seemed mostly intact, though there was no door only a dark opening leading inside. He walked over to the building and peered inside. He saw a large shiny stone floor with a few scattered round tables on it. At the back of the room a wall stood. The bottom half was made of wood, the top half metal mesh with doors in it every few feet. On either side of the room, wooden desks and chairs were scattered everywhere, mostly nothing more than kindling.

He looked up at the writing on the wall. In big letters it said, 'Provincial Savings and Loan."

"Pro…" Starbucks tried to use the words Misterwizard had taught him. "Savins…and…Lon."

He gave up, for some words were still too hard from him to read, especially if they made no sense.

"Super! Deb! Are you in here?"

Starbucks couldn't think of any reason they would have come into the drafty, depressing building, but he had to look somewhere. He walked inside and shivered involumtarily. It was very cold inside, probably caused by the shiny stone floor and the open door.

Suddenly he heard a hiss. He looked to his left and saw a small, black beastie with yellow eyes on the floor near a broken desk. It bared its teeth and glared at him.

Starbucks smiled. It was a cat-beastie but a small one, no bigger than a loaf of bread. Some used to live in Sanctuary, wild and hard to catch. One family tamed one once, and they kept it for a long time until something happened to it and it just disappeared. They were good for catching and eating rat-beasties, though if you got too close they would scratch at you.

Starbucks walked towards the cat-beastie with a smile. "Hello, cat-beastie. You're a tough one, aren't you?"

As Starbucks grew closer, the cat-beastie rose up on its legs, arching its back. Starbucks looked past it and saw why it was so angry. There on the floor under the desk lay five little baby cat-beasties, mewing and looking up at him.

"Don't worry, cat-beastie, I won't hurt your babies. But you better watch out, there's a bad wolf-beastie roaming around. He'll eat your babies in one gulp."

The cat-beastie continued to arch its back and hiss so Starbucks backed away, chuckling. If Super and Deb had come in here, they'd have gone over to look at the cat-beastie. He was pretty sure they hadn't been inside. He walked back out into the sunshine.

He looked down the street again. He saw no sign of

the girls anywhere. What could have happened to them? He checked out his Harley. It seemed safe and no one seemed to be around, so he decided to check out the building across the street. They must have gone somewhere, but why? What would make them suddenly stop following him and go off exploring, not even telling him where they went? Starbucks couldn't figure it out.

The building on the other side of the road was only one story high, and it said, "O'Flaherty's Pub" on it in gold letters. The outside was painted green and brown, and it had a red door. It looked like an interesting place, so Starbucks decided he might as well check it out too.

He opened the red door and walked inside. This room was pitch black and everything was covered with dust. A wooden wall that came up from the floor and ended waist high traveled the length of the room on one side. In front of it, steel stools stood, some tipped over and lying on the floor. Starbucks saw two skeletons. One sat on a stool with a drink on the counter in front of him as if he died about to take a drink. The other one lay on the floor next to some big tables with green coverings on their tops and holes on the sides.

Behind the wooden half wall, a huge sheet of reflecting glass hung. On either side of the glass, shelves held bottles of colored liquid.

On the other side of the room tables and chairs lay scattered about, as well as padded benches along the wall. He walked inside, and the door creaked shut behind him, making his heart jump. The air inside was dusty and stale, as if he was lying with his face under a blanket. For a moment he forgot about the girls and just enjoyed exploring the strange room. He walked in and noticed his steps made footprints in the dust. No one had been inside for a long time.

He pulled out his sword, just in case, and tiptoed over to the half wall. Then he saw someone behind the bar! It was a black person, just like him, and even looked to be the same height. He yelled and crouched down, sword held high. Nothing happened. Slowly, he rose up, until he could just see over the counter. There was no one there.

He stood up, and then the person was back again! But as he stared with amazement, he realized the person was him! He was staring back at himself! He smiled, and his double smiled too. He laughed, and so did the other Starbucks. He moved his sword around, and so did the other one.

It was some kind of magic glass that showed you your own self, he realized. He'd never seen anything like it, not even in Misterwizard's castle. Amazed, he looked at the glass and could see the whole room around him, and even weirder, if he looked at the corners of the glass, he could see parts of the room not even in front of it.

Starbucks had never seen something so fascinating, and he wondered if Misterwizard knew about it. The image in the glass was hazy and indistinct, and the glass was cracked and looked old, but it was still wonderful in Starbucks's mind.

Starbucks looked at the glass bottles, dusty and full of strange liquids. He wondered why anyone would put glasses of different colored water on a shelf, and whether the water was safe to drink. He climbed over the half wall and picked up a bottle. Then he saw something on the floor and yelled. He dropped the bottle and it hit the floor and broke with a crash.

It was just another skeleton, another man from before the Great War. He lay on the floor in tattered clothes, his bones covered in dust and cobwebs. Starbucks mentally made fun of himself for being such a cowardie after not being scared of other skeletons. He figured it was just the surprise of seeing him when he wasn't expecting it. He picked up another bottle. On its side was written, "BSB," and below the words, "Brown Sugar Bourbon."

Starbucks unscrewed the top and sniffed it. It smelled strange and sweet. He began to suspect it was not plain water. He decided to take a sip, just to see what it tasted like. He raised the bottle to his lips. And then he heard the yell. He dropped this bottle too, and it broke with another crash.

From outside, somewhere in the distance, barely audible through the door. "Starbucks! Super! Deb! Where are you?" It was Johnny! Starbucks jumped over the counter and ran for the door. Flinging it open, he ran outside as fast as he could.

Back in the sunshine, he squinted and covered his eyes with his hand, unable to see because of the brightness. When his eyes finally adjusted, he looked around, trying to spot Johnny. He didn't see him, but Starbucks smiled anyway, sure he'd be reunited with his friend soon.

Starbucks ran out into the street, looking everywhere for Johnny. Then he saw the wolf-beastie.

Starbucks scowled at it. "I thought I killed you!"

The wolf-beastie's side had a large red gash and its fur was matted with blood, but it still looked strong and very dangerous. Its teeth were bared and it stared at Starbucks with fierce, hungry eyes.

Starbucks backed away, more irritated than scared. He was just about to find Johnny, now he had to deal with the wolf-beastie. And he still hadn't found the girls. He decided there was nothing else to do but fight and kill the wolf-beastie and this time, make sure it was really dead.

"You didn't hurt Super and Deb, did you, you rotten wolf-beastie? If you did, I'm going to carve you into steaks and eat you."

Starbucks was about to advance on the wolf-beastie when he saw something that gave him a great idea. It was a huge hole in the concrete where a bomb had exploded, leading to who knew where.

Starbucks grinned. "Come here, wolf-beastie, I have a surprise for you."

The wolf-beastie padded towards Starbucks. Starbucks circled around until he was near the hole. "Come and get me, wolf-beastie!"

The wolf-beastie leapt for Starbucks. Starbucks yelled and hit it with his sword. Then he pushed the wolf-beastie towards the hole. Just as he'd hoped, it sailed into the hole and disappeared from view. He heard a distant yelp as his hit the ground, somewhere far below.

Starbucks raised his sword and cheered. "How do you like that, wolf-beastie? Who's the smart one now?"

Starbucks walked over to the hole and looked inside. It was so dark, he couldn't see the bottom. "Enjoy your new home, if you're still alive, you dumb beastie."

Starbucks, pleased with himself, forgot about the wolf-beastie and went back to looking for Johnny.

At the bottom of the hole, the wolf-beastie stood up. It shook itself off and looked up at the small round opening of light. There was no way it was getting back up there. It looked into the darkness and padded off, looking for new prey.

CHAPTER 21

Misterwizard and Sephie walked up to the main floor of the Museum to see the people of the Tribe all in a state of excitement. They all ran up to Misterwizard at once and surrounded him with anxious looks on their faces.

"Sephie, you're safe with Misterwizard," Abercrombie said, smiling. "That's a mercy."

Misterwizard smiled and lowered Sephie down. Sephie ran to her mother and Abercrombie picked up her and hugged her.

"MIsterwizard!" Miscrosoft said, with a look of worry on her face. "Starbucks left and he took Deb and Super with him. Johnny left too. And the rest of the Tribe is wandering all over."

"MIsterwizard!" Jayceepenney said. "Half the tribe went next door to see where the big fight happened. The other half are out picking fights with the Wildies!"

"That's not true," Abercrombie said. "He's making some of that up, Misterwizard. But some have wandered off. "

Misterwizard chuckled darkly and stroked his beard. "Well, well, it seems while the shepherd slept the sheep scattered. That is partially my fault, I'll admit. I do like to sleep in late. But all is not lost. I'm sure we can get the flock back together and close the gate."

"Misterwizard! MIsterwizard!" It was Cinnabon and her son Wheaties. She pushed their way to the front of the crowd until she was next to MIsterwizard. "Johnny has done something without even asking you! He made a decision you may not like!"

"I'm sure whatever decision Johnny made was the right one. But pray tell me, dear Cinnabon what was Johnny's possible transgression?"

"He didn't do a transgression," she said, "he made a deal with the Wildies. He said they could live with us and share our food and beds! And we don't have enough for us, let alone their mangy hides!"

All the Tribespeople talked at once, and Misterwizard raised a hand. "Peace be still!"

The Tribe quieted down. Misterwizard opened his mouth to speak, but then he saw the very people they were talking about. In the door leading outside the Museum, Yellowtooh and his family stood, peering in meekly.

"Ah! It seems your words have been proven to be accurate, Cinnabon, for here stands the evidence of what you relayed."

"What?" Cinnabon said. But then she turned and saw the Wildies in the doorway. Her eyes opened wide and she grabbed Wheaties tight. She pulled him back behind Misterwizard as he strode towards the door.

The rest of the Tribe shrunk back as well, even though Yellowtooh and his family didn't seem the least bit threatening. They were just the opposite, frightened and shaking, as if they thought they might be attacked at any moment.

"That's Yellowtooth," Cinnabon said, pointing and acting as is she knew everything. "And this is his wife Marbleskin and his daughter Funnygiggle. I heard him tell Johnny that. They're very strange, and probably dangerous."

MIsterwizard walked to the door, smiling in a warm, friendly way. "They don't seem to be exhibiting any threatening gestures or making any demonstrations of hostility. In fact, I would say they seem perfectly harmless."

The Tribe watched, holding their breath as Misterwizard greeted the Wildies. Misterwizard stopped in front of Yellowtooh and smiled at him. "Hello, Yellowtooth. I am Misterwizard. Welcome to our humble abode. We are known simply as the Tribe. I understand you have been in negotiations with our leader, Johnny, as to the possible cessation of hostilities and a mutual agreement of cooperation."

Yellowtooth's mouth opened wide in shock and confusion, not understanding half of what MIsterwizard said. He looked at his wife Marbleskin and at his daughter Funnygigle. They shrugged, not understanding, either.

"Good day, milord," Yellowtooth said in a shaky voice. "I be Yellowtooth, and this be me wife Marblekin. Yonder is our daughter Funnygiggle. We be a mite slow to understandin' your speech. Meanin' no harm, sir, we're just not very smart when it comes to that sort of thing, bein' just ordinary folk of no stature at all. But be of a surety, we come with the humblest of intentions. This Johnny ye speak of, he be a good man. He's what said we should take up our matters with ye, beggin' your pardon, sir."

Misterwizard nodded, his eyes sparkling with interest. "Your mode of speech is most fascinating. It seems to be a melding together of eighteenth century English with local gibberish, to create a language indigenous to your people. I've found it very interesting, ever since I heard Lord Algon use it."

Misterwizard gestured towards the interior of the Museum. "Let us not stand here on the doorstep as if you are unwanted sellers of insurance policies or Jehovah's Witnesses. Let me invite you inside, like a good host should do."

He moved back and motioned for Yellowtooth and his family to enter. They smiled and walked in as the people of the Tribe backed away, looking frightened. MIsterwizard led the Wildies over to a stone bench where they sat down, looking scared. Misterwizard sat down on a bench near them, and the people of the Tribe stood by the opposite wall, watching.

"May I be a good host and offer you a beverage?" Misterwizard turned to Abercrombie. "Abercrombie dear, would you fetch our guests some water?"

Abercrombie ran off to comply. Cinnabon scowled and narrowed her eyes, not happy about it.

"Thank ye kindly, milord," Yellowtooth said gratefully.

"So, tell me," Misterwizard said, as he rested his back against the stone wall behind the bench, "what was it specifically that you and Johnny discussed? Please fill me in on the details."

"Well," Yellowtooth said, taking a glass of water from Abercrombie and sipping it with relish, "as I said to your young master, there be many of us who be not of the same mind as Lord Algon. We have no desire for war, nor killing nor even eating man flesh. But what choice have we? For Lord Algon be powerful and has swayed many to his side, having given them someone to follow and a feeling of belonging. We have long wished for a way to escape his cruelty, and now hope comes to us that ye and your tribe may be the salvation we've longed for."

Marbleskin piped up for the first time. "We be hard workers, and good food gatherers." She looked at her husband, who nodded. "Some of us refuse to eat the dead men. Instead we hunt the wild beasts what roam the land. And we gather what fruits and berries grow in the wild places."

Misterwizard smiled with pleasure. "Excellent. You have already begun to create a sustainable society. Your members will be a useful addition to our growing enterprise."

Yellowtooth nodded, not really understanding.

"There are a few obstructions to overcome, however," Misterwizard said, "before we can welcome you with open arms into our tribe. First, we need to take a vote amongst ourselves. Being a firm believer in Democracy, I feel the Tribe must have some say into whether they will allow you to join us. Though I see no reason why they would object."

Yellowtooth nodded. "Democracy," he said, not having a clue what it meant. "Aye. Ye must decide whether ye be thinking we're showing our true colors, that I understand."

Misterwizard continued. "And then there is the matter of Lord Algon. He most surely will not be pleased to find us stealing from his flock,"

"Ye spoke rightly on that. He be planning to attack ye again, and that very soon," Funnygiggle said.

Misterwizard nodded. "Yes, I suspected as much."

He leaned forward and looked at Yellowtooth. "Would your people be willing to fight against Lord Algon as our allies, if that is what it took to assure our mutual safety and proclivity?"

Yellowtooth frowned, not really understanding the last part. But Marbleskin smiled and answered for him. "Oh, we'll fight, ye can be sure of that. For a chance to escape from his evil ways, many would risk not only the fighting but the dying."

Misterwizard sat back, pleased. "Very good. For though we bested him in the first engagement, I suspect he will be better prepared when he confronts us again. The more strength we have in numbers, the better our chance of a successful outcome."

"Ye talk as funny as we," Yellowtooth said, grinning.

They all laughed. Then Misterwizard said, "Yes, I suspect we may have to endure a slight communication discord at the outset until we achieve a mutually beneficial mode of speech."

"Verily," Marbleskin said, not knowing what else to say.

Misterwizard stood up. "We have much to do in the way of setting up defenses and not much time to get it done, I suspect, before your king attacks again. The sooner we combine our forces, the faster the work will be accomplished."

Yellowtooth nodded. "Aye,' standing up himself. The rest of his family stood up as well.

"Come back tomorrow, er, after the next Yellow Eye," Misterwizard said. "By that time, I will have had a chance to meet and discuss this with the Tribe, and we will have a decision for you. Time is truly of the essence."

"Aye, we will do that, be assured."

Yellowtooth and his family walked towards the door. When they reached it, they turned and looked at him one last time. "May the great god Nucleer bless our union and may he look with favor on us."

MIsterwizard frowned, having never heard of their god before. "Nucleer, is it? How interesting. I've never heard of this god before. But that is not to cast disparagement on your beliefs, my dear Yellowtooh. Yes, let's pray he finds favor on us. We need all the help we can get."

Yellowtooth and his family walked to the door. They wore happy smiles.

"Ye know not what joy and hope ye have brought us today. We will spread the news, but stealthily, about thine offer to those who would align with us in joining thee."

"Do be careful," Misterwizard said. "If Lord Algon finds out your intentions, I do not think he will deal with you too kindly."

The Wildies left. Misterwizard watched them go and looked off into the distance. "I wonder what has happened to Johnny. He really needs to be here to discuss matters."

Foodcourt ran as fast as he could back to the main hall of the Museum of Natural History. When he arrived, he was surprised to see Teavana and Bathandbodyworks not there anymore. He strode out into the middle of the room, being careful to go around the big hole in the floor.

As he passed the hole, he looked down inside it one more time, expecting to see nothing. But what he saw made him stop in his tracks with horror.

There at the bottom of the hole, next to the remains of the tiger-beastie, lay the body of Marthastewartliving. Her lifeless eyes stared up at the ceiling far, far above. Her arms were twisted, as if she was a rag doll shaken and broken. And worst of all, her head was bloody on the back.

Foodcourt put a hand to his open mouth and stared with wide eyes. "Poor Marthastewartliving!" Foodcourt said out loud to himself as he put on a sad look of sympathy. "She must have slipped and fallen into the hole!"

He gazed at her for a few minutes, wondering what he should do about her body, for it was obvious she was no longer living. He decided he'd have to wait until he could get some other tribe members to help him lift it out. Then they could give her a proper burial. Marthastewartliving was alone, and she had no living relatives, for all her children had died of the Sickness over the years. At least he wouldn't have to tell them the sad news.

"I'm so sorry, Marthastewartliving," Foodcourt said to the old lady as he gazed at her somberly. "But you shouldn't have been wandering in here alone. It's very dark and slippery."

He looked around, wondering where his wife and Bathandbodyworks could be. "Teavana! Teavana!" Where are you?" He walked over to the passageway on the other side of the room and peered down it. From inside, he heard Teavanna and Bathandbodyworks chatting happily to each other. He sighed with relief and rolled his eyes. Then he walked down the passageway to find them.

Meanwhile in the other passageway, Thegap woke up. He sat up, looked around, realized he was all alone and became instantly afraid. He looked forward again and saw Leader Nordstrom's body again. He yelped and struggled to his feet. He stood still, leaning on a pillar, his head spinning.

"OOOH," he moaned. Then he looked around. He whispered in a intense way, "Foodcourt. Foodcourt!" But there was no answer. He glanced at Leader Nordstrom one more time with a scared frown and turned to run back to the main entrance.

"Hey. You," a whispered voice came from the dark, a sinister, cruel voice.

"Aaah!" Thegap yelled, his eyes widening with terror. He didn't even look back towards the voice, just raised his hands and ran as fast as he could back towards the main hall.

In the dark, the sinister voice laughed. And then there was only silence.

Johnny ran as fast as he could towards the sounds of the Harley. It was a long way from the white stick building across the grassy Mall to the buildings on the other side. Johnny pushed himself, but before he reached the other side he had to slow down and catch his breath. He made the rest of the way to the back of the buildings in a fast walk.

When he finally arrived at the street behind the buildings, the street was empty. All he saw were old junk cars and the dark doorways of the old, rotted structures. There was no Harley, or Starbucks, in sight.

Disappointed, Johnny walked down to the street and looked around. A cool wind blew his face, and the Red Eye was hot on his neck. Where could they have gone, he wondered? He could see down the street for quite a way, but there was no sign of anyone.

Johnny was glad Starbucks found his Harley, but it presented a new problem. Now Starbucks would be way faster than Johnny on foot. It would be hard for Johnny to catch up to him. But Starbucks couldn't fit both girls on the back of his one bike, so did he find Johnny's Harley too? And if so, who rode it? Johnny was pretty sure Deb didn't know how to drive yet, but maybe Starbucks had taught Super. Which meant Deb would have to ride with one or the other one of them, and somebody besides Johnny drove his Harley, which didn't make Johnny very happy.

Johnny walked into the middle of the road. He noticed a huge hole in the street, big enough to swallow a car. The edges of the hole were ragged and cracked, and Johnny didn't feel safe getting too close for fear more of the street might fall in. He stayed far away from the hole and gazed around.

On one side of the road the front wall of the building had a huge hole that rose up two stories. The building also had four big pillars in front. The second pillar on the left side had collapsed in a heap, , making the front of the building look like a mouth with one tooth missing. On the other side of the street was a building with a green and brown front and gold lettering. The front door was painted red. Small windows on the front set high up on the wall were dark, indicating it was dark inside the building.

Johnny doubted there would be any reason for Starbucks and the girls to go into either building, but he didn't see where else they could have gone. He put his hand to his mouth like a megaphone.

"Starbucks! Super! Deb! Where are you?"

The sound of his voice echoed in the empty street, joining the whistle of the wind. There was no reply.

Then Johnny heard a bark. It came from somewhere inside the big building with the columns. It was the sound of a Barker, which Johnny knew meant a whole pack of them. Had Starbucks and the girls ran into more trouble with Barkers? Johnny took out his sword and ran to the building, ready to fight and defend his friends from the hungry dog-beasties.

CHAPTER 22

In the Arena, men carried the unconscious guard out. They also loaded the dead lion-beastie into a rolling cart and hauled it away.

Lord Algon watched the lion-beastie with a dark and unhappy frown. He whispered darkly to the guard who'd been hauled away, though the guard could not hear, "for slaying my good lion ye die a thousand deaths, ye filthy dog."

Lord Algon motioned to one of his guards, a big black man with bulging muscles wearing a gold shirt and black pants. The man leaned down to listen. Lord Algon whispered in his ear. "See yon dog in the Arena be hurt too much from his wounds to live. Never do I wish to see his scurvy face again."

The guard smiled and whispered back, "Yes, my lord."

Lord Algon motioned again, and the guard continued to listen. "And see his death be a long time coming for the life of my pet, 'ere he sail into Davy Jones' Locker. I want him to know what manner of displeasure he brought to his Lord for his bravery and fighting."

The guard smiled darkly. Then he left to do his Lord's bidding.

Lord Algon finally saw the Gangers and his brow furrowed with interest. He motioned to the man surrounding them to have the Gangers brought over.

The crowd watched with interest as the Gangers stopped in front of Lord Algon, wondering what new events were about to occur.

Lord Algon motioned, and the men surrounding the Gangers forced them to their knees. Lord Algon smiled at the crowd.

"Truly this be a day of blessing from Nucleer, my people!"

The people cheered.

"For look what he has put in our hands, none other than the brigands what joined the battle and caused us to lose to the Newcomers."

He strode forward and glared at the Gangers. "Who be ye? Ye be not of the Newcomers."

Facegash looked into the scared faces of the other Gangers then at Lord Algon. He swallowed hard and tried to keep his fear from his voice.

"We are the Doomsday Prophecy. And we also hate the Newcomers. We've come to make a deal with ye, I mean you."

Lord Algon grinned but with no humor. "Deal, ye say. When it was ye who cost me my victory. Ye be the interlopers what attacked my people and caused the

Newcomers to prevail. And now ye seek a parlay. Ye shall instead pay, and that dearly. Ye shall rue the day ye crossed swords with Lord Algon. We shall all see the color of your innards 'ere this day be done."

The guards moved towards the Gangers. The Gangers looked even more terrified.

"Wait!" Facegash said. "We know things about the Newcomers that can help you. We can help you. You'll never win against them without us."

The guards reached the Gangers. The Gangers all looked at Facegash, hoping his words would save them.

Lord Algon stood up and walked over to the Gangers. He stood and stared at Facegash, who stared back, trying to look tough.

"Know things, do ye? Need ye, ye say? And what such things be ye tellin' me?"

Facegash felt a glimmer of hope and he smiled. "For one thing, who their leader is. He's just a boy, not even a man, and his name is Johnny."

Lord Algon stroked his chin with his hand, thinking. "Johnny ye say. This has the ring of truth. The lad said this be his name. What else ye have to say? Speak, 'ere I grow impatient and cut out your tongue."

"I have lots to tell you, all about their weapons and about the wizard who helps them. But first you have to promise you won't kill us. In fact, you have to promise to give us something in return."

Facegash knew the last bit was a gamble which might backfire, but he needed to sound cocky. Facegash knew men like Lord Algon. Any sign of fear from Facegash and Lord Algon would think him less than a man, and the negotiations would be over.

"Give ye something ye say? Thou art a bold one, and

in no position to barter," Lord Algon said, watching Facegash closely to try and read his mind. "And yet, perhaps ye be of some value."

Lord Algon stopped talking and simply stared at Facegash. A contest of wills began. Facegash stared back, trying not to waver. Then Lord Algon grinned, a grin of death.

"Ye shall pay for your part in our defeat, and we shall see what manner of men ye are. And when we see, then we will decide what fate the rest of ye shall find. Choose one of your crew to fight. If he, or she, be victorious, or perhaps if they simply make us merry in the attempting, we will parlay with thee. But if they prove to be spineless, ye shall all join them in the Arena, one by one. Choose. Perhaps it be you?"

Lord Algon pointed at Facegash. Facegash' face went white. He looked at the Gangers. They all stared back in fright, wondering who he was going to pick.

Facegash turned to Badluck. "Sorry Badluck, but your luck ain't changed. Less you can fight real good."

Badluck screamed and tried to run away, but the guards grabbed him. Lord Algon laughed. The rest of the Gangers looked sad, and Lady Stabs bit her lip, trying to keep from crying.

Lord Algon gazed at Facegash, who smiled back. Lord Algon smiled too. "Ye be of the right kind I like, him what protects his own plunder while giving up his weakest member."

Facegash grinned, sensing a kindred spirit. "We think alike, Lord Algon."

They both laughed darkly. Then Lord Algon narrowed his eyes, but his smile remained. "Perhaps too much alike."

As Badluck yelled and struggled, the Wildies dragged him down the ramp and towards the door into the Arena. Lord Algon grinned at Facegash.

Everyone turned to watch what transpired in the Arena. The crowd cheered and jumped up and down as they looked forward to another bloody fight.

Starbucks circled back to his Harley and climbed on. He didn't really know what to do. The wolf-beastie was gone, and he hadn't seen any evidence that it hurt the girls, but they were nowhere to be found. And he knew he'd heard Johnny's voice, but didn't see him anywhere either. He began to wish he'd listened to Deb and not taken the girls on the little trip, even though he found the Harleys.

He started his Harley and it roared to life with a pleasant rumble. He thought about retracing his steps, for maybe the girls simply returned to New Sanctuary. But what about Johnny? If he left, he might miss him.

"Johnny! Johnny! Deb! Super!"

No one answered. Irritated, Starbucks sat for a few seconds, throttling his engine, making it roar. He smiled, for despite his predicament, he loved his Harley. Why couldn't things just settle down so he and Johnny could leave for a while on some nice long trips, exploring the new world they'd discovered? The thought of the four of them, Johnny, Starbucks, Deb and Super just taking off to see what they could find thrilled him and excited him. He bet Johnny would love the idea, and he knew Super would.

But for now, he was stuck looking for lost people. He grumbled to himself and took off, back the way he'd come. The street was choked with rocks and old cars, and he slowed down and weaved among them. He had to stop and almost walk the Harley in a few places because of the broken building pieces in the road.

He saw something to his left and looked. Between the two buildings that stood between him and the grassy Mall, he could see something happening. He slowed down and stopped and looked.

There on the grassy Mall where the shacks of the Wildies stood, a whole gathering of Wildies took place. One old man stood in front of the crowd with an old lady and a young girl about Deb and Super's age. He talked, though he was so far away Starbucks couldn't hear what he was saying. He was very excited though, and he kept pointing back towards New Sanctuary. Whatever was happening, it didn't look good.

Starbucks was really in a tight spot now. He needed to warn Misterwizard and the Tribe, for it looked like the Wildies were planning an attack. But he couldn't just abandon the search for the girls or Johnny.

What should he do? He decided he'd head back to New Sanctuary. Maybe he'd find Deb and Super, and at least he could warn Misterwizard. And if he didn't find the girls, he could come back fast and keep looking for them.

He stepped on the gas and his Harley took off in a shower of rocks. Weaving through the debris, he tried to ride as fast as he could, for who knew how much time they had before the Wildies attacked?

Deb and Super followed Loki down the strange metal tube. The dim light showed a long, narrow hallway going away from them as far as they could see. In the distance they saw another square opening and beyond it another one leading into another section of the tube.

Loki moved fast, loping along, but Deb and Super stumbled because the ground was tilted. "Hurry," Loki said, grabbing Deb's hand and trying to pull her along. "Must show you to Slon. Slon has never sees angels before. And Harp will be excited, too."

"Who's Harp?" Super said, as she felt her way down the middle passage by grabbing metal rungs that ran up to the ceiling from the benches.

Loki smiled in the dark, a little embarrassed. "Harp is a girl in the tribe. She is prettiest girl in the whole world."

Deb and Super grinned at each other, instantly understanding.

"Is she the girl you love, Loki?"

Loki looked at them shyly. "Yes. But she is too pretty for me. Other boys want her, stronger and bigger."

"Don't count yourself out, Loki," Super said with a mischievous smile. "No one knows what a girl is thinking until she shows it. She might just be more interested in how nice you are instead of just who is strongest or biggest."

Loki looked at Deb and Super and smiled. "You think so?"

"Sure."

Deb resisted, making Loki have to stop. "Loki, please

slow down. We're new to your home, and we aren't as fast as you are." Deb's forehead felt hot. The air in the metal tube was stale and stagnant, and it tasted bad. She hoped all that was happening to her and Super wouldn't bring her sickness back upon her.

Super grabbed a metal rail to steady herself and gazed at the benches. "Loki, you live here in these metal tubes? Gross."

"Good place to hide," Loki said, jumping up and down and smiling. "Rat People won't come inside, and we stay dry from the waters falling. The soft places are nice to sleep on. But we don't live in here. We live in our village, up ahead."

Loki pulled at Deb again and reluctantly she started following him again down the narrow, tilted passage.

Super realized Deb was having trouble. "Are you all right, Deb?"

Deb glanced at Super with meaning. "My forehead is getting hot again."

Super looked really worried, understanding what Deb meant, but there was nothing she could do about it.

"Loki," Deb said, "how long have your people lived down here, in this dark, terrible place?"

Loki frowned at Deb, irritated. "Since Loki born and long before, but it's not terrible. Home."

They passed benches and Deb noticed there were pictures and words scrawled on the benches. There were also half eaten rat-beasties and old empty cans. Some of the cans still had liquid in them, as if they'd just recently been opened. Deb wrinkled her lip in distaste.

Super passed an old suitcase and she opened it out of curiosity. Inside lay what used to be clothes, rotted and dirty. She closed it quickly and hurried past it.

As they walked they began to get better at walking on the tilted floor, as long as they held on to the metal rails running from the floor to the ceiling. The dim light flickered and buzzed. Deb wondered how they had 'lectricity, something only Misterwizard had in their world. Did they have their own Misterwizard to help them? And if so, why didn't he tell them there was a whole world above and they didn't have to live in the dark, dank cave anymore?

Loki's pale white body shone in the pale light. Deb wondered why his skin was so white. She decided it must have had to do with the lack of light. He looked like a white slug-beastie she'd seen once in the garden at Sanctuary, and the thought gave Deb the shivers. Were all his people like that? She didn't look forward to seeing a whole tribe of people like Loki.

Deb and Super had put their swords away so they could walk but they were within easy reach if they needed them.

Suddenly they heard voices outside the metal tube ahead. Deb looked up and saw they were coming to a large open space where tunnel expanded to a much bigger size. The metal tube ran right through the larger area and continued far away on the other side where the tunnel narrowed again. Deb and Super had reached Loki's tribe!

Super and Deb looked at each other, both thinking the same thing.

"This is it," Super said, and Deb nodded.

"Let's stick close together, and be ready if we need to run," Deb said.

Super nodded back. "I have Misterwizard's magic if we need it, but I don't know how we're going to get out of here if we have to run for it."

The thought had occurred to Deb too. They were really at the mercy of Loki's tribe, no matter what they did.

CHAPTER 23

Johnny ran past the columns and inside the huge building. The interior was filled with old desks and chairs. The top half of the back wall had fallen, leaving a gaping hole where the top half had been to the street beyond, and the rest of the wall looked ready to fall at any moment. Rock and rubble covered the wooden desks and chairs inside.

Pictures of old men lined the walls, faded and turned white with age. Red drapes hung on the walls, torn and with holes in them from rat-beasties and bugs. A red carpet lay on the floor, so faded and dirty it was black in most places.

Johnny walked around, looking at the rotted wooden desks. What did people do here, he wondered? He couldn't even think of what the desks would be for. Did you use them to hunt, or to make food, or clothing? Did they sit there and talk to each other, or make weapons? There were so many of them, all lined up in rows. All of them had papers in them or on them, faded and some turned into mush from rain and weather.

Johnny walked over and picked up a paper. It was moldy and half destroyed, but he could see it had writing on it. It was so faded he couldn't read it, but there was a lot of it at one time. Did they sit here and read to each other?

Johnny dropped the paper and moved down the row of desks. He saw a metal object on one desk. It looked like two square metal plates, one on top of the other, connected on one side. He lifted the top plate and saw there was a cracked glass screen on the bottom side of it. On the top side of the bottom plate there were buttons with letters on them. What was it for, Johnny wondered? Was this the way books were made?

Johnny shook the metal plates, but nothing happened. He shrugged and threw it down. It landed on the desk and crashed through it, for the desk was rotted. He walked some more and found a metal square with glass on one side. He picked it up and was surprised to see a woman staring at him from behind the glass.

Johnny smiled, amazed. He was looking at someone from before the Great War. She seemed to be about his mother's age, and she was pretty, with long black hair and a nice smile. Who was she, Johnny wondered? Did she sit at the desk? Did she have a Tribe? Did someone love her? Did she die from the Mushroom Monsters? Was she sitting right there where Johnny stood when the monsters came? The questions seemed endless that Johnny could ask, but there was no one to answer them. He could ask Misterwizard, but there were so many things to ask he was sure his wise friend would grow tired of answering before Johnny asked half of them.

Johnny put the metal frame down and looked around. He didn't see any barkers. He was all alone. He walked towards the door opening in the back wall. He stopped and gazed at the strange, sad room one more time, wishing he could go back in time and see it just before the Mushroom Monsters came. How different it must have looked!

He sucked in his breath, put his hand to his mouth for a megaphone and yelled once again. "Starbucks! Deb! Super!"

Suddenly he heard a loud creaking. He looked up. The wall was collapsing! Johnny ran to get away but didn't make it. The wall fell on top of him in a shower of dust and rocks.

When the dust cleared, Johnny looked down. He seemed all right, but his leg was caught under a large square stone piece of the wall. He was trapped!

Then he heard the barking again. The Barkers were coming for him.

The Wildies' loud cheers filled the air with the sounds of death and cruelty as Badluck was pushed into the Arena. He held a sword in his hand and shook all over, terrified. The Gangers sat on the wall next to Lord Algon, who smiled and watched the spectacle with dark glee.

Lady Stabs turned away, not able to watch. She'd had her share of death and horror and felt sick to her stomach. Some of the other Gangers, though, wore smiles and seemed to be enjoying the fight.

Facegash didn't watch the fight, he was too busy thinking. The crazy king could be flat out lying, and planning on putting them all one by one into the Arena. The Gangers were stupid to try and see what was going on. They should have run away until they had more strength in numbers. *Ripper never would have been caught so easily,* Facegash thought. He wished Ripper was there now. He'd know what to do.

Badluck ran to the wall and stood as close to it as he could. He stared at the gate, his knees shaking, wondering what monster was going to be sent to fight him. Whatever it was, Facegash knew Badluck didn't really stand a chance. His only hope was to run to the gate and find a way out before whatever entered found him.

Lord Algon stood up, and the Wildies quieted down. He raised his hand.

"I be a fair man, as ye all know. And if this here fellow is able to survive for just an hour, I will set him free. But if he die quick, then we'll know what measure these men are, and then perhaps we feed them all to our pets."

The Wildies cheered and laughed, and Facegash scowled. It was just as he feared. Badluck better survive for at least a while, or they were all dead.

"Which animal should he be facing, my mateys?"

"The bear-beastie!" Some yelled.

"The gorilla-beastie!" Others said.

"The snake-beastie!" Another yelled.

"The lion-beastie!" Still others yelled.

This last put Lord Algon in a bad mood, for the guard killed the lion-beastie. He glared at the crowd, wondering who said lion-beastie. Those who did realized their error and tried to shrink down so they wouldn't be seen.

Lord Algon tried to recover his good mood. He turned to the Gangers to enjoy the looks of fear on their faces.

"What say ye, fellows? Since it be your matey in the thick of it. Which woulds't thou be thinkin' to pit him against?"

"Please, don't do this. We're here to help you!" Lady Stabs begged.

Lord Algon sneered with disdain at her fear, and Facegash hurriedly said, "The lion-beastie," hoping that picking the dead animal might invoke some kind of rule that might save Badluck's neck.

Lord Algon walked over and looked at Facegash. "The lion-beastie, ye say? I be wonderin' if ye know something of what occurred early in the day, when the lion-beastie was killed by my infernal guard. Nay, I think twill be the snake your mate be fighting."

"Then why'd you ask me?" Facegash said, glaring at him.

Lord Algon glared back, angry at his insolence. "Watch thy tongue, and keep a tempered gaze on how ye try my patience, or I'll cut thee tongue out and feed to my pets. Ye better hope yon mate of yours can run mighty fast, for my pet snake-beastie be fast as he slithers along."

Lord Algon walked back to his throne, and as the people watched, he held up a hand and made a slithering gesture with it. The crowd roared.

Badluck looked up at Lord Algon in terror, wondering what he meant. He soon found out, as the gate to one of the cages opened. The snake-beastie slithered out. Badluck screamed and ran as far to the other side as he could get. The snake slithered quickly towards him.

Now even the hardest of the Gangers had a hard time watching as they waited for the inevitable outcome. Facegash wondered how long Badluck could last. It didn't like he was going to make it five minutes, let alone an hour.

Badluck ran and the snake slithered after him. He screamed in fear, and the crowd roared their approval. The snake was fast, but Badluck managed to stay one step ahead of it. He ran behind an old car, and the snake slithered on top of it. Badluck ran behind a stone wall, and the snake slithered around it.

Badluck made a mistake and ran into a corner of the Arena. The snake came towards him. He was cut off and trapped.

The crowd was so intense on watching the battle that no one saw the strange figure in a dark cloak near the entrance where the cages stood. They didn't see him raise a rifle, and because of the crowd noise they didn't hear the gun fire. But they all saw the giant snake suddenly writhe in pain and the hole in its head. Then the snake lay still, dead.

The crowd grew silent and Lord Algon stood on his feet, mouth open in amazement.

"What trickery be this?" He turned to Facegash. "Be ye also holders of the magic like the Newcomers?"

Facegash, mouth open with shock of his own, quickly tried to recover and act as if he'd planned the attack on the snake. He put on a look of arrogance and scowled.

"That's right," Facegash said, not believing his good luck and clueless as to where it came from. "We would have told you, but you didn't want to listen. So, we decided to show you."

Just then, as if to prove his point, the crack of a rifle

shot filled the air. One of Lord Algon's new guards screamed, grabbed at his side and fell down, blood pouring from a hole in his chest. Lord Algon's eyes opened wide with fear. He turned to Facegash hastily.

"Aye, ye have shown us yer magic. Belay the killing of us and we strike a bargain."

Facegash felt his confidence and swagger come back. He stood up and scowled at Lord Algon. "From now on, we're calling the shots, got it?"

"Aye, for now it seems ye have the upper hand," Lord Algon said, glancing at his guard with a look of amazement. "Truly be there strange devilry come upon us of late."

Facegash pointed into the Arena. "Get my man out of that hole down there. And then give us something to eat."

"Aye. 'Twill be done as ye say."

Lord Algon motioned to his guards and they hurried to comply.

Facegash looked around, wondering who he could thank for saving their lives. Whoever it was, Facegash would be grateful to them forever.

MIsterwizard sat on a bench in the entry hall of the Museum with Sephie on his lap. The whole Tribe, two hundred of them, crowded in front of him. Sephie held Kermit and smiled, happy to be on his lap.

"Dear friends and fellow sojourners on the journey for a new world with me. I have assembled you all together to discuss some matters of state that, upon their resolution, will solidify our position in our new home and ensure our survival and ultimate success."

Cinnabon rose a brown hand and spoke up. "Misterwizard, can you please try to talk so we can understand? And where's Johnny? Shouldn't he be here?"

Misterwizard chuckled. "As to your first request, I will strive to make my conversation simple enough that you won't have to struggle to understand. I am sorry if my speech sometimes mystifies and confounds you. I assure you, it is not intentional. I have a tendency to speak eloquently in words of complicity due to a fondness of the memory of my father, who taught me to speak with sophistication ."

"There you go again," Cinnabon said with a frown of irritation.

"As to your second question, dear Cinnabon, I do not currently know the whereabouts of our erstwhile hero. He is no doubt on a noble mission to save fair maiden and slay some mischievous dragon. I would prefer that he be here, but time and necessity dictate that we proceed without him for the moment. I truly hope you and the other members of the Tribe have enough confidence in me by now to trust my intentions for you or only for your betterment. I believe if Johnny were here, he would allow me to proceed without disagreement."

"What'd he say? Wheaties said, tilting his head and looking confused.

"Be quiet and listen," Cinnabon said. "Okay, go ahead Misterwizard we're listening."

Misterwizard set Sephie down, to her disappointment, and stood up. As the Tribe watched he walked over to the front door.

"We are currently in negotiations with the local

current indigenous population on a mutual agreement of cooperation and unity. But we cannot wait for their acquiescence to proceed. We need to expand our territory out of this Museum. I propose we begin to take over the whole area of grass known as the Mall. We will build walls between the buildings surrounding the Mall and essentially make a fortress out of the area, with this Museum being our castle. This way we will have a much more defendable position against enemies."

"I thought you said you were going to speak plain," Cinnabon said, frowning irritably. "Say that all again so we can understand it." The other nodded.

Misterwizard smiled. "We shall build walls and make a fortress. And then we'll be able to defend ourselves."

Cinnabon nodded. "Why didn't you just say that?"

Misterwizard walked out the door the marble porch and the Tribe followed. When most were outside, he pointed towards the Mall and the buildings surrounding it.

"We will need to use the broken remnants of the buildings as well as old cars and possibly even our buses to make the walls. We will want to find a way to make the walls scaleable and wide enough to post guards on. We have a lot of work ahead, my friends, but when we're finished, we can sleep soundly at night, knowing we have a place of relative safety in which to live."

The members of the Tribe nodded and smiled.

"We'll do whatever we have to, Misterwizard," Abercrombie said. "Just tell us what to do."

Just then, Foodcourt, Teavana, Thegap and Bathandbodyworks came running from the the Museum they'd been exploring, excited and out of breath. Misterwizard and the whole Tribe turned towards them in curiosity.

"Misterwizard," Foodcourt said, his face sad. "Something happened to Marthastewartiving. She's dead!"

Misterwizard frowned with sorrow and the members of the Tribe all talked to each other in surprise and alarm.

Then they all heard a now familiar rumble. They turned the other direction to see Starbucks roar up on his Harley. Starbucks jumped off and ran up to Misterwizard as the Tribemembers talked animatedly.

"Misterwizard! I just saw a whole crowd of Wildies. It looks like they're planning an attack!"

CHAPTER 24

Loki led Deb and Super out the other end of the tube to a large open area. As they left the confines of the metal tube, they walked into the strangest scene they had ever seen. Here the rounded ceiling was lit up with torches set on the tunnels walls, showing a bizarre underground wonderland.

A small village splayed out before them, made up of makeshift walls of old parts from the metal tube behind them and bits and pieces of trash from the suitcases. The village was made up of two rows of tents on either side of a middle pathway, stretching off into the distance. It finally ended far away near where the tunnel shrunk down again.

From the ceiling of the vast structure far above, streamers made up of old paper hung down, painted in weird colors. Some were fashioned to look like beasties, others to look like people of the village. On the platforms on either side of the tunnel near the village, a strange art exhibit existed, with crude paintings and sculptures of beasties and people made of old posters and mud.

But the most amazing thing was the giant statue of white stone laying on the right platform halfway down a tunnel. The statue leaned over, as if it had fallen and landed crookedly. The statue was partially hidden by shadow, but Deb and Super could see it was of a huge man with a beard sitting on a giant chair. The man wore a suit, and he looked wise and sad at the same time. The statue was twice as tall as the girls, and it seemed strangely out of place among the old shacks and paper sculptures. Plates full of food and other odds and ends, buttons and pieces of shiny metal and odd bits of clothing lay at the statue's feet.

In the village, people milled about in the tents, talking, making food, or doing chores. The platforms on either side of the lower area were filled with makeshift homes as well. Children played in the village and on the platforms next to the statues, running around the older people and the tents, kicking balls or just sitting and talking. Just as Deb imagined, they were all just as white as Loki, even the women. They women had long, white hair and the men white hair cut very short, so it stuck up, just like Loki's. They all had the large, dark eyes and long fingers, and they were all very thin.

Deb saw a tunnel beyond the statue. This tunnel seemed larger than the ones before, almost as big as the tunnel they'd been walking down. This tunnel was different than the others for another reason. It had colorful strips of cloth running from the ceiling to the floor, all down the passage.

"What's that?" Super said, wrinkling her nose and pointing at the statue.

"That's not a what, it's a who," Loki said. "That's our great god Lincone."

Deb and Super looked at each other and smiled, amused and mildly alarmed.

Then Deb pointed beyond the statue at the tunnel with the strips of cloth.

"Loki, where does that lead?"

Loki looked where she was pointing and then back at Deb. "That leads to the Door to Heaven." Loki looked at them curiously. "If you are angels, why don't you know all this?"

Super hastily replied, "We were just testing your knowledge."

Loki frowned, looking unconvinced, but then he nodded.

Deb and Super looked at each other then back at Loki. Deb asked, "Show us you know, Loki. What is the Door to Heaven?"

Loki smiled with pride. "I know the Story of the Ancients," he said. "That is the door where we will all ascend to the Heavens one day, when the Govermint Representives tell us Order had been retored and the monster Half-life has been vankished."

"The Heavens," Super said to Deb. "Do you think he means what I hope he means?"

Deb nodded, hope on her face. "The door out of this dark hole. But is sounds like it's sealed."

"Well, maybe we can open it," Super said, pointing with her head towards the green ball she had hidden in her coat. Deb nodded, grinning back at her.

Deb turned to Loki. "Loki, how will you know when

the order has been restored?"

But Loki wasn't listening anymore. He turned towards the shacks and the people inside them and raised his hands. He smiled with pride and spoke in a loud voice.

"Behold! Loki has brought you angels!"

Silence fell as everyone stopped what they were doing, turned and gazed with open mouths of amazement at Deb and Super.

"Well, this is it," Super said. "Hang on to your toenails. The beastie fur is about to fall into the mixing bowl."

Ever so slowly, the people recovered from their shock and surprise. Then they all talked at once. The whole village ran towards them, until the spot at the front of the metal tube was packed with so many people none of them could move. The excited people pushed each other and smiled up at Deb and Super with eyes wide in wonder. Deb and Super grew a little scared, and they backed up into the metal tube again. Loki joined them and all three stood at the door watching the hysteria unfold.

Loki stood tall with pride. He looked over the crowd and then smiled as he spotted one girl. At the back of the crowd stood a young girl, slender with long white hair and a long, pretty face. She had a long, elegant nose and soft eyes. It was Harp. She smiled as she looked at Loki and the angels with curiosity, and Loki smiled back at her, happy to see her being impressed.

It didn't seem to Deb as if the people were going to attack the girls, they were just so excited that they pushed each other forward to get closer. Soon those in front began to be crushed against the metal tube and they yelled. The scene grew wilder by the minute, and

Deb and Super became afraid that things were going to turn into chaos at any moment. But then a male voice, strong, forceful and with a touch of anger, sounded above the din.

"STOP!"

Everyone in Loki's tribe became silent. They all turned towards the passageway to the right, next to the statue and watched, waiting. From behind the colorful cloth streamers, a tall, thin white man with black eyes, a pointed chin and a long, thin face that looked as if it rarely smiled. He wore a hat like a turban on his head made of golden cloth, fancy gold slippers on his feet and a purple cloth robe lined in gold. He held a long staff in his hand. Taped to the top of the staff was a metal object. One end of the object had two handles. The other end had three flat metal tabs with holes in the middle of them.

"Who is causing all this disturbance?" The man said, raising himself up to his full height. He was so thin and comical that Deb had to keep from giggling. She put her hand to her mouth, and Super frowned at her in warning. Deb tried her best to smother her laughter and tried to look serious.

The whole tribe raised their right hands and pointed at Loki with their index finger. All except Harp, who just stood in the back and stared. Loki, confident before, now looked nervous and a little afraid. Deb and Super both held their breath and waited. Deb realized this must be the leader, Slon.

"Oh great and wise leader Slon," Loki said, but Slon raised his hand.

"Stop! You know the scriptures, Loki. You should be ashamed."

Loki looked embarrassed and crushed, and Deb felt sorry for him, wondering what he'd done wrong. She soon found out.

"Yes, oh great leader. I am sorry. I grew too excited."

Slon raised his head and sneered in contempt, and Deb decided right then and there she didn't like him at all.

"There is no excuse for your disobedience." Slon turned towards the giant white statue. "Let us give homage to our great god Lincone, as we should."

Everyone turned towards the statue and knelt down, Loki as well. Deb and Super looked at each other and stayed on their feet, watching.

Slon knelt down and put his arms out straight towards the statue. He lowered his head and looked towards the floor. "Oh great Lincone, god of the Undergrounder people, ye who fell from Heaven at the beginning of time, grant us your wisdom as we travel the path back to Heaven someday."

"AMEN!" All the people chanted.

Super looked at Deb and whispered, "Creepy." Deb nodded, feeling her skin crawl. They worshiped the statue like it was a god. Whatever weird things did they do? Deb began to really wish Super hadn't pretended they were angels.

Yellowtooth stood in front of the shacks n the grassy Mall. In front of him stood a small group of Wildies, mostly women and children but a few men as well. These were the Wildies who didn't want Lord Algon as their leader, the ones who hated his cruelty and war like ways. They didn't follow him and obey, like the ones now cheering at the Arena of Death. They only wanted peace and a chance to build a life, but Lord Algon was strong and had many fierce followers. If they didn't do as he said, they would be the next ones facing his beasties in the Arena, or worse.

On the night of the fight between Johnny's tribe, Lord Algon and Ripper's gang, the night the Wildies now called the Night of the Loud Monsters because of the explosions and gunfire, most had been forced to fight for Lord Algon. Some of their loved ones had been killed by Ripper's Gangers or by the explosions from Misterwizard's weapon. Now they gathered and listened as Yellowtooth told them of his meeting with Misterwizard.

Yellowtooh and his family faced the crowd, Yellowtooth in front. He spoke in a low and quiet but urgent voice, like a conspirator afraid to be caught.

"This be secret, and 'tis not to be shared with any unless ye be sure of the color of their jib," Yellowtooth said. "If Lord Algon get wind of what I say, we will all walk the plank, or be fed to his beasties."

The Wildies looked around, as if suspecting a spy in their midst, then back at Yellowtooh. Yellowtooth continued.

"This be the lay of it. The Newcomers be good folk, with not but good intentions, if we be willing to strike our colors and lay anchor aside them. But it won't come without a cost, ye can be sure of that. If ye want to join them, then fight by their side against Lord Algon, ye surely will. If ye have not the stomach to fight, then ye can remain Lord Algon's puppets."

The Wildies whispered among themselves. Marbleskin spoke up.

"It be up to thee to decide what flag ye will sail under. But be ye sure of this. One way or t'other, ye will have to fight. I says, let's fight for something, and someone what can give us better then just the killing and torturing of folk and the eating of man flesh only for the cruelty of it. Let's join them what want to make a better life, ones with good intentions and peace for all as their course."

The Wildies smiled, for the first time in their lives seeing hope for a better life. They whispered among themselves, while Yellowtooth peered around nervously, sure that the longer the stood in t a group the more chance Lord Algon would hear about it.

Finally, an old man named Bigears, for the big, flat ears on the side of his head, stepped forward. "Long have we endured the fear and cruelty of Lord Algon's reign. Many's the night Redhair," he pointed to his wife who stood beside him, whose hair was no longer red but gray with age, "and I have longed for a place we could raise our children in peace."

Bigears turned and looked at the other Wildies. They all smiled at him in agreement. "I speak for all here when I say, let's parlay with the Newcomers and be their mates, if they be willing. If we die because of it, at least we'll have done it for a chance at freedom."

The Wildies all spoke in agreement, and Yellowtooth put a finger to his lips and hushed them. Then he smiled.

"Anon, I reckoned the answer t'wood be thus. Ye be the good people, as I knew ye were. Than that settles it. We be mates with the Newcomers."

They all nodded. Then Bigears spoke again. "What

happens now, Yellowtooth?"

"I will tell the Newcomers of our decision. Ye all keep a low profile, and keep this to yourselves. Tell no one, unless ye be certain of the cut of his jib. If the wrong ears hear our plans before we can sign a treaty with the Newcomers, it will be all our necks in the noose."

They all nodded and headed back into their shacks. Yellowbeard, Marbleskin and Funnygiggle hugged each other, happy for the outcome of the meeting. Then they left to go back and talk to Misterwizard.

But at the back of the crowd, Yellowtooth's worst fears became real, for a man watched the crowd leave, one who was definitely of a different cut of jib. He was a loyal follower of Lord Algon, in fact he was one of Lord Algon's spies. They were men he placed amongst the Wildies for the very purpose of catching any hint of disloyalty or rebellion. This one's name was Wolf Fang.

None of the Wildies knew him by that name, of course. He assumed a false name, one meek and mild, to throw off suspicion. They knew him as Simpleman, for he acted as if he had been kicked by a horse-beastie when he was a child. If they really knew who he was, they would have been shocked into speechlessness, for he was a great actor at playing his part.

Wolf Fang was a thin but strong man with black hair and a black beard. He was only twenty- five seasons, but he acted as if he was much older, and always drooled. He spoke in a slurred speech, and most of the Wildies took pity on him and fed him from their tables. Many had even treated him as if he was their own child, letting him sleep in their shacks when it was cold or making him clothes when his became worn out. Now, he would repay their kindness with treachery, for he had no love for anyone but himself.

He knew he had to hurry to Lord Algon, before a deal was struck between the Newcomers and the Wildies. He waited until the crowd had dispersed, then turned to run quickly to Lord Algon's fortress.

But just as he was about to leave, someone grabbed his arm. It was a middle-aged stocky woman with huge breasts and a big, round head named Boomvoice, for her loud, booming voice. She didn't speak loudly now, however. Instead she whispered in a loud voice.

She grabbed Wolf Fang's arm and shook it. "Simpleman, ye heard what Yellowtooth say? Ye understand what we are to do?"

Wolf Fang bent over and drooled. "Yesh, I tink so," he said, nodding in a way that made him look simple.

"'Tis good. We need not you, what hasn't the sense of a monkey-beast spouting off and running our ship aground 'fore it has a chance to sail."

She began dragging him to her tent.

"Gotta go! Gotta go!" He said, and tried to pull away, but she held him firm.

"Nonsense. Ye look weak and wasted. Ye come with me, and I'll feed ye."

"Nay!" He said, "Nay hungry, thank ye."

"NO ARGUING. Ye have no sense when ye are hungry. Ye need meat on yer bones, and a good bathing. Ye stink. Now come along."

Wolf Fang had no choice but to comply, for the moment at least. But at the first chance, he would escape, and then the traitorous Wildies would know Lord Algon's revenge.

CHAPTER 25

Johnny struggled desperately to get his leg free from under the large piece of stone which held it fast. Panic gripped him, but he mentally forced it down. Now was not the time to lose his head. He stopped struggling and looked around for something close enough to grab that he could defend himself with. He saw a broken stick, but it was just out of reach. The bark came again, this time closer. The Barker was on its way towards him. In a few seconds it would see him.

Johnny thought how stupid it would be to die, eaten by Barkers while trapped under a rock, just before his dreams of a new world for his tribe came to pass. And he was almost sixteen seasons. It wouldn't be long before he could ask Deb to be his mate. The thought of dying before that could happen was almost enough to drive Johnny mad. He had to get free, he just had to.

The bark came again. It was almost on top of him! He strained with all his might, and just managed to touch the stick with his fingers. But it wasn't enough to grab it!

The Barker arrived. There was only one, so far. It was a big barker, with a black body and a splash of white on its chest and nose. Its black ears pointed straight up. Its eyes were slightly slanted and its red tongue lolled out of its mouth.

"Good Barker," Johnny whispered, hoping it wouldn't see him. "Just wander off again and lead your pack somewhere else to eat some nice Wildie or Ganger."

But the Barker turned its head and saw him. Johnny knew he was in trouble, for immediately the Barker trotted over to him. Johnny made a fist, ready to fight it off.

The Barker looked at him with intelligent eyes and sat down on its haunches. Johnny couldn't help but smile. It was almost as if the Barker was waiting for Johnny to entertain him.

"Good Barker," Johnny said. "You're not hungry, are you?"

Something about the Barker made Johnny stop being afraid, for it didn't seem threatening at all. It wasn't snarling and it didn't have the hungry, wild look in its eyes the Barkers got before they attacked.

Then the Barker did something that made Johnny laugh. It walked over to him and licked his face!

"Hey, knock that off!" Johnny said, smiling. He looked up at the Barker. It lay down in front of Johnny and moved its paw towards him, as if wanting Johnny to grab it. Johnny reached out and petted the Barker's paw, and it wagged its furry tail. It licked his face again.

"You're not a bad Barker at all, are you boy?" Johnny

said. He began to feel a strange affection for the animal, almost as if he'd found a friend. He reached his hand to the Barker's muzzle, the real test. But the Barker didn't bite his hand, just rubbed his cold wet nose against it. Johnny rubbed the Barker's head and it wagged its tail some more.

Suddenly a strange idea came to Johnny. What if he made this Barker his pet! The thought filled Johnny's heart with a strange joy and elation. He didn't know of the centuries old connection between man and dog, he only knew that somehow it seemed right, as if it was meant to be.

But first he had to get out from under the stone. "Hey fella, can you pick up a rock?"

The Barker wagged its tail but didn't seem to understand. Johnny chuckled. He rubbed the Barker's head again and went back to concentrating on how to get out from under the stone.

Then he heard another bark, and he knew this one came from a Barker that definitely wasn't friendly. It had a fierce hungry quality, and Johnny knew it meant a bad Barker was coming.

Johnny's new friend stood up, and instantly Johnny feared for friendly Barker's safety. After he'd just found the Barker, he couldn't see it get killed by a pack of mean dog-beasties!

Johnny doubled his struggles to get free, just as another Barker appeared. This one was black and hairless, with a big square brown muzzle. It was as big as Johnny's Barker, even a little bigger.

It saw Johnny. It saw Johnny's Barker. And it snarled. Johnny's Barker snarled back and barked but not near as fiercely as the other one. Johnny was sure it would get killed by the mean Barker, if Johnny didn't get free to help it.

The mean Barker ran towards them. Johnny yelled, trying to distract it. And then in a flash, the Barkers fought.

Johnny looked around desperately. He saw that his Barker has brought the stick over to him and laid it in front of him, which was strange. But Johnny didn't have time to wonder at his good fortune. He grabbed the stick, shoved it under the rock and pried it up.

Snarls and yelps of pain filled the air as the Barkers snapped at each other and rolled around in a fight to the death. Johnny screamed and pushed with all his might. Finally, the stone budged.

Johnny heard his Barker yelp. It was losing! The bigger and meaner Barker was just too tough for it. Johnny got his leg free. He leapt up and grabbed his sword from the ground where it had fallen. He ran at the combatants, but they were a ball of fur, rolling over and over. Johnny didn't want to hurt his Barker by accident.

Finally, he saw a chance. He stabbed at the mean Barker. It yelped and stopped fighting. Johnny's Barker pressed its advantage, and soon the mean Barker jumped up and ran away.

"Yay!" Johnny yelled, happy in the victory. But then he looked at his Barker friend.

It lay on the ground, covered in blood. Johnny's heart sank with sadness.

"Don't die, Barker. Please, don't die!"

For some reason tears came to Johnny's eyes. He put his sword away and picked up the Barker. He had to get the Barker to Misterwizard and fast. Johnny ran out of the building, faster than he'd ever ran in his life. For some reason he didn't understand, he wanted that Barker to survive more than he'd ever wanted anything in his life. It had risked its life to defend him. It was his friend, and now Johnny had to save it.

Facegash, Lady Stabs and the rest of the Gangers lounged on the floor on a rich red carpet in Lord Algon's throne room. They gazed up at the walls, decorated with skulls of men and beasts, and the bones of strange animals Lord Algon had taken from the museums.

Rich red tapestries hung from the walls as well. The furniture in the room came from the museums as well, antique couches and chairs in beautiful golds and purples, tables of rich dark wood and statues in white marble of beautiful maidens.

In front of the Gangers lay glasses of wine and plates full of food. Facegash and most of the Gangers ate ravenously, but Lady Stabs just picked at hers, wondering just where the meat came from. She glanced around nervously, for most of the Wildies seemed friendly, but she'd noticed dark looks in their eyes, and she didn't think any of them would hesitate to kill them if they had the chance.

Beautiful women, at least beautiful for Wildies at least, stood behind them holding food and drink in case they wanted more. Some of the women were disfigured or missing teeth, but they were the best Lord Algon could find in the wasteland.

They dressed in fancy robes as if they were Greek maidens, but somehow the luxurious clothing just pointed out their ugliness more clearly.

Lord Algon sat in his throne at the head of the room with a plate of his own, held by a maiden where he could pick at it, and a glass of wine held by another woman. He didn't eat though, but sat brooding, looking at the Gangers with a dark frown full of resentment. They had somehow tricked him, killed one of his best guards with their magic, and now he felt a certain uneasiness, even a touch of fear. What if they had enough power to force him to give up his throne? He knew what would happen then. If he became just another Wildie, there were other Wildies would take no time to get revenge for things he'd done to them. Many had felt Lord Algon's cruelty, many times just for his entertainment, and they would love a chance to get back at him for what he'd done to them, he had no doubt.

He had to find a way to steal this magic from them. The problem was, he didn't even understand what it was. The Newcomers had possessed magic that was terrifying and beyond understanding. They had thrown balls in the air that exploded, tearing flesh and metal as if they were invisible monsters. He'd watched Wildies and some of the Gangers too, simply seem to disappear when the round balls exploded next to them. And he'd even seen the old metal hulks lying around fly in the air from the Newcomer's magic. The thought of this magic made him tremble in awe and fear, and lust after so much his mind burned.

But what the Gangers had done, this was the other magic, the one that only hurt one Wildie at a time. It was like a bee sting, but it killed instantly. Lord Algon had seen this during the fight too, men walking and suddenly fall, with blood pouring from their bodies. This magic always came after a loud bang, and Lord Algon began to fear the sound as much as what happened after. When he thought back to the fight, he still shook from the fear he'd felt, and the explosions, and the loud bangs.

Now the Gangers seemed to have the magic as well, which was a new development. The night of the big fight, they had been killed by it as much as the Wildies had, but something was different now. And if they could find this magic, then Lord Algon knew he could find it as well. He had to, before the Gangers decided to kill him and take over.

He smiled his most pleasant, and oily, smile at the Gangers. "How be ye likin' your meal, mateys? Is it to your liking and such?"

Facegash scowled at Lord Algon. He knew the crazy king was scared now, though he tried to hide it. Thanks to their secret friend, the Gangers were now the ones who held all the cards. If Facegash played his cards right, he and the Gangers would be in control of the whole bunch of them, and Lord Algon would get a taste of his own Arena.

"This food is cold. We want fresh, warm meat. And this wine. Is this the best you got?"

Fear gripped Lord Algon, but he tried to hide it. This Ganger knew he was in charge now. He was no fool. Lord Algon would have to be very careful. "Aye, 'tis a pity ye be not enjoyin' it. We will fetch ye a new batch, for sure, and this be more to yer likin.' But tell me, matey, what be your plans now? Shall we be beginnin' negotiations and planning together now, or do ye want to wait until ye've had a chance to digest a mite?"

Facegash took a bite of meat and chewed, not even looking at Lord Algon. "We'll talk when we're good and ready. How about some entertainment while we eat? You got any funny people, or people you can torture for our amusement?"

Lord Algon smiled. Despite the danger, he liked this man. He was of the same cut of jib as Lord Algon, and under other circumstances, would most likely be mates. "Aye, we can scare up some fun to entertain ye. Nothin' helps the digestion like watching a man in misery and pain."

Both Lord Algon and Facegash laughed, and the other Gangers looked at them with smiles that hinted they were crazy. Still they joined in the laughter, all except Lady Stabs. She was getting sick of the whole thing. She didn't know how much more she could take. She had made a decision. At the first chance she got, she was going to make a break for it. She was going to go to Johnny and the Tribe and tell them what was going on. Then she was going to ask them if she could join them. Even if they only let her be a slave, it would be better than the life she lived now.

But Lord Algon had not achieved his position by being stupid. He thought of something and smiled darkly. As he looked intently at Facegash to see how he would react he said, "Now before we go getting' all chummy and such and makin' of the treaties and what not, how's about ye show me this magic that killed my guard? I be thinkin' we need to know ye really have it and are not just takin' advantage of a lucky mistake of Dame Fortune."

Facegash stopped eating and his face went blank, telling Lord Algon all he wanted to know. He didn't have the magic! Lord Algon chuckled to himself. The tables turned again.

Facegash tried to play off his surprise, acting nonchalant. "We'll show it to you in good time. We're not going to show you everything at once. How do we know you won't just try and steal it from us and stab us in the back?"

Lord Algon stood up and walked towards Facegash. "And how know we ye really have it at all, and are not just bluffing, matey? We find ye been lying to us, what might have happened to ye before be child's play to what will happen to ye now."

Facegash knew Lord Algon was just toying with him, feeling him out to see what he really knew. He had to be as tricky as Lord Algon, or the Gangers were doomed.

"In good time, we'll show you some of our magic, but not all of it. But for now, where's that entertainment?"

Lord Algon frowned glumly, knowing he'd been fought into a stalemate. Then he smiled again, back to the game with Facegash. "Aye, the entertainment."

Lord Algon walked back to his throne and sat down as an old man was led in by two guards. One of the guards turned to Lord Algon. "This man be caught stealing, me lord. We cotton you'd enjoy watching us hang 'im."

"Aye, sounds like good clean fun. Be lively with it."

As the crowd watched, the guards threw a rope around a beam, getting ready for the night's entertainment.

As Starbucks walked inside the Museum to join the others, Misterwizard would have smiled because at his lack of understanding the situation with the Wildies but hearing the news from Foodcourt about Marthastewartliving made him frown with sorrow instead.

The Tribe didn't know which one to look at or listen to first either, and they kept looking back and forth between the two of them. Finally, Misterwizard turned to Foodcourt and everyone in the Tribe followed.

"Tell us Foodcourt," Misterwizard said, "how did this tragic and unfortunate circumstance happen to occur?" Misterwizard asked.

Before Foodcourt could speak, Teavana butted in. "We don't know, Misterwizard. But we think she wandered into the building and didn't see the big hole where Johnny and Ripper fought."

The Tribe members all looked sad and whispered to each other, their faces downcast. Starbucks listened impatiently. "Look, I'm sorry about Marthastewartliving, but I think we have a bigger problem."

Misterwizard walked up to Starbucks and put a comforting arm on his shoulder. "It's all right, Starbucks. We have information on that subject that you do not possess. We have been involved in negotiations with our unpredictable neighbors and may have come to a mutually beneficial arrangement with the more reasonable of their clan."

"A what with who?" Starbucks said.

"Wait a minute, Misterwizard!" Thegap said, interrupting them. "I was the one who found Marthastewartliving. But that's not all I found."

Foodcourt, not wanting to lose his part in things, walked up and piped in as well. "I was with Thegap when we found it, Misterwizard. It was horrible."

Thegap gave Foodcourt an irritated look. "I was only there because you forced me to go."

"Or you wouldn't have found it," Foodcourt shot back.

"Gentlemen," Misterwizard said. "Please tell me just what it is you are at long lengths trying to describe."

Misterwizard and the Tribe listened with growing horror as Thegap and Foodcourt took turns describing how they'd found the body of Leader Nordstrom.

"It's a message, Misterwizard," Foodcourt said, his face dark and somber. "A warning."

"Of course, it is," Thegap said, looking smug.

The Tribe members all talked at once, looks of fright on their faces. Misterwizard didn't speak, just looked at the floor, pondering this new development.

Bathandbodyworks wrung her hands and wailed, "Misterwizard, what do we do? Maybe we would be better to take the buses back to Sanctuary."

"No way!" Starbucks piped in. "This is our home now. We're not going to run like a whipped Barker with its tail between its legs."

The Tribe members all started talking again. Foodcourt looked at Misterwizard. "What do you think, Misterwizard? I say we stay and fight!"

A roar of agreement and raised fists greeted his words.

Misterwizard said, "I too am of the sentiment to stay. For as the old saying goes, you can't run from your problems, you must turn and face them. Washington D.C. is the capitol of this once great nation, and here we should begin to rebuild. Wherever we go, there will be challenges."

"So, who do you think put Leader Nordstrom's body

like that, Misterwizard?" Starbucks asked.

Misterwizard smiled somberly. "We knew that there were still Gangers in the vicinity, as well as Lord Algon and his Wildies. It could have been any of them. We have a herculean task ahead of us, friends. But be of good cheer; we shall overcome and be victorious in our endeavors, if we faint not."

They all nodded and talked amongst themselves. Then Cinnabon turned to Starbucks. "Hey. Weren't Deb and Super with you?"

Starbucks nodded with a look of sadness. "They were behind me, but when I went back to find them, they were gone."

Starbucks turned to Misterwizard. "I heard Johnny, but I couldn't find him either. I'm going back to look for them some more."

Suddenly Cinnabon screamed, making everyone jump. She pointed her finger to what she saw outside the front door, and they all turned to see what she was looking at that made her so scared. What they saw shocked and amazed them all.

"Misterwizard!" Cinnabon said, pulling her son Wheaties close for protection. "It's Johnny! And he's carrying a horrible beastie with him!"

Misterwizard, Starbucks and the tribe members all watched as Johnny, dirty and stained with blood, ran towards them holding the Barker in his hands.

CHAPTER 26

Slon finished praying. As one, the Undergrounders rose and now turned to gaze at Deb and Super, their eyes wide with a mixture of fear and interest. Slon rose from his knees and also turned to look at them, but he frowned with suspicion. Deb felt her insides tighten, and in the back of her mind she thought about her and Super running back down the metal tube if the Undergrounders grew hostile. How far could they get before they were caught? And where would they go, back to the Rat People? It didn't seem like they had any other choice but to hope the Undergrounders were friendly.

Slon stepped forward, this tall white frame eerie against the semidarkness behind him. Loki smiled with joy and pure excitement. "Oh, mighty Slon, look what I have brought to you! They are angels! I saw them fall from the Heavens. They helped me escape from the Rat People. Surely this is a sign from Lincone. He has sent them to save us!"

The people turned and talked to each other in loud, excited voices, looks of hope and joy on their faces. The voices echoed off the close walls of the cave, creating such a loud noise it hurt Deb's ears and she covered them. It hurt Super's ears too, and she scrunched up her face and looked pained.

Slon didn't speak. He just stared at the girls, looking unconvinced. Deb began to get a bad feeling about him, hoping he wasn't another Leader Nordstrom. It seemed everywhere you went, there were more people like Leader Nordstroms. But, she thought, that might also mean that everywhere you went, there were also men like Johnny. That thought made her smile to herself.

Slon raised his hand, and the people quieted down, though they continued to stare at the girls with looks of hope and excitement. Son walked forward haughtily and the Undergrounders all watched him intently. He came right to the door of the metal tube and stared at the girls, turning his head this way and that, making them feel uncomfortable.

"Hey, Toots." Super said. "What's up?" Deb jabbed her in the side, and she looked over at her and shrugged.

"They're angels, Master Slon!" Loki repeated, full of excitement. "It's just like we prayed for. They've come to open the Door to Heaven!"

Slon spoke, and it was clear he didn't believe Loki. He stared at the girls with a harsh look. "Are you really angels? Were you sent from Lincone to save us?"

Deb and Super looked at each other, not sure what to say. Finally Deb said, "We are from what you call Heaven, but we are not-"

Super bumped her, and Deb stopped. Then Super said, "We are here to help you. We can open the Door to Heaven."

Slon remained unconvinced. He smiled cagily. "If ye are angels, prove it. Pray tell me, what is the fifth law of eating?"

"Oh, oh,' Super whispered. It looked like they were caught.

Deb suddenly felt woozy. The interrogation and the weakness from her recent illness combined to make her suddenly feel weak. Her forehead felt hot and she had to grab the side of the doorway to steady herself. She decided to answer truthfully, for there didn't seem to be any choice. "We don't know."

"Aha!" Slon said, victory in his eyes. He turned to the people. "They do not know the fifth law of eating!"

He turned back and stared at the girls again. "The fifth law of eating states, 'always cook the worms before you eat them, for they may carry parasites.'"

"Oooh," Super said, scrunching up her face. "Gross."

"And what is the Supreme Law of the Holy Book? Surely you know that, since it is all about you?"

"We don't know it, okay?" Super said. "Why don't you just tell us?"

"The Supreme Law states that no one is to open the Door to Heaven or venture out into the lands of Radee-active Fallout until the Govermint Representives come to tell us that Order has been retored and the monster Half-life has been vankished."

It was the same thing Loki had told them earlier. Super rolled her eyes. "It's just like Sanctuary all over again."

Deb nodded and decided to speak boldly. "We know of this law. We lived by a similar law in the land where we come from. And we are the Govermint Representives, from the new Govermint. And we're here to tell you, Half-life has been vankished. It is time to open the Door to Heaven!"

The people erupted into excited talking, even louder and more boisterous than before. They turned and smiled at each other and hugged each other.

"Wait!" Slon said, raising a hand again.

"This guy is hard to convince," Super said.

"So, you say. What proof do you have that you are who you say you are? How do we know you aren't spies sent from the Rat People to trick us?"

"Do we look like rat-beasties?" Super said, hands on her hips and head tilted to the side. "We're people, just like you, only from Heaven, got it?"

Slon smiled slyly. "But you just said you were angels. Now you say you are only people."

Deb, worried that Super had said the wrong thing, spoke hastily. "Angels are just people who have gone to Heaven and come back, isn't that right? And we've come back, to lead you to Heaven."

Slon continued to smile an oily smile, and Deb began to dislike him even more. He glanced at the Undergrounders and back at them but spoke to his people. "Do not be so ready to believe these strangers, my people. They do not even know the law or the holy book. They speak of things they do not know."

"You haven't given them a chance," Loki said, frowning sadly. "They're very nice. And they are beautiful. Look at their skin and hair. They have to be angels!"

Slon looked at Loki sternly. "You are still a child, and not very bright."

Loki looked crushed, and Deb wanted to punch Slon in the face. Super felt the same way. She said, "Hey, that wasn't very nice. He's smarter than you, you creepy old man. And a lot nicer too."

"Super!" Deb said, afraid Super was going to get them killed.

But Slon just smiled. "You are defending your friend. This is a good sign."

He turned to his people. "We shall test them and see if they truly be from Lincone or not. If they pass all three tests, then we shall accept them as angels."

"Oh, oh," Super said to Deb. "I don't like the sound of that."

"Me either," Deb said, and felt woozy again. She hoped she wasn't getting sick again. Now would not be a good time.

Slon turned back to Deb and Super and spoke to his people again, but it was plain he was really giving the girls a message. "We shall find out just who, or what, they are. If they be truly angels, we will find out. But if they be spies of the Rat People, we will show them the punishment for being false."

Slon backed up and put his hand out, welcoming them to join the tribe. Loki smiled, happy again. He looked for Harp and saw she smiled back at him. Deb and Super reluctantly walked towards the Undergrounders. Soon they were surrounded by the pale white people with their big, black eyes. The Undergrounders stared at them, turning their heads this way and that and looking them up and down.

Deb and Super looked at each other. "Boy," Super

said. "Did we ever pick the wrong hole to fall into."

Outside Lord Algon's castle on the grounds of Arlington Cemetery, the man who'd saved Facegash and the Gangers stood behind a giant stone statue of a man on a horse-beastie. It was night now, and the Yellow Eye, half closed, shone in the sky. The dark night helped him blend with the shadows, making him disappear unless a person stood very close and saw the whites of his eyes. He leaned just enough to peer into the window of Lord Algon's throne room. A cheery light poured from the window, making it easy to see the people inside. The rifle the man used to kill Lord Algon's guard hung on his back. Through the window, he watched Facegash and the Gangers being entertained by Lord Algon.

He smiled, pleased. It looked like the Gangers and Lord Algon were making a pact, no doubt involving a plan to kill Johnny and the Tribe. A warm glow spread through the man's heart and he congratulated himself for his part in helping the Gangers. He decided he'd done all he could for the Gangers that night. He needed to find some food and a place to sleep.

He wandered through the dark space full of strange stones, feeling the warm night breeze. The scars on his face still ached, especially when it was cold, and his right eye was useless in the dark. He could only see through it in the brightest sunlight. A long ugly scar ran from his left shoulder all the way down to his hand, and his chest was covered with red gashes that still hadn't healed completely. And he limped from where the muscles in his knee had been torn. He felt barely alive, but there was enough fight left in him for what was important: revenge.

Up ahead he saw the flickering light of a fire. It made shadows on the white stones, black figures that danced merrily. He slowed down and crept up to where he could see the fire from behind one of the stones sticking out of the grass.

A Wildie woman sat alone on the crumbled remains of one of the stones next to the fire, roasting some kind of animal over it on a stick. She sang to herself happily in a sing-song voice, and the man saw that she had a bottle she was drinking from. Whatever was in the bottle was making her very happy, and she kept dipping the beastie too low and it would hit the flames and catch on fire for a few seconds, until she lifted it out again and waved it around, putting the flames out.

The man looked around. There was no one else around. He smiled and walked up behind her.

"You, stupid old witch, you're burning that food."

The old lady turned. She gazed on the man's scarred face and gouged eye, horrible in the flickering light and shadows of the fire. She screamed in terror and dropped the stick with the beastie in the fire. She even dropped her bottle as she ran off into the night, still screaming.

The man chuckled, pleased that his looks had scared her. Maybe being disfigured wasn't so bad after all. He picked the stick with the beastie out of the fire and picked up the bottle. He gazed at himself in the bottle's reflection from the firelight. It was Ripper who stared back, a dark smile on his now scarred and disfigured face. His smile disappeared as his mind filled with anger, hotter than the embers of the fire. Johnny did this to him.

Johnny, who now sat in that Museum, like a king on his throne. Johnny made a fool of him, caused him to be attacked by a tiger-beastie and now had even scarred him for life. But he would get his revenge. He'd already killed an old lady in the tribe, and he'd kill more, too. He'd kill them one by one, if that was the only way to get rid of them. And one day, he would face Johnny again, and this time, Johnny wouldn't escape until at least one of them was dead.

He wandered off into the night, eating the beastie on the stick and drinking from the bottle.

The man being hung had been entertaining, and after him Lord Algon had brought in an old man and had him whipped for dropping a basket of food. They'd all laughed and pointed, enjoying the man's misery, all except for Lady Stabs, who claimed to be ill and left. After the tortures, they sat around and ate and drank until they were all very merry. Lord Algon entertained them with gruesome stories of people he'd killed and ghost stories of dead people coming back from the grave and eating their families.

Now it was late. The fire in the fireplace had burned down to embers. Most of the Wildies and Gangers lay on the floor, asleep. But Facegash was still awake, for wariness and caution had kept him sober. He looked over and noticed Lord Algon was awake as well, watching him. He decided now was the time to about their alliance.

Facegash, gaging Lord Algon's reaction, said, "Let's join together. Together we can kill the Newcomers."

Lord Algon nodded, showing Facegash that he was thinking about the same thing. "Aye, 'tis my thoughts as well. Ye, with your magic, and me with my numbers of men. Take them easily we will."

"But when we do, there's one man that I get to kill myself."

Lord Algon smiled, chuckling. "Ye be speaking of this Johnny lad, don't ye? Seems he's made quite a few enemies, and not just lately. But I too have a score to settle and wish to have a part in seeing him pay for his disgustingly courageous deeds."

"He crossed us first," Facegash said stubbornly. "He killed our leader Ripper. We have more right to kill him. Besides," Facegash said, looking off into the distance with a look of pure hatred, "I want to make it last a long time."

"Aye, 'tis how I feel as well. We want the lad to know he's been killed. I say, him what finds the lad first gets first crack. But whichever it be, save him alive for the other to have a share in the killing."

Facegash nodded, and then he looked even uglier and more sinister. "And he has a girlfriend named Deb. I want to kill her, right in front of him, after doing whatever I want to her."

"Aye!" Lord Algon said, his eyes lighting up with unholy fire. "Truly I like thee, matey. Ye and I be cut from the same stock, we be. Perhaps this union of ours be lasting a long time, even after our victory."

They grinned at each other and laughed, both knowing they were in the presence of another man who knew how to lie and be deceitful very well. They were alike in many ways, so both knew they couldn't trust the other for a second.

"Now tell me, young master, about this old man they have amongst them. He it seems to be what gives them their magic."

Facegash nodded. "His name is Misterwizard. And he's the one to really be afraid of. He knows things. He knows how to use the old things from before the Great War. And he can even read the ancient words."

"Hmmm," Lord Algon said, rubbing his chin. "Perhaps this would be a good man to capture alive. He may be useful in the teaching of the magic."

"Yeah, but you'll never get him to do what you say."

Lord Algon sat back, thinking. "There are ways to make a man do what we want, matey, ways of persuasion shall we say. Has he a girl of his own, or someone what might be used in the form of blackmail, as it were?"

"Yeah! Facegash said, snapping his fingers. He turned to Lord Algon.

"Be it a lady friend?"

"It's a lady friend all right, but not like you think. It's a little scrabbler named Sephie. You take her, and Misterwizard will do anything to keep her from being hurt."

"Aye," Lord Algon said with a smile. "Seems we have a plan in the works matey, you and I. On the morrow, carry it out we will." Lord Algon lifted up his glass. "To victory!"

Facegash raised his glass in return. "To victory!"

They both drank, looking into each other's eyes.

In the shadows, Lady Stabs watched. She'd had enough. She was going to go that night and tell Misterwizard everything. She couldn't stand by and let Facegash and Lord Algon do anything to little Sephie. She tiptoed away. When she was clear, she ran for the door. Running outside, she disappeared into the night.

In the Wildie camp, Wolf Fang opened one eye from where he lay inside Boomvoice's shack. Boomvoice had insisted in making him sleep there, had even gave him dinner and forced him to take a bath. Finally, she let him lie down when he acted like he was so sleepy he could barely move, and then she laid down on her blanket on the other side.

Wolf Fang could hear her snoring now. Cursing her annoying kindness, he slowly sat up, trying to make no sound. If she woke up this time, he decided, he wouldn't put on the act, he'd just kill her quietly and leave anyway.

But she didn't wake up, even when he accidentally bumped into the cooking pot hanging from the middle tent pole, making it bong against the wood loudly. She *must be a heavy sleeper,* he thought. He dressed quickly in a dark cape and cowl he kept for traveling to hide his identity and slipped out into the darkness.

Once outside, he ran as fast as he could through the dark night, his cape billowing behind him. He looked like a dark ghost as he ran down the dark streets and across the grassy Mall, and many of the Wildies would have been terrified if they saw him, but no one did.

It was a long way to Lord Algon's castle, and it would take him most of the night on foot, but he kept running even though his legs ached with the strain. He ran silently across the bridge over the running water and on into the darkness beyond. Once again, he thought of how much he hated Boomvoice for delaying him so long. When Lord Algon came to take his revenge, Wolf Fang would make sure she was rewarded for her kindness with death.

After running for what felt like forever and just before he was forced to stop or fall over from the pain in his legs, he finally arrived. In front of him, the gray stone walls of the Cemetery loomed high in the darkness. He followed them, staying in the shadows, until he reached the heavy black gate where torches on long poles illuminated the entryway. A lone guard with a sharp spear walked back and forth inside.

Wolf Fang slowly crept into the torch light, just enough for the guard to sense his presence.

"Anon! Stop, ye dark spirit of the night. Who be ye, sneaking about for mischief no doubt? Speak quick 'fore I coma at ye and spear ye like a fish!"

Wolf Fang lowered his cowl just enough for the guard to see who he was. When the guard did, his face paled with fear. All the guards knew about Lord Algon's spies though few of them had ever seen one. They knew, however, that they all wore the same dark cowls, and if a guard were to delay them on their mission, it would mean a slow, painful death.

"Forgive me, milord, I knew not who ye were. If I caused ye any delay-"

"Let me in, fool," Wolf Fang whispered with venom, scowling impatiently and covering his face again. The guard, hands shaking, quickly opened the gate. Wolf Fang slid past, keeping low to the ground, much like a real wolf-beastie.

The guard watched him run past and disappear into the darkness on the other side. He closed his eyes and sighed with relief, praying to himself the spy was too busy to remember the guard's transgression.

Wolf Fang snuck up to the castle, being careful not to be seen, staying behind the white stones whenever he thought he heard someone near. None of the Wildies were supposed to know of his existence as anything but the simpleton he pretended to be. If they saw him no, it would blow his disguise, and the witness would be quickly killed.

When he was sure no one was watching, he crept to the secret entrance Lord Algon had fashioned at the back of the building, down a broken set of concrete steps to an old door that looked abandoned and long unused. Wolf Fang dug a key out of his pocket and quietly slipped it into the keyhole. He turned it and heard a soft click.

He glanced around one more time to make sure no one saw him. Then he slowly pulled the door open. It scraped on the dirt on the floor, and Wolf Fang slowed down until he could move the door slow enough that it didn't make any sound. When it was just wide enough to slip through he went in and pulled it closed behind him.

Once inside he climbed a rickety set of wooden stairs, some that looked barely strong enough to carry his weight. He walked slowly, for some of the stairs creaked. At the top of the stairs another door faced him. He opened it slowly and peered into a long, narrow hallway with a red carpet and fancy gold paintings on the floor. This hallway led to Lord Algon's sleeping chamber. With a smile, he crept through the door.

He moved quickly now, knowing there would be no one to see him. He reached the door into Lord Algons room. He didn't bother to knock, for he was always welcome by Lord Algon's orders. He opened the door and hurried inside.

Lord Algon's room was even fancier and fuller of luxurious treasures than his throne room. Statues of beautiful maidens stood everywhere. A stuff tiger-beastie Lord Algon has taken from one of the museums stared lifelessly at Wolf Fang as he hurried towards the bed.

Lord Algon lay in bed, snoring loudly, dead to the world. He still wore his elegant clothes, and it was plain he'd been so drunk he didn't bother to change. Wolf Fang looked at his sleeping king and pondered. He thought of how right then he could kill Lord Algon, slit his throat, and assume the throne for himself. It would be so easy. But was he ready to deal with the possible consequences? What if the people didn't accept him as king? What if the guards decided to get revenge?

Someday, he thought, he would have the courage to do it, but not that day. He looked and saw a bowl full of jewels and gold rings. With an eye on the king's sleeping form, he helped himself to a handful of them, stuffing them in his pockets. Lord Algon was no fool, he thought, but he wouldn't miss a few trinkets. Besides, he like to reward his spies, and would likely give Wolf Fang a very nice prize for discovering the plot by the Wildies to join Johnny.

Wolf Fang put his hand on Lord Algon and shook him and was surprised to see the king come instantly awake. It scared him to realize just how light a sleeper the king was, and he decided he was glad he didn't decide to try and kill him.

Lord Algon's eyes opened and he sat up. Wolf Fang, even though he was on Lord Algon's side, still felt a thrill of fear at having the king concentrate on him. He'd seen what happened to Lord Algon's enemies.

Lord Algon recognized him immediately and knew Wolf Fang must have something important to tell him. "What news have ye for me?" Lord Algon whispered even though they were alone, as he stared at Wolf Fang intently.

"A plot, my lord," Wolf Fang whispered back. "One ye shall find mighty interesting. It seems there be a scurvy scalawag amongst yer people who would betray thee. His name be Yellowfang. He be an old man, but not very bright, as ye can surely see."

Lord Algon nodded, his eyes gleaming. "Aye, ye be a good man, Wolf Fang. Tell me more."

A quiet joy filled Wolf Fang's heart at the compliment. It meant good things were coming his way. "It seems there be some of your people what don't have a stomach for the killing and eating of flesh. They talked this Yellowbeard into making a pact with the Newcomers. They be planning on fighting on their side, if there be a battle."

Lord Algon scowled, furious. "They be traitors, be they? We shall make an example of al of them. Have ye their names?"

"Aye, milord. I know all of them."

"Good," Lord Algon said, pleased. He put a hand on Wolf Fang's arm. "Keep that close to thine chest. But now there be another matter I need thee to attend to."

"Anything ye say, milord."

Lord Algon motioned with a finger for Wolf Fang to lean closer. When he did, Lord Algon whispered in his ear. "There be a little lass whose catching may help turn the tide in the upcoming battle. I need thee to go to the Newcomer's home, snatch her and bring her to me."

Wolf Fang looked worried. "In the Newcomer's

home, milord? That will be dangerous."

"Aye," Lord Algon said. "Which is why I reward thee handsomely if ye accomplish the deed."

Wolf Fang knew he had not choice but to comply. He nodded, acting as if he was happy to do what Lord Algon asked.

"I know not what she looketh like, nor her seasons of age. But she goes by the handle of 'Sephie.' She be a sweet little lass, and we'd like to have her here for dinner."

They looked at each other, grinning and chuckling darkly.

"It shall be done, milord. She's as good as yours."

Johnny ran up carrying the Barker. Everyone except Starbucks and Misterwizard shrank back and gasped in fear, for the beastie was covered in blood.

Carny sheltered Mary Poppins Miracle and carried her to the other side of the room, afraid of what the Barker might do.

"A Barker!" Abercrombie yelled.

"Eeww," Sephie scrunched up her nose and frowned at it.

"It's dead!" Thegap said.

"No, it's not, it's going to attack us!" Cinnabon said, as she pulled Wheaties away.

"Don't be silly," Foodcourt said. "Johnny wouldn't bring it in here if it was dangerous. It must be dead."

Johnny's face was a mask of sorrow and urgency as he hurried to Misterwizard. "Misterwizard! It's hurt!

Please save it!"

Misterwizard looked at the Barker and smiled. "A dog-beastie, Barker as you like to all them, and a handsome one at that. A husky, if I'm not mistaken. A very beautiful animal though it seems it's been involved in quite an altercation."

"Please, Misterwizard. It got hurt defending me from another Barker." Johnny's voice broke with sorrow and worry. "It saved my life."

"Come then, not a moment to lose!" Misterwizard led the way back down the stairs to the tunnel into the Bunker. "There are medicines and bandages below. We will do everything we can to save its life. I only hope we are not too late."

As the Tribe followed, all talking excitedly, Johnny and Misterwizard hurried as fast as they could down the steps to the basement.

The trip down to the Bunker never seemed so long to Johnny. He couldn't feel the Barker breathing, and inside, he felt sadness fill him. He was afraid it was already too late.

They finally reached the Bunker, but Misterwizard didn't stop. He led the way down a side passageway to the Dispensary. Going inside with Johnny right behind, Misterwizard pointed to an exam table.

"Place him down, Johnny, and we'll give him a good examination."

Johnny placed the dog on the table and stepped back, feeling utterly helpless. Outside the exam room, the people of the Tribe crowded the doorway, looking in with interest. Misterwizard saw them, walked over and closed the door. As Johnny watched, Misterwizard got to work.

Upstairs. Starbucks watched the crowd head down the stairs. He wanted to go along, but knew he had to go out and look for the girls again, now that the crisis with the Wildies seemed to be over. He looked outside to see night had come, and the Yellow Eye, half-closed, rose into the sky. Dark or no dark, he decided he was going to stay out there until he'd found the girls, even if it meant days and days.

He hurried outside and got back on his Harley. He didn't see Sephie watching him until she spoke.

"Starbucks, can I come?"

"Sorry, Sephie, not this time."

Sephie frowned, disappointed.

Starbucks started his Harley and it roared to life. Sephie smiled, but then went back to frowning.

"Go inside, Sephie. Don't you want to see the Barker Johnny brought?"

Sephie smiled again and nodded. Starbucks waved goodbye and took off. Sephie watched him, wishing she could ride his Harley, it looked like so much fun.

She was just about to turn and go back inside when she saw a lone figure heading for the Museum. It was a girl, and as she grew close, Sephie gasped. It was a Ganger! With eyes wide with fear and excitement, Sephie ran as fast as she could back into the Museum. No one was in sight in the main room, they had all followed Misterwizard and Johnny to see what happened to the Barker. Sephie ran, arms in the air, her heart beating wildly with fear. As she ran she yelled, "The Gangers are attacking! The Gangers are attacking!"

CHAPTER 27

Deb and Super followed Loki who walked ahead of them with his chest held out and a look of pride, as if he had caught them, and they were his prize. As they passed through the middle passageway of the village, people peered at the girls from behind curtains and around cloth doors with looks of awe and pleasure. Deb made sure to smile at them warmly, trying to let them know she was friendly. Super kept turning her head and gazing around, a grin on her face. "Wow, this place is really creepy. Everything they own is some kind of junk from those suitcases, and it's all old and moldy."

"Look, Deb, at that girl over there," Super said, pointing a Harp, who stood peeking out from behind the flap of a tent. "I wonder if that is Harp."

Deb looked at Loki to see him gazing at the girl with longing. "Yep," Deb said.

Super walked over and stood next to Harp. She moved backwards with mild fright and stared.

"Hi! You must be Harp!"

Harp smiled, intrigued and pleased that they knew her name.

"Yes," she said, softly.

"Loki has told us that you are one of the nicest people in the tribe."

"I didn't say that!" Loki said, embarrassed, then he realized his mistake. "Though I thought it." Loki looked even more embarrassed and uncomfortable.

Harp gazed at Loki and then looked at Deb and Super again. "Loki is the nicest, and bravest boy in the tribe too."

Loki couldn't help but grin at her, looking goofy.

"He will someday be in charge instead of Slon. Loki is smart."

"Aw, shucks," Loki said, looking uncomfortable.

"Come on," Deb said. "We've embarrassed these two long enough."

Super grinned, and Deb and Super started walking again. Loki quickly followed, feeling odd, and Harp watched them leave.

"Hope we didn't embarrass you too much, Loki," Deb said.

Loki grinned. "It's okay. I'm glad you talked to her. I've always been too shy to."

"Well, it's obvious she likes you, Loki. Now you know." Super said.

"Loki," Deb asked, "how long have your people lived here?"

Loki looked at her but kept walking. "Since before I was born. Before my mother and father were born, too.

Nobody knows how long." From behind him, Deb saw Loki frown. "We can't stay much longer though. We have to get out."

"Why is that?" Super asked, ducking a low hanging basket of moldy fruit.

Loki glanced at them and then looked forward again, glum. "Because of the Rat People. They are so mean. They won't leave us alone."

Deb and Super looked at each other with mild alarm. Deb asked, "Where are we going now?"

"To my place," Loki said. "I want to show you to my mother and father."

The girls smiled at each other and kept following Loki.

They came to one room and Loki turned and smiled at them. "Come on!" He walked inside and they followed.

They found a small square room with walls made of blankets. Inside, benches taken from the long metal tube sat next to the walls. A fire pit sat in the corner, for there was no roof. Paper pictures, mostly faded and dirty, hung pinned to the blanket walls. At the back of the space, blankets lay on the floor with a makeshift pillow, someone's bed. A few feet away lay another one, though it was smaller, probably Loki's.

Two people stood in the room when they entered. One was a man of about forty seasons, though his lined white face looked older, as if he'd been through tough times. He was short and squat, with a square body like a box. Next to him stood a plump but attractive woman with long white hair, about the same age. She was short but thin and petite, with delicate, small hands and an attractive face. They both turned as Loki and the girls entered. When they saw Deb and Super, the man and woman ran to each other and hugged with fright. Then they stared, not unkindly but nervously.

"Don't be afraid, mother, father. These are the angels. And they're my friends."

Deb smiled warmly and walked forward to greet them. "My name is Deb. And this is Super. Hello."

Loki's parents smiled, though they still seemed a little scared. They separated and stood looking uncomfortable, staring.

The man said, "My name is Bot, and this is my wife, Pak. Welcome to our home."

"Nice place," Super said, though it didn't sound as if she meant it.

Pak walked forward, seeming to lose her fear. She smiled, but in her eyes, there was a hint of sorrow. "We are so glad you are here. It is a miracle." Her lip started to tremble, and she looked like she was about to cry. Bot walked over and held her again. "We are all so afraid. If something doesn't happen soon, we will all die."

Deb and Super glanced at each other. The whole thing was getting weirder and weirder. "Look," Super said. "About us being angels, don't expect too much. The only thing we might be able to do is open the Door to Heaven. And we're not really sure about that."

"But we are here to help, in any way we can." Deb said. "Please tell us what is going on?"

Bot and Pak looked at each other meaningfully and then walked to one of the benches and sat down. Deb and Super sat on the bench on the other side, and Loki sat on the floor on his blanket.

"Loki didn't tell you?" Pak asked Deb.

"He told us about the Rat People."

Pak wrung her hands and looked miserable. "That is the worst of it, yes. The Rat People come every night. We fight them off, but many die. But there is also the food. We grow some things, but nothing grows well. We eat the beasts we can catch, but they are growing smarter, and harder to find. And there is the water."

"Water?" Super said.

Pak nodded. "I'll show you."

Pak stood up and walked back into the main passage. Deb and Super followed, with Bot and Loki right behind. Pak led them down the main aisle, past more and more home spaces. She walked fast and Deb and Super hurried to keep up. Finally, she reached the end of the Village on the other side. Beyond it lay another long, dark passage, for the torches stopped just past the village. Pak walked down the metal rails into the darkness, and Deb wondered how far they would have to go.

Suddenly Deb felt something wet on her feet. She looked down to see they were walking in water. As they walked, it grew deeper, until it covered her shoes. She slowed down, about to tell Pak to stop, but then Pak did. In the dim light that came from the lights above the village, they saw her point to a wall.

"There."

Deb and Super looked. A large crack extended from the floor of the raised platform all the way up to the rounded ceiling. And from it, water seeped out.

Pak turned to them. "It grows worse every day. The crack grows bigger. And do you hear that sound?"

They all tried to be quiet and listen. Soon they heard a roaring sound, somewhere deep in the wall.

Pak spoke again, her face grim. "Bot says it is a river. He has seen old books and showed them to me, ones he found in Train. They show a blue ribbon that is water flowing. The river is fast and mighty. And soon it will break through the wall and wash us all away."

"What is Train?" Super asked.

Loki laughed. "You walked through it."

Then Super realized that must have been the name for the long metal tube. "Oh, that," she said.

"How long do you have, Bot?" Deb asked him.

"I don't think very long. And the sound gets louder every day too."

The girls looked at each other, both thinking the same thing.

"We have to convince this Slon guy fast," Super said. "I don't want to drown down here."

"Me either," Deb said.

Johnny paced outside of the exam room where Misterwizard worked on the Barker. Surrounding him was the whole Tribe, whispering among themselves and wondering about all the strange things that had been happening lately. It seemed like every few minutes, some new and surprising event took place, and they were all having a hard time keeping up.

"Johnny," Foodcourt asked his son, when Johnny happened to walk towards him in his pacing. "Where did you find this Barker? Why are you trying to save it? I don't understand."

The rest of the Tribe nodded in agreement. Johnny looked at his father with a confused expression, trying to find the words to explain. "Father, this Barker isn't like the others. It was friendly. It protected me. It was almost as if it wanted to be my friend."

Foodcourt shook his head in bewilderment. "A good Barker? What is the world coming to? So many changes. I don't know if I can keep up."

Teavana spoke up. "Johnny, are you sure it wasn't just pretending, acting friendly until it could gain your trust, just so it could attack?"

"No Mother," Johnny said, "It's different. You'll see," he turned and looked towards the exam room, "If Misterwizard can save it."

"Well," Carny said, pulling Miracle closer, "I'm never letting that beastie near Miracle. You may trust it, but I won't."

"I think it should be shot," Cinnabon said.

Johnny glared at her. "No one is hurting it. It's my friend." The rest of the Tribe glared at Cinnabon, and she just shrugged and held her son Wheaties closer.

Just then Sephie came running down the tunnel. "The Gangers are attacking! The Gangers are attacking!"

Everyone in the Tribe yelled at once and confusion reigned once again. Half the Tribe tried to run enter the tunnel at once, and it became choked with people. Sephie ran back down the tunnel to avoid all the people heading for her. Johnny yelled, trying to be heard over the din, but it there were too many people yelling.

The stairs were so clogged that finally everyone had to stop moving and the noise lessened. Johnny could finally be heard over the crowd.

"Listen to me! Listen!"

Everyone settled down and turned around, looks of fear and excitement on their faces.

"Go back and get some weapons, knives and spears. I will go check it out. If the Gangers have already taken the Museum, we'll need to make a stand here. Now clear out of the way so I can go see what's happening."

The people all nodded and slowly cleared the way for Johnny. He pushed his way past them and entered the long, dark tunnel. "Sephie!" He yelled. "Sephie, come back!" But she was already far down the tunnel. Johnny worried if the Gangers really were attacking, she'd be running right into them. He ran as fast as he could up the narrow passageway.

When he reached the Museum, he stopped and looked around. There was no sign of Sephie in the basement. He ran up the stone steps to the first floor.

The first floor of the Museum was like a maze, full of glass cabinets with old things from before the Great War, and papers hanging from the ceiling with words all over them. Narrow passages led in both directions making it hard to see. Johnny ran down one as fast as he could towards the Main Hall.

When he made it to the Main Hall, he looked everywhere for Sephie. The floor, a sea of white marble, stretche from one side of the room to the other, dotted by stone benches and paper displays. There was no Sephie. But standing in the middle of the floor, one person stared at him. It was a Ganger.

Johnny scowled and took out his sword. He moved towards the lone figure slowly, cautiously. He looked behind the figure, but there was no one else. As he reached the Ganger, he realized with surprise that it was a girl. She simply stood there, watching, him. She didn't raise a weapon or even look like she was ready to fight, she just looked at him.

He was even more surprised to see her knife on the floor five feet in front of her, as if she was surrendering. Johnny stopped ten feet away. "What have you done with Sephie? If you hurt her, I'll kill you, I swear."

The girl looked confused. "I don't know who Sephie is. Is she the little girl I saw run past?" She pointed to a left passageway. "I think she went down there."

Johnny glanced behind the girl again, even more confused. "What do you want? Were you sent by the Gangers who are left?"

The girl smiled nervously. "No, I came on my own. If he knew I was here, Facegash would kill me. "

"Facegash?" Johnny said, wondering just what she was talking about, and suspecting some kind of trick. He circled around behind her and went to the door. She kept talking to him as he walked to the door. "Facegash took over after you killed Ripper. He's gathering what's left of the Gangers together. He's made a pact with Lord Algon."

Johnny reached the door. It was open, but there was no one else in sight. He closed the door tight and faced her again. "So, are you here to spy on us, find out our strengths and report back, is that it? Let me tell you, we're ready to fight again. We're stronger now than we've ever been."

"I know you are," Lady Stabs said. She looked sad, and she blinked hard. Her lips trembled. "I-I'm Lady Stabs. I know you have no reason to trust me. But I'm here to surrender and tell you what they're planning. I want to join you."

This was something Johnny didn't expect. He lowered his weapon, but only slightly. He stared at her, trying to decide if she was telling the truth. "A Ganger, join us? W   h   y   ?   "

Lady Stabs wrung her hands together and bit her lip. "I'm not like the other Gangers. I grew up in the Gangers. My mom and dad were Gangers. They treated my mother terrible, and finally she died when one of their Barkers attacked her. They just laughed. My father died when a group of Wildies attacked a scouting party he was in. They just ran away and let the Wildies kill him. I had to become tough and mean and act like them. But I always hated them. I never had no choice. Until you guys came along."

Johnny moved towards her, cautiously, wondering if she was telling the truth, or just making it up. "Why didn't you join us at Sanctuary?"

"'Cause you were always behind them walls, and there was no way to get in. And I didn't know you, Johnny. There was only that mean Leader Nordstrom. Now everybody has seen what a good, fair man you are, and how you want to make a good world for everybody. I just want to be part of it, that's all."

Johnny smiled. Could it be true? Could she really want to join the Tribe? And what if there were more Gangers who felt like her, who just wanted to live a good life and turn their back on the killing and robbing? It was a nice thought, Johnny decided. But what if it was all a trap?

Suddenly Stephie came around the corner. She was on the other side, and Lady Stabs stood between them. Johnny's heart jumped and he ran to try and get to Stephie before the Ganger girl could.

But he was too late. Stephie walked right up to the Ganger girl, carrying her green frog. Lady Stabs smiled at her and knelt down in front of her.

"Hello. Who's this?" Lady Stabs said, petting the green frog. "

"That's Kermit," Stephie said. "I thought you were the Gangers, but it's just you, isn't it? Are you going to attack us?"

"No, of course not," Lady Stabs said. She saw Johnny coming and backed away. Johnny ran up to Stephie and scooped her up in his arms.

"Listen," Lady Stabs said. "I'll do anything. I'll do the chores nobody wants to do. I'll be your slavey. Please don't send me back to Facegash. He'll kill me for sure."

Johnny and Sephie stared at Lady Stabs, Johnny with a mixture of suspicion and uncertainty, Sephie just with a happy smile.

Johnny pondered. What should he do? If she were a spy, she could be pretending to be nice just to find out their defenses. Then later she'd leave again, and this Facegash would know what weapons they had and where the weaknesses in their Museum were. But if she was serious, it could mean a chance to show the Gangers that they didn't have to be the Tribe's enemies.

Johnny made a decision. "Sit on the bench over there," he pointed to a stone bench by the wall, "and wait. Misterwizard is busy, but when he's done, he'll talk to you. Then the Tribe will have a say. If everyone agrees, then we may give you a chance."

Lady Stabs smiled, her face full of joy and hope. Her eyes moistened with tears and it looked strange to see a tough looking Ganger with half her head shaved and a skull tattoo in a leather jacket with chains crying. "Thank you, Johnny. I knew I was right about you."

Lady Stabs walked over and sat meekly on the bench, her hands folded. Sephie looked at Johnny. "Johnny, is she going to join us? She's nice."

Johnny smiled at her. "I don't know, Sephie. We'll have to find out if she really is nice, or just pretending. Carrying Stephie, Johnny walked over to where Lady

Stabs' knife lay. He set Stephie down and picked up the knife. As Stephie watched, Johnny looked at it, wondering how many people from the Tribe it had killed. He looked at Lady Stabs. Could a Ganger really change? It didn't seem very likely.

He stuffed the knife into his belt, put his own sword back in its scabbard and picked up Stephie again.

Then Johnny had a terrible thought, but one he had to ask about. "Lady Stabs, did the Gangers have two girls captive, one a blond and the other with black hair?"

Lady Stabs smiled. "You mean your girlfriend Deb and her friend? No, Johnny. They didn't have them, at least not where I could see. And the Wildies don't have them, or they'd be parading them around, for sure."

Her words gave Johnny hope that at least the girls weren't captured. But where could they be? He had to get back out there looking for them. They might be trapped somewhere, waiting for him and Starbucks to rescue them. Johnny walked back to the stairs to the basement, glancing back at Lady Stabs now and then to make sure she wasn't trying anything. When he reached the stairs, he called down.

"Foodcourt! Father, can you hear me?"

He waited a moment, hearing hushed voices all speaking at once. Then he heard the hurried shuffling of feet and soon saw Foodcourt hurrying up the steps. His eyes were wide with excitement and he smiled, happy to be called on to do something important.

"Yes, Johnny?" His eyes twinkled. "Are the Gangers attacking?"

"Not yet," Johnny said. He turned and led Foodcourt back to the Main Hall. When Foodcourt saw Lady Stab sitting on the bench, he gasped in amazement.

"A Ganger!"

"Yes, Father," Johnny said, watching her.

"But they're not attacking?" Foodcourt said, looking confused.

"No. She came alone. She claims she wants to leave the Gangers and join us."

Foodcourt smiled wide with humor and interest. "Does she know? Isn't that a new twist?"

Johnny smiled too, for Foodcourt's excitement was contagious. "Can you watch her for me until I can get Misterwizard to talk to her?"

Foodcourt nodded eagerly. "Oh yes, my boy, gladly. I'll make sure she doesn't try anything!"

As Foodcourt grinned from ear to ear, happy to be part of something interesting, Johnny gave him his own sword and positioned him on a bench nearby where he could watch Lady Stabs and still be comfortable. Then Johnny carried Stephie back down the steps to the tunnel to tell Misterwizard he was going to leave again and go looking for the girls. He hoped he didn't just let an enemy soldier come into his camp.

Facegash woke up and stretched. He sat up and look at his surroundings and smiled. He lay in a huge bed with gold blankets, sheets and pillows. Above the bed some kind of fake ceiling hung, draped in the same gold fabric. It was the nicest bed Facegash had ever slept in. The sheets felt like he was sleeping on water, or the sky, and he'd never slept so well in his life.

He looked around the room. The walls were also

painted a dark gold, and were covered with huge, elegant paintings. Laying on the rich carpet were two serving girls Lord Algon had told to serve him, surrounded by empty wine bottles and half eaten plates of food. Fancy couches and chairs filled the room in elegant green and blue fabrics with gold thread mixed in.

If this was what it was like to live like a king, Facegash could get used to it, he thought. No wonder kings fought so hard to keep their thrones; once you lived like this, how could you go back to living in old abandoned buildings and rusted out cars?

It gave you a fever, one of desire and greed. It made you want to do anything to keep it, even murder. Facegash felt the fever taking hold of him. His mind raced with dark thoughts, and a bead of sweat formed on his brow.

Kill Lord Algon and take over the throne yourself. The Wildies won't care; as long as you act tough, they'll follow you.

The idea swam in his mind like a shark-beastie, making small circles.

After all, Lord Algon is crazy, no one will miss him. And don't the Gangers deserve to be the ones in charge?

He nodded to himself. The only question was how. Lord Algon had guards, big, strong ones, and Facegash had no idea how loyal they were. But then, the guards had seen what Lord Algon did to the others, putting them in the Arena, and even worse, cooking and eating some of them. Surely if they had a chance to serve a lord who was less crazy, less likely to go on wild insane rampages, they would jump at the chance. And Facegash was smarter, meaner, and more ruthless. If he could just show all of Lord Algon's men these facts, they would surely be glad to help him give Lord Algon a taste of his own medicine.

How to start? He decided the first thing he'd have to do is feel out the guards, see which ones seem most likely to join him. In other words, the ones that hated Lord Algon the most. Surely there were at least a few with ambitions of their own.

Facegash stopped making plans and yawned. He looked around for a cup with something still in it and found a glass half full of wine. He drank it down and then reached onto the floor for a hunk of meat on a plate to nibble on.

The door burst open. Facegash looked up. Badluck stood there, staring at him with wide eyes. Facegash scowled, feeling like a king, his face full of indignant fury. "How dare you burst into my room, you stupid worthless piece of dirt? Why aren't you down in the main hall sleeping with the others?

"I-I'm sorry, Facegash," Badluck stuttered. "There's just something I think you need to know."

Now what, thought Facegash. "Okay, spill it all ready."

Badluck nodded his head, looking like a stupid bird-beastie looking for worm-beasties. "Nobody's seen Lady Stabs anywhere."

Facegash laid back on his golden pillow, relieved. "Is that all? She's probably off using the Necessary Room." He laughed at his own joke and took a bite of the meat.

Badluck grinned at the joke but then frowned again. "Nobody seen her since we left Lord Algon's throne room. In fact, she was gone halfway through the meal."

An alarm went off in Facegash's mind, the one that always went off when his mind sensed possible danger. It was an alarm he'd learned to listen to, at least until he was sure it was false, for listening to it had saved his skin many times.

He put the meat down on the covers and frowned, thinking. Then he smiled again and said, "She's not bad looking. Have you looked in Lord Algon's chamber?" Badluck grinned again but remained nervous. "She ain't there. He left with two serving girls."

"Do you think he might have decided to take us out, one by one?" Facegash said. Badluck shrugged.

Facegash groaned inside. He was hoping for a nice quiet morning, maybe spent getting to know the servant girls better, but he should have known that wasn't going to happen. They were in the enemy's camp, and there was never a moment to let your guard down. And ever since they started tangling with Johnny, they hadn't had a day of peace.

"What do you think, Badluck?" Facegash said, taking a big risk asking for advice. It was not something to do as a leader very often, for it made you look weak. But there was no one else there, and if Badluck mentioned that he did it to anyone, he'd live to regret it.

Badluck walked further into the room, almost falling when he stumbled over a sleeping servant girl. He bumbled his way over to the bed and leaned close to Facegash. Facegash, despite his irritation at Badluck coming into his room at all, leaned toward Badluck and listened.

"One of the girls said," he paused and looked around, as if someone were listening in.

"What? What did she say?" Facegash said, impatiently.

"She said she heard Lady Stabs once say she thought

we should all just give up and surrender to Johnny."

Badluck's words set a thousand alarms off in Facegash's head, for his battle instincts told him they were nearing the truth. He himself had heard Lady Stabs say many times that they should leave Johnny and the Tribe alone and go back to Misterwizard's castle. And even before that, way back when the Tribe still lived in Sanctuary, he remembered something she'd said. She said, "Do you think if we asked, maybe they'd let us live with them in there?"

Lady Stabs was always a strange one, never as tough or cruel as the other girls, even though she put up a good front. She spent a lot of time by herself too, staring up at the lights in the sky. Facegash knew they were in big trouble. He knew now without a doubt Lady Stabs had run off to warn Johnny.

The thought filled his mind with such anger and hatred for Lady Stabs that he physically reached out his hands and pretended to strangle her. Badluck watched him nervously, wondering if Facegaash had finally lost his mind.

"That-that-that rotten tramp!" Facegash finally stammered out. He looked at Badluck. "Do you have any idea what she might have done to us? Lord Algon may think we're spies and kill us all."

Badluck nodded, looking scared. "She really stabbed us in the back, all right."

Facegash scowled. "When I catch her, the things I'm gonna do to her."

"Forget about that now, Facegash. What are we gonna do?"

Facegash got up and put on his clothes, his pants and white tee shirt and black leather jacket, while Badluck walked around in a nervous circle.

Facegash grabbed Badluck and jerked him around until he was looking in Facegash' eyes. "I tell you what we do. You go down and tell the rest of the Gangers not to say nothing. We're gonna have to make something up, get this Lord Algon to attack today. We got to hit Johnny and the Tribe again before they get even more set up, before they turn that place they're in into another Sanctuary."

Badluck nodded and turned to go, but Facegash gripped his arm tighter and made him look at him again. "Not a word, got it? And when we kill Johnny and all the others, Lady Stabs is mine. I'll make sure she wished she'd never been born."

CHAPTER 28

Wolf Fang ran swiftly, keeping himself hidden behind buildings and piles of debris. The Red Eye was already creeping over the horizon, which disappointed him. It would be much harder to get the girl in the daylight. Still, it could be done, if he was very quiet, and lucky.

Arlington cemetery where Lord Algon had his castle was on the opposite side of a large river that ran through the city from where Johnny and the Tribe had set up their new Sanctuary. The river split the city into two parts, making a perfect defense for either side from the other. Wolf Fang knew if Johnny and his Tribe managed to gain all the land on the other side of the river, it would be very hard for Lord Algon to beat them. But that was Lord Algon's problem. Wolf Fang wasn't an expert at war, and he didn't really care. His specialty was killing in the dark and doing dirty deeds when no one was looking.

He reached the river and had to stop. Now that the Red Eye was rising, there was very little concealment on the bridge that crossed the river, so he had to make sure no one was watching. When he was fairly sure there was no one in sight, he hurried across the bridge as fast as he could. In the far distance between the tall white buildings he could see the grassy Mall, full of the Wildie's shacks. He reached the other side of the bridge and hurried to the nearest building to hide behind it. He looked at the shacks and sneered. He was disappointed his news about the traitors didn't cause Lord Algon to come in force and destroy them all that very night. He couldn't wait until Lord Algon paid the cowardly ones there for their betrayal. They could join Johnny and the Newcomers, only to die with them. It wouldn't be long, he knew. Lord Algon would surely attack that very day. He had to get the little girl quickly, so Lord Algon could use her in the battle.

He ran from building to building, silent as a shadow, as fast as a blink. He was good at hiding, had been all his life. He was a master thief, and his parents kicked him out when he was young for stealing from them. He paid them back though. He stabbed them in their sleep and left them where the beasties could eat them. The thought of his revenge on them still made his heart warm.

As he reached the buildings on the near side of the grassy Mall, he heard voices. He slowed down and hid, then peeked out. It was the Wildies, all right; they were meeting in a big gathering. As he watched, they talked to each other excitedly, gesturing with their hands and arguing with each other. He saw Boomvoice, talking loud as usual, and being bossy.

He carefully walked around to the other side of the building he was near and ran behind it so they wouldn't see him. Then he ran from building to building until he reached the Museum of American History where the Newcomers lived. He positioned himself at a corner of the Museum next to it, and watched, waiting to see what would happen.

A young man came out, fifteen seasons or so. He was black and he wore leather pants a, a red cotton shirt and a leather vest. And right behind him came a little girl. Wolf Fang's eyes opened wide with dark delight. This had to be Sephie, his target. But to his dismay, she went back inside. The young man climbed on some kind of contraption. It made a loud roar and he zoomed off. Wolf Fang had never seen such a thing, and it amazed him, but he put it aside. He didn't care about such things, he only cared about killing and thievery.

He wasn't sure what to do, so he decided he'd just wait, and see what happened. Sooner or later, he's see his chance.

Deb and Super were followed everywhere they went, not only by Loki, but always by two or three other members of his tribe. They began to find that most of the people were friendly. But there was a desperation, a fear in their eyes that never left. The girls began to realize that things were very bad for Loki and his people, and they didn't have long to survive if they didn't escape their dark, underground dungeon.

Deb and Super were given a room of their own, and it

was the best the Undergrounders could give them, but they quickly found out the bed and blankets were dirty and unpleasant. And then they had their first meal with them.

The Undergrounders sat in a large circle on the raised platform on the opposite side of the village from the passage that led to the Door to Heaven. On this side, piles of cloth served for seats on the cold, marble stone. Near where they all sat, pots of some kind of food were heated over an open fire. Deb and Super sat next to Loki and his parents.

The girls were both starving, having eaten nothing since they arrived. Deb felt her fever coming back, probably from lack of food, and she just hoped there would be enough to eat to at least stop the rumbling in her stomach.

"Loki," Super asked him, "where to you get food down here?"

Loki shrugged, as if it was obvious. "From the ground, mostly. We dig them up. And sometimes flying things come, we don't know from where. They are a gift from Lincone. And the rats too. We eat them when we catch them."

Super looked at Deb. "Bug-beasties, bird-beasties and rat-beasties. Yum."

Deb grinned at her. "Right now, I'd eat anything. I'm starving."

The woman stirring the pot, large and husky, her white skin looking strange in a polka-dotted dress she must have found in one of the suitcases, nodded to Slon and he smiled.

"It is time for blessing of the food." Everyone looked at him, and he in turn looked at Deb and Super. "Why don't we let our angels give the blessing? I'm sure they know how."

Deb and Super looked at each other with concern then back at Slon.

Slon watched them a sly smile on his face. "This will be their first test, to see if they truly are angels."

Deb and Super hesitated, not sure what to do. Then Loki leaned towards Deb and whispered in her ear. "Just use Lincone's name a lot and say you're thankful."

Deb nodded at him, raised her hands and closed her eyes. Super followed suit, and soon the whole tribe did as well.

"Oh, wonderful Lincone," Deb said, "Ye who came down from the Heavens. For what we are about to partake of, may we be truly grateful."

She finished. All the people smiled and clapped. Slon looked disappointed, as if he was hoping she'd be exposed as a fraud. He nodded to the woman at the pot, and she cheerfully began dipping a wooden spoon into the pot and pouring gray liquid with lumps in it into bowls.

Deb and Super looked at the mixture, trying their best not to grimace or show any disgust, but it wasn't easy.

"Well," Super said, "It's food."

"Is it?" Deb said back to her.

Suddenly someone screamed. Everyone looked to see what was wrong. Deb and Super looked too. It was a little girl and she looked terrified. She stared at something in the dark, and Deb and Super looked to see what she was looking at. Then they saw it.

In the shadows next to the train, the wolf-beastie stood, its teeth bared and a look of hunger in its eyes.

The people all jumped up in fear and ran the opposite direction.

"What is it?" One woman wailed.

"A creature from Hell!" Another yelled.

"Run, run!" Another screamed, and the people began to do just that, running down the passageway into the darkness.

But the little girl, terrified into immobility, stood in place, her little white knees shaking. She had long white hair, and she held her hands to her face, staring at the slavering beastie.

The little girl reminded Deb of Sephie. Without thinking, Deb jumped up and ran towards the wolf-beastie, drawing Sting from its scabbard. Super quickly followed and together the girls ran as fast as they could, hoping to get to the girl before the wolf-beastie struck.

The wolf-beastie started towards the little girl, and soon it was running. It was so intent on the little girl it didn't see Deb and Super run up. Just before it leapt on the little girl, Deb reached her and she slashed her sword at the wolf-beastie, hitting it good and solid on its head.

Surprised and shocked, the wolf-beastie fell to the ground, flailing. It quickly got back to its feet and tried to figure out what just happened. Then it saw Deb and Super. It snarled and circled around them, its dark eyes flashing with hatred.

"Get out of here you mangy wolf-beastie," Super said, trying to act tough, but really just as scared as the rest. She'd never faced down a wolf-beastie before, and though she held the sword out in front of her, she wasn't sure she'd even know how to use it to defend herself.

"Listen," Deb said. "I'm going to circle behind it. You keep it distracted."

"Oh, sure," Super said. "Use me for bait. What if it decides to pounce?"

"Then run," Deb said, as she slowly moved far enough away so the wolf-beastie lost sight of her.

"What kind of a plan is that?" Super said.

"The only one I got," Deb said. When she was sure the wolf-beastie was no longer watching her, she snuck up behind it. "Make some noise to keep it looking at you."

"Hey, wolf-beastie. Look at me." Super said. "Don't I look good and tasty?"

The wolf-beastie stared at her but kept glancing at the little girl, who still stood frozen, with desire. She looked like a tasty morsel to it, but bigger girl just looked dangerous. It tried to think of how to get to the little girl, snap its jaws on her and carry her off without the girl with the sharp thing getting it first. It tried to move towards the little girl, slowly, hoping the girl with the sharp thing didn't notice, but she did. She moved to block its way and it stopped, disappointed.

Deb snuck up behind the wolf-beastie. She moved until she was at its side. Then with a mighty thrust, she stabbed it in the side with Sting. The wolf-beastie yelped in pain and spun. It tried to snap at Deb, but Super rushed in and stabbed it from the other side.

Quickly it was over. The wolf-beastie lay dead. Deb and Super grinned at each other, not believing that they actually did it. They walked over and high-fived each other.

"Yippee!" Super said. "Look what we did!"

"Wouldn't Johnny be proud of us?" Deb said.

The Undergrounds slowly came back, wearing looks of amazement and joy. The little girl walked up to Deb.

Deb put her arm around her and the little girl gave her a hug.

"You saved my life," the little girl said. "You're a wonderful angel."

The Undergrounders surrounded them. They stared with wonder down at the dead wolf-beastie.

"They killed the demon from another world," one man said.

"They really are angels!" a woman said.

Loki ran up, his chest out, full of pride. "Didn't I tell you?" He grinned from ear to ear and strutted around. Bot and Pak ran up as well.

"You have saved us," Pak said. "Thank you."

"And you know what the best part is?" Super said cheerfully. "Now we have some nice wolf-beastie to eat, instead of that, whatever it was."

The Undergrounders cheered. Some of the men came and picked up the wolf-beastie. They lifted it over their heads and paraded it towards the cooking pot.

Slon walked up and surveyed the scene. Bot turned to him. "Surely this is test number two. They have saved us from a monster."

Slon stared at Deb and Super intently. And then he did something they didn't expect. His frown lessened, and he looked almost friendly. A small measure of hope came to his face. Deb suddenly realized Slon was not trying to be mean or bossy like Leader Nordstrom, he was just trying to be a good leader, and he was scared for his people.

"Yes. This qualifies as test number two. Maybe they really are angels." Slon looked so sad and hopeful Deb felt a little frightened. What if they couldn't help the Undergrounders? What if it turned out they were all trapped in the tunnel until the water came and drowned them all?

She put those thoughts out of her head. They had to help the Undergrounders, that's all there was to it. Together, they had to find a way out, before it was too late.

CHAPTER 29

Lord Algon awoke and opened his eyes. He sat up in his huge four-poster bed with its black silk sheets and thick fur blankets made of many different beastie hides sewn together. Immediately two serving girls ran up to him with wine and meat on trays. He grabbed a glass of wine and motioned them away, crossly.

He had not slept well, for he knew that the morning would be a day of destiny. This day he would once again attack the Newcomers. But this time, he would use every weapon and trick he had to fight, and he had the Gangers' magic to help them. And yet, he felt afraid, as if the battle was already lost. The Newcomers were making deals with some of his own people, and he didn't trust the Gangers. He knew perfectly well their leader, this one with the gash on his face, would kill Lord Algon the first chance he found. And where was that spy of his with the little girl? He wanted to wait until he came back with her, but he didn't dare hesitate. The longer he waited, the more of his own people might defect to the Newcomers. And the more time the Newcomers had to prepare, the better defenses they would have. He had to strike now.

He climbed out of bed and, with the help of his servant girls, dressed in his clothes for battle. They consisted of a white shirt streaked with blood, a long black leather jacket with bones attached to it, black leather pants, long black leather boots and a wide brimmed black leather hat. He looked at himself in the reflecting glass. His rugged and frightening appearance cheered him slightly, but not enough to allay all his fears.

There was still the other option, he thought to himself as he put on his black leather gloves with the metal spikes, though he hated the thought of it. He could take as many treasures and trinkets as he could carry, and leave, before anyone else knew he was gone. It meant going back to being a traveling thief and murderer, which was what he'd been before.

Lord Algon started out his life in a small village south of Washington D.C., in a place with the words Portsmouth on the signpost. He lived with a small group of Wildies who lived by the ocean and lived off the fish-beasties they caught. They lived simple lives, and many died from the Sickness, but enough survived to eke out an existence, and for the most part, they were happy.

Then when Lord Algon was five, the Piratts came. They arrived one night in big wooden boats. Lord Algon, who was simply Algon then, awoke to the sounds of screams and fires burning outside his little wooden shack. He ran outside to see the Piratts killing and looting. One of them, a Piratt who called himself Blackbeard ran up to him brandishing a long sword. The Piratt was huge and wearing a long, velvet coat. He didn't have a black beard, in fact his hair was red, but he was still terrifying. As Algon screamed, Blackbeard grabbed him and carried him away. Algon's last sight of his village was of the houses all burning, men and women, just shadows in the dark, yelling and screaming as Piratts chased them.

Algon spent all his years growing up with the Piratts, learning to speak the language they made for themselves and how to rob and pillage. He soon became one of the most ruthless and cold hearted Piratt and became well respected by the others.

Then one night when he was fifteen seasons old, he decided he wanted to be in charge. He snuck into Blackbeard's cabin on his ship and stuck a knife in him, killing him. The next morning, he declared himself to be the Captain. But the first mate, a scurvy dog named Crooked Walk, had plans of his own. One day Algon found himself waking to a bag over his head. Before he could even yell or fight back, someone hit him with a hard, wooden stick and everything went black.

He awoke to find himself stranded on the shore near Washington D. C. with a huge headache. The ship and his crew were long gone. That was years ago, but he always vowed he would someday find Crooked Walk and pay him back. But in the meantime, he had to find a way to live. And so, he learned to steal and kill. His few days as Captain helped him learn how to convince people to do what he wanted, and so soon he had a band of thieves and murderers following him.

He kept building his band, until he was now Lord

Algon of the Wildies. The thought of having to turn tail and run, just because of the Newcomers, filled him with anger and fright. What was even worse was who he would be losing to, this Johnny who was still merely a lad and an old man with long white hair and whiskers. It was too humiliating to even think about.

He decided he would prepare a travel bag full of food and valuable things and have it staged. If the battle started to go bad, he would turn and run. And then he would come back someday and get revenge on this Johnny and his old man, just like he would on Crooked Walk and the scurvy dogs who betrayed him.

He ordered the servant girls out and called for his first mate Hardhitter. Hardhitter came in, holding a servant girl around the waist and looking as if he'd already started drinking. Lord Algon grew angry. "Send ye that maiden away, ye nonsensical fool. Know ye not what day is today? We've plans to make and a battle to fight, ye brainless mutton-head!"

Hardhitter scowled and looked tough, and for a moment Lord Algon felt fear again. He wondered to himself if he was just losing his touch, everyone seemed to be scaring him lately. Maybe it was time to simply disappear and find a new place to be Lord. He shook off the feeling and scowled back.

"I be knowing that, milord. Ye prepare yeself in your way, and I in mine."

Lord Algon scoffed angrily. "Ye be doin' what I say, and not talking back, 'fore ye find yerself not me first mate no more, savvy?"

"Aye," Hardhitter said, nodding woodenly, but not with much conviction. Lord Algon gritted his teeth and tried to ignore the affront to his power.

"Go ye and gather me the men, and the women too. Even the older ladies and lasses. We're gonna need 'em all to fight these Newcomers. Have 'em meet in front of the Arena for battle. Then send ye a message to them cowardly Wildies in the grass. Tell them they be fightin' for us, or they better hide inside the Newcomers' new place, for the first ones we be killing will be their traitorous hides."

"Aye, 'twill be done." Hardhitter turned and led the servant girl away, still taking swigs of his bottle.

Lord Algon watched him leave, furious. He hated the feeling that someone was disrespecting him, and even worse the feeling that he couldn't do anything about it. He turned back to his room to eat, for it was going to be a long day.

He stopped. There standing by his window was a dark figure. He couldn't make out who it was, for the light of the Red Eye was behind him, casting him into shadow.

Lord Algon put his hand over his eyes to try and see better, but it didn't help much. "Be ye one of the Gangers?" he said, casting his eyes around to see where he'd left his sword.

A deep dark voice answered him, one full of malice. Lord Algon could also tell something else: this was the voice of someone who was really mean, someone not in the least afraid.

"You fight Johnny today. You beat him. But don't you dare kill him."

Lord Algon's eyes opened wide with confusion and interest. "And why should I not, whoever ye be?"

"Because he's mine, that's why. And you let the Gangers be in charge, or you're going to die, before you step one foot outside this castle."

Lord Algon gulped. Whoever this was, he was a very scary and dangerous person. Lord Algon squinted and looked closer. A dark, evil scar ran from the man's eye down his cheek. Still, Lord Algon recognized the man. Wasn't it one of the Gangers from before?

"Ye might want to be careful, matey, threatening a king in his own castle. That just might be a way to get your innards turned outside, 'fore ye even know have time to see what be happenin.'"

The man laughed. It was a dark, ugly laugh, full of venom, and for a moment the thought came to Lord Algon that maybe he was talking to a ghost.

"You be the one who will not see what's happenin.' Don't kill Johnny. And don't do anything to his girl Deb. Just catch 'em for me. I'll be watching."

The dark figure leapt back out the window. Lord Algon took a deep breath, realizing he'd been holding his breath for a while. He thought about just leaving again. The idea was started to sound better and better.

Starbucks stopped his Harley back where he'd last seen the girls. He climbed off and wandered around, frustrated. What could have happened to them? He looked up and down the streets. There was not a sound, just empty buildings and old cars. Then his eyes went back to the hole in the ground. It finally occurred to him in a flash of horror. Could they have fallen into the hole?

He rushed over to the hole, cursing himself for being too stupid to think of it before. Of course, they fell in the hole, where else could they be? He peered down into the darkness. But how? And why? Surely, they would have seen the hole and avoided it. He thought back to when he passed this spot, and it came to him in a flash. The hole wasn't there when he passed it. It must have opened up just as the girls passed.

He crawled as close as he could to the edge and peered down. He could see nothing but a big, black hole that seemed to go on forever. He held his breath and tried to be totally quiet, and he swore somewhere down inside he heard a banging.

He looked around the surrounding area, frantic. If they did fall in the hole, they might be lying there, wounded. He had to find a way to make sure. And then an even more terrible thought came to his mind. He remembered the wolf-beastie. He personally had knocked the wolf-beastie down there, into that hole. At the time he thought he was smart, but now he cursed his stupidity. Why didn't he think, was he totally an idiot? He might have sealed the girls' doom. If they had been lying down in the hole unconscious, then when he tricked the wolf-beastie down there, he'd sent it right to them.

Despair and sorrow filled Starbucks' heart. Tears threatened to fall from his eyes. Had he just killed the only girl he would ever love, and Johnny's girl too? How could he live with himself if it was true? It was too horrible to contemplate.

He breathed deep, trying to get control of his emotions. He had to get down there and find out, no matter what it took. He needed a rope or a ladder, something, anything to let him climb inside. He stood up and started a frantic search of the nearby buildings. He had to be fast, even if he was too late.

Johnny ran through the basement, past the members of the tribe who threw questions at him but he didn't have time to answer. He ran back into the dark tunnel to the Bunker, taking the steps two at a time. Why did everything have to happen at once, he wondered? It seemed like there was never a moment to catch your breath or think about what was happening before something else came along. All he knew was, he had to get back out there and find Deb and Super, but he was worried about the Barker too. And there was the Wildies and Gangers coming to attack, and the Ganger girl upstairs to think about...

As Johnny ran, he thought how nice it would be to grab Deb and his new Barker friend, get on his Harley and just take off. Explore the world they had just discovered, find new places and people, see the land called America the Bootiful. The thought of leading the tribe full of grumpy, complaining people held less and less appeal to him. He was only fifteen seasons, soon to be sixteen. He didn't want to sit on a throne and figure out people's problems.

As he reached the Bunker he put his thoughts aside, thinking grumpily how he really didn't have much choice. The Tribe relied on him as their leader. He'd led them out of Sanctuary. Now he was stuck with them.

He ran through the large main hall with its semidarkness lit only by the white lights on the walls and down the passageway where Misterwizard and the Barker were. He reached the door to the exam room to find Misterwizard and a small group of tribe people standing outside. Misterwizard wiped his hands on a towel and wore a satisfied smile.

As soon as he saw Johnny run up with his look of concern, Misterwizard spoke. "He's out of danger for the moment, Johnny. Only time will tell if it's strong enough to recover from his wounds. Some of them were fairly deep. What it needs now is rest."

"Is it okay to leave it in there alone, without anyone watching it?" Carny, who was nearby holding Miracle, said. "What if it wakes up and attacks us?"

Misterwizard smiled at her. "I understand your apprehensions and concern for your young daughter, Carny, but I think we are relatively safe. It is locked in the exam room, and as long as no one else ventures inside, it won't be able to escape. Johnny or I can be the first to go back inside, if that will allay your fears."

"I'd like to be the first," Johnny said, smiling.

Misterwizard slapped Johnny on the arm. "That is perfectly understandable, Johnny. After all, it is your dog-beastie, I mean, Barker."

My Barker, Johnny thought. For some reason hearing that made him feel happy inside.

"Misterwizard, there's something else we need to talk about. There's a Ganger upstairs, a girl. She says she wants to join us and turn her back on the Gangers. But it's possible she's a spy."

Misterwizard finished wiping his hands and threw the towel on a table. Together they began walking back towards the main hall of the bunker. "A girl, you say? Interesting development." Misterwizard looked at Johnny. "What do you think, Johnny?"

Johnny thought about it. "Something inside me says she's telling the truth. But what if I'm wrong?"

Misterwizard put an arm around Johnny's shoulder and gave him a hug. "You have good judgement, Johnny. I think if you feel she's all right, we should give her a chance. We can always keep an eye on her and keep her from learning too much about us."

Johnny nodded. But then he frowned, remembering his real reason for coming down. "Misterwizard," Johnny said, looking at Misterwizard worriedly. "I have to get back outside and find Deb and Super. Starbucks can't find them. Something terrible might have happened."

They stopped in the Ready room, where they were all alone for the moment. Misterwizard frowned gravely. "I understand your concern and desire to leave, Johnny. However, we must get the Tribe working on our defenses I am fairly certain that the Wildie king, Lord Algon, will not wait for us to be prepared before he attacks again."

Johnny looked frustrated and irritated. Misterwizard put his arm around Johnny again. "Johnny, if you really feel you need to leave to find Deb and Super, then so bit it. I will soldier on without you, for I cannot fault you for wanting to save the girl you love. Just think about this, Johnny. Starbucks also departed to look for Deb and Super and I am sure his search will be quite thorough. And you have a responsibility to these people as well as to Deb and Super. They look to you as their leader, and you have been gone quite a while. Nothing has happened to strengthen our position, and this is a perilous situation."

Johnny knew Misterwizard was right. Every fiber in his being wanted to help search for the girls, but he couldn't leave the people helpless against the attack that was surely coming soon. He nodded. "You're right. I need to stay and help the Tribe."

Misterwizard nodded. "I know that was a very hard choice for you to make, Johnny. As soon as we have an adequate balustrade built against the coming storm, you should leave and find yon fair maidens. Let us hurry in our tasks so you can be on your way."

CHAPTER 30

"Hurry, we must hide." Loki grabbed Deb's hand and pulled her, trying to get her to move.

"Why, Loki?" Deb said.

They had just finished a fairly filling meal of wolf-beastie. The elders of Loki's tribe took the wolf-beastie pelt and placed it at the feet of Lincone. The people were all bowing down now to the statue and thanking it for sending them the angels.

Super walked up and said, "This place gets creepier and creepier. Once you're done worshiping beastie fur, can I have it? It will make a nice pair of warm boots. I hate to see it go to waste."

"Loki's trying to tell us something, Super," Deb said.

Loki grew more urgent, pulling at Deb's arm. "Come! It is night time!"

"How can you tell?" Super said.

"It is night time," Deb said. "It's chillier and there's more breeze. Can't you feel it?"

"I just know after that wolf-beastie, I'm ready for a nice, long nap."

"No napping!' Loki said, his face twisted with fear. "They come soon!"

As if to point out the truth of his words. Slon walked up to stand by the statue of Lincone. He held a brass plate that looked like a wheel cover from one of the old cars and a stick with a piece of rock on it. When Deb saw his face, it filled her with alarm, for he looked even more terrified than Loki. He hit the plate with the stick, making a dull bonging sound.

The people instantly reacted. They all screamed in fear and leapt to their feet. As one they turned towards the tunnel at the far end of the village and ran towards it.

Deb and Super let Loki drag them in the same direction, beginning to feel the urgency. They ran through the center aisle of the village towards the end where most of the people were already heading down the dark passage.

"Oh, oh," Super said. "I'm getting a really bad feeling about this."

"Me too," Deb said. "Loki, what's happening?"

"The Rat People come. The Rat People come! Deb and Super looked at each other. "This place just keeps getting better and better," Super said.

They picked up their pace and soon joined the throng of people crowding into the dark tunnel. A feeling of dread and impending doom crept over the girls. The people didn't even care about splashing through the water, they seemed too terrified to care about anything but what was coming.

They all reached the very end of the tunnel and all turned. Barriers made of old steel and wood went up in front of the tribe. The men of the tribe produced spears and sharp sticks from somewhere and handed them out to everyone. And then something very unexpected happened.

"You see lots of light now!" Loki said, looking at Deb with a smile, despite his fear.

The villagers took out torches from a large wooden box. They were passed out until everyone had one. Then Slon came from the passageway to the Door to Heaven. In his hand he held a flaming torch. As Deb and Super watched, he passed it from villager to villager. Each one lit their torch and held it high. But it came at a cost to them, for the light seemed to hurt their eyes. They blinked and turned away from it, trying their best to shield themselves. Deb felt bad for them, living in the dark for so long so that even torchlight hurt them.

Everyone stopped talking, as if by a signal. They all stared forward, looks of fear and even despair on their faces. Deb and Super tensed up and waited, looking towards the now empty village, for the tension was as taut as a bowstring.

And then slowly, very faintly, they heard the shuffling of a thousand little feet, coming towards them. Along with the shuffling came faint squeaks and a scrabbling sound. Deb felt sick to her stomach and began to feel very afraid. She took out Sting, and Super took her Cling-on sword out too. They stood next to each other, touching shoulders, waiting.

It seemed like an eternity of terror before they saw anything. And then it was a terrible but amazing sight. Like a living carpet, the rat-beasties came, thousands and thousands of them. The people cried and screamed in misery, and Deb couldn't remember feeling so low in her life. This was way worse than anything they'd faced in Sanctuary. It was like something from a person's nightmares.

The rat-beasties kept coming. The tops of the tents of the village started moving, and they could see the rat-beasties were crawling inside and over everything. A tent near the back fell down from the weight of the rat-beasties. Somewhere a metal pot banged as it was knocked off a shelf. Soon all the tents moved and swayed, from an unseen and horrible source.

"Oh my god Lincone!" Super said, "What did we ever do to deserve to die down here, eaten by rat-beasties!"

Deb grabbed Super with her free hand. When Super looked at her she said, "Listen. If we have to, we run for the Door to Heaven. And we try to open it."

"That's the smartest thing I've heard in a long time," Super said. "Let's go now!"

"Too late!" Deb said. The horde had arrived.

The creepiest thing to Deb was how now that the rat-beasties came down the tunnel, they melded in with the darkness. The only thing she saw was their horrid rat-beastie bodies reflected in the torchlight.

Deb screamed and stabbed at them as they ran. Super did too, stabbing and poking at the moving horde. Then they saw something strange. The villagers were ignoring the rat-beasties! And the rat-beasties were running past the villagers, thousands of them.

Confused, Deb turned to Loki. "Loki, aren't those the Rat People?"

Loki shook his head. "No, those run from the Rat People."

Deb and Super looked at each other again.

Super said, "Things are about to get a whole lot worse."

Deb nodded. "Get ready to fight. I think we're going to be lucky to survive."

Johnny and Misterwizard headed back up the long tunnel to the Museum.

"Have you heard about the Wildies that want to join us as well, Johnny?"

"No," Johnny said. "We're suddenly getting friends from everywhere."

"A very fortuitous circumstance, indeed. But we still have enemies, unfortunately. However, this should not preclude us from implementing the doctrines and laws pertaining to Democracy. And no time is better to begin than the present. With your permission, we will meet with the Tribe and get their vote on whether we should allow the Wildies to join us. Then we can move forward in unity."

"What should we do with the Ganger? Should we have a vote about her as well?"

"No, I think that is a decision for you, the leader. Let's go talk to her. I'd like to meet her."

After talking to Lady Stabs, they decided to put her in the Gift Shop of the Museum while Johnny and MIsterwizard had a meeting with the Tribe. They gathered in the Main Hall of the Museum. The Tribe totaled two hundred and filled the Hall from one end to the other. Johnny and Misterwizard stood on a bench so they could be heard over the crowd. MIsterwizard spoke first.

"Dear members of what we call the Tribe. Welcome to this, our inaugural and most monumental voting session, the first of many in our new republic, I hope, as we re-institute the institutions of Democracy."

Foodcourt looked at the others in the Tribe and then at Misterwizard. "Misterwizard, do you mind if Johnny speaks for you? He's easier to understand."

Both Misterwizard and Johnny grinned. "Totally acceptable, dear Foodcourt, and justifiable. I do have a tendency to wax philosophic and use my larger and more verbose vocabulary."

MIsterwizard pointed to Johnny. Johnny looked over the crowd with a serious look and began to talk.

"We're in a new home, and it's a good place, but we as you know, there are some people who want to take it from us. But we also have some people who want to join us in rebuilding the world to be a place for everyone. Some of the Wildies want to join us. And there is even a Ganger girl sitting in the next room who says she wants to join us too."

The people all started talking at once, creating a loud roar that hurt Johnny's ears. He waved his hands to try and quiet them, and finally it became possible to speak again.

Microsoft, Sephie's father barged through the crowd with his large bulk and stood in the front. "We knew about the Wildies, but not about this Ganger girl. What do you think, Johnny?"

Everyone looked at Johnny with anticipation, wondering what he was going to say.

Johnny looked over the Tribe and smiled. "I believe

that she is being truthful. I think that as we start to rebuild this country, many people will come to want to join us. At least I hope that is what happens. The more people we have, the faster we can be strong and make good laws."

The people all smiled and talked, agreeing.

Foodcourt walked forward to address the crowd. "You all listen to Johnny. He's a good man, and he knows what he's talking about."

The people of the Tribe all talked among themselves and then they all started nodding.

Abercrombie spoke. "We all agree, Johnny!"

Cinnabon looked out the door to the grassy Mall. Her eyes widened and she grabbed Wheaties and held him close. "Aaah! They're coming!"

Everyone looked outside. As if by some secret signal, the Wildies came in a group towards them. Johnny and Misterwizard walked to the door and outside as the rest of the Tribe watched from the doorway. They walked up to the Wildies and both groups stopped a few feet from each other.

At the front of the Wildies, Yellowtooth, Marbleskin and Funnygiggle stood, looking nervous and afraid. "Here we be, come to join ye, if ye still be willing."

Misterwizard walked forward and extended a hand. "Welcome to the Tribe, good friends and neighbors. You are now officially part of our small but courageous band of new world pioneers."

Yellowtooth, Marbleskin and Funnygiggle all smiled, and Funnygiggle giggled. They turned to the other Wildies and grinned at them, and soon all the Wildies were smiling with pleasure.

Johnny and Misterwizard smiled too. But then

Misterwizard looked serious. "This is a splendid and momentous occasion, but I fear we do not have time to dwell on it. As you most surely are aware, Lord Algon is planning a new attack, and I fear the time is very imminent."

Yellowtooth looked confused, so Johnny translated. "Lord Algon is coming to attack again, and we need to build up some defenses. Are you willing to help us?"

Yellowtooth smiled and all the Wildies behind him nodded. "We be willing and able to help ye, young master. We have strong arms and no fear of hard labor. 'Twould be a shame if we were to join thee, only to sit at port while Lord Algon tore ye asunder."

"You're almost as hard to understand as Misterwizard," Johnny said, laughing. He turned to the Tribe in the Museum and motioned with his hand. "Come on outside, everybody!"

When the Tribe had all joined the Wildies on the porch, Johnny looked at Misterwizard. Misterwizard and Johnny surveyed the grassy Mall. The Tribe and Wildies stood all around them.

Misterwizard pointed to the buildings. "You see, Johnny, how the large grassy field called the Mall is rectangular in shape? And how on all four sides, building surround it. This makes for an excellent layout for the creation of the walls of a fortress. All we need do is fill in the openings between the buildings to make a solid barrier on all sides."

Johnny nodded. "We can use some of the old rocks."

Misterwizard said, "And the old junk cars. I believe if we use the busses, we can drag the old hulks close to the buildings. Then it will simply be a matter of finding a way to lift and secure them on top of each other. A pulley or crane system is what we need."

"Pully system?" Johnny asked.

MIsterwizard chuckled. "Don't worry, I'll look for those. There must be something I can find or rig up in one of these buildings."

"And I'll get the people to start building the wall. It's going to take some time. I hope we have it to spare."

Misterwizard left to start his search. Johnny returned to the Tribe and explained to them what they needed to do. He split the Tribe into two groups, one to drive the buses and haul the cars, and another to collect old rock and stone. Most were happy to have a purpose and a direction and went to work willingly, but a few grumbled at the hard work. But before long, they were all occupied.

Once more Johnny thought how nice it would be to get on his Harley and ride. If only he knew where it was. If nothing else happened, he hoped he would at least find it again and get one more ride before he died in a war he didn't even want. And more than anything, he hoped he would see Deb again. The thought of never seeing her before something happened to him was too terrible to contemplate. He had to quickly put that thought out of his head or he knew it would drive him crazy.

Lord Algon stood in front of the Arena dressed in his battle armor. Next to him stood his First Mate Hardhitter, Facegash and the other Gangers.

"This day we reclaim what be ours!" Lord Algon said.

"The Newcomers be scurvy dogs who think they've bested us. But one small skirmish be not a war, and they've only managed to bring death and destruction upon their own scurvy heads. Ready yourselves for fighting, mateys, for we not come home until we've sent everyone of them down to Davey Jones Locker!"

The crowd roared and shook their fists. Lord Algon grinned, feeling back in control. Suddenly he wasn't afraid anymore, it was as if things were before the Newcomers and Gangers arrived. He looked at Facegash, still grinning. But when he saw the way Facegash was staring at him, as if contemplating when he was going to kill him and take over, Lord Algon's smile faded away. The fear crept back inside his heart and he scowled unhappily.

"I can't wait until I never have to hear that stupid gibberish you people talk again." Facegash said, staring stonily.

Lord Algon stared back with a sneer. "Ye won't, matey, when ye be dead. Perhaps that's what be happening to ye soon."

"Maybe to somebody," Facegash said. "We'll see who, won't we?"

Lord Algon smiled, trying to restore friendly relations. "Maybe it be this here Johnny lad, his old man and his tribe."

"Maybe," Facegash said, but he didn't smile.

Lord Algon looked again at his cheering people, but inside he felt no joy or confidence, only fear.

The lone figure watched the Wildies and Gangers prepare for their attack. He smiled, looking forward to the mayhem to come. He took out his rifle and aimed it at Lord Algon. He looked down the sights of the gun with one eye, watching the Wildie king. When the time was right, once the battle was mostly won, he would put a bullet in Lord Algon's head. Then Facegash could take over. It would be a simple matter for him, Ripper, to show back up. Surely Facegash would step down when he saw him. And then he would be the rightful king of the land. Best of all, there would be no more Johnny.

Thinking about Johnny made him realize he had to hurry. He wanted to be there before the battle began, to make sure the foolish king didn't disobey his warning not to kill Johnny. If the battle went the way Ripper hoped, the Tribe would soon be dying. When that happened, he had to be ready to step in and kill Johnny. No one deserved that pleasure but him.

He smiled and shouldered his rifle again. Let the foolish Wildie king think he was still lord of these realms for a little while longer. When the time was right, he would die. And then Johnny would be next.

Wolf Fang crept back into shadows, cursing. Just when he thought things were getting nice and quiet, those stupid Wildies had shown up, Boomvoice, that stupid old man Yellowtooth and his silly mentally weak daughter Sillygiggle. How Wolf Fang hated them all! Now everything was all stirred up again, the Newcomers were all milling about and making noise. He decided he'd have to find a safer, more remote place to get inside.

He walked around to the back of the Museum, looking for a place to enter. He looked up and saw a window, high up on a stone ledge on the second floor. It was perfect. He looked around for a way to get up to it.

Suddenly the whole crowd of Newcomers burst out the back door with the Wildies in tow. He ran as fast as he could and barely made it back to hiding before he was spotted.

He watched as they swarmed over three long yellow metal things on the street. Then they went inside them, like inside a hollow shell of a beastie. What happened next was even more strange and amazing. As Wolf Fang watched in disbelief, the yellow things began to roar like beasties! As he watched with his mouth open, the yellow things moved with all the people inside them! This truly was magic. A thrill of fear coursed through him. The Newcomers were truly powerful.

The yellow things moved until they each came to a rusted old hulk of metal sitting on the street. Then Wildies and Newcomers climbed out. As Wolf Fang watched with interest, they tied ropes to the old hulks. Then they got back inside the yellow things and they drove off, towing the rusted hulks behind them!

Wolf Fang couldn't figure out, no matter how hard he tried, what they were up to. He shook his head and stopped trying. He turned back to the Museum. And he smiled. In their haste, the Newcomers had left the back door open.

He looked around. No one was near. Crouching down, he moved swiftly and silently and disappeared inside.

CHAPTER 31

Starbucks came back to the hole with a loop of wire he found in one of the old buildings. It was the only thing he could find, for every rope he found was so rotted he could pull it apart with his hands. The wire would be hard to hold onto, but he didn't care. He had to find out what happened to the girls.

The wire was thick and covered with red rust. He looped one end through the rusty carcass of a car near the hole and tied it a knot in it. He pulled on it, and it seemed to hold, though the wire was so thick he had to knot it twice. By the time he was done, his hands were covered with rust and scratched up, but he barely noticed.

He ran the other end of the wire to the hole. He looked at the length that was left. Would it be enough to reach the bottom? He didn't know. If he climbed down it and didn't reach ground, he didn't think he'd have the strength to climb back up it. He decided he'd just have to chance it.

He dropped the other end of the wire into the hole and listened for the sound of it hitting the ground. He heard nothing. Disappointed, he readied himself to climb down, realizing he might be risking his own life on a hunch. The girls might not even be in the hole. But what choice did he have but to check?

He walked over to the hole and peered down one more time. This time he could see the ground! The Red Eye was directly overhead, and so it shone down directly over the hole. The ground was far below. He didn't see the girls lying there.

Was that a good sign or not? Had the wolf-beastie found them and dragged them off? Or was it right now chasing them somewhere in the dark? Were they hiding from it somewhere, waiting for Johnny and him to rescue them?

These thoughts forced him to move faster. He grabbed the wire and prepared to swing his leg over it. And then he saw something!

In the gray light, hulking shapes, huge and terrible, sped past the opening. They ran fast, as if pursuing something. Starbucks stopped climbing and watched them. One after another bolted past the hole. They looked human, but like beasties as well, running on their hands and legs like Barkers. He watched as the last ran past. If the girls were down there, they were in big trouble. Those things looked way more dangerous than even the wolf-beastie.

Starbucks ran to his Harley, climbed on, and roared it to life. He took off in a squeal of tires, headed back for

New Sanctuary. He needed to get some more firepower, some of Misterwizard's magic bombs, and he had to hurry.

Johnny and Misterwizard watched the progress of the building of the wall from the porch of New Sanctuary, the Museum of American History. Misterwizard found something better than a pulley system, he found an old mobile crane with a hook. He soon had a member of the Tribe running it to lift the cars and position them on top of each other. The first few cars came crashing down, one almost killing someone who leapt out of the way at the last moment. But after a few tries, the men had gotten the hang of it. It was still slow work, but eventually the work progressed.

The wall was a jumble of different old rusty vehicles, from buses and small sportscars to large trucks and vans, all in different colors but all sharing the orange color of rust. Many of the vehicles were without doors and most had no windows. They were stacked on top of each other but there wasn't a straight row of cars anywhere. Some cars tilted up, others down. The wall resembled a strange quilt of rusted metal.

The progress was frustratingly slow, but finally the wall began to take shape. Johnny told the Tribe to concentrate on the side facing the direction that Lady Stabs said the Wildies would come from. This was the side with the Capitol at the end where the President of the old country the United States held court. The work took a long time, for there was a large gap between the

Capitol and the buildings closest to it on either side of the grassy Mall. It took even longer because Johnny wanted two rows of cars and rocks, so men could stand on top of the wall for defense. The wall had almost reached the Museums on either side, but there was still a lot of wall to build.

Johnny saw something coming in the distance. It looked like Starbucks on his Harley! Johnny turned to Misterwizard. "Misterwizard! Look!" Johnny pointed. Misterwizard looked and saw Starbucks approach.

Johnny ran up to Starbucks as he skidded to a stop and hopped off.

"Did you find them?" Johnny said, his face anxious.

Starbucks frowned. "No, but I think I know what happened. There was a hole in the ground."

Johnny's mouth opened with surprise. He remembered seeing it.

"Why didn't we realize it before?" He said, feeling terrible.

Starbucks nodded. "I was thinking what a dummy I was for not realizing what happened. But Johnny..."

Starbucks stopped, having a hard time saying the next words as his throat tightened with emotion. "I did something even stupider. I knocked a wolf-beastie into the hole, not knowing the girls were down there. And now there's something even worse down there, some kind of monsters."

"That settles it," Johnny said. "Misterwizard-"

MIsterwizard patted Johnny on the arm. "Say no more, Johnny. Go. Foodcourt and I will finish the wall and carry on the fight. Go."

Johnny nodded. He turned to Starbucks. "What are you doing back here?"

"I came to get some of MIsterwizard's magic bombs. I think we're going to need them."

"Well, let's hurry!" Johnny said, and together he and Starbucks ran back inside the Museum.

Inside the Museum, they ran through the empty main hall quickly. They ran so fast they didn't see the stranger hiding behind one of the columns watching them.

Luckily Misterwizard had made one of the side rooms into an arsenal. They ran in to find a stack of the green little bombs, rifles and long thick tubes that sent fiery explosions far away. Starbucks grabbed bombs and stuffed them in his pockets. Johnny picked up one of the rifles and slung it over his shoulder. Then he picked up one of the long tubes.

"Let's go!"

Starbucks nodded, and they ran back out. Outside they both climbed on Starbucks' Harley, Johnny riding on the back.

"If I knew we were going to do this, I would have brought your Harley back with me."

"You know where it is?" Johnny asked with pleasant surprise.

"Yep. No time now though."

Starbucks took off with a loud roar and soon they sped across the grassy Mall for the hole, hopefully to get to Deb and Super in time.

Deb and Super held their swords in front of themselves and waited, both afraid and tense as bowstrings. The water was up to their ankles, and their clothes were wet from sloshing through it. Both of the girls were wet and miserable, but the fear made them forget about it. Deb looked at Loki. "Loki, who are the Rat People? Where do they come from?"

Loki continued to stare forward, looking grave. "Old tales say they were the disobedient ones. They did not listen to Lincone, who told them to come down from Heaven. They stayed above in disobedience and were punished by the monster Half-life."

"They got the Sickness," Super said.

"Then how did they end up down here, Loki?" Deb asked.

"After they were punished, they came down, but they were shunned by the good, obedient people of Lincone. They were forced down deep into the dark holes in the ground."

They all stared into the darkness. A new sound began. This one sounded like distant drumming. Deb began to feel panic, and her fever started coming back. She willed it to go away and forced herself to be calm.

"And now they're back," Super said.

"Yes. They come every night now, to kill and eat us." Loki looked scared, like what he was, just a little boy afraid. "And we have no place to go to run away."

"Those creeps!" Deb said. "I wish we could get to Misterwizard and Johnny. They'd take care of 'em."

"Deb,," Super said, leaning towards Deb so that only she could hear, "Let's go to the Door of Heaven now. We can open it, and all the people can escape."

Deb thought about it. Then she nodded. She turned to Loki.

"Loki, you know we are angels, isn't that right?"

Loki looked at her, his face drawn with fear. "Yes."

Deb pointed to Super. "My fellow angel Super and I are going to go to the Door of Heaven and open it. Then we will lead you away from the Rat People."

"Hurry!" Loki said, nodding, hope in his eyes.

Deb and Super turned to see Slon standing in their way. He had been listening. But then he nodded. "Go angels, and free us, for that is what you were supposed to do."

Deb and Super hurried past him. They sloshed back through the water, which was like walking through quicksand, until they finally reached the place where the water receded. Then they ran as fast as they could.

They climbed up onto the platform next to the statue of Lincone and hurried down the passageway. Beautiful furs, bright clothing and bits of jewelry adored the walls and floor. Here and there offerings to Lincone lay, rotted food left long ago and trinkets.

They ran down the hall until they came some strange metal bars in weird shapes coming up from the floor and raising up waist high. The bars curved into loops, four loops on each post. Three posts stood across the opening.

"What are those?" Super said.

"Who cares?" Deb said, as she vaulted over them. Super shrugged and did the same thing. They kept running.

They ran up some stairs to another hallway. Here the decorations were even more elaborate, with old paintings on the walls and figures made out of mud and sticks.

"Yuck," said Super, as she ran by them. Finally, they reached a wall. Set in the wall was a set of two metal doors. The metal doors had metal bars in the middle of them. And around the metal bars—

"Chains." Deb said. That's what's barring the Door to Heaven?"

The chains were rusty and looked like they hadn't moved in ages, but they still looked strong.

"Not for long!" Super said. She took the explosive out of her coat. Just as she'd seen Misterwizard do it, she pulled the metal pin and threw the bomb towards the door. "Run!"

Deb and Super ran down the hallway until they were far enough to barely see the door. Then they waited. And waited. Nothing happened!

"Are you sure you did it right?" Deb asked.

"I did it just like Misterwizard did."

They waited some more, hoping. Nothing happened.

As if by some invisible signal to each other, they both started walking back. When they reached the door, there sat the bomb, right up against the door, doing nothing.

Super walked towards it. Deb looked alarmed. "Don't go near it!"

Super got close and stared at it. "I think it's dead." She picked it up and examined it.

"How can you tell?" Deb asked.

Super looked inside it. "There's nothing inside it. I picked up an empty bomb."

Super sat down on the ground. "I feel like crying. I don't want to be stuck down here anymore."

"And those monsters are coming."

"We just have to get back out the hole where we came in," Super said.

"Past the monsters?" Deb said. "I like Loki and his tribe but seeing them again right now is going to make me sick."

Super got up. "Well, we better get back before those monsters come."

They shuffled back down the passageway slowly, dejected.

"I want to see Starbucks again," Super said. "And I want to see Johnny."

"We will. We have to have hope."

They passed the statue of Lincone. Super stopped. She looked up, mouth open. Deb kept going.

"Deb?"

"Yeah?" Deb said, still shuffling on.

"Come back here."

Deb stopped, curious, and came back. She saw how Super was looking up towards the ceiling and she looked too. They looked at each other with blank expressions. Then they both burst into wild laughter. They laughed so hard they fell over, weak from exhaustion.

Deb sat up, tears in her eyes. "See? All you had to do was ask Lincone."

Above them and surrounding the statue of Lincone was a pile of rubble, leading up to a giant hole where Lincone had fallen through. It led into the building above.

"I could kiss him right now! You wonderful, creepy old statue!" Super jumped up and kissed the side of the statue.

Loki walked up. "Did you open the Door to Heaven?"

"We don't need to, Loki. Look!" Deb pointed up. We can get out right here.

Loki frowned, unhappy. "You cannot go there. No one is allowed to touch our god. To touch him is to die."

"Oh, please!" Super said. "I've had just about as much of this nonsense-"

Deb put a hand on Super stopping her.

"Loki, we're angels. We can touch Lincone, can't we?"

"No one!" Loki said, getting angry.

Slon walked up. "What is going on? Did you-"

"No, we didn't," Super said. "But we found a way out. Up there."

Slon looked angry, so angry he looked dangerous. "No one touches Lincone. Did you touch Lincone?"

The girls both thought of how Super had just kissed the statue but kept it to themselves.

Deb said, "Slon, we have to touch Lincone. We have to use him to escape to safety!"

"NO!" Slon said. He raised a spear and pointed it at them.

Suddenly from far down the tunnel, the sounds of distant drums came, ominous and terrible. Slon looked at them. "The Rat People are here. They will kill us if they find us here, unprotected. We must get to safety!"

Slon pointed the spear at the girls, making it clear he wasn't going to let them near the statue of Lincone again. Reluctantly but without any choice, the girls walked back down the passageway.

"Thanks for nothing, Lincone," Super said grumpily.

CHAPTER 32

Lord Algon sat on his new portable throne on its wooden platform. The carrier sat on the ground with poles along the sides, waiting for him to order his guards to pick it up. This time he wasn't alone, for on his right, Facegash sat on another throne on a king carrier. Lord Algon looked at him, and his smile faded. Facegash looked way too comfortable, as if he'd been a king for his whole life. It made Lord Algon uneasy.

They both sat in front of Lord Algon's castle in the cemetery looking out at the army of Wildies assembled and waiting. The army, more than two hundred, filled the grounds. At the head of the army stood Hardhitter, Lord Algon's first mate. Lord Algon felt a surge of power and confidence. His smile returned. They would win, and then he would get his revenge on everybody who had crossed him, including the Gangers.

"So, what's your plan, just to run up and attack?" Facegash said. Lord Algon didn't like his tone, it held a hint of mockery.

Lord Algon frowned again, for that was exactly his plan. Why did this Ganger have such a good knack of spoiling his good mood? He sneered and said,

"Be ye not concerned with me plans for battle, Matey. I be fighting enemies since before ye be born. We be unprepared last time, and they caught us by surprise, but this time be different. I have vanquished many a foe in my time. Look yonder and see what treats we have for your newfound friends."

Lord Algon pointed, and Facegash looked. On the far end of the cemetery, he saw large wooden structures with wheels. They each had a long arm with a rope attached.

Lord Algon smiled at Facegash's expression of surprise. "These be what called catapults. And over yonder, look see."

Facegash looked the other direction to see metal tubes on rollers.

"Old friends from my days at sea. They be cannons. And they pack a mighty good shot, they do. And then there be me the Wildest Wildies." Lord Algon pointed to the back of the cemetery. Facegash looked there as well.

At the back of the army stood five huge men. They snarled and shook with rage. Dressed in dirty rags, other Wildies held them by chains.

"They be called the Crazies, trained to kill since they was lads. Made mean by cruelty, they be looking for anyone to get their chance for payback."

Facegash nodded, admitting they looked fierce.

"And don't be forgetting me best weapons of all."

Lord Algon pointed in another corner with pride, like a man showing off his trophies.

Facegash looked. There sat the three in cages. One held the bear-beastie and another the gorilla-beastie. The third now held two huge mean looking Barkers. The cages sat on rollers, and Wildies stood behind them, ready to push when the time came.

"See ye now?" Lord Algon said, sitting back with a self-satisfied look on his face. "The Newcomers be begging for mercy soon, but we'll give no quarter, until they all be dead."

Facegash stared at Lord Algon, not seeming impressed. It made Lord Algon uneasy. Facegash said, "They still have their magic, you know. And that Johnny is tricky. He may be only fifteen seasons, but he's a smart guy. He'll be prepared. We need more strategy than just run up and attack. Only an idiot would do that."

Lord Algon was really beginning to hate this man, and all the other Gangers as well. He decided to himself when it was all over, they would cook and eat them all, this arrogant dog last of all. The thought made him feel warm inside. Then he realized what Facegash had said, and it made him suspicious. He eyed Facegash warily.

"Ye be sayin' ye had the magic as well, Matey. Be ye tellin' me now ye have naught but your swords to fight with?"

Facegash was caught by surprise, but he quickly recovered. "We have magic. And you'll be seeing it too, when we get into battle. But that doesn't mean you don't have to a have a plan." Facegash hoped Lord Algon believed him, at least until they were in the thick of the battle. He had plans of his own once that happened.

Lord Algon sat back and smiled, feeling confident

again. He was beginning to suspect the Gangers really had no magic but had somehow been saved by a lucky chance. It would be easy, once they were in the thick of battle, to kill this annoying arrogant Facegash. Then he would take care of the rest of the Gangers nice and slowly, enjoying their suffering.

"There be other plans already in motion to cement our victory," Lord Algon said, acting as if he and Facegash were still fellow conspirators. "By the time we start the battle, their wizard be already wantin' a truce, I wager."

Facegash wondered what Lord Algon meant, but he just shrugged and sat back. "Let's get going. I'm getting bored."

"Aye, let's." Lord Algon stood up. All the Wildies looked at him. "Let's go teach these Newcomers who be the masters of this here city! To war!"

The Wildies roared and marched. Lord Algon's guards picked up his king carrier by the poles. They placed the poles on their shoulders and walked as well. Four more guards picked up a chair Facegash sat on and did the same thing. The catapults rolled forward. The beasties in their cages rolled as well. The Crazies screamed and leapt up and down and ran along the ground on all fours, making it hard for their captors to keep up.

Lord Algon's army marched to war.

A lone figure ran swiftly down the empty street, past the junk cars, rotted metal boxes that once held mail and the little metal stumps coming out of the ground with the rounded tops. Around him the windows of empty buildings seemed to stare at him like dead eyes.

Ripper wore a dark cloak and a thick cowl to hide the gashes on his face and his missing eye. Every time he passed one of the looking glasses and saw how ugly his face was, his anger and hatred burned hotter. The man, who was actually merely a boy, who did this to him would pay.

The street Ripper ran on was on the opposite side of the buildings facing the grassy Mall. He wanted to be next to New Sanctuary when the battle between Lord Algon and the Tribe started. Once the fight started, he would have a chance to sneak in to the Museum. There were a thousand terrible things he could do then, all of them to hurt his enemy Johnny.

He ran past a hole in the ground. He stopped, looking at it curiously. He walked over and peered down into it. Reminding him of the hole he fell into where the tiger-beastie mauled him, he scowled and spit into it. Then he thought of something. This would be a great place to throw members of the Tribe, a place where Johnny would never find them. He smiled at the thought. Who would he throw in the hole? Carny, or maybe her new baby Miracle. He'd love to throw Misterwizard down the hole. If ever there was a more meddlesome and annoying old man than him, Ripper didn't know who they could be. Foodcourt, Johnny, father, Teavana, Johnny's mother. The list went on and on. Maybe all of them, once they were dead. It would make a nice big grave for them.

He stopped and leaned over. He swore he heard someone yelling, and explosions. Was there someone living in the hole? Maybe it was best to stay away from the hole until he was ready to throw someone in it.

He heard sounds far behind him, not in the ground but on the surface. He turned and looked down the empty street. Somewhere far in the distance, men shouted war cries and horns blasted. He smiled. The fight had started!

He turned and ran faster. He had to make it to a place near the Museum before the fight raged hard and heavy. He couldn't wait until all the killing began.

Misterwizard and Foodcourt walked through the grassy Mall and surveyed the work building the walls. Having finally finished the wall from the Capitol to the buildings on either side of it, work continued for the gap between the Museum of Natural History where Johnny fought Ripper and New Sanctuary, the American History Museum on one side. The Tribe also worked on the gaps between the museums on the other side of the Mall.

The men of the Tribe worked steadily on the wall for hours, and Misterwizard worried that after all their exertion they wouldn't be strong enough to fight. There was nothing he could do about it, however. Misterwizard doubted they would have much time before Lord Algon attacked. The day had almost passed again. He glanced up at the Red Eye in the sky. It crept closer to the horizon, and a beautiful sunset in reds and oranges blazed forth, filling the sky. Nighttime would soon be on them. Misterwizard didn't like the idea of fighting at night, but it seemed that was Lord Algon's plan. He turned to Foodcourt. "If the Wildies attack at night, our battle is going to be much more difficult. We need to rig up torches, so we can see by their light."

"I'll get some of the men on it right away," Foodcourt said. Misterwizard looked at Foodcourt and smiled.

"You have become a quite a reliable overseer yourself, Foodcourt," he said. "In Johnny's absence, you have taken the mantle of leadership and worn it most efficiently."

Foodcourt smiled humbly at the compliment. "I know everyone thinks I'm crazy because I talk about Australia so much." He looked at Misterwizard with eyes full of hope. "But now that Johnny has led us out of Sanctuary and give us such hope for the future, we don't need to go to Australia anymore. For a young man, he is quite a son, don't you think?"

Misterwizard chuckled and nodded. "He is. And part of the credit for that goes to you and Teavana. You have raised a good boy in Johnny. But I must tell you something."

Misterwizard and Foodcourt stopped. Facecourt looked at Misterwizard with curiosity. "What is it, Misterwizad?"

Misterwizard stroked his beard and looked thoughtful. "I'm beginning to suspect that the mantle of leadership and the burden of politics is becoming quite odious to Johnny. He is developing a natural desire in one his age for freedom and exploration."

"What?" Foodcourt said, his face blank.

"I think Johnny may not want to be leader much longer. He wants to go explore our new country, and I don't blame him. He is young and wild, and wants to live a life of adventure, not sit in a chair talking politics. Which means it may fall to you to become the leader of the Tribe. First, we would engage in free and fair elections, but I suspect that you would be the one chosen by the Tribe. Do you think you could fulfill the role of the first president of New America, Foodcourt?"

Foodcourt smiled with joy. He nodded his head up and down. "Yes, I think I would like that. I'd like that a lot."

Foodcourt stood taller and tilted his head back. "Mr. President. I like it. I've always had ideas about what should happen, but no one would listen. It will be nice to be heard for a change, and not just ignored as a crazy old fool."

They walked again. Misterwizard said, "Once we are victorious in this coming conflict, we will discuss it at greater length. And I may be wrong about Johnny. Still, it is something to expect and not find surprising if it happens."

"I understand," Foodcourt said. "Johnny has done so much for this Tribe already, he deserves to do what he wants."

"My feelings as well."

Suddenly in the far distance beyond the walls, they heard yelling and horns. Lord Algon and the Wildies were on their way. Misterwizard and Foodcourt looked at each other.

"The wall will have to be enough. We need to get ready for battle!" Misterwizard said.

"I'll spread the word!" Foodcourt said. "And get torches rigged up. He ran off towards the crew wrestling with a car on the far side of the Mall.

"I'll get the bombs and guns," Misterwizard said and ran in the opposite direction.

"Johnny, where are you?" Foodcourt said as he ran. "I'm not sure I'm this ready to be leader. You're the fighter, not me!"

In the distance, the yelling and horns grew louder. "Maybe Australia is still a good idea!"

Inside the museum people ran everywhere, yelling and crying. The approach of Lord Algon's army sent most of them into a state of panic. Cinnabon kneeled in the corner, clutching Wheaties to her. Thegap and Bathandbodyworks stood in the middle of the main hall, yelling at each other. And Microsoft and Abercrombie ran into the weapons room and gathered weapons and bombs, not sure what they were even supposed to do with them.

Lady Stabs walked out, carrying a rifle. They all looked at her. In the excitement, everyone had forgotten about her, even Foodcourt, who was supposed to be watching her. The Tribe members in the main hall all stared in fear, wondering what she was going to do.

"I'm a good fighter," she said. "If I'm to be a part of this Tribe, let me prove it. Abercrombie came out of the weapons room, holding an armful of rifles. She saw Lady Stabs. She smiled.

"We'll trust you. Don't make us wish we hadn't."

"I won't," Lady Stabs said. "I want to earn my place."

Abercrombie nodded. As the rest watched, Lady Stabs shouldered the rifle and ran outside.

Hidden in a corner, Wolf Fang scowled with contempt. He would make sure the Gangers knew of her treachery and that she paid for it. All the activity was making him nervous. He was sure he was going to get caught if he wasn't very careful.

Then he saw what he'd been waiting for the whole time. He smiled evilly.

Sephie walked up from the stairs to the basement, holding Kermit. She gazed around at all the activity going on with wide eyes.

"Psst. Little girl." Wolf Fang smiled.

Sephie looked at him. Her eyes filled with fear and suspicion.

"The old man sent me to get you and take you to a safe place."

"Misterwizard?" Sephie asked.

"Yes, yes." Wolf Fang nodded. "He doesn't want anything to happen to you, because you're his special friend."

Sephie smiled at that, but a hint of suspicion stayed on her face. "I've never seen you before. Are you sure you're not a bad man?"

"I'm a good man," he said, chuckling darkly to himself. "You'll see. I'll take you to Johnny."

"Johnny?" Sephie said, and she smiled brightly, her suspicion disappearing.

"Yes, Johnny!" He motioned to her with his hand, glancing up to make sure no one was seeing them.

Sephie frowned again. "Are you sure? I don't know."

"He gave me something to show you. Come here."

Sephie slowly, cautiously tiptoed over, her face showing her distrust.

As soon as she was close enough, Wolf Fang produced a burlap bag he'd staged just for the occasion. Before Sephie could react, he popped it down over her head and scooped her up.

She screamed, but it was muffled by the bag. Quickly,

before anyone could hear, Wolf Fang ran for the back door. As Sephie struggled and thrashed, he chuckled to himself, thinking about the great reward waiting for him. Little girls were so easy to catch. Tasty to eat, too.

CHAPTER 33

"Deb," Super said, "we have to escape and climb Lincone. We can't die here because of their silly superstitions."

"It's too late," Deb said. "Here they come!"

Deb and Super saw the first of the Rat People emerge from the darkness. They were huge, larger than ordinary men, with gray skin and flat faces and large ears. Each one was disfigured somehow. Some had missing eyes or only holes for a nose, others had clubs for hands. One even had two heads! Their teeth were sharpened to points and they ran on all fours like animals. To the girls they were terrifying.

Deb and Super backed up, waiting for the first attack. They didn't have to wait long. But when the Rat People arrived, Loki's tribe lifted the torches high, filling the tunnel with light. The Rat People stopped and held their hands up to shield their eyes.

Loki's people didn't like the light either, and they tried to keep from looking at the light as well. Then men ran out to meet the Rat People, spears in hand.

Deb and Super looked at each other, nodded, and ran out too, swords ready.

Soon a pitched battle began. The Undergrounders fought hard, stabbing the Rat People. Deb ran up to one creature and with a yell slashed at it with Sting. The creature had never seen a sword before, and as the sword cut a gash in its head it looked at it with surprise. Then Deb stabbed it in the heart, and it fell to the ground with a look of confusion on its face.

"Take that, you monster!" Deb said, smiling.

Super ran up to one of the monsters and screamed. She slashed and slashed at it, but it was a little smarter than the one fighting Deb. It stepped back out of Super's reach and grinned evilly at her.

"Come here, you freak!" She yelled and advanced.

It reached out and grabbed her arm. She yelled in pain and slashed at its arm. It yelped and let go, an expression of surprise and hurt on its face.

Meanwhile the Undergrounder men stabbed at the Rat People with their spears. The creatures were big and strong though, and they grabbed some of the men and held them above their heads.

Deb ran after another creature, but suddenly she felt weak. Her head grew hot and she realized she had to keep from overdoing it, or she'd faint and be easy pickings for the creatures. She stopped and waited until she felt steadier on her feet, and then she moved forward again but at a slower pace.

Super kept slashing at her foe and finally it couldn't

back up any further. Super stood in front of it as it bared its teeth and snarled.

Suddenly she realized what she was doing and fear gripped her. She was fighting a monster! She gritted her teeth and forced the fear away. "Take this, you sicko!"

She stabbed it in the chest, pushing the sword in as far as hard as she could. The creature howled and grabbed its chest. Super stabbed it again and again until it didn't move anymore. Then she sat against a rock, worn out.

"Fighting monsters is hard," she said out loud to no one in particular. Then she took a deep breath and started looking for another one to fight.

She looked down the tunnel. A hundred more of the creatures filled the tunnel, coming their way.

"We're dead!" Super said, as all the strength left her.

All around her, Undergrounders fought. A few stood over the creatures, winning their battles but most were losing, being beaten into the ground.

A creature grabbed Deb around the waist. She screamed and dropped her sword. Super yelled and ran to help her, just as another creature blocked her way. She slashed at it, cutting its arm. It roared and flinched but didn't move.

The creature grabbed Super's sword arm. She screamed and fought back, but it was too strong. The pressure on her arm made her drop her sword. She stared at the creature's deformed gray face, sure she was going to die.

Suddenly the tunnel lit up with a bright yellow flash and a deafening explosion. Two of the creatures flew up into the air. The others all stared, mouths open with surprise. Another explosion shook the tunnel, and what was left of one of the creatures splattered on the tunnel wall.

The rest of the Rat People stopped fighting and took off back down the tunnel. The one holding Deb dropped her and took off running. The one holding Super's hand let her go.

"Run, you rotten cowards!" Super jumped up and down with joy.

Then her joy doubled when she saw who had saved them. At the end of the tunnel stood Johnny and Starbucks.

Despite her best efforts to stop it, tears filled her eyes and emotion choked her throat. Her lip trembled and she sniffed, for her nose suddenly wanted to run.

She didn't need to worry about showing her emotions, for Deb didn't bother hiding hers. Bursting into tears, Deb ran into Johnny's arms.

Super really had to try hard not to turn into a mess as she walked over to Starbucks. Johnny held Deb as she sobbed into his shoulder, kissing her head.

Starbucks was emotional too. As he and Super grew close they were both on the verge of tears. Silently, Super walked up and kissed him. Then they held each other.

The Undergrounders walked out and stood around them, cheering. Johnny and Starbucks looked with amazement at the strange people. Johnny looked at Deb. She wiped her eyes and smiled. "It's a long story."

"I bet," Johnny said. "But all I care about is you, Little Debbie." He lifted her chin with his finger. Then he kissed her. She closed her eyes and let him for a long time.

In the distance, the yells and cheering from Lord Algon's army grew louder. The Red Eye was almost over the horizon, and little natural light remained. Bright torches flickered in the breeze on top of the makeshift wall and scattered throughout the grassy Mall.

MIsterwizard and Foodcourt stood on a makeshift platform on top of the old cars on the left of the old White House. Next to them and along the makeshift wall, men from the Tribe stood, holding weapons from the Bunker, guns and bombs. Misterwizard wore an old Army uniform and helmet he'd found. A string of grenades was wrapped over his shoulder and around his body, and he held a grenade launcher in his hands.

Foodcourt wore an old police bulletproof vest and helmet with a face-shield. He kept the face-shield up though, for the first time he tried wearing it down, it fogged up so much he couldn't see anything. He held a short, black metal rifle Misterwizard had told him was an "AK-47." Misterwizard assured him it would do considerable damage when fired in the enemy's direction.

Misterwizard looked down the wall and tried to estimate how many men the Tribe had to fight. Since the Wildies had joined them, their ranks had swollen. Now they had, he estimated, almost three hundred and fifty to four hundred men. And yet, it seemed such a small number. In the distance, the shouts of Lord Algon's army made them sound as if they had a considerable larger force.

Where was Johnny and Starbucks, Misterwizard wondered? Had they found Deb and Super, or did they fall to the same fate that made the girls not return? If it wasn't for the upcoming war, Misterwizard would have liked to take a force of men and go find them. He hoped Johnny and his friends were not in grave danger.

Next to Misterwizard stood Yellowtooth. He wore a home-made piece of armor out of a bunch of old car hubcaps nailed together, as well as a helmet made of hubcaps as well. In other circumstances, Misterwizard would have found Yellowtooth's 'suit of armor' very amusing, but on this day, nothing seemed to cheer him up. Other Wildie men stood on the wall as well, holding spears and rocks to throw. A quick training session with the Wildie men and the guns proved they were quick learners, but still, Misterwizard didn't suspect their aim would be too accurate. It was almost better giving them spears and rocks instead of wasting the ammunition.

Some of the women wanted to fight as well, and those that did also stood on the wall. The rest, along with the Scrabblers, were told to barricade themselves in New Sanctuary. If the men were overrun, they would mount a last-ditch defense. The buses were primed and ready at the back of the Museum of America History, just in case. If it seemed like defeat was certain, the remaining Tribe members would jump on the buses and try to escape. Misterwizard hoped it wouldn't come to such a grim ending, for if it did, it surely meant the end of their hopes for a new America.

Foodcourt pointed, his face full of excitement. "I see them! Gosh there's a lot of them!"

Misterwizard squinted his eyes and looked. The other men of the Tribe saw them as well, for excited talking rippled up and down the wall. It was as Misterwizard feared. The force coming towards them was so large it passed out of sight. What he could see must have been at least five hundred.

MIsterwizard turned to Foodcourt. "Give them the instructions, Foodcourt."

Foodcourt nodded. He turned and looked up and down the line. "Remember everybody, don't fire until they're close enough to make sure you can hit them. We don't have the bullets to waste. Try and get the bigger ones first. And whoever shoots Lord Algon and kills him will get a hero's reward."

The men all cheered and raised their hands, but there was a definite lack of conviction in their voices. To Foodcourt, they all sounded a little scared. *Most had never been in a real war before,* he thought. He doubted many of Lord Algon's men had been in one either, which he hoped would put both armies on even footing.

Misterwizard stared out at Lord Algon's army. It weaved back and forth between the buildings, which trouble Misterwizard. They seemed to know not to stand in the open and present too easy of a target. Then he saw something that he found more troubling. Huge wooden structures rolled down the street towards them.

"Foodcourt, look!" Misterwizard pointed.

Foodcourt squinted, frowning. "What are those?" he asked.

"Those are his catapults," Yellowtooth said. "He used them last season when the piratts attacked. They launch balls of fire. And he's probably got his cannons coming, too."

"Well, isn't that wonderful?" Foodcourt said.

"We will have to take the catapults out as soon as

they are in range," Misterwizard said. "And hope that his cannons can't hit us from too great a distance. If they destroy the wall, we will be in quite a precarious situation."

Suddenly Abercrombie came running across the grass from New Sanctuary, yelling at the top of her lungs. Misterwizard and Foodcourt turned to see what was wrong. As she grew close, they could see she her face was twisted with grief and fear. She ran up to the side of the wall and waved up at Misterwizard.

"Misterwizard! Help!"

"What seems to be the problem, Abercrombie?"

"We can't find Sephie anywhere. We've looked and looked!"

Misterwizard frowned, deeply troubled, and stroked his beard in thought. Foodcourt looked worried as well. MIsterwizard spoke gravely. "This is not an opportune time for Sephie to choose for an exploratory sojourn."

Misterwizard looked down at Abercrombie again. "Have you searched the whole Museum and the Bunker? It is quite extensive, and there are many places she could find to entertain herself."

"We've searched everywhere!" Abercrombie wailed. "We even went and searched through the whole next building, the one with dead beasties. She's nowhere to be found!"

Foodcourt turned to Misterwizard. "I'll go looking for her."

Misterwizard looked over the wall. "I'm afraid it's too late, Foodcourt. Lord Algon's army has arrived!"

The first of Lord Algon's army came within range of the guns. The battle was on.

CHAPTER 34

Johnny held onto Debbie, not wanting to let her go, as she explained what happened to her and Super. When she came to the description of the Undergrounders, Johnny and Starbucks both listened with interest.

"And then you rescued us," Deb said, smiling as she looked up at Johnny from her position under his arm.

"Don't you know better than to look out for a hole in the ground?" Johnny said, teasing.

"I guess not," Deb replied, laughing. "But there wasn't a hole until we walked over it. Then suddenly, whoops! Down we went."

"I've never been so glad to see anyone in my life as when you guys showed up," Super said. "But I knew you would. You guy can't live without us."

The Undergrounders surrounded them. Loki walked

up to Johnny wearing a smile of joy.

"You are also angels! You have come to rescue us! Thank you!"

The Undregrounders all nodded and cheered. They crowded around the four 'angels.' Some came up and offered Johnny and his companions gifts, trinkets of gold and jewelry and other strange treasures they had found on the trains. The also offered them handmade gift fashioned out of scraps of cloth or wood.

Deb put her hand up to block them. "You don't have to do that," she said.

"Please," a tall, thin woman said, "let us thank you. You are sent from Lincone to save us."

Slon walked up humbly, smiling at them. "I am sorry I doubted you, friends. You told uus the truth. It's been so long, we began to doubt the ancient prophecies."

Johnny walked up to Slon. "Slon, if I understand Deb right, you've lived down here, in this tunnel since when the Great War happened hiding from what you call the Half-life monsters."

Slon nodded and all the Undergrounders did too. "We have been waiting for Lincone to send us angels to save us, and here you are!"

Johnny turned to Deb. "Did you girls tell them you were angels?"

"Not exactly," Super said. "But once they decided we were, it was hard to change their minds."

Slon frowned. "I do not understand."

Johnny looked at him. "Slon, we are not angels. We are just people, just like you." Johnny pointed up towards the ceiling. "I don't blame your people for creating a faith to sustain you in this dark and terrible place. But you don't have to live down here anymore.

There was a war, a terrible war. The Mushroom monsters came and killed many people. I think they were the same ones you call the Half-life monsters. Sometime long ago in the past, your ancestors brought you down here to survive, and you learned to live down here the best you could. But the danger is over. We are proof of that. You have a choice now. You can leave this place."

Deb looked at Loki. "Loki, Super and I are not really angels like we let you believe. We're just girls, just like the ones in your tribe. But we do care about you and your people."

"I don't understand," Loki said, frowning. "You killed the monster."

"Monster?" Starbucks asked.

"A wolf-beastie that got down here," Super said. "It attacked us, and Deb and I killed it."

"Oh," Starbucks said, suddenly looking guilty and shrugging. "Wow, I'm glad to hear that."

"Starbucks," Super said, suddenly suspicious, looking at him. "Is there something you want to tell us?"

Starbucks pulled Super close to him. "Only I'm sorry you had to fight it, and I'm glad it didn't hurt you."

"Uh-huh," Super said, wondering if there was more to the story than Starbucks was sharing.

Loki looked hopeful. "You are going to open the Door to Heaven now?"

"The Door to Heaven?" Starbucks asked.

Super answered him. "So, there's a door that leads out. The Undergrounders call it the Door of Heaven. But it's barred with a chain. We tried to blow it up, but our bomb didn't work."

Johnny's face scrunched up with determination. "Well, yours might not have, but mine will. Show me where it is. I'll open it right now."

Deb and Super led that way, with Johnny and Starbucks right behind them. The Undergrounders followed, all talking excitedly amongst themselves. Loki ran up to be next to Deb and Slon marched behind Johnny.

The came to the doors leading out. Everyone looked at Johnny. He raised the long tube he had taken from Misterwizard's weapons. "Everybody stand back."

They all hurried to get far enough away that if felt safe, almost back to the statue of Lincone. Johnny aimed and fired.

With a loud hiss, a rocket sped out of the tube. It sailed through the air as everyone watched it, yelling and jumping up and down. Then it hit the doors. With an ear-rending explosion and the sound of tearing metal, both doors to the outside exploded backwards, flying to land on the stairs leading up and out.

Everyone cheered. From above, faint light from the Yellow Night Eye shone on the smoking remains of the doors. Johnny grinned and looked at Deb. She ran over and put her arms around him.

Slon walked up, but he looked scared, uncertain. He spoke in a wavering tone of unhappiness. "You have opened the Door to Heaven."

"You don't seem very happy, Slon," Deb said, looking at him with concern.

Slon stood still, as if not sure what to do. "What do we do now? We have waited for this moment for all our lives. Now that it has come, the Ancient Book doesn't tell us what to do.

Pak, Loki's mother walked up. "Should we continue to worship Linone?"

Johnny set the metal tube down, let Deb go for the moment and stood in front of the Undergrounders. "Undergrounders," Johnny said, trying to speak as kindly as he could. "I hope you understand what I'm saying is only for your own good. Your god is not really a god. He's just a stone carved to look like a man. The stone fell from the building above you. He isn't alive, and he didn't help you do anything. We helped you, but now you can help yourselves. You can leave this place and join my Tribe. I promise you, we will welcome you. There's a whole world for you to explore. Join us."

Slon looked at the rest of the Undergrounders. They stared back at him, unsure what to do. Then Loki stepped forward. He stood next to Deb and looked back at his people.

"I never really thought he was a god," Loki said. "He never helped us when we were hungry, or when the Rat People attacked. Now we can leave this place and Lincone for good."

Pak looked at Slon, afraid of what he was going to say. Slon just stared at Loki, not looking angry, just unsure. Then he spoke.

"I am the leader of my people. I don't say I believe everything you are saying, but this I do say. I believe it would be a good thing to join your people. If they are all as good as you friends are." Slon smiled. Johnny, Starbucks and the girls grinned at each other and then looked at Slon again.

"And," Slon said, "I think we should see this new world you speak of."

The Undergrounders all cheered and hugged each other. They ran over and shook hands with Johnny and the others.

Slon turned to Deb. "Will you show us this new world, Deb?"

Deb said, "Johnny and I will show it to you, together. Follow us!'

Johnny grabbed Deb and she grabbed Loki's hand. Together all three walked out the doors, leaving the dark, dismal tunnel behind. Starbucks and Super fell in behind them. Slon and the rest of the Undergrounders followed slowly, looking fearfully but with excitement ahead as they entered a new existence.

Lady Stabs ran outside New Sanctuary with the rifle in her hands. She scanned the horizon and saw Misterwizard and the other men on the top of the wall. She looked at the wall the Tribe built on her left, the one next to the Museum. It spanned the gap between the Museum of American History and the Museum of Natural History. Made of junk cars and old pieces of fallen buildings, it wasn't very high and didn't look to tough to scale, but it would at least slow anyone coming to it down long enough for the Tribe to mount a defense.

She looked to the other side of the Museum. Here there was no wall yet, in fact the whole area to the broken stick building on either side of the Mall lay wide open. Lady Stabs worried about it. If Lord Algon came from that direction, there would be nothing to stop him. She decided she would patrol that side, so she could give the alarm if the Wildies tried to attack from there.

She trotted over to the far side of New Sanctuary and peered around, but no one seemed to be coming yet.

Then she saw something strange.

From the back door of the Museum of American History, a lone figure in a cowl and cloak ran. He carried a large burlap bag over his shoulder, and he looked very sneaky, as if he was trying not to be seen. The way the man was crouching low and peering around made Lady Stabs very suspicious. She grew even more concerned when she saw something inside the bag moving, thrashing about.

Instantly she knew this man was up to no good. She decided to follow him and see just what he was up to. Crouching down herself, she hurried to follow him, staying far enough behind that he wouldn't spot her.

Ripper watched Lord Algon's men begin their attack with a quiet feeling of joy inside. Even though the fight had just begun, it warmed his heart to see the Tribe being attacked again. He stood behind the long, white stick building with the broken top at the far end of the grassy Mall, listening to the yells of the men fighting, and the occasional sound of an explosion.

He squinted his eyes and could just make out the men on the makeshift wall. He saw what he thought was Misterwizard, and that fool father of Johnny's, Foodcourt. He didn't see Johnny, which disappointed him. Made of junk cars, the wall didn't seem too safe to stand on, as if the wall might collapse at any moment. The Tribe had made a lot of progress in building a fortress. It wasn't finished though, the side of the grass Ripper stood on was wide open. *Why didn't Lord Algon see it and bring his army around to this side? Because he was stupid,* Ripper thought. He always suspected that the crazy king of the Wildies was an idiot, and his tactics in this battle proved it.

Ripper looked at the Museum of American History that the Tribe now called New Sanctuary. That was where he wanted to go, to get inside before he was spotted. Things were so chaotic though, with people running in and out, he doubted he could get inside without being spotted. He might have only one more chance to kill Johnny, and he didn't want to waste it by doing something stupid like being caught because he was in too big a hurry. Still, he thought, smiling evilly, there was something he could do to help Lord Algon a little. He took his rifle off his shoulder. Raising it up, he looked through the scope. He aimed at Misterwizard and prepared to fire.

CHAPTER 33

Like wild hyena-beasties, Lord Algon's Wildies ran towards the makeshift fence laughing insanely. They weaved back and forth in a crisscross pattern, making it hard to get a bead on them with a rifle. In the distance, the yells of the rest of Lord Algon's army drifted on the night air.

The men of the Tribe and the Wildies who had joined them aimed and fired. Lord Algon's men fell or screamed in pain as bullets hit them. The others didn't stop, but kept running, filled with bloodlust and the craziness of war.

Suddenly a loud whistle shattered the air. It came from Lord Algon's s direction, but swiftly traveled towards Misterwizard and the men on the wall. It passed over their heads and ended with an explosion that tore up the grassy Mall behind them. Two tents turned into went down and a large furrow appeared in the ground where they had been.

Foodcourt looked at Misterwizard. "Is that what I think it was?"

MIsterwizard nodded, his face grim. "I'm afraid it is, Foodcourt. Lord Algon's cannon fire. Fortunately for us, his accuracy is currently lacking. Let's hope it stays that way."

The Wildies who had joined the Tribe and stood on the wall pointed the guns down at Lord Algon's men running towards the wall. One took aim at a Wildie and fired. The concussion knocked him backwards and he almost fell off the wall, grabbing onto a car window at the last moment. The bullet missed the man, making a puff of dust in the dirt.

"Take your time, dear friends, and aim!" Misterwizard said. "Remember my instructions on operating your weapon." He looked at Foodcourt, who was busy aiming to shoot himself. "I'm afraid our new allies are not going to impress us with their marksmanship. It is a shame we didn't have time to institute formal training."

"If you mean, they're going to waste a lot of bullets, I think you're right," Foodcourt said, nodding. Foodcourt aimed his rifle. In the crosshairs he saw a huge man with wild eyes and a crazy smile. He fired. The man went down.

"Got one!" He yelled.

"Excellent shooting! And now to light the night up a bit!" Misterwizard picked up a grenade and threw it. On the ground below it exploded, sending three Wildies flying into the air. A few Wildies reached the wall and began to climb. The men of the Tribe aimed down at them and shot as many as they could. Many fell, but a few began to slowly make their way to the top.

Lord Algon grinned, his heart soaring with the feeling of imminent victory. "Release the beasties!" He yelled.

The Wildies shouted and began to open the cages to let the wild beasties out.

Made in the USA
San Bernardino, CA
13 January 2020

62967247R00224